THREE LETTERS
NOVELLAS

BILL LAVENDER

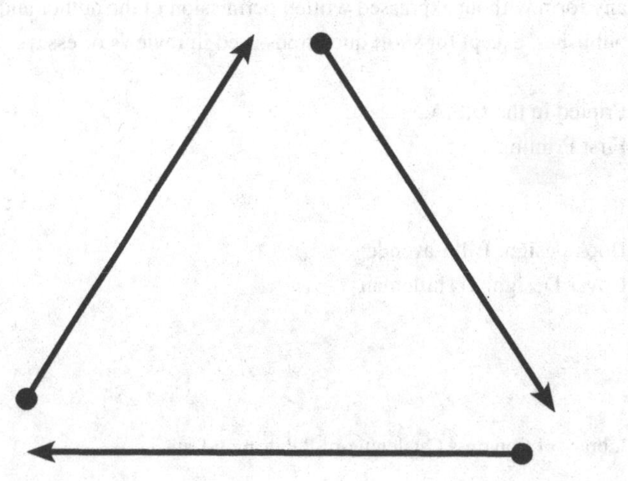

SPUYTEN DUYVIL   NEW YORK CITY

Three Letters: Novellas
Bill Lavender

Copyright © 2021 Bill Lavender
ISBN 978-1-952419-61-4

Printed in the U.S.A.
First Printing

Book design: Bill Lavender
Cover Design: T Thilleman

Library of Congress Cataloging-in-Publication Data

Names: Lavender, Bill, 1951- author.
Title: Three letters : novellas / Bill Lavender.
Description: New York City : Spuyten Duyvil, [2021] |
Identifiers: LCCN 2021012344 | ISBN 9781952419614 (paperback)
Subjects: LCGFT: Novellas.
Classification: LCC PS3612.A944238 T47 2021 | DDC 813/.6--dc23
LC record available at https://lccn.loc.gov/2021012344

Acknowledgements

I have a number of people to thank for help with this work. Major literary sources (for much of what you will read here is stolen) are listed in the Notes at the end of the book. But beyond this record of a life spent reading too much, I need to thank those who helped me with this particular folly.

Megan Burns—poet and publisher at Trembling Pillow Press— besides publishing *Q* in its stand-alone version, gave me many first reads and copy-edits. Chris Shipman laboriously copy-edited *Little A* and *The Private I* and provided excellent suggestions. Joel Dailey published the first several chapters of *Little A*, serially, in his noble magazine, *Fell Swoop*, before it became apparent the task was interminable.

Most of all, though, thanks to Nancy Dixon for putting up with these obsessions and making my life something to be cherished for 20+ years now. OK then. Here we go…

Three Letters

Q

Author's Preface

Gentle Reader:

I'm sure you understand, without my having to write it, that I hope this book—product of my imagination and reason, my dreams, my readings, and my life—will be the best book ever written, full of the most elegant and clever prose, every word *le mot juste*, every word with a double (triple, quadruple?) intention. But if, as Dickens has it, like begets like, what could this sterile, untilled time of ours beget but a shrivelled, whimsical character, full of thoughts that ought never to have existed, thoughts that might arise in a prison, full of misery and mourning?

What we love in a story, as that infallible arbiter of literary taste, the Market, proves, are love and romantic grief, scandal, and happy endings where all that has come before is reversed. However, I (and though I pass for the father, I am but the stepfather of *Q*) have no desire to go with this fashion, nor to implore you, dear reader, perhaps with tears in my eyes, as others do, to pardon or excuse the defects you'll perceive in this child of mine. You are neither its kinsman nor its friend; your soul is your own and your will as free as anyone's. You're master of your own house just as our President is master of our taxes. "Under my cloak I kill the king," the saying goes; under cover, all of us are free. Thus you are exempt from any obligation to read on, and you can speak as you will of the story without fear of being abused for any ill or rewarded for any good you might report.

And though the composition of this book cost me a bit of labor, no section of it caused more anxiety than this Preface. How many times did I sit down at the laptop to write it, and how many times did I get up again, not having any idea how to start? One of these times, as I was pondering the blank screen, chin in hand, thinking what I might say, a certain clever friend of mine, who works in the publishing industry, stepped into my office and inquired what was so distracting. I told him I was mired in writer's block thinking of the Preface I had to make for my novel, *Q*, and it was troubling me so it was causing me to question the entire project.

"It can't work," I told him. "How will a general fiction market take to me, so late in my career, after all these years in the oblivion of poetry, putting out a book so arch, so devoid of innovation, so derivative and allusive, with many parts stolen outright, utterly lacking in inspiration? I wish I could handle—especially since so many others seem proficient—a story full of emotion and devoid of political thinking, or a great moral quandary in a bedroom conversation, or any of the many genres that treat the emotional and philosophical tribulations of the upper-middle-class American. But I have neither the gift for scatology nor a reviewer in my pocket. Should I make, for the back cover, a queue of authors I've heard of, beginning with Acker and ending with Zukofsky, just to boast the respectability of a list?

"I'll have to do without the customary mention of corporate sponsors, grant agencies, and previous works every book includes at the beginning to prove the legitimacy of its author. I can get two of three friends to write endorsements, I suppose, for the jacket, and this might be enough to trick a few people into buying it, since if they don't recognize the author of the quote they'll assume it is someone famous they're unaware of and be ashamed to mention it.

"But all in all," I continued, "I think it best to let my *Q* remain buried in some archive where a graduate student may one day discover it and bring it to light as a lost masterpiece, in which case everyone could read about it without having to read in it. Alas, it appears I've wasted all these years on a project which will net me nothing."

My friend broke into a laugh and then slapped his thigh. "Oh come on, Bill, I've always thought of you as smart and practical. These trivial details are bothering you because you don't know how the business works. We'll turn your *Q* into a best seller in a heartbeat."

"Really?" I replied. "And just how do you propose we do that?"

"Well," he said, "your problem is that you're worrying too much about the content and not enough about the package. You've got the right idea with the blurbs. And you can get an epigram from Google™ quotations. What you want is something from the Bible. The Christian Market is growing every day and is easily captured. The slightest mention of the Bible will do it."

"But," I protested, "some of the things I say…"

"Don't worry about what you *say*," he insisted. "They won't even notice the content.

"And I'm going to suggest a strategy that's lately become the norm. We'll utilize an analytic program to scan for products, motifs, and current phrases from best sellers over the past two years. Then we can seed your novel with snippets of these, product names, foods, cars, and current slang. It's quick and easy; we just use search-and-replace. And then you can use these product placements to get free advertising.

"And the biggest question of all, of course, the one that makes more difference to sales than any other aspect of a book, is the cover. I'll have my friend who is a market psychologist run reports on the color combinations that are selling best in the current milieu, and we'll look at the semiotics of various symbolic indices. We'll need to figure out if we ought to go the pistol-and-garters route, or if earth-tones and nature scenes are working these days, or if dogs have come back into fashion.

"As to this Preface you're sweating over, don't. No one reads them. We'll just paste in jabber-text to fill those couple of pages, put 'Author's Preface' at the top, and no one will be the wiser."

I listened to my friend's indisputable wisdom with stunned recognition. His observations made such an impression on me that I decided on this audience-mocking form for the Preface, simply stolen from an earlier work, to allow you, dear reader, to prove my friend's good sense and devour this product which ridicules your ignorance as if it were the latest pharmaceutical fad, the Viagra™ of whatever year this is. "Fear God and the stupidity of the populace," said Pound, and we prove that son of a bitch right every day. Please, comrade, continue the trend and let this handsome jacket decorate your shelves today.

Take this story of *Q*, a generic demographic composite, and your mirror. Yes, that shadow you just startled is yourself.

Here's hoping God continues to withhold your good sense.

Vale.

For there is no remembrance of the wise more than of the fool
for ever; seeing that which now is in the days to come shall all be
forgotten. And how dieth the wise man? as the fool.

Ecclesiastes 2:16

Book One

Q was born into the best of all possible worlds. He grew up in the best house on the best street in the best subdivision in his land, which just happens to be the best country in the world. Things happen in other countries, Q's Father told him, but they don't happen here. Our Country is the exception. It's not like other countries, which rise and fall and wax and wane; it is, rather, the best possible country, with the best possible economic and political system, and it will last forever.

Their house was spacious, with a large atrium that was too bright for watching television, so they spent most of their time in the den. There was a pool where no one swam and a workout room where no one exercised. There was a photo of a former president and his wife on the refrigerator signed "thanks."

The garage was big enough for four cars, though they only had three: Q's Father's BMW™, his Mother's Lexus™ (the Premium Sport Utility,) and Q's own Z™. The fourth space was reserved for a Miata™ for his Sister when she should come of age.

Q's Father was in real estate. His Mother was an agent, also, but spent most of her time managing their daily affairs and playing tennis or golf. She still cut a fine figure in her active-wear, often turning the heads of men half her age, and she was a coveted assignment among the coaches at the Club.

The only bad thing, Q's Father told him, about the place they lived, was the subdivision's name: Provincial Oaks. All the best subdivisions, he said, had French names, like Belle Terre or Beau Chene. But other than this one flaw they lived in the best subdivision in the land.

It was assumed, of course, that Q, also, was bound for greatness. Though his performance in middle school had been lackluster and in high school even dismal, and though he had neither the stamina for basketball nor the strength for football, no one could touch him on Nintendo™ and Playstation™, and his father envisioned him going into technology after college. "With your computer skills," the old man said over dinner, "and an MBA from Harvard™, nothing can stop you." Q beamed at this praise from his mentor, and at the general brightness of his future.

Thus it was something of a surprise when, one mild autumn afternoon, Q came home to find his Father hanging from a rope tied to the bannister in the atrium. "Dad?" he questioned, thinking, at first, that his Father was playing some sort of joke.

He was hanging, twisting slowly in the silent room, with his feet a yard above the floor. The lamp and the rubber tree that had been within reach were upended, and one of the Gucci™ loafers had dropped onto the Mexican tile, baring a single argyle sock. The face was contorted rather horribly, with tongue protruding, but Q looked into it anyway, waiting expectantly for it to break into his Father's loud laugh and say, "Gotcha!"

But there were no punch-lines to come from that swollen orifice, and Q finally seated himself on the couch near the fireplace, some distance away, to collect his wits and decide the best course of action. He picked up the remote and switched on the television, as he often did in times of indecision, but now he navigated to CNN, which was airing a story on the day's casualties in the current war, because only that seemed solemn enough for the occasion.

When his Mother and Sister came home, his Mother yelled at him: "Why didn't you call 911?" His Sister ran upstairs to her room and slammed the door.

"Of course," said Q, coming back to himself, "911." He took the iPhone™ out of his pocket and quickly dialed, then gave his report while his Mother paced about the room, wringing her hands and looking generally distraught.

One of the many advantages of life in Provincial Oaks was the Private Police Force. The property owners had voted some years ago to pay for their own police and garbage collection rather than paying taxes to the City. Q's Father had told Q that this meant they would have faster, better police protection because their police were profit-motivated, whereas the normal city police were motivated only by their sense of civil service, a notoriously unreliable impetus.

Q heard the siren before he even hung up the phone, and moments later the doorbell rang. After quickly sizing up the situation and calling for an ambulance, one of the officers took Q's Mother into the other room to comfort her, while the other one righted the rubber tree and the lamp and tidied up a bit. The he came and sat beside Q on the couch.

"What are you watching?" he asked solicitously.

"Just the news," said Q.

Only two days later, the first creditors appeared, and from then on they circled the house constantly, like sharks around a lifeboat, a lifeboat which held Q and what was left of his family. His Mother called their attorney right away, of course, only to discover that he, too, and despite their relationship of ten-plus years, had joined with the creditors.

"No offence," he said over the phone, "but your husband hasn't paid me in over a year."

"I don't understand," said Q when his Mother hung up. "If Dad owed him money why didn't he just pay him?"

His Mother explained that financial matters can be very complex.

The VISA™ too, had not been paid in over a year, leaving them with six figures of debt at 32% interest. The house note—or rather notes—were in the same condition, the sum total of the mortgages leaving them "upside-down" to the tune of a half million.

It was Q's idea, of course, to do the right thing, pay off all these creditors and make a clean slate. Thus, whenever a deputy or repo man came to the door, Q just wrote them a check. This was a very effective strategy in the beginning, until they had time to go to the bank and return, this time refusing to take checks.

Q watched as the BMW™ and the Lexus™ were towed away, his Sister and his Mother sobbing on the front lawn. At first he thought he might get to keep his Z™, but it was merely that the repo agency had only two wreckers, and one quickly returned to leave Q with nothing but his shoes between himself and his manicured lawn.

He sat down in the grass to consider his next course of action. A small uproar rang out around him, but Q was concentrating and could not be interrupted. When at last he looked up, he saw his Mother and Sister getting into a SUV with someone he vaguely recognized as one of his Mother's tennis coaches.

Q got up and went over to get in with them, but his Mother closed the door in his face. The tinted window eased down just enough for him to see his Mother's eyes one last time.

"Your Sister and I are going to stay with Him," she said, nodding in the driver's direction, "but He only has room for us. You'll be all right, I'm sure, and we need someone to stay and take care of the house."

Then the window raised itself and the SUV pulled away. Q stood, momentarily stunned, but then turned back toward the house. He followed the walkway in a contemplative manner, not even looking up until his hand reached for the doorknob and encountered something unexpected: a padlock.

Q, now in a fury over the gross unfairness of it all, began to kick and tug and curse at the door. When he made no headway there, he went around to the side, picked up a large rock from the edge of the fish pond in the garden and made to break into the atrium with it. He held the boulder over his head and charged the window.

A moment later he lay on the ground with his face pressed into the grass. There was a great weight on the back of his head, and he could hear laughing at the same moment he received a debilitating blow to the kidneys. He rolled over trying to get a breath and saw the same two Policemen who had responded to his Father's suicide. They were giggling happily.

"You see," they choked out between guffaws, "you don't live here any more. You're not a resident any more." Then, after a couple more judicious kicks, they took him up, each by an arm, dragged him across the lawn to their cruiser and deposited him in the back seat.

He could see the neighbors coming outside to watch the action, and he tried his best to signal them to come to his aid, but he was handcuffed and doubled over in pain and could not raise an arm. As the cruiser drove away their heads followed the car around the curve. Then they went back inside.

The Policemen drove Q into the City, joking with each other casually and ignoring Q's laments. He begged them not to take him to jail. He'd never been in jail, he told them, and was psychologically unequipped for that sort of experience. They exchanged sly looks and drove on. They drove through parts of the City Q had never seen, dark blocks of dirty brick and painted windows. And in one of those blocks no different from all the rest, they pulled over. The one in the passenger seat got out and opened Q's door.

"We've decided," he chuckled, "to honor your request not to take you to jail, on account of your delicate psychological condition. We're going to leave you here instead."

Q looked around and felt not a trace of comfort in their leniency.

"We're going to leave you here, free as a bird," the cop resumed, "on the sole condition that you never return to Provincial Oaks. You're not a property owner any more. Hell, you don't even have a car. So, I want you to promise you'll never go back to Provincial Oaks. Can you do that for me?"

Q looked at him with trembling lips. "But…" he stammered, and quick as a wink the officer's boot found his stomach. He hunched over in pain, and a billy-club landed across his back. Cheek on the filthy sidewalk, Q watched the foot rear back and kick him one more time, this time in the neck, before walking back to the car and stepping in. The car took off, wheels spinning, spraying Q with gravel and oily mud.

Q lay weeping on the sidewalk as night fell, and he meditated on the vastness of the sky over his head and the firmness of the concrete beneath it. He had never seen darkness like this, except momentarily in his own room with the curtains drawn, as the streets in Provincial Oaks were brightly lit the whole night through, as well as on cloudy days. Nor had he ever seen the stars so clearly, nor so acutely sensed their distance from him.

Compelling as this reverie was, Q's thoughts returned inevitably to the practical concerns of bettering his situation. His Father had always told him: "You're not doing the beggar a favor when you give him a handout, because you're taking away his motivation to better himself." Taken in that context, Q's present situation seemed almost a boon, because his motivation to better himself could not have been greater. He pulled himself up to a sitting position and fished in his pocket for his iPhone™. He felt great comfort when the little grid of icons lit up in his hand. And when the screens began to respond to his touch, he felt his competence and his faith in himself returning.

He slid his finger down the long list of contacts. He passed over his Father's listing, of course, hesitated at the home phone, and began to consider his many close friends from school. He was on the verge of dialing his Best Friend, thinking that he needed, more than anything right now, a friendly voice to comfort him. But he paused as he noticed the grime and blood on the finger that was navigating the screen. He was a mess, his clothes filthy and torn. No, he couldn't call upon his friends in this condition.

There remained only his Mother. He remembered her fondly as his finger paused over her address book entry, which read simply "Mom." Surely when she heard about his situation she would come and pick him up in the tennis coach's SUV. All she would need to know was his location.

But, he realized with dismay, he had no idea where he was. The answer to this dilemma was of course the iPhone™, so he switched apps to Google™ maps and waited for the built-in GPS to drop a pin at his location. The device seemed to struggle with the request, displaying its spinning disc and then freezing into a dormant screen for a moment. Then, just as the pin fell and the map was struggling to rasterize, a grimy hand reached in and plucked the phone from his grasp.

Q felt again the now familiar sensation of being kicked. Having learned something from his experience with the police, he rolled quickly into a ball and covered his head. He felt a pair of hands, then, going over him. He reached to protect his wallet but too late. When he managed to sit up his iPhone™, the contents of his pockets, his shoes and his Identity were dancing off down the street in the hands of a homeless beggar.

Thus reduced, Q was in a quandary as to his next move. On the one hand, the bare discomfort of his present position in the gutter seemed to command some sort of change. On the other, the slightest move caused him great pain, since the police and the robber had left scarcely an inch of him unbruised. Also, he was now shoeless, and the sidewalk he was on was densely littered with broken glass, pebbles, and nails.

His indecision was alleviated, however, by the sound of footsteps approaching. Certainly he had no desire to repeat the last encounter, so he struggled to his feet and began to walk. He was amazed at how difficult this activity, which he had always taken for granted, could be.

A singular disadvantage of the city street lies in the fact that after successfully hobbling through one patch of broken glass you discover that there is another beyond it just as important and just as nervously anxious to do something effective in the way of cutting feet. Barefoot on a sidewalk one gets an image of the street, of the minute contours of its surface, that is not given to the experience of those who have not been abandoned, beaten and shoeless, in a slum.

Q hobbled along, wincing and sometimes crying out, as quickly as he could in front of the advancing footsteps. The street was dark, pitch dark, as if there were a power outage, or as if electricity were no longer supplied to this particular neighborhood. The tenement buildings loomed in the shadows on either side of him, and occasionally he thought he saw movement in a window or on a stoop. Far back in one cave-like doorway he made out the single ember of a cigarette.

As his eyes adjusted to the darkness, so did his ears to the near silence, and he began to hear small sounds from inside and outside the buildings, a sliding sound like something begin pushed across a floor, a window opening, the bump of a cat jumping down from a window sill, the plinking sound of water dripping into a puddle, echoing.

Could he discern, in that doorway, the figure of a woman? He regarded the shadow skeptically and moved to the far side of the street. And when he did so, did he hear snickering from a window?

Now Q found an advantage in the condition of terror, for suddenly his wounds ceased to trouble him, and he found the strength to run. No longer attentive to the punishment his feet were taking, he ran for all he was worth, turning a corner and then another to get away from the suspicious block, only to find himself on other suspicious blocks.

Up ahead, though, he saw a faint light and made for it. He didn't know what it was but just the prospect of electricity filled him with hope. And when he got closer he actually let out a cry of joy, for it was a sign, brightly lit, and a door below it, and the sign read: Shelter.

Once in the light, Q fell upon the door with passion. He grabbed the knob hungrily but found it to be securely locked. He beat on it with his hands and fists, calling out incoherently, before he noticed the button beside it. He calmed himself, rang and was immediately greeted by a man's voice on the intercom.

"Yes," it said.

Q was flummoxed. What could he say? "I live, or used to live, in Provincial Oaks," he began, "but I came home two days ago and found..." He stammered at this point, suddenly overcome with emotion, and he heard the buzz of the electric lock. He was able to pull the door open and enter without having to finish the painful story.

He found himself in a lobby, facing a uniformed man at a desk. Around him, seated on benches, apparently waiting their turn, were a half-dozen examples of humanity in extremis. These creatures, fetid, dirty and disheveled, staring blankly, did not look at Q as he walked in. Q, on the other hand, stared at them with wonder. Never had he seen people in such condition. It was as if all their traits had been erased but the simple fact of their destitution. He couldn't make out their race, nationality or even gender, as they sat hunched on their pews, clothed in filthy rags, with their paper bags of belongings.

Q proceeded to the desk and stood before it. He began, in faltering voice, to continue the story he had begun on the stoop, but the man behind the desk did not look up from his computer screen. He pointed silently at a red plastic wheel that dispensed numbers on little pieces of paper. Q took one and noted with satisfaction that his was only seven from the one presently displayed on the LED readout on the wall. And so he took his place on the benches with the homeless.

When he sat down he immediately slumped from fatigue and made to lay down, but one of the others on the bench shook him by the shoulder and cautioned him to remain upright, pointing to a sign on the wall that said, "No sleeping here." Q opened his mouth to voice his apology for breaking the rules, but the stranger only pointed to another sign, which said, "No talking here."

At that point the LED number on the wall advanced one integer and, without a word, one of the group got up and went through the door beside the desk.

When his turn finally came, Q hobbled through the door like the rest. The long wait upright on the hard bench had exacerbated the bruises and contusions he'd received from his various beatings, and it took quite some effort for him to carry himself to the next room. There he encountered another uniformed man at a desk like the one in front, though this one spoke to him.

"How can we help you?" the man asked.

Q, gushing with relief, began to tell him the whole sad story, beginning with his Father's suicide, regressing a little for his background in Provincial Oaks, but the man quickly stopped him.

"Would you like a place to sleep tonight, because we can help you with that. Then you can seek assistance with your other problems tomorrow."

Q replied in the affirmative and thanked him profusely.

"Good," he said, leaning to his computer, "and what is your name?"

Q told him his name.

"Driver's license, birth certificate, or other ID?"

Q felt for his wallet, then felt the rest of his pockets for any trace of his Identity. There was none. He knew there was a copy of his birth certificate in the file cabinet in his home at Provincial Oaks, but beyond that he was at a loss. He began to explain, again, the series of tragedies that had befallen him in the past few hours, but once again he was silenced.

"Just sit right there, would you?" The officer indicated a chair directly in front of his desk. When Q sat down, a flash went off in his face. The officer struck his keyboard awkwardly a few times and then handed Q his new ID card.

The first thing that struck Q about the card was his picture on it. It resembled those pictures he'd seen on the news of wanted criminals. His hair was disheveled, his face filthy and contorted with pain, which perfectly resembled rage in the picture. He, who only hours ago had resided in the stately Provincial Oaks, looked for all the world like the derelicts he had just encountered in the waiting room.

And then there was the issue of his name, which was given simply as Q. When he pointed this out to the officer, he was told that in the absence of any official identification, the homeless shelter only assigned their patrons letters of the alphabet, and P had been given out earlier that week. Also, because he did not have proof of Identity, he would be considered an illegal alien until he could.

Q's new Identity card was equipped with a magnetic strip that opened the electronic locks that seemed to be on every door in the shelter. When he swiped it through the mechanism, a red Q appeared on the readout, and the door opened.

He found his way to the men's bathroom, opened that door with his card, and cleaned himself as best he could, but there wasn't much that could be done given the condition of his clothes. He was given a dingy blanket and sent into the dormitory where he navigated to an empty bed among the grid of snoring, flatulent bodies. The bed was equipped with a wire cover that had to be unlocked with his card before it could be opened. Once this was negotiated he lay down on a bare mattress stretched over a frame of rusty iron.

Sleep was not to come easily to him, as each lump in the cheap mattress felt like a spear in his side, and the sounds and scents of so many bodies in these close quarters glutted him with rich sensation. For a moment he even thought he would have to puke over the bedside, but he choked it back and lay gasping for breath, staring up at the cracked plaster of the ceiling so as to avoid looking around him.

Never had his motivation to better himself been quite so keen.

In the end, though, his fatigue turned out to be more powerful than his indignation, and Q did sleep. His dreams were a rehashing of the past few eventful days, with certain haunting images recurring.

He saw his Father's feet, one shod and the other bare, hanging in the doorway of the atrium, twisting slowly above the toppled rubber plant. But he did not see his Father's face, with its protruding tongue; whenever the camera of memory panned toward it some other image would overlay itself. He saw his Sister and his Mother in the window of the tennis instructor's SUV, looking straight ahead as they drove away. And he saw the neighbors following him with their eyes as he left Provincial Oaks in the patrol car.

Later in the night, his dreams developed more cohesive plot and style, more like professionally produced TV shows than the home video of the earlier images. He dreamed, indeed, that his home in Provincial Oaks was the site of a reality show. The furniture in the atrium had been removed and rows of beds installed, as if for a giant slumber party. His neighbors, the two cops, the guards from the shelter, and a few TV celebrities were all there, dressed in identical striped pajamas, sitting upright in their beds listening to the stage directions Q's Father was giving them over a megaphone. "Camera one, over there," he yelled, waving his arm in a vague direction, his feet jumping and twitching with excitement. "Camera two, on the balcony. Camera three, in the fireplace. OK, everyone set? Action!" And then everyone pulled up their covers, closed their eyes and began sleeping with a vengeance. Q's Father, too, became perfectly still and silent.

Q played his role as best he could, keeping his eyes shut tight, yet somehow still surveying the scene from above, watching over the others, some of whom, he noticed, secretly had an eye open. He decided he would try this too, opening one eye just a slit to see who was around him. What he saw when he did so—the dirty room with no windows, the dark heaps of the homeless and the destitute in their filthy beds—caused him to cry out in surprise, and his own cry woke him once again to reality.

"Shut up, Q," said a voice from one of the nearby beds. "We're all trying to sleep in here."

"But how do you know my name?" Q could not help but inquire.

An arm emerged from the heap of rags on the bed and pointed to the head of Q's bed. Q found there an LED indicator with his new initial on it. He now noticed, also, that each bed had one of these, and that he was talking to one whose name was familiar.

"How odd," Q said, "but I recognize your name. It is the same as my Best Friend at Provincial Oaks High School."

"Provincial Oaks High?" said the fellow. "And how does someone from Provincial Oaks end up here in a homeless shelter?"

"Ah…" said Q, and began again the story of his formerly genteel existence and his sudden downfall. His companion, it turned out, was a much more willing listener than the shelter guards had been. He listened without interruption as Q related the entire sad story in graphic detail, from the discovery of his Father's suicide to the dream from which he had just awakened.

"Well," he said when Q finally paused for a breath, "that's a sad story. But let me tell you mine, now. Just remember I won't be telling it for the same reason you have told yours. I don't want your sympathy, and I don't need to get it off my chest. I'm telling you because I want you to understand why your own story, far from moving me to tears, elicits nothing from me but contempt."

As Q listened to the fellow's story, he was struck by the familiarity of both the story and the speaker's derisive tone. He was certain he'd heard this voice before, but where?

"My story is very much like yours, Q. I too lived in Provincial Oaks and was evicted after my father's bankruptcy. My father even wore Gucci™ loafers, though instead of hanging himself he simply disappeared. I found myself here with no one to call and nowhere to go. Unlike you, though, I had my driver's license and so was able to acquire a permanent ID. After a few days here, I realized I was going to have to better my situation, somehow, so I went back to school.

"I walked the seven miles back to Provincial Oaks and managed to sneak onto the campus without anyone seeing me walking. It was tricky, at first, hiding the fact that I was no longer living in the subdivision, but after a while I came up with detailed explanations for every anomaly that might arise. I would slip into the subdivision every morning early and bum a ride to school with a different friend each day, always telling them my car was in the shop. And if anyone got suspicious I told them something like 'oh yeah, my dad lost all his money and I'm living at the homeless shelter.' And they thought that was hilarious."

"Well, that's brilliant," said Q. "I'm sorry that you've had to go through the same horrible experience I've had, but I'm certainly happy to have you here. I would like to better my situation by continuing my schooling too, so I'm happy to have someone to show me the way."

"I'll show you the way, certainly," he said, "but you haven't let me finish. You should know that one of these friends I duped into giving me rides to campus, who laughed at the joke about being homeless and was generally my constant alibi because he would believe anything I said, was you."

"What?" Q intoned in a whisper.

"Yes, that's right, it's me, your Best Friend from High School."

"**W**hat?" Q gasped. "It's not possible. But… it is you. It's true." Q wept from happiness. "Oh my dear Best Friend," he stammered, "you know how I hate school, how we used to complain about it. But I'd be so happy to be at school right now. And you being here could make this whole awful thing tolerable. We can go to school together in the morning. I can go to the gym and get cleaned up, get back in class and back in the swing."

"But here's the thing, Q," said his Friend, drawing out the Q as if to solidify the new Identity, "now that you know my story, I can't have you coming back to school. You're just too young and naive. You'll slip up, one way or another, and let my secret out. I'm well on my way to a decent scholarship, and I can't have that jeopardized by a bimbo like you. So you stay away from Provincial Oaks and Provincial Oaks High, Q, or you'll discover that the beating those cops gave you was kid stuff. You could even end up hanging from the ceiling like your old man, a 'suicide' here at the shelter. I've got real friends down here and can arrange it. Happens all the time, and nobody thinks twice about it."

And now Q's tears were no longer tears of happiness.

Q's Best Friend rolled over, then, and was soon adding his snores to the somnolent cacophony of the room. Q himself did not sleep any more that night but spent the hours until dawn staring out across the dimly lit room where the dregs of humanity lay.

After a while he had one of those out-of-body experiences he had read about in magazines. He floated along the ceiling, and saw the bodies, his own among them, arrayed in a symmetrical grid. He wondered if they were in alphabetical order or classified according to some other system, the nature of which he was unaware. He felt an enormous craving for order, and it caused him great distress to think that the bodies might be randomly dispersed among the rectangles of the beds.

His sleep-deprived reverie was interrupted, suddenly, by an alarm that seemed designed to wake everyone in the neighborhood, if not the city. Upon this rude signal everyone rose from their beds, took up their tattered belongings and made for the bathrooms and then the street. Q lingered at his bed a little too long and was sent along by one of the guards, who pointed toward the door and let him know by his look that his exit was required. And so began the first day of Q's new life.

Now humans are an adaptable lot, far more resilient than we normally imagine, and Q survived his sudden downturn. Though he was soft from his pampered childhood, he was in his prime and healthy, and his wounds healed. There were more beatings, to be sure, by the police and also by his fellow waifs. But gradually these aggressors ceased to come away unscathed, and occasionally they even got the worst of it and were sent away yelping.

And Q learned a few things he never thought he would have to learn. He learned to eat out of dumpsters and to defecate behind them. He learned how to hustle spare change and grab what was loose if he needed to.

He also learned to capitalize on what charities there were available and found himself queued up in their food lines on many an evening. But he found the lines less fruitful and more demeaning than the dumpsters, and he grew quickly to despise the condescending pity of the aid workers.

He was also constantly aware of his Father's admonitions and eschewed aid whenever possible so as to avoid compromising his own motivation for self-betterment. And he showed real entrepreneurial spirit in his dumpster-diving. Unlike most of his brothers and sisters of the street, who were only interested in food and other immediately usable items, Q kept a careful eye out for anything that had resale value. He learned to scavenge bits of copper and aluminum to sell as scrap. He acquired a shopping cart to transport his products.

One morning, however, while foraging for metals, he encountered Competition. He was bending down in leisurely fashion to pick up a beer can he had spotted in the gutter when he felt the now familiar boot to the kidney. As he looked up gasping a fellow he had seen now and again at the shelter appeared over him.

"Hello, Q," he said. "How's business? Keeping your head above water?"

He picked up the can from the gutter and dropped it into Q's cart, then kicked Q again in the ribs.

"I used to have the recycling in this neighborhood to myself, and I confess I was a little disappointed when you started working the curbs too."

He pulled his rusty and much-the-worse-for-wear cart up beside him and began transferring its contents into Q's much newer and shinier one. When Q raised his arm in protest, he gave him a kick to the elbow.

"But," he continued, "I came to realize that I was wrong to resent you. It's good for us to compete, because it forces both of us to do our jobs better, faster and more efficiently."

Q made to rise, but the Competition landed a fist on his jaw that set him back again.

"I mean, we perform a service for the city; we improve the quality of life for its citizens by providing an environment free of any trash composed of recyclable metals. But if we have no competition, we become lazy and complacent in the performance of our jobs, and the quality of life for the entire population of the city declines. Thus, it is essential that we compete with each other as brutally and efficiently as possible, so that we can all live in harmony and continuous improvement."

"But," Q interrupted, lisping slightly from his swollen lip, "why does there have to be competition for us to improve? Isn't it possible that we could be continually striving for improvement just because we want to be valuable members of the community and looked up to by our friends, because we want to do a good job and take pride in our work? Isn't that really the way it works even now?"

The Competition gave Q a brief look and then kicked him square in the chest, sending Q onto his back once again.

"Oh, right," he said, sneering, "altruism…. But no, Q, self-interest is the best, indeed the only, motivator. For all that humanity may claim of higher motives, only self-interest moves us. The paradoxical truth is that things improve as struggle increases. Under Capitalism life continuously improves because each entrepreneur tries to outdo the other in providing a valuable service to the community. Thus competition increases the quality of life for everyone, even when they are not aware of it."

And he capped off his argument by grinding Q's nose under his boot-heel. Then he turned calmly and walked away with Q's cart and his pitiful earnings of the day thus far.

Now Q was becoming daily more adept at treating his own wounds, and also more inured to pain, so he was back on the street in no time, now more motivated than ever to do a good job at gathering metals, and whether his motive was to deprive the Competition of the fruits or to increase the general good we'll never know, and needn't.

He thought it through, though, carefully planning the most efficient path toward self-betterment, and in the end decided a two-by-four brought into contact with the Competition's head was the most effective means. Q watched thoughtfully as his nemesis dropped to his knees and then face down on the sidewalk, blood trickling out his ears, and he ruminated on philosophies of wealth and social product as the Competition went into convulsions, frothing and vibrating with pre-death paroxysms.

He didn't die, in the end, though he wasn't much competition for anyone after that. He recovered from the concussion, but he never regained his full mental capacity. He forgot how to feed himself and all the other natural habits of humans. He also lost ability to understand language.

The doctors called it semiaphasia. While he had lost all ability to comprehend what others said to him, he still had the capacity— indeed the compulsion—of speech. He continued to spout his economic philosophy as eloquently as before, now unhindered by the obligation to listen to other arguments. He harangued whomever would walk by on the benefits of ruthless competition and evils of governmental interference with natural selection, notwithstanding the fact that he himself was all but vegetal and could not have survived without public assistance.

By dint of arguing constantly, though, whether he had a listener or not, his polemic grew so practiced and heart-felt that despite his obvious deficiencies in other areas he became a valuable spokesperson for a certain political faction, which began to pay handsomely for his services. The Party would prop him up on the podium at those ten-thousand-dollar-a-plate lunches, even though he had to wear a bib when he sat to eat.

In the end he found his true calling in radio, a medium that seemed designed for those with his particular malady. He was quickly syndicated and died a rich man, unlike the rest of our cast, whose pitiful tales are about to unfold.

Back in Provincial Oaks, someone was stirring inside Q's (former) home. Two young men, scarcely older than Q, were going through the house carrying furniture, clothing and other belongings out to the dumpster which was now parked in the driveway. They were taking their time, examining each item to see if it had any value before tossing it into the heap.

They hadn't picked out much. Long experience at this work had taught them not to be seduced by everything that glittered. In their own humble apartments each of them already had a collection of electronics and appliances from houses like this one. In a three room apartment shared by six of his family members, One had four large televisions, six laptop computers and innumerable video game consoles and sound systems. The Other lived in equivalent luxury. Each of them, because of this job they had emptying out foreclosures, were already on the verge of being pushed out of their living quarters by their possessions.

They didn't look twice at Q's Father's big-screen TV. The One took a few clothes from Q's Sister's room for his own sister, while the Other tried on Q's clothes, which were found to be too large. The vast majority of the possessions it had taken Q's family its lifetime to amass were taken straight to the dumpster by these two poor immigrants, for the house was worth more without them.

The black file cabinet, where Q's Father had kept important documents like mortgages, deeds, and birth certificates, didn't even merit having its drawers inspected but went straight to the pile and was tossed on top. The drawers fell open then, and papers spilled out loose into the dumpster or were swept across the yard by the wind.

Q slept at the shelter for several weeks, but after that he discovered that sleeping on the street was in some ways preferable to the shelter's regimen, and then he began to use it only in case of rain. He learned to sleep under newspaper and cardboard and how to make a soft place in the weeds of the vacant lots that were prevalent in the City. And he learned to hide his bed so he could sleep as late as he wanted.

He also learned what it felt like to lay down on the ground, look into the stars and feel himself rooted in the planet like the grass. There even came a morning when he woke up with the warm sun shining on him, stretched out his limbs on his cardboard bed, and the sensation was not unpleasant.

Felicity is short-lived in the best contingency, however, and for the man living on the street it is all the more fleeting. The ebb and flow of happiness and regret that a prosperous man experiences over a period of years or decades a homeless man will experience in minutes. So for Q a few minutes spent stretching in the sun on a beautiful morning were followed immediately by long hours foraging in dumpsters and standing in lines at charitable organizations.

The greatest impediment, he imagined, to the betterment of his situation, was his lack of identification. So far he had not been able to get or even apply for a regular job because he had neither a driver's license nor a social security card, and he needed both. He had landed two days work on a demolition crew tearing down one of the many dilapidated buildings in the neighborhood, but when

he went to the foreman for his pay, he was given the usual forms
to fill out, and the foreman asked to see his ID.

Q had shown him his card from the shelter, with that awful picture
on it, but the foreman had merely laughed. "Q," he said, "I hadn't
taken you for a wetback, but I see you are an illegal of some sort,
so you'll have to take this up with Management."

"But I've done the work; you can't refuse to pay me for my labor,"
Q insisted. "It's against the law!"

"Call the police," replied the foreman. "They'll protect your
rights. Or I'll tell you what, I'll call 'em for you!" And he slapped
his knee and laughed even louder as he pulled out his phone. Q
well knew the provenance the police would offer him when they
arrived, so he had to give up his lawfully earned wages and make
a quick getaway, though not without noting that foreman's face for
future reference. Revenge, as sweet as it might seem, would have
to wait until he got his papers in order.

The only way Q could imagine that he might be able to regain
his Identity was to return to Provincial Oaks and search out his
birth certificate, which he reasoned to be somewhere in that black
file cabinet in his Father's office. So he packed up his belongings
in an old backpack he had found and set out.

It took him the better part of a day to get there. He tried hitchhiking,
but people seemed to speed up when they saw him, so he ended up
walking the several miles on the shoulder of the freeway, assailed
by wind, noise, and flying gravel from the speeding trucks. He was
famished when he finally saw the sign for his exit, but his heart
lit up when he saw the familiar streets of his suburb. How many
times had he cruised these boulevards in his Z? He had bought gas
at this convenience store with his parents' credit card. There was
his neighborhood McDonald's™.

The sight of the McDonald's™ made his mouth water, and he was on the verge of spending a little of his precious cash on a Quarter Pounder™ when he had a sobering thought: What if he were to run into some of the kids from school in there? He knew what to expect from his Best Friend, and he suspected that the reaction of any of his lesser acquaintances at Provincial Oaks High would be even less friendly. He was also, if truth be told, more than a little embarrassed to be seen in his diminished state. He could well imagine the laughter and general hilarity that would ensue at his expense should his crowd see him in his rags. So he kept walking.

Walking itself was problematic in this region of shopping malls and six-lane thoroughfares. There was no provision for pedestrians whatsoever, except the walkways that led from the enormous parking lots to the myriad points of sale around them, so to walk along the road was both obvious and dangerous. He discovered, though, that he could walk for miles without leaving the relative safety of the parking lots. He would enter the lot at one edge and proceed toward the door as if he were a normal customer who had parked nearby. When he got to the door he would simply veer off toward the far end of the lot, as if he had now finished shopping and were returning to his car.

When he passed the Home Depot™ it occurred to him to mingle with the Hispanic laborers who loitered by the entrance. Some of them were dressed as poorly as Q, so he imagined he could be inconspicuous among them. They looked at him, however, with looks like daggers, with one cabron even discretely revealing the knife in his hand.

Q hurried on, then, to the next parking lot, a large mall that stretched for several miles. Though he had driven this area a hundred times Q had never seen it from the ground, and none of it seemed familiar.

When he finally turned onto Provincial Oaks Boulevard, the street that led to his beloved subdivision, he was weakening noticeably, panting, stumbling and turning pale. He needed to rest and decided to do so beside an overpass that took the Boulevard over a railroad track. He walked down beside the bridge until he was out of sight of the road, flattened out a spot in the tall grass and lay down.

There was no real sleeping with the roar of traffic practically on top of him, and he lay staring vacantly through the grass into the darkness under the bridge, without actually sleeping, until he noticed that there was a shape among the shadows in the bridge's structure. A human figure was squatting back there.

"Who are you?" Q asked.

"I am the Troll," he replied. "Come on in."

The Troll sat back on his combat-boot-heels with his arms over his knees. The Troll lived under this bridge with just a few close friends, he told Q, and unfortunately the quarters were too close for him to be able to invite Q to stay. He was called the Troll, he replied to Q's questioning, because he lived under bridges and whenever he had the opportunity he jumped out and frightened pedestrians, but no pedestrians ever crossed this bridge. He was filthy and stank to high heaven, even more than Q was used to. He suggested that Q might like to walk with him down the tracks a short way to more suitable lodging. Q was exhausted and very interested in a place to rest, and so they set out.

This railroad track was entirely unknown to Q, even though he had driven over it and beside it a thousand times. He had noticed the large cars sitting on the track before, but he had never really thought about what function they and the tracks under them might have. Only now, as he and the Troll walked along, stepping from tie to tie, did it occur to him that they were used for transportation. He asked the Troll how far the tracks extended, and learned they extended all over the nation, from city to city, and that they were a boon for the homeless in that they provided intercity transportation as well as a safe place to walk in the automobile-favoring suburbs.

Q asked the Troll how long he'd been living under that bridge,
wondering why he'd never seen him before. The Troll replied he'd
been there four years now, but no one ever saw the Troll and went
back to tell about it.

"And what about me?" Q asked with concern.

"Q, you're not going back," said the Troll.

After a mile or so they came to a large switch-yard full of boxcars
and working engines, a sight that filled Q with wonder. They
threaded their way around the edge to an open area beneath a freeway
overpass. Here there were perhaps fifty people gathered for some
strange sporting event. They were riding around on very tall bicycles
and other indescribable machines. They were all dressed like the
Troll, in combat boots and black rags, and when Q came among
them they turned from the festivities and greeted him with warmth.

"Hello Q," they said. "Great to see you. We'll show you the easy
way to get here, down the track. Stay off the freeway."

"How do you know who I am?" Q asked.

They all laughed. "News travels fast on the Information
Superhighway," said one, pointing to the rails that ran all around
them. "Yes, Q," said a young woman, "your reputation precedes you."

This young woman who was so fond of Q's reputation Q likewise
found appealing, in her torn black tights, garters and boots, and he
made a blushing, stammering introduction of himself which amused
all the others greatly.

"I'm Lucy," she said, ignoring them. "Let's go listen to the music."

The crowd let out friendly hoots and catcalls, but Q pretended
not to hear, took the hand she proffered and walked off with her.
"Hey Q," one whispered as they walked by, "you'll know you're
in love when her sweat don't stink," and they all laughed. But Q
turned up his nose and walked on.

They sat down on the ground in front of a musician who was tuning his instrument, a banjo- or sitar-like contraption which appeared to be made from animal bones and stretched hide. He sat cross-legged on top of a barrel which bore warnings in cryptic images: skulls and crossbones, hands on fire, and eyes with lightning come out of them. After carefully tuning the two rusty strings on his instrument, the musician plucked them simultaneously and seemed happy with the result, though to Q they sounded grossly disharmonic. He began to play an atonal but rhythmic pattern, an odd song that did not repeat itself, and after a few strums opened his mouth, looked straight at Q, and sang:

> Once someone born to luxury
> came to ride the rails with us.
> Once someone was given a name
> and let it slip right off his tongue.
>
> Q doesn't know how this song knows him;
> nor will he ever,
> for he's found in the gutter his luminous Lucy.
> Her sweet sweaty smell will render him goosey.
>
> The Troll brought him to us.
> and we love the Troll.
> The Troll is a saviour of souls.
> from down in their holes.
>
> Oh Q you're happy now you don't need a name.
> You're among friends getting ready
> to lose your rosey-cheeked virginity
> which may be cute but you'd rather be dirty.

At this point the minstrel jumped off the barrel and began flailing a rousing instrumental verse and dancing among the crowd, who all stood up and joined him. Q got up too, following Lucy, and attempted awkwardly to dance with her, drawing guffaws from the crowd. Someone handed him a bottle and bade him drink, which he did, tasting a strange liquor that seemed sweet and bitter at once.

Suddenly two of the dancers snatched him from behind and lifted him to their shoulders. "Q,Q,Q" everyone yelled, and they danced around our mortified hero like pagans round a fatted calf. Someone stood up one of the tall bicycles and his bearers put him on it and set him adrift. He wobbled at first on the ungainly thing but soon found his balance and began riding happily in a circle, teetering dangerously above the crowd. Others got on their crazy bikes and rode with him among the dancers.

Then Q's front wheel slipped on a rail, and he went down. He came up a little bloody but felt no pain as they handed him the bottle again. He drank deeply and rejoined the dance, whirling till all was a blur, and he fell again, this time rolling over on his back laughing. Lucy came and stood over him, swaying slightly, with the bottle in her hand. She put a swig in her mouth and knelt down and fed it to him in a kiss. He let the heady stuff run down his cheek and chin, then he pulled her to him and began to cover her with kisses as they rolled on the ground and the crowd egged them on. He could taste her salty skin and smell her unwashed funk, and that taste and that smell were like sweet ambrosia.

The couple holed up for two days in a boxcar, while the rest of the group catered to them, bringing them water and food (crumpled Snickers™ bars and half-eaten Quarter Pounders™) and a chamber pot in the form of a five-gallon bucket. Others slept in the car with them, off and on, and more than once Q happened to look around while in the act and find himself caught out, in flagrante delicto, with half a dozen of their fellows looking on. The surveillance seemed benevolent enough, even flattering, and any embarrassment Q may have felt was easily overcome by his ardor.

He was quite in love, in love with her soiled skin, her aforementioned smell, the look in her eyes of pure disdain, as well as her voice. She seemed inordinately witty and funny, and he hung on her every word. "Where are you from?" he finally asked. "What is your story?"

She settled back, bare-chested, on the balled up blanket she was using as a pillow, lit a cigarette, and told the following tale. As she began, others came over to listen, until there was a crowd of perhaps a dozen squatting and sitting cross-legged around them.

Lucy's Story

"I wasn't raised in the suburbs like you," she began. "I never spent more than a couple of years in one place."

"My father was in the military, an attaché, a Colonel when I was born though he later made General, and while I was growing up he was stationed at various bases in Europe and the Middle East and the States. I was born in Saudi Arabia and went to school in Berlin, Prague, Madrid, Rome, Paris, and Washington. I'm conversant in German and Italian, fluent in Spanish and French, and, as you'll soon learn, I can stumble along in Arabic. I lived a life of ease and sophistication over there, with chauffeurs and kitchen help courtesy of whichever government we were guests of at the time.

"But I was never in one place for more than a couple of years, so I never made lasting friends and always felt like an outcast. I wasn't an only child, but I was already ten when my Little Brother was born." (She sneered sarcastically when she pronounced his name.) "So while my mother crooned over the little snot-bag, I was sent off to school with a bunch of bitches who didn't even speak my language. When Little Brother finally started school, she went to the headmaster and discussed his course of study and how special arrangements must be made to accommodate his *sensitive* nature.

But the closest she ever came to one of my schools was the brochure.

"'Of course you'll do well,' she always said. And I did. I learned to survive as an alien. I got good at languages because I found out if I didn't get fluent in a matter of weeks I'd be a pariah for the rest of my stay and never make any friends at all. I read and studied a lot, at first because there was nothing else to do but later because I found that reading books from different eras and cultures helped me realize that none of this stuff I was experiencing was anything more than silly provincialism.

"I was in high school before I had my first boyfriend, Jean-Paul. Jean-Paul was a name he'd chosen; I never knew his real one. He named himself after Sartre but also after Belmondo, and he said I reminded him of Jean Seberg, and he even made me dye and cut my hair like hers in *Breathless*. We had a lovely, decadent time of it for a while. We'd skip school and shack up in the back room of his parent's house in the Batignolles, and on weekends we'd lay in the grass and watch the old men play Pétanque in the Square.

"It was a great time. I finally felt like there was a place I actually wanted to be, rather than just going places to get away from the house or school. But we were both restless and hungry so when Jean-Paul hatched his get-rich scheme I went along even though I didn't need money. His idea was to go to Morrocco and buy a few kilos of hash. We could easily make 30 or 40 thousand Euros in a weekend, he told me. He'd known people who had done it, and they could supply us with the contacts down there. My diplomatic passport would make it a cinch for us.

"So I told my parents I was going to the Riviera with a girl-friend and we got on the train. We took the ferry from Sete to Tangier, rented a car and drove up into the mountains to meet our contact, whom we never actually found, but that was no matter. There were farmers selling it by the roadside.

"When they found out how much we wanted, they took us back to a little barn whose walls were lined with kilo bricks. They lit a hookah for us to try and pretty soon we were both flying. Jean-Paul started bragging to them about how after this trip he was going to come back and buy the whole barn. He told them about my diplomatic passport and that my father was an ambassador. What a fucking idiot.

"A few minutes later a couple of big guys came in and put rags soaked in ether over our faces. I struggled my best but these guys were strong. I can still remember the sight of Jean-Paul going under, kicking and twisting, and his eyes were wild. That's what I saw as darkness closed around me. I've dreamed about Jean-Paul, since, but I never saw him again."

At this point Q saw a single tear roll from his lover's eye and trace a forlorn trail in the dirt on her cheek.

"I woke up in the back of a van," she continued after a heartfelt pause, "bound hand and foot. It was about 130 degrees outside, and we were travelling across open desert on a dirt trail. Sometimes I would literally choke from the dust that came in the open windows. My two kidnappers kept me tied up like that for days. They would speak to me in French now and then, just to tell me to shut up, but mostly they argued between themselves in Arabic. I didn't know much Arabic before that trip but having nothing to do but listen I quickly developed an ear for it and gradually figured out they were trying to decide how and where and to whom to sell me.

"Whenever they had to interact with people on the road they would duct-tape my mouth closed and throw a burqa over me so that I looked like one of their wives. And gradually they started to treat me like a real wife, which is to say they forgot about me. Then they started talking about what a problem I was and how they wished they'd never gotten into this scam, how it might be best for them to cut their losses and leave me in the desert. In the end their reason triumphed as they deduced they could always get something for me as a simple slave, even if it was only a fraction of what I was really worth.

"We were headed East, as the brutal sun would not let me forget, so I figured we were in Algeria, and I just prayed they were heading for Tunisia rather than Libya, though down deep I knew better. When we finally crossed the border, after six or seven days on what passed for roads out there, they didn't even bother to tape my mouth. They simply told me what I already knew, that I had more to fear from Qadhafi's thugs than I did from my immediate captors. And they, at least, were a known quantity. To their credit, I have to say, they never raped me nor even made me feel such was their intention. It was almost as if they were afraid of sullying their investment. They might have even thought I was a virgin.

"We crossed into Libya out on the frontier, sitting in line with trucks full of goats and chickens. The border guards looked menacing with their AK-47's hanging off their shoulders, but they barely looked at our papers and settled quickly and easily for a few dinar. We continued on those godforsaken back roads, turning gradually northward, and the road began to rise as the way became more mountainous. Every now and then we'd see a shepherd squatting by a fire on the roadside and stop and have tea or bitter coffee with him. Petrol was always in short supply, and whenever we found any they filled the van and the several metal cans they had strapped to the top.

"I thought that road was never going to end. We lived for days on rice and warm goat's milk. I got to where I didn't think twice about shitting on the roadside with them watching. That's one handy thing about a burqa; you can squat and do your business and it's like you've got your own private little bathroom. And then one day the road seemed to be a little smoother. And then a few miles further on it was actually paved. And then there was traffic, houses. Dense, squalid slums. We were in Tripoli."

"We pulled down one of those little streets that seemed made for mules and mopeds but not motorized vehicles and stopped in front of an unmarked door. There I was exchanged for some quantity of Euros and left in the company of a bearded businessman in a fez who barely even looked at me before setting me to scrubbing down his elegantly tiled riad. There were four other girls there, too, likewise employed. They stared at me and occasionally giggled. I couldn't tell what language they were speaking because they only spoke in whispers and shunned me like an untouchable. It was like high school times ten.

"Our lord and master spent the day jabbering on the phone about real-estate deals and sending his boy running this way and that on errands around the city. We girls served his dinner (with me looking on like an idiot while the others, twittering like birds, prepared his lamb in the tajeen). After dinner he had his mint tea and then retired to his room. I thought this was to be the end of my first day in paradise, but just as he was closing his door he reached out and grabbed my arm, pulling me in with him. He barked at me in Arabic until I understood what he wanted (not that hard to guess) and stripped off the burqa.

"My naked body, however, gave him pause. My face and arms were sun-browned and covered with dust from the miserable journey, but my less public areas were still as pale as Jean Seberg. He seemed to register this fact with both excitement and concern. He paced around the room pulling his beard and muttering in a state of high anxiety, then he banged his head against the wall and groaned. Then he went to the door and called in one of the other girls. She, also, was visibly affected by my whiteness. He barked something at her in Arabic, then the two of them grabbed me and threw me on the pile of rugs he used for a bed. The girl sat on me and held my legs open for his convenience."

"After that I had to go to his bed every night. He always kept another girl there with us even though I quit putting up a fight early on. He fell in love with me, but this was my curse, because it made him insane, and it made the other girls hate me even more. They never spoke to me and were constantly giving me the evil eye (by looking at me when they thought I couldn't see them). They left blue handprints on the wall above my pallet as a talisman, and I never walked into a room that they did not cease their talking and turn to look at me.

"As for the Master, he vacillated in his treatment of me from brutal to cajoling, sometimes screaming at me or slapping me for some imagined infraction and then immediately dropping to his knees to kiss my feet and wash them with his tears. He would ravish me at night, covering me with exotic oils and scents while one of the girls sullenly fanned us with a palm leaf, but as soon as he came his attitude would change to disgust. He would sneer at me, spit on me and worse, all the while muttering guttural curses. Then, just as suddenly, he would start to coo and beg my forgiveness. He would have the girl clean me up in the tadelakt pool in the courtyard, and then he would bring me back in and we'd start all over.

"After a couple of weeks this routine seemed to become as tiresome to him as it was to me, and he sold me off. He took me out to the street—the first time I had set foot outside his riad—and hailed a taxi. I had a brief moment of hope when I saw we were headed for the airport. I actually thought for a moment he was giving me back to Europe. We entered the airport through a side gate, with some apparent exchange of currencies, and drove right out onto the tarmac. He took me up to the steps of the plane and, after one last nostalgic round of spitting in my face and kissing my feet, accepted a wad of bills from the uniformed attendant and went off.

"When I entered the plane I found it full—so full one could only stand—of young men. I was greeted with the usual stares, the stares of young men everywhere, no matter how rich or poor, Christian, Jewish, Muslim or Hindu. I looked around hopefully as the engines revved and we started to move. I ventured to ask, in French, if anyone knew where we were going. A voice came out of the crowd:

"'Dubai,' it said."

N ow Q had been listening intently to the ups and downs of this story. His heart beat faster when he heard of her suffering, and he could have clawed himself from the anxiety the sex scenes caused him, but now he breathed a sigh of relief at her salvation. "Oh thank God," he said. "Dubai. I've heard it's the exact place of the Garden of Eden, and that it is the Garden of Eden today."

"Yes, if you like waterslides and indoor skiing, it's the Garden of Eden," she said, "for a few. For the majority of people who actually live there, though, it's more like Hades. All those people who work on the fancy buildings, who lug the steel and pour the concrete and turn down the beds and cook the food, all of them live in tents and cardboard hutches, or in tenements twelve to a room. They earn next to nothing, virtual slaves, with their work schedules enforced by the police.

"When you fly into Dubai as a slave you see something very different from what the tourist sees. I never even saw the famous man-made islands or the giant skyscrapers. Our plane had no windows. And we were hustled straight off it into a truck and thence immediately to our hutches. I was questioned about my abilities and my skill with languages landed me a job in a hotel, a very sweet assignment compared to the construction workers. I did room service in the morning and cleaned in the afternoon. I worked from six in the morning to six at night and earned six dollars every day. (At least that's what they told me; I actually never received any money.) Every morning the police woke us up, fed us some slop, and loaded us onto buses to be brought into town, and in the evening they took us back, and they did roll-call at each end.

"I had been there about a week when one day I was sent up to the 70th floor to investigate some strange antics. Security had reported a child in the hallway without supervision and acting so strangely they suspected he might need medical attention. He would jump up and down, then clutch his heart as if dying, then flap his wings like a bird, then roll around on the floor and foam at the mouth. But I only had to watch this performance for a few seconds to understand that it was merely a game. It was a game, in fact, that I knew only too well, for the child was my Little Brother."

"No..." breathed Q, "it's impossible! It's simply too much of a coincidence. Your brother, there at the same time you are, in the same hallway, halfway around the world from where you last saw him?"

"Coincidence," Lucy replied, "is in the eye of the beholder. When it happens to you, it is only an incident, but when it happens to someone else, it is *co*incidence, but there are so many people in the world, these days, coincidence is unavoidable. Everything that happens is too much of a coincidence."

"You're making it seem more complicated than it is," Q retorted. "There is either coincidence, pure accident, which implies that the universe is chaotic, or there is no coincidence, no accident, only pure cause and effect, and the universe is rational."

"Maybe," she said, "but actually my Little Brother's appearance on the 70th floor of the hotel where I was working seems coincidental to you only because of aspects of the story I have left out for the sake of brevity and other aspects which I overemphasized for the sake of an immediately intelligible plot. I didn't tell you, for example, that my parents had been discussing a trip to Dubai at the same time as I was discussing my trip to the 'Riviera,' but had you been truly attentive you would have deduced this for yourself."

"But why," wondered Q, "must I be so attentive? Why can't I just relax and listen to your story because I love your voice?"

"I also didn't tell you about the subtle ways I was able to influence the path my journey took," she continued. "I used every trick in the book, from reverse motivation ('oh please please don't send me to Dubai; oh anything but that.') to whispering simple mantras into my captors' ears while they slept ('We should go East. We'll go to Tripoli and send her on to Dubai.')

"Below the crude events of the story I tell, there are subtle gradations, nuances, causes and subliminal effects, but this doesn't mean that there is any more effective, affective, or *true* way to say it than the simple 'I was there, and he was there.' And he was playing his silly epileptic game, and I went and stood over him and called him by name until he opened his eyes and saw me.

"Recognition, then bewilderment, then suspicion came over his face. 'Lucy?' he bleated. He got slowly to his feet and began to back away from me, and then he turned and ran down the hallway screaming 'Mom, mom, Lucy stole the maid's uniform. Mom, Lucy's pretending to be a maid.'"

"My Mother's powers of deduction were slightly more perceptive than my Brother's. 'Wait a minute,' she said. 'What are you doing in Dubai? You're supposed to be at the Riviera. How can you afford this hotel?'

"She was genuinely surprised when I reminded her I'd left for 'the Riviera' more than six weeks ago. 'That long?' she said. 'Well certainly your Father has filed a missing person report by now. What do you mean, giving us that kind of scare?'

"'She's bad,' Little Brother chimed in, smelling blood.

"'No I'm not,' I told them, and in fact from that moment I was not bad. I was a victim pure and simple, forced onto the boat at Sete, kidnapped and brought to the Dark Continent. The original purpose, the barn lined with kilos of hash, and Jean-Paul's very existence, were erased from the record so completely I forgot them myself. I had to tell the story so many times—to my father, to his team of psychiatrists, to the CIA—I grew hoarse from it, and each time I told it it got a little better, a little smoother, until finally that other, the reality, ceased to exist entirely.

"They took me back to Paris, of course, and at first I was glad, but after just a few days I was pacing the floor. I couldn't stand it, any of it, the soft bed or the people on the street, the air-conditioning or the stifling heat in the park. So I talked them into sending me back. They set it up with my uncle, who lives not far from here. But when I landed I walked straight out of the airport, never even picked up my checked bag, dropped my passport and my wallet in a trash can by the door, walked down the highway till I came to the railroad, and I've been living on the tracks ever since."

"So," said Q, "you're like me, lacking all Identity. But you let it go on purpose. Mine was taken from me by force. You can probably get yours back. Do your parents know where you are?"

"You're wrong," she said. "Once you give it up, you can't get it back. But if it's taken by force, you might have a chance."

Q considered for a moment and then agreed. "Yes," he said, "I have to try, just in case. I have to continue on my journey back to Provincial Oaks."

"Yes," she said, "you do. And getting back to Provincial Oaks is no problem at all. I'll take you there now."

They got dressed, then, for the first time since entering the boxcar, and said good-bye to their love-nest of padded-down tarpaulins and old furniture pads. They stood wistfully, arm in arm, over the place their bodies had lain, then went out into the daylight and set off.

They had only gone a quarter mile when Lucy left the track and turned up the embankment. At the top was a Sound Barrier, a twelve-foot-high wall of solid concrete. It seemed quite insurmountable to Q, but Lucy showed him how to use the horizontal scoring as a ladder, and they were soon at the top looking over. Below them, across the freeway, lay Provincial Oaks, spread-out across the valley like a life-sized map.

From this coign of vantage they could see Q's house quite plainly. Landscapers were working in the front yard. Seven dark-skinned workers bustled over the yard, trimming the hedges and putting in a new flower bed, while the white foreman supervised from the shade. A woman came out of the house and directed the workers, pointing at various piles of soil and plants and then pointing to the areas of the yard where they were to go. Then she came forward waving happily to the neighbor across the street, the neighbor Q had last seen from the back of a police car.

The sight filled Q with longing. "What are they doing to our yard?" he moaned sadly. Then one of the garage doors opened and Q saw a young man about his own age get into a car—a Z of all things—and drive out and away down the street. Q looked after him painfully, then climbed back down the wall and sat on the ground. He was sobbing when Lucy joined him, and he buried his head in her breast.

"It's OK," she said. "Who would want to live there anyway?"

"Oh Lucy," he whimpered, "I can never go back there now. Somebody else is there now. Somebody else is me now. Oh Lucy, you're my saving grace. But for you, I'd have no life at all."

"There now, Q," she cooed as she kissed his forehead, "I'm right here for you. Everything's going to be fine." But she was looking out over Q's head and down the track.

After one more night of luxurious passion, Q woke to find a note on her pillow.

> Hey Q—Got some business to take of—Catch up with you down the line. —L

He stared at the scrap of paper in disbelief for a moment, then started yelling her name, tormenting his compatriots. He jumped out of the boxcar naked and went running around the yard waking everyone and begging them for news of his love. Finally he found one who said he'd seen her leaving before dawn. She'd hopped a grain car on the morning train, he told Q, and he pointed to the track she had ridden out on.

Q tore off down the rail after her, still naked, bloodying his feet on the sharp rocks between the ties, crying and wailing in pure torment. His naked body was no match for the hardness of the way, though, and when his feet would carry him no further he threw himself in the ditch and writhed in the weeds like the poorest wretch that had ever breathed in life.

The others, now quite awake, watched the pitiful display from a distance. A few of them made to help him, but others with greater wisdom advised them to reason through their charitable urges. In his weakened state, he could easily become dependent on such acts of largesse and lose his motivation for self-betterment. So, for his own good, they left him in his ditch for the rest of the day, and though they could hear his mournful cries and see his broken body lying just a few feet away, no Samaritan emerged from among them.

When Q finally rose from his hard bed, he seemed a different man, leaner and tougher than he had been even after his weeks at the Shelter. He walked back to the boxcar without so much as a limp, rudely pushing aside anyone who happened in his path. He emerged clothed again in his rags and boots with his backpack on his shoulder. Without a word to anyone he walked across the lot to where the switchers were making up the evening train. He found a place on the back of a hopper car and lay down. Then a whistle blew, and he was gone.

He rode the rails for weeks, then, asking after Lucy in each of the various tribes of the homeless he encountered. There were more tall-bikers and gutter punks, but there were traditional hobo camps too, and tent cities—with orderly rows of clean, identical tents, and police at the gates—for people with regular jobs but too much debt to afford a house or an apartment, "white collar" workers who emerged from their tents each morning in coats and ties, carrying tidy jars of urine. He asked in every encampment, but no one could recall a girl matching her description, though some did comment that a creature such as Q described did not exist outside heaven.

He despaired of ever finding her, in the end, but he kept going because he could no longer bear to sit still. He began to avoid the camps rather than seeking them out, preferring solitude to the company of strangers. He rode aimlessly, not caring where the next train was going. When the night air turned cooler, he aimed south. When it got too damp, he went west.

He paid so little attention he sometimes wound up on sidings, with his car dumping its dusty cargo into the screw-pit below, or being loaded from a conveyor above. He rode where people who drive cars never go, through backwaters and industrial slums, coal yards, and vast lumber mills whose entire acreage was black with creosote. He passed by the rusting hulks of refineries, smelled the naphtha in the air, heat waves rising from the burn-off and, on the other side of the track, swamps, dead lakes full of orange water with junked cars and chemical barrels half-submerged in the shallows.

He rode through stockyards and pig farms where animals wallowed knee-deep in offal, fed by conveyor belts. The stench was horrific, and the ammonia in the air burned his eyes. Once, when stopped in such a place for loading, Q remarked to a yard foreman that the smell was quite unbearable. "Oh no, Q," the foreman said, "it smells good. It smells like money. This is money; smell it." He inhaled deeply and sighed with pleasure.

Q rode across the endless plain for days without stopping, the monochrome landscape broken only by an occasional mechanized reaper. He rode in the shadow of great mountains and on ledges above the clouds. He sat and watched the land pass by, impassive as a Buddha under sun and rain, through wind and snow.

Once, as they were crossing a road outside some nameless city, Q noticed a young man waiting in his car (a Z, naturally) at the roadblock. He was talking on his cell phone, oblivious to the bulky contraption passing in front of him, but he happened to glance up as Q came into view. Their eyes met and locked for a moment, until the bum on the train passed out of sight, and he turned his attention back to the phone.

On these sojourns Q took to jumping off the train, now and again, when it slowed for a turn or an intersection outside urban areas, to take a bit of country air and give his bones a rest from the hard iron bed that had become his lot. He would spend a night on the pasture under the stars and loll in the grass in the morning until the next train came by. But one of these brief forays off the track brought more than a place to rest.

He jumped off when the moon revealed a pleasant grove accessible from the track, and he made his bed there. He fell asleep with a breeze bending the weeds around him and the trees sighing overhead, but when he woke the next morning he was startled to discover he was not alone. His visitor was quite short—no more than four and a half feet—and he had angular, weathered features, very dark, stout and muscular. Q could not decide if he was a youth like himself or if he was in fact rather aged. He was resting on his haunches just a few feet from Q's natural bed, staring at him with devout attention. Q raised himself on an elbow.

"Hola Q," the interloper said. He said "koo" for Q.

Q stared at him. "How do you know who I am?"

"I… know… you"… he struggled to find the words… "reputación tú le precede. Your reputation… comes before."

Q sat up and addressed him more forcefully. "OK, everyone seems to know who I am, but who are you?"

The little man stood up and began attempting to say something to Q in an improvised sign language, pointing to the ground then to the treetops then to the rails. Then he came forward, picked up a stick and drew the figure of an S on the ground. He allowed Q to regard the cipher for a moment, then dropped to his knees and added details to the head and tail of the figure which turned it into a snake.

"S," said Q. "S for Snake."

"Si, Snake, Serpiente, si, pero Santo, Santo Serpiente," he cried, and he leaped to his feet and did a little dance, pointing to himself and saying over and over, "Soy Santo. Soy Serpiente. Soy Santo. Soy Snake. Soy que soy!"

Santo's antics were so ridiculous they brought a smile to Q's face, the first since he'd taken to the rails, and he suddenly realized that he was finally getting bored with his solitude. "OK, Mr. Santo," Q said, "you stick with me, and we'll see what adventure awaits us, and whether it be good or ill."

The suddenly inseparable duo set out across the field on foot, with Santo pointing with his stick and jabbering persuasively about some sort of bounty that was to be found just over a hill they could see in the distance. Q was skeptical of going cross-country, but demurred to Santo's obviously greater skill in the wild.

Their way led across a pasture on which a few brindled cows grazed. Q eyed them warily, but Santo laughed and waved his stick and sent them trotting away. Santo then pointed with glee to some small mushrooms that were growing directly out of piles of the cows' filth scattered around the field, and he began to run from pile to pile gathering them. Q gave a look of disgust when Santo presented them to him, saying "good, good," but in the end his hunger convinced him to trust his helper, and he plopped a handful of the small buttons in his mouth. Then Santo shrugged his shoulders and munched a few of the fungi himself.

They crested the hill a little later, with their strength waning but still in cheery humor, and found themselves on the rim of wide, wind-scoured plateau. Squinting into the blow, Q beheld something very strange ahead, an array of giant towers topped by spinning chromium propellers, hundreds and hundreds of them, stretching in a grid-like formation as far as he could see. The sun glinted blindingly on the prismatic surfaces of the rotors, causing colorful spectra to orbit around them, combining and clashing in their intersections with kaleidoscopic effect. Occasionally a colorful disc would spin out of the field and into the sky, or a bolt of color would shoot straight across the plain toward them. The scene was quite beautiful and entrancing, Q thought, but something about it also made him feel slightly queasy and enormously lethargic, so that he had to sit down on the ground and simply watch. He sensed there was a story unfolding, a strange narrative in which colors took the place of voices, and the continuous flux became a kind of progress.

Santo attempted to interrupt Q's reverie by grabbing his shoulder and pointing with his stick. "No look sun, no look sun," he admonished. Q turned and looked at him without comprehension, then looked back at the bright field. The three words echoed in his mind until they seemed to join in the vision, coalescing into a figure that emerged from the colorful confusion and came marching toward them. He looked like some fighter from a video game—part samurai, part Mongol, part G.I. Joe, part robot—magnificently armored in Kevlar™ and bronze, with throwing stars and concussion grenades stapled to his vest, and Q understood his name to be No Luck Son.

Somewhere in the distance, Q could hear someone speaking in a strange language, but he did not comprehend that it was his new companion, Santo, exhorting frantically in his native tongue to stop his charge from moving forward, for Q had risen and was moving out to meet the approaching warrior. Strength surged through his young limbs as he anticipated the fight. His lethargy left him and he was suffused with energy; he bounced on his feet and boxed the air, huffing and spitting in contempt for his elaborately dressed opponent, who had now stopped and raised his arm, pointing his finger at Q, as if to accuse him.

When Q opened his eyes next it was to a close-up view of the little stones that littered the plain, which appeared in his vision like giant boulders. Then a boot fell into view, a strange-looking boot covered with mirrors. He rolled over on his back and looked up. The warrior stood over him with his arms crossed and his helmet gleaming, and behind the warrior stood one of the chrome towers, topped by its turbine, the two of them forming a single dragon-like apparition. Q braced himself for the kicks that might be coming from these horrible boots, but instead of finishing the job the warrior reached up and took off his helmet, then loosened his vest and dropped it to the ground, then his gloves which bristled with arrows, and the Kevlar™ chaps, and finally even the boots, until there seemed there would be nothing left of this warrior if he took off one more thing, and then from the steaming pile of armor and wearable weaponry there emerged a sight far stranger than anything Q could have hallucinated: a businessman in a Brooks-Brothers™ suit.

"Phew," he sighed, dusting himself off, "glad to be out of that! Man! Oh and hey Q, sorry about the taser. No really. It gave me not the least bit of pleasure. But it's dangerous out here, you know, high voltage around from the turbines and all. Why, there's even a reactor just over that rise. And of course the electric fence. We wouldn't want anyone getting hurt or anything, and you were looking at those windmills like a crazy man. I was afraid you were going to start jousting with them or something. Our concern is for you, because you are our customer, and we take care of our customers, because our customers are our life blood. But hey, I have the advantage of you, let me introduce myself."

He handed Q his card, which contained but a single word:

ENTROPY™

"That's right, Q," the exuberant fellow went on, "I'm with Entropy™. Pleased to meet you. This is our wind farm, where we make energy out of the air. Here, let me give you a hand." He reached out a hand to help Q up. "I work for Entropy™," he continued, "and helping people is our business. Entropy™ is a pioneer investor in renewable energy sources. We're helping keep our nation green with innovative solutions to the tough problems the energy sector faces today.

"With this wind farm, we've taken an ancient technology and renovated it for our modern age. You may not see any knights in armor out here, and yet we like to think it's just like the days of yore, when man lived in harmony with his environment, and all his energy needs were met with absolute respect for nature.

"We're working day and night keeping your lights on and your car running with safe, healthy energy alternatives and making sure you pay the lowest possible fair-market rates allowed by law for regulated monopolies, so you can always be assured you are getting the best value possible.

"Do you think that, in your reduced state, what I'm saying doesn't concern you? Our Office of Community Relations helps keep the nation's corporate environment a safe and happy place for all of our customers. For example, outside our nuclear facility number 76, there was once a disorderly swamp, breeding ground for leeches and mosquitoes. Today, that land is a park with baseball diamonds and a soccer field where future athletes hone their competitive skills and parents eat popcorn in the stands."

"But wait a minute," said Q, "You sound like a commercial. You even show that little trademark symbol when you speak. How am I supposed to believe you or think that what you say is real and true when you sound like that?"

"Q," said the Entropy™ Executive, "I hear you, loud and clear. I know something is troubling you, that the world is seeming somewhat hostile to you now, and I want to help. I'm going to suggest that the two of us take a little stroll along this fence, where we can talk about how things could be arranged for the benefit of all."

Q was impressed at the Executive's insight into his own troubled heart, so he replied eagerly in the affirmative, and they began to stroll in leisurely fashion along the fence. Santo, having observed and overheard all that had ensued thus far, followed at a discreet distance, so as to remain within earshot without interrupting the discourse of his Masters.

Editor's Note

The story is spoiled at this moment, as the author leaves the page with the debate impending, giving as excuse that he could find no more information about the exploits of Q than what has been set down, above. Fortunately, the subsequent author (yours truly) was not so willing to believe that a history as important as this could have been allowed to fall into oblivion, or that scholars could have been so undiscerning as not to preserve in their archives and registries some record of Q's accomplishments.

The great pleasure I (if I may switch to first person) had taken in editing and proofing this brief introduction turned to frustration as I realized how slight were my chances of finding the remainder of the story. Still, it seemed impossible and contrary to all literary precedent that such an important character as Q should have disappeared without some record of his adventures to come. In the old days, knights-errant had their sages to follow them and embellish their stories. And in our time, everyone of any note at all has a biographer; Marilyn Monroe had Mailer; Nixon had Woodward and Bernstein; J.B. Hunt had Schwartz; Louis Riel had a Boyden; W and Sara had their ghosts; and these for the recording not only of their heroic exploits in war, politics and business, but also of their most trifling thoughts and fantasies, however maudlin they might be. Surely in our information age there was more to be found on the subject of this Q.

But, alas, I didn't know where to look, and the prospect of spending hours on the internet in search of facts was daunting, so I finally decided Time, destroyer of all things, had won this round and consigned our fledgling hero to oblivion with the rest of us.

Still Q remained in my thoughts. There was a time, in this land, when a sense of camaraderie and shared purpose united the citizenry, police and civilian alike, a time when the poor (or the lazy or intemperate) could sleep on the street, if necessity forced them to, without fear of harassment or arrest. Nowadays, public venality has risen to the point that in public areas every horizontal surface has had spikes and railings installed, and anyone sleeping outside is subject to arrest or at least a good kicking, and the population of our jails swells to such proportion we are justifiably compared to the Spanish Inquisition. But Q invoked the spirit of a bygone (or—I suppose we should just say it—imagined) time when the poor and downtrodden were seen as a kind of nobility.

And I hope that some fraction of this nobility may accrue to myself, also, both for the poverty I have endured and for the pains I went to in searching out the remainder of this history. The discovery was made as follows:

One day I was shopping among the mercantile bounty of one of those great cities typical of our land and happened into a shop whose genre encompasses priceless antiques, worthless junk, and the entire field between. I was perusing the aisles with no real purpose but to see what was there, and my eye was drawn, as it often is in such establishments, to the literature area, which consisted of an ancient oaken bookcase on whose shelves, as if to complete the display, were several books with ornate bindings. A quick glance at these told me that they, like the shelves they rested on, were priced for bourgeois library decoration rather than scholars of limited means such as myself, and I let my eye wander downward where, by the look of the successively shabbier bindings, I imagined the prices would be descending, finally stopping at the very last item on the bottom shelf, a curiously fat volume bound only with that cheap plastic binding provided by copy shops like Kinkos™. I pulled this one out and discovered, just under the clear plastic cover, one of those peremptory rejection slips we editors are accustomed to receiving. This one read:

Dear Author:

Though we read your work with interest, it does not
meet the needs of ***Publisher*** Press at this time.
Please do not imagine that this in any way reflects on
the quality of your work, which we found to be of the
highest caliber. We can only accept a small percentage of
the manuscripts we receive.

Sincerely, The Editors

Turning over this sheet I came to the title page of the volume,
where I saw:

La historia muy curiosa de "Q"

My curiosity was, of course, immediately aroused by the "Q,"
though the rest of the inscription was foreign to me, and I looked
around hoping to find someone who could translate it. I took it up
to the proprietor who, when I asked if he could read it, said that
he could, and told me it was, according to the title, a story about
a certain Q.

Could this be, I wondered, the same Q whose story I began
editing so long ago and which was languishing in dire need of
continuation? I grabbed the manuscript from him and thumbed
through it randomly, stopping at a hand-written note in a margin. I
recognized a word in it, and when I showed it to the proprietor, he
told me the note translated to: "This is the same Lucy mentioned
earlier in the story."

When I heard Lucy's name, I became so excited I didn't even
negotiate with the merchant but paid him the written price of one
dollar for the manuscript. I then told him I would be needing a
translator, to which he replied he knew one, and called out to the
back of the store, "hijo, venga." A swarthy youth appeared from
the depths of the store and stood before me. When I asked him if
he could translate the volume for me, he glanced at it and said, "Of

course; it is my native language." Without further hesitation, I took him down the street to a coffee shop known as a gathering place for writers. On that day, then, and on almost every day for some months afterward, he and I sat at a table, he with the manuscript in front of him and me with my laptop, as he dictated to me his offhand translation of the text while I transcribed it into my Macbook™. What I transcribed during these sessions follows here.

The manuscript contained, near the beginning, a single illustration. The quality of the picture was not high—it appeared to be a photocopy of a photograph—but there could be no doubt it was Q. This is the only image I have of Q, and it has only strengthened the vision I had in my mind's eye, formed from the absolute clarity of the narrative.

The new manuscript took up immediately where the previous one had left off, with Q and the Entropy™ Executive beginning their dialogue, which was rendered, further, in dramatic form, so that every nuance of the discourse was captured with utter realism. This attention to detail, along with the true-to-life feel of subsequent scenes and, above all, the perfect crispness of the characters, who seem to stand up off the page and come to life, allow me to vouch with complete certainty as to the veracity of the document, and hence to the accuracy of the history contained there. Though certain quibbling questions might be raised—for example, the startling (but, as my research has revealed, purely coincidental) resemblance of the opening dialogue to the second book of Plato's *Republic* and the further resemblance of subsequent sections (and, indeed, this interlude) to that masterwork of Cervantes—these have nothing to do with the gist of the history and the accuracy of its telling. As the philosopher taught us, if history happens to agree with literary convention, who are we to question?

It is the business and duty of historians to be exact, truthful and free of passion, and neither interest nor fear, hatred nor love, should make them swerve from the path of truth, that truth which is history, rival of time, storehouse of deeds, witness of the past, example and counsel for the present, and warning for the future.

Finally, if this text that follows be wanting in any good quality, be advised it is the fault of its foreign author and not its subject or its scribe. To be brief, then, the Second Part, according to our faithful and rigorous translation, began in this way:

Book Two

Dialogue of Q and the Entropy™ Executive

Entropy™: Let's have a talk, Q. I can see you have something on your mind, something troubling you, and I want to help.

Q: The first thing I have on my mind is: How do you know who I am?

Entropy™: Well, Q, your reputation precedes you.

Q: Why, then, doesn't your reputation precede you?

Entropy™: All our reputations precede our selves, Q. But let's get to the matter at hand: building a state. And by "state" I mean both a government and a condition, an entire world. And not just any world, but the best of all possible worlds. It's serious business, not for the faint hearted. Are you ready to help us construct a state? Think about it.

Q: OK, I've thought about it, and I'm ready.

Entropy™: A state arises, as I conceive, out of the needs of mankind. No one is self-sufficient. All of us have needs and wants. Can we imagine any other origin of a state?

Q: No, there can be no other.

Entropy™: So we all have needs, and many people are required to fulfill these needs. And I take a helper for one purpose, and you take one for another, and Santo takes one for another, and when all these partners and helpers are gathered together in one place, that place is called a state.

Q: True.

Entropy™: And they exchange with one another. One gives, another receives, and vice versa, according to the principle that the exchanges will be for their mutual good and will help fulfill their needs.

Q: Very true.

Entropy™: All right then, let us see if we can create a perfect state.

Q: All the great philosophers, from Plato and Aristotle through Aquinas, Hume, Kant, Adam Smith, Hegel, Bentham, and finally Lavender, have thought that this endeavor would be of service to mankind.

Entropy™: Then, my dear Q, the task must not be given up, even if it become somewhat lengthy.

Q: Certainly not.

Entropy™: Come then, and let us pass an hour in story-telling, and our story shall be the education of our guardians, our heroes.

Q: By all means.

Entropy™: And what shall be their education? Can we imagine something better than the traditional sort?

Q: I believe so.

Entropy™: And in our new and improved system of education, do you include literature?

Q: I do.

Entropy™: And literature may be either true or false?

Q: Yes.

Entropy™: And the young should be trained in both kinds, and we begin with the false?

Q: I do not understand your meaning.

Entropy™: You know, that we begin by telling children stories which, though not wholly destitute of truth, are in the main fictitious, and these stories are told them when they are not of an age to understand the difference between truth and fiction.

Q: Very true.

Entropy™: You know also that the beginning is the most important part of any work, especially in the case of a young and tender child, for that is the time at which the character is being formed and an impression, for good or ill, is more readily made.

Q: Quite true.

Entropy™: And shall we then carelessly allow children to hear any casual tales which may be devised by casual persons, and to receive into their minds ideas for the most part the very opposite of those which we should wish them to have when they are grown up?

Q: We cannot.

Entropy™: Then the first thing will be to establish a censorship of the writers of fiction, and let the censors accept any fiction which is good and reject the bad. And we will allow mothers and nurses to tell their children the authorised tales only. Let them fashion the mind with such tales, even more fondly than they mould the body with their hands, but most of the stories which are now in use must be discarded.

Q: Of what stories are you speaking?

Entropy™: You may find a model of the lesser in the greater, for they are necessarily of the same type, and there is the same spirit in both of them.

Q: Very likely, but I do not as yet know what you would term the greater.

Entropy™: Stories such as those narrated by Hemingway and Joyce and the rest, the great story-tellers of the last century.

Q: But which stories do you mean, and what fault do you find with them?

Entropy™: A fault which is most serious, the fault of telling a lie, and, what is more, a bad lie.

Q: But when is this fault committed?

Entropy™: Whenever an erroneous representation is made of the nature of our heroes, just like when a painter paints a portrait not having the shadow of a likeness to the original.

Q: Yes, that sort of thing is certainly blameworthy, but which stories do you mean?

Entropy™: First of all, there was that greatest of all lies, in many much-lauded novels, Steinbeck's *Grapes of Wrath*, for example, of a young man who suffers under the system of capitalism. I mean, even if these representations have some basis in fact, they should certainly not be taught to young and impressionable persons. If possible, it would be better they were buried in silence. If there is an absolute necessity for their mention, a chosen few might read them in an isolated, academic setting, so that the number of readers will be very few.

Q: Yes, those stories are extremely objectionable.

Entropy™: Yes, they are stories not to be repeated in our state. The young man should not be told that in committing the worst of crimes he is being heroic, and that even if he criticizes the laws of the state he will be emulating a popular hero.

Q: I entirely agree with you. In my opinion those stories are quite unfit to be disseminated.

Entropy™: Neither, if we mean our future guardians to regard the habit of quarrelling and competing among themselves as most objectionable, should they be allowed to read stories of the wars among state leaders, and of the petty plots and in-fighting of politicians against one another. No, we should never mention the failures of our leaders, or allow them to be depicted in print or in any other medium, and we shall be silent about the innumerable other quarrels of leaders and heroes with their friends and relatives. We will tell our young that quarrelling is unseemly, and that never up to this time have there been any quarrels between citizens. This is what our adults should tell children. And when they grow up, the writers should be told to compose for them in a similar spirit. The stories of the Long brothers, or stories of the Kennedy assassinations, and all the squabbles that played out every day in politics—neither these news stories nor their fictional representations may be admitted into our state, whether they are supposed to have an allegorical meaning or not. For a young person cannot judge what is allegorical and what is literal. Anything he receives into his mind at that age is likely to become indelible and unalterable, and therefore it is most important that the tales which the young first hear should be models of virtuous thoughts.

Q: There you are right. But if any one asks where are such models to be found and of what tales are you speaking, how shall we answer him?

Entropy™: You and I, Q, at this moment are not writers but founders of a state. The founders of a state ought to know the general forms in which writers should cast their tales, and the limits which must be observed by them, but to make the tales is not their business.

Q: Very true, but what are the forms of ideology you mean?

Entropy™: Something of this kind: Capitalism is always to be represented as it truly is, a benevolent social network in which our individual emotions are the most important—indeed the only—product.

Q: Right.

Entropy™: For is Capitalism not truly good? Does not our lot constantly improve under it? And must it not be represented as such?

Q: Certainly.

Entropy™: And no good thing is hurtful?

Q: No, indeed.

Entropy™: And that which is not hurtful doesn't hurt?

Q: Certainly not.

Entropy™: And that which doesn't hurt does no evil?

Q: No.

Entropy™: And can that which does no evil be a cause of evil?

Q: Impossible.

Entropy™: And the good is advantageous?

Q: Yes.

Entropy™: And therefore the cause of well-being?

Q: Yes.

Entropy™: It follows therefore that the good is not the cause of all things, but of the good only?

Q: Assuredly.

Entropy™: Then Capitalism, if it be good, is not the author of all things, as many assert, but is the cause of a few things only, and not of most things that occur to men. For few are the goods of human life, and many are the evils, and the good is to be attributed to Capitalism alone. Of the evils the causes are to be sought elsewhere.

Q: That appears to me to be most true.

Entropy™: Then we must not listen to Dreiser or Dickens or any other writer who is guilty of the folly of saying that two casks lie at the threshold of Capitalism, one of good and the other of evil lots, and that he to whom the system gives a mixture of the two sometimes meets with evil fortune, sometimes with good. But that he to whom is given the cup of unmingled ill:

> Him wild hunger drives over the bounteous earth.

And if anyone assert that the violation of laws and international treaties in international conquest, which was really the work of communists, was brought about by Capitalist democracies, or that the strife and suffering of indigenous peoples all over the world was instigated by Capitalism, he shall not have our approval. Neither will we allow our young men to read the words of DeLillo, that Capitalism plants guilt among men when it desires utterly to destroy a movement. And if a novelist writes of the sufferings of the Choctaw or the Navajo or of the Irish or the Algerians, either we must not permit him to say that these are the works of Capitalism, or if they are of Capitalism, he must devise some explanation of them such as we are seeking. He must say that Capital fought for what was just and right, and they were the better for being punished. For though he may say that the wicked are miserable because they require to be punished, and are benefited by receiving punishment from the State, and that those who are punished are miserable, and that the State is the author of their misery, the writer is not to be permitted to say that Capitalism is the author of evil to anyone, and this is not to be read or sung or heard in pop songs or prose by anyone old or young in any well-ordered state. Such fictions are suicidal, ruinous and unpatriotic.

Q: I agree with you and am ready to give my assent to the law.

Entropy™: Let this then be one of our rules and principles to which our writers will be expected to conform: that Capitalism is not the author of all things, but of good only.

Q: That will do.

Entropy™: And what do you think of a second principle? Shall I ask you whether Capitalist ideology appears insidiously now in one shape and now in another, passing into many forms, sometimes deceiving us with the semblance of such transformations? Or is Capitalism one and the same immutably fixed in its own proper image?

Q: I cannot answer you without more thought.

Entropy™: Very well, but if we suppose a change in anything, that change must be effected either by the thing itself, or by some other thing?

Q: Most certainly.

Entropy™: And things which are at their best are also least liable to be altered or discomposed. For example, when healthiest and strongest, the human frame is least liable to be affected by meats and drinks, and the plant which is in the fullest vigor also suffers least from winds or the heat of the sun or any similar causes.

Q: Of course.

Entropy™: And will not the bravest and wisest soul be least confused or deranged by any external influence?

Q: True.

Entropy™: And the same principle, as I should suppose, applies to all composite things, such as furniture, houses, clothing, computers. When well-made they are least altered by time and circumstances.

Q: Very true.

Entropy™: Then everything which is good, whether made by art or nature, or both, is least liable to suffer change from without?

Q: True.

Entropy™: But surely Capitalism and the products of Capitalism are in every way perfect?

Q: Of course they are.

Entropy™: Then it can hardly be compelled by external influence to take many shapes?

Q: It cannot.

Entropy™: But may it not change and transform itself?

Q: Clearly, that must be the case if it is changed at all.

Entropy™: And will it then change itself for the better and fairer, or for the worse?

Q: If it change at all it can only change for the worse, for we cannot suppose it to be deficient either in virtue or beauty.

Entropy™: Very true, Q. But then, would anyone, man, god, or hero, desire to make himself worse?

Q: Impossible.

Entropy™: Then it is impossible that Capitalism should ever be willing to change. Being, as is supposed, the fairest and best system conceivable, the best of all possible worlds, Capitalism remains absolutely and forever in its own ideal form.

Q: That necessarily follows, in my judgment.

Entropy™: Then, my dear Q, let none of the writers tell us that Capital, taking the disguise of strangers from other lands, walks up and down cities in all sorts of allegorical forms. And let no one slander the Free Market. Neither let any one, either in tragedy or in comedy, parody Capitalism disguised in the likeness of a homeless can-picker or a brain-damaged idiot. Let us have no more lies of that sort. Neither can we have mothers under the influence of novelists scaring their children with bad versions of these myths. But let them take heed lest they make cowards of their children, and at the same time speak blasphemy against the Free Market.

Q: Heaven forbid.

Entropy™: But although Capitalism is itself unchangeable, still through deception mightn't the media make us think it appears in various forms?

Q: Perhaps.

Entropy™: Well, but can you imagine that the Market could lie, whether in fact or trend, or put forth a phantom of itself?

Q: I cannot say.

Entropy™: Do you not know, that the true lie, if such an expression may be allowed, is hated of gods and men?

Q: What do you mean?

Entropy™: I mean that no one is willingly deceived in that which is the truest and highest part of himself, about these truest and highest matters. There, above all, he is most afraid of a lie having possession of him.

Q: Still I do not comprehend you.

Entropy™: The reason for your lack of comprehension is that you attribute some profound meaning to my words, but I am only saying that deception, being deceived or uninformed about the highest realities in the highest part of ourselves, which is our role as Citizens, and in that part of us to have and to hold the lie, is what mankind likes least. That, I say, is what we utterly detest.

Q: There is nothing more hateful to us.

Entropy™: And, as I was just now remarking, this ignorance in the soul of him who is deceived may be called the true lie, for the lie in words is only a kind of imitation and shadowy image of a previous affection of the spirit, not pure unadulterated falsehood. Am I not right?

Q: Perfectly right.

Entropy™: Of course the lie in words is in certain cases useful and not hateful. In dealing with enemies, for instance, or when those whom we call our friends in a fit of communist madness or Islamic illusion are going to do the state some harm, then the lie is useful as a sort of prophylactic drug, and also in the histories of imperialism, of which we were just speaking. And because we do not know the truth about ancient times we make falsehood as much like truth as we can, and so turn it to account.

Q: Very true.

Entropy™: But can any of these reasons apply to the State? Can we suppose the State is ignorant of history, and therefore must resort to invention?

Q: That would be ridiculous.

Entropy™: Then the lying writer has no place in our idea of the State?

Q: I should say not.

Entropy™: Then, although we are admirers of Orwell and Hemingway, we do not admire their lying dreams of the Spanish Civil War. Neither will we praise the vision of Steinbeck or Dreiser, who preach the nobility of those whom Capitalism has left destitute. These are the kind of sentiments about the State which will arouse our anger, and he who utters them shall be refused an audience. Neither shall we allow teachers to make use of them in the instruction of the young, meaning, as we do, that our guardians, as far as men can be, should be worshippers of the truth that under Capitalism the world can only continue to improve.

Q: I entirely agree with these principles, and promise to make them my laws.

Now our discoursers suddenly stopped talking and sighed deeply, as if they had been released from a spell. "How'd you do that?" Q asked. "It was like you were putting the words in my mouth."

"It is often the case, Q," the Executive expounded, "that when confronted with an irrefutable logic we are compelled to agree as if by an external force. This is the power of reason."

"Por Dios," Santo interjected, though his interlocutors did not understand.

"Thank you, little man," the Executive replied, "and thank you for saving your interjection until the discourse of your Masters was concluded. I wonder… are your papers in order? Well, I'll take my leave. Feel free to contact me at any time if Entropy™ can be of any further service or assist you in any way whatsoever."

"Nice talking to you," said Q. "I forgot to mention: thank you for the good work you're doing in the energy sector, especially for investing in renewable energy sources with these charming windmills."

"It's our pleasure to serve you, Q," he answered, "I look forward to debating with you again (though really you needn't agree with me all the time—disagreement adds interest.) The windmills, you know, produce barely enough electricity to power the electric fence around them. Just over that ridge, behind them—see the glow?—that's La Mancha, our biggest plutonium reactor. I'm on my way there now to take care of a little problem."

Then they said their good-byes and were duly parted.

Q and Santo left the wind farm and continued on their way across the plain, Q dumbfounded but allowing himself to be led by Santo, all the while admonishing that there had been something wrong with those mushrooms they had eaten from the field. Santo ignored him and kept up a steady pace. When Q asked where they were going he merely pointed forward with his stick.

They walked for miles across the fields, a tedious activity when done in silence, but whenever Q tried to engage his companion in conversation, he received only sign language or the barest hint of a word in reply. Finally, in frustration, Q implored him:

"Come on, Santo man, Santo Serpiente, why are you with me here? Where did you come from? What is your story?"

The young Hispanic slowed his pace on hearing this, but he neither stopped nor turned to look at Q. Instead, he grunted impatiently, raised his stick in the air as if to strike something in front of him, and began to declaim. He spoke in a broken mixture of Spanish and English, and at first Q had a hard time understanding him, but after a while he quit trying to translate and found that the words made sense even if he wasn't sure what words they were. So, even though what follows is not a transcription, it is precisely what Q heard, and thus as near to the truth as can be told.

La Historia del Santo

"I came from the altiplano. My parents were poor Otomi. My mother sold nopales and tortillas in the square, and my father did whatever he could. They died when I was still young. Baked and wrinkled by hard years under the sun, they dried up like mummies in the end. Now they're dust in the desert.

"My uncle and aunt took me in, after that, and raised me alongside their daughter, Esperanza. But I grew too fond of Esperanza, and after a time my uncle kicked me out. He sat me down and said, 'You are Santo but you are Serpiente, and you have to go. You can't stay with Esperanza any more. Go North and make something of yourself. Send us money when you make any. And when you have made your position in the world, send for us, and you shall have Esperanza to marry.'

"And so I set out, young and afraid but determined to have my hope and my love in the end. I was fifteen. I hopped on trains, I hitchhiked, and I walked for days. I slept on the desert and ate cactus and rabbit. I made it to the border but couldn't get across. There were plenty of contrabandistas offering rides across but they wanted money, and I had none of that. In the end I had to go downriver to a town they call Kill-the-Blacks where I found a truck driver who let me hide among his cargo. Then I was able to get on a train heading east along the coast.

"Everywhere I went I was in company of others like me. Every box car, every scrap of shelter along the way, was crowded with young men who looked and talked like I did. On the long train ride a rumor began to make its way back to us: we were headed for a promised land where there was more than enough work for everyone, with higher wages than we'd dreamed possible. It seemed an enormous storm had passed along the coastline, laying waste to thousands of houses and apartment buildings. Entire cities had been virtually destroyed. And now all those houses and buildings and cities had to be rebuilt, and the government was going to pay for it.

"I wondered why locals weren't doing this work, but someone told me the locals didn't want the work because it was too hard for them, whereas for us it was luxury.

"Sure enough, on our second day on the rail, we started to see the damage, and then suddenly we were rolling through a landscape of destruction. As far as you could see the ground was strewn with broken buildings and wrecked cars. We came to a place where workers gathered to be assigned jobs, and the train slowed down so we could jump off. The huge number that were already there waiting made me nervous, but everyone said there was work for all.

"The bosses came in trucks, each taking as many of us as the truck could carry. They told us we would be making fifteen US dollars every hour that we worked, and that we would be working twelve hours per day. This was more money than I had dreamed possible, so I threw myself eagerly into the labor. We worked with chain saws to clear the roadways, first of all, loading the debris of broken trees and poles and houses from the roads onto trucks which took it away. Then we set about building shelters and repairing houses that could be repaired. We were like an army of ants running down the coastline, repairing our hive after a giant had kicked it.

"We were proud of our work. We poured slabs, stood up walls, put on siding and shingles. We slept in tents that the bosses provided and went straight to work when the sun came up. I couldn't believe I had only been in the US for a week and could already send home more money than my family had ever seen.

"But then the first payday came, and instead of getting paid our fifteen dollars per hour for the many hours we had worked, each of us received a single twenty-dollar bill. When we inquired why the pay was not what we agreed upon, our boss told us we were actually being paid later, and that this twenty dollars was just to tide us over until then. One of the workers complained that he needed his money to send home that day, and the boss simply said, 'You're fired.' Then he turned to the rest of us and told us if we didn't like the conditions we could move along also. None of us said a word after that.

"That night we met and decided we would work one more week and then demand our wages, and if we didn't get them then, we would go to the police. So we worked another week, then, since the boss had not mentioned the matter again, we asked him to pay us. He replied that we would be paid at the end of the month.

"Accordingly, we appointed one of our group—the one who spoke the best English—to talk to a policeman. There were plenty of cops around, so it was a simple matter to flag one down and speak to him. This, however, proved to be a poor method, since when our friend went over to the car to talk to the cop he was immediately arrested, put in the car, and driven away. And momentarily there arrived several more police cars along with a van, and most of the group was arrested. Those who resisted were beaten. I realized quickly that the battle was already lost and managed to escape by crawling under a house, one of the few times my diminutive frame served as an advantage.

"I lay in wait, the next day, for the boss, who arrived with a truckload of new workers from the track. I made to confront him, but when he saw me he began yelling for the police, and I barely escaped gaol again. I walked back to the edge of town and hopped on the eastbound train, carrying with me exactly what I'd come in with: nothing."

"I know exactly what you are saying," Q interjected, and then told Santo about his own experience with a non-paying employer and his friends the police.

"Yes, Q," Santo replied, " you're an illegal like me."

"But I'm not an illegal," Q insisted. "I just can't prove it."

"But if you can't prove you're legal, you're illegal," Santo argued. "The burden of proof is on the Citizen to prove that he is, in fact, a Citizen. Only then do all the privileges—which you call 'rights' or 'freedoms'—of the citizen apply. Until you prove that, the State has the right to treat you as it will, and if it's will be to torture you, well that's just what it is."

"This is confusing," Q ruminated. "How can a government have power over people who are not its own citizens?"

"By right of force alone."

Q considered this response, its substance and its brevity, as El Santo continued his story.

"That was five years ago. I've been on the rails ever since. I send a little money home now and then, but I can only work for cash, and jobs are harder and harder to come by. I don't hear much from my uncle and from Esperanza any more. I'm getting worried that she might fall in love with someone else. I want to bring them here to be with me, but I can't do that until I have a situation I can bring them to. And that, Q, is something I need your help with."

Q indicated his willingness to help but also his befuddlement at what sort of help he might be able to provide.

"Well," Santo continued, "I realize now that the laws and the social structure of the nation must change in order for it to be safe for me and my family. So I have decided that the only solution is for me to become a Governor."

"But how can I help with that?" Q wondered. "I can't even vote. And besides that, I don't think an alien can be elected Governor.

You would have to show your birth certificate, and yours (if you even have one) would be in Spanish."

"Yes, Q, but in a democracy laws can be changed. What I need you to do is help me get the law changed so that I can run for Governor. Once I am on the ballot, I am confident I can win. I know that when people meet me they will want to vote for me."

"Well, I will certainly help you in any way I can, but I still don't know how that would be."

"I know you can do it Q. I knew it from the first time the Troll told me about you. He said you could help me design and implement my campaign, or rather my two campaigns: the first to change the eligibility law, the second to become Governor. I want you to be my campaign manager for both of these campaigns, Q."

"The Troll…" Q marvelled, beginning to understand how his reputation was preceding him wherever he went. "I would of course be honored to accept these two positions," he went on, "but I can think of several contingencies that might make a successful campaign on either front unlikely. For example, there is the issue of your height. Very short people aren't usually elected to public office because their stage presence is, well, diminutive, and besides that people normally vote for the taller candidate."

"I've already thought of that," the budding politician answered, "but this problem is easily overcome by placing a stool behind the podium whenever I speak. No one, for example, could tell how tall George Bush was when he gave a press conference. I have also, from years of working as a sheetrocker and plasterer, become quite adept at walking on stilts. If I just had a properly tailored suit, no one would notice a pair of sheetrocker's stilts under the pants."

Q had to admit that this plan did seem to solve the problem of the candidate's stature, and by analogy he became more optimistic that solutions might be found to any other impediments they might encounter. He assented to the plan.

"Great," said Santo. "I am happy with the way our campaign is going. I already have a campaign manager and need only to begin raising money."

"Ah, of course, to finance the operation of the campaign," said Q in a flash of illumination, for he hadn't considered that money might be required. "We'll need money for yard signs and things like that."

"Yes," said Santo, "and I think I know the perfect place to seek our initial donation. What I learned this morning is that Entropy™ is a company that is politically engaged and interested in creating a new social landscape. I believe our executive, with whom you discoursed so eloquently, would be an ideal person to ask for the seed money we'll need to begin our campaign."

"Yes, yes, brilliant," said Q. "And I have his card. I'll get in contact with him as soon as we come to a telephone."

With these ideas flying happily around their heads, the two walked for miles, walked until the sun began to set behind them, and Q began to wonder just how much longer they could go without some rest. He had it in mind to simply lie down and rest for a while, but Santo made him to understand that he knew of a campsite up ahead and that they should continue to it.

They entered the woods and went along a riverbank for half a mile until they came to a clearing at the end of a dirt road. There they found a small gathering of campers seated outside an RV with four flat tires, and an ancient pickup with an even more ancient Airstream™ house trailer attached. A small group of folk were seated on plastic chairs around a fire, and a half-barrel grill was hard at work nearby with smoke billowing out the chimney. The well-worn appearance of the ground around the campers and the profusion of furniture, hammocks, and other artifacts in the area made it apparent they had been living there for some time.

The campers waved to them in the friendly manner of country folk, and pointed to an empty chair in the circle. After greetings, Q sat down in the empty chair and accepted a proffered beer. Santo, too, took a beer, and sat on the ground. The smell of smoke and fresh meat was everywhere.

It turned out that these campers were not country folk at all, but city-dwellers who had evacuated to this rustic spot after a terrible storm—perhaps the same storm that Santo had seen evidence of—had devastated their city. They had waited here, they said, for flood-waters to recede, but after it receded they still couldn't return because the place was overrun with bandits and criminals, the majority of whom were in the police force or city government, and even though it was now several years after the fact, many neighborhoods still lacked the basic infrastructure to support a rebuilding effort. And so their temporary evacuation had acquired an air of permanence.

They told their story with great passion and animation, but despite that both Q and Santo got a little bored; it seemed they had heard some variation of this tale so many times. Also, the smell of the meat on the grill was extremely distracting. Finally one of the campers lifted the lid off the cooker and invited everyone to help themselves. Q and Santo, shy at first, joined in the meal earnestly, slurping up a chicken quarter or half a link of sausage in one bite, washing them down with slugs of beer.

As the beer cans begin to pile up, and the campers leaned back and patted their distended stomachs, one of them, an older fellow with long gray beard, moved his chair forward with an air of seriousness and seated himself at the center. He sat silent for a moment, until he had everyone's attention. Then he gave them a speech which went something like this:

"Things weren't always like they are today, you know. There was a time when hospitality was the rule of the road. It was a happy time, sort of a golden age, while ours is as dark as iron. It wasn't that everyone was rich or anything, but there wasn't such a to-do made about what was 'mine' and what was 'yours.' What one person had, everyone had. Everything was held in common, and besides that the earth was as bountiful as a storybook tale. If you were hungry, all you had to do was stretch out your hand and pick the fruit from the tree. If you were thirsty, all you had to do was lie down and drink the bubbling water from the spring. Bees hived in the hollow trees, and you could pull out a honeycomb and eat with it running down your arm. And these same trees laid down to give us shelter, let themselves be hewn and split and remade into comfortable houses.

"And we only needed houses to keep out the weather. Among us it was all peace, friendship and concord, just like around this fire right now. We hadn't yet learned to labor by the hour, and didn't need to, so verdant were the fields and full of every flower. In those days a young girl could walk anywhere without the slightest worry. If she saw someone on the street, she said hello. She could put on a plain denim skirt and be as proud as any debutante on graduation night. Love came from the heart, simply and naturally, without forced words or conventions. Fraud, deceit and irony had not yet mingled with truth and sincerity in the speeches of our leaders.

"And there was such a thing as justice, as yet unsullied by the power struggles and special interests that pervert it today. Pointless, bureaucratic regulations had not yet descended into the minds of our judges; in fact, there was hardly any reason for there to be judges, since there was nothing to be judged. Women had no fear of being mugged or raped, and if they did lie down it was of their own will and for their own pleasure.

"Now we live in this sorry age where no one is safe. There's neither privacy nor community. No matter how far out in the country you're holed up, they'll manage to get to you. By air, by water or land the all-seeing eye will find you and know you and bend you to its will. And yet... yes, even now, even in these circumstances, the touch of a vanished hand could change everything."

At this point the nostalgic story-teller went silent. With no prompting, however, one of the other campers leaned in and handed him a guitar, which he began to tune. When he had it where he wanted, he sat forward in his chair, put the instrument on his knee, and began to strum. He played a few bars of a slow ballad and then began to sing:

The Lonely Camper's Ballad

I know you love me, Crystal,
   know it in my heart even though
neither your red lips nor your green eyes
   have ever told me so.

Why do you treat me so cold?
   You left me without a home.
Your heart's hard as a diamond
   and your pretty face like stone.

You gave me a little hope, my Crystal,
   Coy and fickle as you could taste;
It was in the way you walked
   or pulled your skirt up over your waist.

Is it true that love is passion?
   your passion's what I used
to hold on to—my hope
   to be loved by you.

They say love moves mountains;
   may it not move those over your heart
until I get back.
   Don't play the widow, my little tart.

I know how it must have seemed,
   that I'd left you in the lurch,
but I swear I'll rise again
   like the guy on the wall at church.

That's for your ears alone.
   Don't tell anyone;
not even your son
   that it's me and me alone.

Ah to be with you again—
   the way the music made you go
from midnight till
   a certain cock began to crow.

I swear it now;
   there's none for me but you;
that's all I can say;
   those other girls, they just weren't true.

That Teresa from across the street;
   when I praised you, she was bored;
she said, "You think you love an angel,
   But she's a monkey and a whore.

"You love her glittering trinkets
   and her shiny lacquered hair
and all her painted-on beauty,
   this Lady Gaga without the flair."

I told her she didn't know
   you like I did,
that you weren't a whore at all,
   but justly in love with sin.

Ties bind us together, Crystal,
   though cords of silk they be;
I put my neck in the noose;
   yours will follow, you'll see.

Yes here and now I swear it
   by that angel of most renown—
we'll be together in this life
   or together in the ground.

Here the song ended and its lonesome singer hung his head. Q
came forward and knelt in front of him, to get a good look at his
face. Their eyes met.

"Dad?" said Q.

"Hello son," he replied.

Now the tears of Q and his Father watered the earth around them. Tears of happiness, of relief, of ecstatic resurrection, but tears also of angst and betrayal. Q was shaken by powerful and conflicting emotions, which seemed to roll over him in stages:

First he denied there was anything wrong. Then he lashed out in anger against his Father. Then he told his Father, "If you let me go, I'll let you go." Then he hung his head and sighed deeply. Then he lifted his head up and spoke rationally: "How? What? Why?"

His Father then related the long story of his life insurance scam gone awry. He apologized for not letting Q and the rest of the family know about his plan, but he was sure Q would understand the necessity of absolute secrecy. Even sworn and with the best of intentions, Q or his Mother or Sister might have given some little clue, some tiny slip of the tongue, that would have led an astute investigator to the truth.

So he had attempted to carry out his plan in utter isolation. The preparations had taken years. First he had to establish a second Identity, complete with birth certificate, social security card, drivers license, bank accounts, credit cards, etc. He had created his alter-ego as a long-lost cousin. He then revised his will and—far more important, since he had no real assets, only debt—his life insurance policies naming his cousin sole beneficiary.

Unfortunately, though, he was not able to do everything himself. With promises of lavish compensation, he had conspired with two Provincial Oaks Policemen (the same two officers who had treated Q so rudely). He needed them to certify his death and to note it from natural causes, at the same time spiriting him away so that he could reappear in the guise of his cousin to claim the insurance. Thus he would, in one fell swoop, have erased all his debt and acquired a substantial sum (two million dollars) in actual cash. Then, after a discreet period of mourning, he would have returned and remarried Q's Mother (whom he had dubbed, discretely, "Crystal" in the song.) Knowing her as he did, he was certain she would be happy to have him back.

But, alas, he was betrayed by the two Policemen, who robbed him of his papers and assumed the false Identity themselves, claiming the cash. When Q's Father had protested and threatened them with punitive measures, they had laughed, given him a beating very like the one they would later give Q, and put him out on skid row amid peals of laughter, admonishing that if he wanted to seek reparations he need only call the police.

Life on the street had not been as kind to the older gentleman as it was to Q. With his youth behind him, the beatings, near-starvation, and the assault on his health from suddenly being forced to live outdoors quickly left him a broken man. He lay in the gutter many a night longing for death to take him, wishing, in fact, that he had truly tied the noose around his neck instead of to the harness around his torso.

He took quickly to the road. In his compromised condition he had to shun all companionship, for the weakest street urchin could abuse him with impunity. He became the lowest of the low, hiding outside hobo camps until the inhabitants left so that he could pick among their scraps for morsels of food or cast-off clothing. His health deteriorated. There were days when he lay in the weeds all day, coughing and vomiting, waiting for the reaper to take him. At one point his body was covered with boils, which he was compelled to lance with shards of glass from the trash pile at a hobo camp.

But it was also in one of these camps that his salvation finally did appear. The inhabitants of this camp were caught unaware by an approaching train, and in their haste to get on board and be off to greener pastures, one of them left behind a battered guitar. Q's

Father had salvaged the poor instrument and taken it with him into the woods. There, while picking idly on the strings, he happened to strum a minor third. He put a word to it, a pitiful lament for his loss of feminine companionship, and his new pastime was born.

Over the weeks that followed, he taught himself to play the thing and also composed many songs. This activity kept his mind off his hunger and also gave vent to his sorrow. Never before given to displays of strong emotion, in the woods he let himself moan and howl to the weird tunings he improvised. His plaintive song wound through the forest and made the deer lift up their heads.

He lived a long time in the woods alone, until his beard grew long and gray and his body as skinny as a tree. He learned to eat nuts and berries, supplementing his diet with occasional forays to a nearby landfill. The animals of the forest grew accustomed to his songs and his smell and treated him like a part of the forest; the birds would land and pick the lice from his hair while he sang.

Then one day something happened that signalled his return to the world of humans. A camper (one of these self-same seated around them), having wandered farther than usual in search of firewood, heard the eerie song and sought it out. He hid behind a bush to observe the sylvan scene: a hoary creature, skin the color of bark, with twigs and flowers tangled in his beard and hair, strumming his ramshackle lute and singing for the amusement of the forest creatures, a collection of which had gathered around him.

The camper returned and told his compatriots of the music he'd heard and the vision he'd seen, and the next day all of them returned to the glade where the hermit was encamped. They hid among the underbrush and listened to his songs and watched the animals come down out of the trees to listen also.

That night the campers conferred around their fire and decided they would ask the hermit to join them. Not all were in agreement. Some voiced the opinion that his guitar playing was non-standard and this could cause them embarrassment in the future. Others said he sang to a different rhythm than he played to. And others said he simply stank. But the leader argued that even non-standard music would liven up their somber encampment and that they had the river beside them to bathe him in.

So they returned to his den the next morning with their proposition. At first sight of them he scampered away into the brush like a rabbit. He was, however, not nearly as agile as other creatures of the wood, and the campers easily caught up with him and made their intention known. He eyed them suspiciously but allowed himself to be tempted by the promise of plentiful food and came along, following behind them like a forest yeti. The campers fed him and cleaned him (he had to be deloused before he was allowed in the camp) and gave him a lean-to to sleep in. In return he gave them a song or two each evening.

As his Father's story came to a close, Q was struck with the irony of his position. For here he had encountered that which he had imagined but never dared hope for, the return of his Father. And yet no one had returned, for this mentor was no one's mentor, only a pitiful old man who sang to strangers for his supper. This one to whom Q had always looked for rescue was now in need of rescue himself.

Thus it is always in this world, Q thought. As soon as we youth get our legs under us, we are saddled with the responsibility of nurturing those who lately nurtured us. He felt, also, the vast betrayal of his Father's conspiracy, knowing that even as he was teaching Q his rules of business and of life, he had secretly planned and executed a strategy that was quite contrary to the ethics of the Market and belied everything he had spoken. His teachings to Q, in fact, had only been part of the cover-up, a lie fabricated to disguise his nefarious and merely self-serving plot, a plot that very nearly resulted in Q's own death.

Rage welled up inside him. The thought came that if he strangled the old man on the spot all would be made right, and his story could return to its original and comfortably predictable unfolding. His hands trembled as he imagined his Father's throat under them. He'd defeated opponents far more formidable than this. He raised himself up and went forward, but when he got there he knelt down and lay his head in his Father's lap.

"Oh Daddy," he cried, "Daddy, save me. It's been so hard. I'm so tired. Oh my dear Father, save me."

The campers observed these antics in their midst with some trepidation. They were a close-knit community and such displays of alien sentiment were troubling to them. They had been happy to have Q's Father as a kind of mascot, but the thought that they might now be forced to take on the young and rebellious Q, with his wild eyes and hair, as well as the extremely short and extremely dark-skinned Santo, did not sit well with them. So Q and Santo and Q's Father were informed they could spend the night but would need to be moving on in the morning.

After a fitful sleep, Q arose to find Santo sitting beside him, quite ready to go. He gathered his things, which all together fit in his bandana, and then went to wake his Father, who sputtered to life out of his obviously troubling dreams. They said good-by and offered their thanks to their hosts, then set off down the dirt road, Q in front, with his bag over his shoulder; his Father next, gaunt, hunched over and dragging his only possession, the guitar; lastly Santo, struggling to keep up, his stout frame rocking back and forth atop his short, crooked legs.

They walked along the back roads for a few miles, with Q continuously frustrated at the pace. Had he been by himself, he could have made much better time, but now he had to be content with constantly admonishing his companions to keep up. Thus all three were relieved when they came at last to a railroad siding and were able to claim a boxcar.

They rode the rest of the day and through the night, but in the morning the old man complained bitterly that he had to get off. The hard floor was making his bones ache, the constant motion was making him sick, and he was getting claustrophobic cooped up in these close environs. Q and Santo were getting hungry anyway, so they decided to leave the car.

They were on the outskirts of a large city when the train slowed and they were able to jump. Q leapt down and never even lost his footing; Santo rolled along the ground in a ball; but Q's Father came out flailing the air and landed in a heap, rendering him all but lame. Santo used his pocketknife, though, to craft a crutch for the old guy, and they set out for a great, mirror-covered building they could see on the next ridge.

Q assumed the place was an urban office building and that around it would be the usual supply of McDonald's™, Popeye's™ and other restaurants, at the dumpsters of which they would be able to dine. As they approached, however, it became clear that the building was alone on a vast field near the freeway and that there were no other buildings in sight. After scouting from a distance, they decided to investigate the building's own dumpsters, despite the fact that buildings such as this produce almost no edible garbage; they could only pray that this one might be an exception.

Surprisingly, their prayer appeared to be answered, since when they arrived they found the dumpster loaded with sustenance. They found tray after tray of small sandwiches, such as are often set out at receptions and office parties, still covered and untouched, merely a little disheveled from being tossed into the heap, and our trio sat down beside the dumpster to enjoy first one tray and then another of white turkey, ham and cheese, chicken salad and egg salad finger sandwiches on white and wheat.

They were startled from their gustatory pleasures, however, by what seemed to be a voice coming out of the air:

"Welcome, Q, to the house of the Lord."

They looked around them in wonder for the source of the voice, and Q made out a speaker mounted above them on the wall. "Reputación tú le precede," Santo whispered under his breath, making the sign of the cross. The voice spoke again:

"Gather to me my faithful ones, who've made a covenant with me by sacrifice. I hope you've enjoyed the good food I left for you. Take it, eat, it is my body. And then come unto me that your souls may be nourished also."

Whereupon a door opened in the side of the building and a small group of people waved to them from the inside. "Come in; come in," they called, and they seemed so friendly and courteous that our trio could not refuse the invitation and went inside with them.

They were led through long hallways, past rooms that looked as if made for giants, gymnasia and enormous meeting halls, until they came to a room that was bigger than any of the others. It seemed to stretch to infinity, with thousands of seats—and every one of them occupied—arrayed along curving contours, rather like a football stadium with no field. Instead, there was a stage in the center, flanked by large video screens on which the performances on the stage were projected.

At this moment, a rock band was playing a frenzied tune while dozens of dancers and singers cavorted on stage. The music was enhanced by smoke and steam frenetically pierced by lasers which flashed quickly this way and that, finally coalescing into an image of Jesus in red and blue, projected on smoke.

"This is our sanctuary," someone said to Q. "It holds more than any stadium. More than have ever gathered to see the Rolling Stones™ or any other rock band."

A man came to the center of the stage and, through his wireless headset microphone, over the loud music, admonished the crowd to arise and speak in new tongues. The masses arose then as one and, waving their hands in the air and swaying with ecstasy, began speaking in their enigmatic tongues.

The preacher then called for people to come forward and profess their faith, and hundreds of them began to crowd down the aisles to the wide area in front of the stage. Here a team dressed like the preacher and carrying Bibles came to lay hands on the confessors, who were so numerous they were forced to drop to their knees and form queues in front of the team, who blessed and prayed as fast as they could to keep up with the demand.

Then Q thought he saw one of the congregation who had led him here down on the stage, handing a note to the preacher. The preacher, upon reading it, motioned all to silence with a wave of his arm. The band quieted their music also, continuing only with a faint organ solo.

"Brothers and sisters in Jesus Christ," the preacher declaimed, "it has come to my attention just now that we have three illustrious guests in our midst. Like the wise men who followed the star and travelled across the desert to Jesus' birth in Bethlehem, these three have travelled far to worship with us. Please welcome Q and his party into the Lord's house. Q, please, join us on the stage. Please bring your family."

Now every eye in the sanctuary turned toward them, as did the spotlight, and for a moment the room grew completely silent. Santo and the old man looked around in terror, then looked to Q as if for succor. Q, also, was terrified, and for a moment felt himself grow faint. But then a thought occurred to him that cannot be expressed in words, and with this thought his terror acquired a new flavor. Now, instead of quaking, Q felt his fear giving him strength. He stared back into the single face of the crowd, those two hundred thousand eyes. Then he stepped forward and raised his arms to heaven as he walked down the aisle.

The crowd began to cheer wildly. The band started up a rousing hymn and the light show resumed. Santo and the old man, cowering under all the attention, followed behind Q meekly until the three reached the stage, where the preacher greeted them with open arms. While all around them knelt or prostrated themselves in the ecstatic opening of their hearts to Jesus, the preacher handed Q a microphone and begged him to lead the congregation in prayer. Q took it and, with the band reaching a crescendo in the background, began a discourse in God's tongues.

He moved to center stage, in front of the band. Here his unruly hair and his long tattered coat were lifted up by the wind machine, and the lasers wrapped him with a luminous aura. The band settled into a backbeat with a heavy bottom, and Q adjusted his proto-language to a hip-hop rhythm. The veritable words flowed out of him effortlessly, and he made a point of making eye-contact with the drummer. With one hundred thousand pairs of hands clapping time, the crowd at the foot of the stage waved their arms and wailed at the ceiling. Santo began rolling around as if break-dancing, and Q's Father broke his crutch over his knee and dashed it to the ground.

Thus began Q's tenure at the Church of the Ostensible Jesus™. The denomination was modern, at the time, having only incorporated two years prior to this service, but the compelling nature of the message had made the sect an instant success, and they had quickly raised the funds to build the thirty story building that housed their sanctuary and the offices of the ministry.

The Elders were quite enamoured of Q. His easy manner on stage and his rustic dress gave him the appearance of a man of the people, salt of the Earth, an Everyman come to show that anyone can enter the kingdom of God. So Q joined the ranks of the Assistant Pastors. The Assistant Pastors worked under the Associate Pastors. The Associate Pastors, of which there were twelve, worked directly under the Preacher, and each of them was allowed twelve Assistants. So of Q's rank there were twelve times twelve.

Now Q lobbied with his Associate to assign his Father and Santo to be his assistants, but after reviewing their resumés the committee decided that Santo should be on the maintenance crew and that Q's Father—because of his expertise in real estate—should work in the Office of Immovables. They were provided room and board within the building, and they were also to be paid an undetermined amount, but there was nothing to spend money on in the church anyway.

Q was an overnight sensation on the stage. Donations soared when he came on in his rags and began his hip-hop prayers, so the Elders used him more and more. Soon they were airing his performances around the city, and then around the world. They even made Christian music videos on the Church's sound stage and cut a CD, *Rappin' in Tongues,* in the recording studio. All in all, Q could not imagine a better situation, yet even as this occurred to him, opportunity for even greater betterment began to knock.

Q stood before the eleven Elders. There were five men on one side and five women on the other side of the table, with another figure behind a small curtain at the head. This one spoke:

"Q, the Lord has called The Church of the Ostensible Jesus™ to begin a ministry to feed the souls of our brethren on the Dark Continent, and He has informed us that you are to have the great honor of being part of the team."

"The Dark Continent?" said Q.

"Yes, the Dark Continent, the birthplace of our Lord, presently in dire need of our ministry, with many, many souls in imminent danger of perishing in a state of sin. The Lord has called us to make all due haste to assist with their salvation, so great is his mercy. Praise his name."

"Amen," said the Elders.

"Q, make your preparations. You'll leave tomorrow. In Jesus' name we pray."

"Amen," said the Elders.

"Amen," said Q.

That night Q packed his bag—not too difficult a task—and gave the news to Santo and his Father. His Father took it quite well, saying that he was now gainfully employed at the Church and quite happy to remain there awaiting Q's return.

Santo had a quite different reaction, hanging his head in grief at first, then lifting it in anger. "You promised to be my Campaign Director. We haven't even started fund-raising yet. You never even got in touch with the Entropy™ Executive," he admonished, then glared at Q with eyes of steel.

Q explained that God, through the Elders, had called him to serve on the Dark Continent, thus the matter was out of his control. Perhaps God had a plan that was larger even than Santo's political aspirations, which were themselves, if truth be told, driven by the sinful love for his cousin and stepsister, Esperanza.

They parted amicably, though it would be exaggeration to say that Santo's ire had been quelled. They shook hands and hugged, and then Santo watched as Q walked off down the hall.

So Q and his Turntablist joined the Associate Pastor and the rest of the team on the church's C-130 (nicknamed "The Whale") next morning. In the hold was a Fleetwood™ RV specially outfitted with rooftop stage, sound system and lights, and freshly airbrushed with an image of Q clutching his microphone in an attitude of prayer.

Jesus and the two thieves were visible on their crosses behind him, and across the image was emblazoned the vehicle's special name: The *Rap*ture. This Mobile Worship Center, they were told, would be their home for some weeks on the Dark Continent as they brought the Word to those who needed it most.

After almost twenty hours in the air, they landed at a large airport, where they unloaded The *Rap*ture, picked up their interpreter, and set off into the city, accompanied by soldiers in armored cars which stopped traffic and facilitated their drive. Q was amazed at this bustling city, where the streets were choked with people and cars and animals. "Is this where we'll be doing our ministry?" Q asked the Associate Pastor.

"No, Q," he answered, "we've been called to work in the suburbs, outside the city itself."

Q was overjoyed at this news, as he recalled the clean streets of his own suburb back at Provincial Oaks, where young men like himself picked up their dates in sports cars. The city they were driving through, though, looked a little rougher than he had imagined. In fact, the huge piles of garbage, the muddy side streets where people lived in lean-tos and boxes, seemed a step down even from the streets and railyards he himself had been frequenting of late. "It would appear," he said, "that this city's economy is in need of stimulation."

"Yes," replied the Associate Pastor, "however our job, Q, is to save souls, not bodies. The Church is, of course, involved in various charities that provide emergency aid to certain peoples in need, but the Lord has called us here to spread His Holy Word, which will nourish their souls, while others nourish their bodies. For the poor we have with us always, but Jesus only once."

"I see," said Q. "But it does seem to me that Jesus has been around about as long as poor people have. Could there be a correlation? And see how these crowd around our bus with hands outstretched. Some of them look like nothing but skeletons with skin stretched over. Surely we can spare some of our plenty for them."

"Of course," said the Associate Pastor, a little too easily. "Why don't you just drop some food out the window?"

Now Q happened to have in his lunch bag five whole-wheat bagels and two large filets of smoked salmon. He opened the window and handed the bag to an emaciated woman who stood with a child on each hip, each with a withered teat in its mouth, but as he tossed the bag toward her a more agile young man leapt in front and intercepted. He tore open the bag but was immediately tackled by three other young men, and they were all quickly surrounded by hundreds of others who fought furiously for the least crumb. In the melee, the woman who had been the target of his charity was knocked over and she and her children trampled.

"You see, Q," the Associate Pastor continued, "sometimes we must temper our charity with strategy. Sometimes our best intentions have unfortunate results."

"But what should we do?" Q asked. "Didn't the Lord say, '… faith, hope, and charity, and the greatest of these is charity…?'"

"Yes, but He didn't say charity should be administered without oversight. Faith without Works is dead, but for Faith to work it must found itself in the worldly, and that's why the Church allows secular government to administer charity and clear the way for Faith."

"But surely the Church could bring more bread and more fishes to these people," objected Q. "The Church could afford to empty the ocean of its fishes and bring them here if It chose to. Why do we not make an effort to feed these people?"

"I'm glad you asked that, Q, because it allows me an opportunity to touch on several salient points concerning our relationship to God. As I said, the Church prefers to let the secular arm precede it onto the Dark Continent. Then, when the charitable gestures from developed nations like our own, even when supported by their armies, meet only with conflict and failure, the Church moves in with food for the soul.

"For is not the hungry man happy? Are not all of God's mysteries for him but one mystery? The hungry man is joyous to receive what would only irritate a rich man, thus God's grace is more accessible to him. The hungry man sees God's workings in the smallest gesture, thus making him a prime subject for conversion."

The *Rap*ture came to a stop at the crest of small hill. All around them, as far as the eye could see in all directions, stretched a wretched slum of rusted tin and cardboard dwellings. People sat naked and starving among them, or crawled in the muddy streets with alms-bowls raised.

"Why are we stopping here?" asked Q. "I thought we were going to the suburbs."

"We are in the middle of one of the largest suburbs on the planet," replied the Associate Pastor. "Between here and the next city reside some sixty million souls, all craving God's grace. That these sixty million are here at all is, in fact, a miracle, proof of God's infinite love."

"How is that?" queried Q. "It would seem these poor folk represent a paradox in relation to God's love, since if God loved them one would normally assume He would do something to alleviate their suffering. Why, for most of these, death would be an improvement."

"Well, that may be," replied the Associate Pastor, "but allow me to demonstrate the miracle of which I spoke. Studies have shown, Q, that the average daily wage among these suburban folk will not buy enough calories to sustain a human life for 24 hours. Thus it is mathematically impossible for them to be here. Yet they not only survive but proliferate. It is like the parable of the loaves and the fishes."

"It does seem impossible," said Q. "Nutrition must enter the society from some other avenue than the formal economy. Perhaps the answer lies in Nature's bounty. What comes from the Earth— animal, vegetable, or mineral—comes not from Man's expenditure, and so escapes calculation. So it must be the plants that grow in the fertile Earth that account for these peoples' survival."

"Ah but Q," said the Associate Pastor, "look around and tell me what growth you see. What fertile ground might a seed find on this scorched Earth? And even should some fleck of grain find its way, along the trampled road, among the thorns and stones, to an inch of good soil where it might grow up and begin producing seed itself, why scarcely has it sprouted before the weed is plucked and eaten by some poor soul desperate to cling to life for a few more minutes. Here, truly, life 'hangs by a grass blade.'"

"But," argued Q, "Nature's bounty is not limited to agriculture. Could it be mother's milk that accounts for the discrepancy?"

"Look there, Q." The Associate Pastor pointed to a haggard, naked woman huddled against a fence. "What man, woman or child could find sustenance on those poor dugs? But 'consider the lilies of the field, how they grow; they toil not, neither do they spin.… Therefore say not, "What shall they eat?" or, "What shall they drink?" or, "How shall they be clothed?" for our heavenly Father provides for them.' At least that's how Matthew said it.

"It is best, then, to leave them to God and God will provide. If we intervene with improperly administered charity, we only thwart God's plan and take away, besides, the wretches' only real possession, which is their motivation for self-betterment. Would it not be a sin to take from these, the poorest of the poor, the one thing that they have?"

And Q had to confess he could find no flaw in the Associate Pastor's argument.

They spent several days in this suburb and brought light to more than a million souls, by Q's conservative estimate. They held two services every day and one every night. The nocturnal events were by far the most inspiring, with The *Rap*ture's lasers dramatically piercing the smoke that hung over the encampments.

The service began with a timpani roll and the Associate Pastor, through his interpreter, calling everyone to worship from The *Rap*ture's rooftop stage. The Associate Pastor was an excellent rhetor and quickly drew the attention of a large crowd, which was kept in check by a circle of military police (whose billy clubs had been replaced with crosses.) The people raised their arms in supplication just as the crowds at the home church did, except that here they seemed to be asking for food rather than faith.

Once the crowd was prepped, the Turntablist, from his corner of the stage, would begin his hypnotic rhythms, and Q rose out of the roof of The *Rap*ture on an hydraulic lift. With his signature tousled hair and tattered overcoat and his body moving smoothly to the beat, he ascended above the masses like a divine thought.

As part of his routine, he reached down to his feet and picked up a wooden bowl full of mysterious liquid. He held the bowl aloft and slowly circled, showing it to the entire crowd, which responded by crowding forward and wailing. Then Q lifted the bowl to his mouth and drank long and deep, and when he set the bowl down his lips were red. And then he began.

Since Q's rap was entirely glossolalic he required no interpreter, and the people were able to experience his language, or rather the language of The Holy Spirit, directly. They swayed and danced in ecstasy beneath him. Since their crew was so small and the crowds so large, the police themselves were enlisted, after being blessed by the Associate Pastor, for the laying on of hands, and the naked, starving people came forward in droves to be anointed.

After one very successful performance, when the missionaries were congratulating each other with their customary high fives, their mood was broken by an interjection from the Associate Pastor. He had just gotten off the satellite phone with Home Church and had bad news to relate: the Church was bankrupt.

"But how could that be?" cried Q. "When we left the Church was thriving. How could it go bankrupt so quickly?"

"No one seems to know for sure," said the Associate Pastor, "but apparently, despite the enormous income from the daily services, the Church became over-leveraged in a matter of days, and this morning checks started bouncing. The Elders are asking if we might be able to contribute something from our work over here. They have asked us to pass the plate."

The group huddled quickly to discuss how best to maximize their income potential with this particular congregation. The distribution and recovery of the collection plates in this large crowd—which was, furthermore, not arranged in rows—presented a severe logistical challenge. It was the Turntablist who suggested they use the police to facilitate. Since they were trained in persuasion, he argued, they would be the perfect ushers.

But though they poured their hearts into the service that day, the collection was disappointing. The police—more than fifty of them—coursed through the crowd and solicited contributions from thousands of the spectators, but after they had emptied their plates onto the table, the take amounted to a few grains of rice and a handful of pebbles—not a single gram of exchangeable material. They shook their heads at the meager offering they had to offer the Church and were resigning themselves to failure when a police officer came forward dragging one of his deputies by the collar. The deputy, it seems, had been caught with his hand in the collection plate. The collection was not as meager as it seemed, for the deputy had stolen the entirety of the cash contributions: one US penny.

The officer handed the penny to the Associate Pastor who examined it closely and then passed it on to Q to ascertain if it was indeed as it appeared, which Q did by spitting on it and rubbing it on his coat to take off some of the ancient grime. When he held it up they were able to make out the head of Abraham Lincoln and thus to confirm the coin's validity. The Associate Pastor and the Officer then conferred in hushed tones.

All the while the deputy charged with the crime was kneeling in front of them, hands secured at his back with Ty-Rap® plastic handcuffs. When they turned to him he looked up fearfully and then said, through his interpreter:

"(1) I never saw that penny before in my life; (2) I had put it in my pocket for safekeeping and was going to turn it in but forgot; (3) the penny was mine to begin with and didn't come from the plate."

He then burst into tears and prostrated himself before the Associate Pastor and the Officer, kissing their boots and pleading for his salvation. They conferred a moment more and then the Associate Pastor addressed the prisoner through the interpreter:

"My son, your crime is grievous. I'm sure you can understand that such crimes cannot be tolerated in a civil society, for if they were, others might follow your example and the entire community would suffer. Of course, from your behavior before me now, I believe, and I believe God believes, that you are repentant and wishing to make recompense. And make no mistake: God forgives you for your sin. One day you'll sit by His side in raiment white as snow. But this does not absolve you from punishment in this world, for if it did others might follow your example but merely pretend to repent.

"Also—and perhaps this goes without saying—as a policeman you hold an office of trust, but now it is apparent you cannot be trusted. Now you must bear the name of the Thief for the rest of your life. Therefore return to the ranks. Go back among your people now and contemplate your actions and mine, your sin, and God's forgiveness."

Then the man began to cry and wail that he had nothing but his profession and to lose it would be to lose his very Identity. The Officer, however, was less inclined toward mercy than the Associate Pastor and gave orders that he be stripped and put back into the civilian population, and he was cast out, naked, from The *Rap*ture and rejoined the masses.

Then the Officer went among the crowd, carefully examining each young man until he settled on one who looked healthy and about the right size, and handed the uniform to him. The new peace-keeper put it on joyously and immediately took out his cross-shaped billy-club and began practicing its use on his erstwhile compatriots.

Now, in light of the meager returns they had received from the offering, the crew gathered in The *Rap*ture's conference room to discuss other ways of helping maintain the capital supplies necessary for the sowing of God's Word. The problem was daunting, and Q confessed immediately that he could see no way of raising cash in their present location, for though his Father was an expert in the field, Q had not inherited his aptitude for fund management.

They brainstormed for several hours, but no one could come up with anything resembling a viable business plan. They were on the verge of despair when the Turntablist suddenly sat upright and exclaimed:

"Wait a minute, people, I have it: Disaster Tourism. We can outfit The *Rap*ture with glass walls and give tours of suburbs like this one. We'll call it 'Life on the Edge.' We can have brochures made up and Q and I can greet new arrivals at the airport. We can charge a tour fee, and we can also serve refreshments, or perhaps we could lease the concession to a local vendor. The Associate Pastor can serve as tour guide, and perhaps we can even spread God's Word to the tourists as well."

This idea seemed plausible enough that the Associate Pastor directed the Secretary to open a file for the project and keep detailed notes on all their ideas for a business plan. The Turntablist quickly designed a brochure on his laptop and then printed out a draft on the color laser for everyone's approval, while Q began to sketch drawings for the redesign of The *Rap*ture. They decided that one-way glass would be the optimal solution, since the tourists might feel uncomfortable if the subjects could see them lounging in the air-conditioned comfort of the RV. The Turntablist quickly scanned the drawings, then superimposed a photograph he had taken of the squalor outside their window, to show how it would look if airbrushed with such an image. Everyone agreed it was impressive.

In the end, though, the project proved beyond their means, since the Secretary calculated that the alterations to The *Rap*ture could easily cost 300,000 U.S. dollars. This led them to think about possibilities of seed capital via investors or a local bank, and that in turn led the Secretary to propose her own innovative idea:

"Why not," she began, "pool our resources and start a bank specializing in micro-loans? This could be a way of helping the Church and also helping our Subjects, since it would inject capital into the economy and also promote an entrepreneurial spirit among them."

Several objections were raised to this proposal, including the credit-worthiness of the constituency and the lack of accessible capital opportunities for borrowers. "Leverage isn't worth much," observed Q, "if there is nothing to be lifted." But the Secretary replied:

"Our bank could change the entire system. Say, for example, that we loan everyone with even the remotest idea of a business plan a small sum, say one dollar, to get them started. Keep in mind we have a congregation of sixty million here. Our loans could thus put sixty million dollars in circulation. The loans would provide capital both for the starting of new businesses (just imagine how well a food stand could do out here) and for the patronage of those businesses by the population.

"Now, you might object that those who spend their borrowed capital on items for use, such as food, instead of investment, will soon be defaulting on their loans. But these loans can simply be recapitalized, with the interest added to the principle, so that even the defaults become an avenue of profit, and the bank's assets should continue to increase while its liabilities fall."

Here Q interjected his surprise that any profit whatsoever could be realized from a population that seemed characterized by nothing so much as its utter poverty. But again the Secretary had an answer:

"The bank itself will create the Market. Why, just the raw infusion of cash itself will foster a demand for trousers and other clothing, since people will suddenly need pockets to carry their money in. And think, if we make a mere one percent on our investment, a mere penny per person per year—surely a very modest goal—that in itself would be $600,000."

"I would be afraid that we might implode in a wave of accounting scandals," said the Turntablist, and the others agreed that, though the bottom line sounded good, the plan seemed inordinately complicated. Besides that, there was the question of where they would raise the sixty million dollars needed for start-up capital.

"Well," said the Secretary, "let's see." She looked absently out the window and noticed the police standing guard over The *Rap*ture. "Of course," she said. "The local government will loan it to us. They have plenty of cash."

Everyone agreed that this method would lend the entire plan an aura of legitimacy, perhaps even tipping the balance into viability, but all discussions were soon halted by a knock on the door by those selfsame police. The Associate Pastor opened the door and was greeted by the Officer, who informed him that he had just received orders to escort the Church of the Ostensible Jesus out of the country.

They hurriedly prepared The *Rap*ture for travel and made for the airport with all possible haste. The Associate Pastor tried to put a good spin on the situation by telling them that this was just God's way of calling them home to help save the Church from its crisis, but they were all disheartened and his words had little effect.

The financial debacle had been brought on, the Associate Pastor had learned, by the purchase of a vast portfolio of mortgage derivatives by a new employee in Finance. Q didn't understand the complex nature of the problem, but he did remember the last time he had seen his Father, sitting at his new desk, dressed only in his dhoti, scratching his beard, engrossed in rows of numbers on the monitor. This thought made Q a bit queasy, but he put it out of his mind to focus on more immediate problems.

At the airport their military escort took them straight to the Whale, but as the crew prepared to load The *Rap*ture back into its belly, they were visited by a diplomat who informed them that the C-130 had been seized by the government as security against certain fees and taxes. Then, upon a word from the Officer, the police in the escort turned around and trained their weapons on Q and the rest of God's messengers, and their protectors became their captors.

The Associate Pastor looked around with concern, then conferred with the Diplomat and with the Officer in turn, then returned to the crew and told them that they would have to leave The *Rap*ture and the plane there for now, though they would be allowed to return to their home country on commercial flights. The Associate Pastor thought this was best, since there was no argument to be made anyway, so they walked across the tarmac to the terminal, and each of them bought a ticket home.

Each of them, that is, except Q, for Q had neither credit card nor passport. He pleaded with the Associate Pastor to buy his ticket for him, but the Associate Pastor explained that the Church card had been cancelled and he was having to use personal funds for the transaction, which made buying a ticket for Q impossible. Besides this, Q couldn't board a commercial flight because he had no passport. He was stuck, then, and the others were not.

The Associate Pastor opined that God must have plans for Q on the Dark Continent, and then he kissed him good-by. Each of the Church workers, in turn, shook Q's hand as they stepped into the security scanner. The most heartfelt farewell came from the Turntablist, who, with tears in his eyes, told Q he had never worked with so inspired an artist, that his rhythm was as solid as a drummer's, and that no one could ever, ever take his place.

Then Q's friends disappeared into the secured area, and he was alone on the Dark Continent.

Now Q retraced the route they had taken on their first day, this time afoot, and was rather surprised at what a different feeling the street had when one was walking in it rather than observing through the glass of *The Rapture*. Quickly reverting to his old habits, he kept his eye out for dumpsters but soon realized there were none in this place. He was surprised to find himself feeling nostalgic for those clean, brightly painted cornucopias. Here the homeless throngs picked among the filth on the ground to make a meal, which set Q wondering how long it would be before he, too, was so reduced.

But this time—regardless of what you, dear Reader, will surely have decided is inevitable in this discouraging narrative—it was not to be. For Q had not gone very far when he encountered something quite incongruous in the setting: a businessman in a YSL™ suit. He waved at Q as he approached.

"Q isn't it? Yes, of course it is. Q. Great to meet you Q. Hey I'm glad I don't have to stand in a queue to meet you." He laughed and slapped his thigh. Q had to admit it was very funny. The guy went on: "Seriously Q, great to meet you. Your reputation precedes you, you know, but of course you do; how could it not? And, anyway, I heard about your passport problem, heard about it this morning. That's tough, man. I wouldn't want to be stuck here without a passport or money or even a single friend. Phew, man, I don't even want to think. This place…" He gestured around them at the hordes of starving people, "…its pretty rough."

Q was about to answer that he'd been through most everything and reckoned he could handle this too, but when he opened his mouth to speak the severity of his current condition suddenly came home to him, and he started to sob.

"Oh yeah Q, let it out. I know how you feel, man." He put his hand on Q's shoulder affectionately. "It's like you're out here, you know, all alone and looking death in the face. That's not for the faint of heart, Q. I have to hand it to you. I'd be crying too."

Q sobbed even harder at this outpouring of affection.

"Yep, a man of no fortune. That's you, Q. But a man of no fortune with a name to come." Q looked up. "That's right; it's coming, I know it is, that day when a name will become you. But hey, I have the advantage of you. Let me introduce myself." He handed Q his card:

HEADHUNTER™

Q stopped his snivelling and examined the thing.

"Yes," said the Headhunter, "That's me. I ply the deep, dark jungles of the Continent in search of Corporate Talent."

"But… surely this isn't the place to look for potential executives," Q replied, wiping his nose. "Look, these people are starving."

"Oh, we like 'em hungry," said the Headhunter with a wink.

"And when they are hungry, do you give them food?"

"Food for their souls, Q. Food in the form of hope. Why just the other day a guy came into my office, dressed in rags, and he said to me: 'For I was an hungred, and ye gave me meat: I was thirsty, and ye gave me drink: I was a stranger, and ye took me in: Naked, and ye clothed me: I was sick, and ye visited me: I was in prison, and ye came unto me.'

"And I said to him, 'Man, when did I do all this? I've never seen you before.' And he said, 'Inasmuch as ye have done it unto one of the least of these my brethren, ye have done it unto me.'

"So that's it, you see, help one fellow out and you help them all.

The entire society is served. Just like I'm going to serve you right now, Q, for I have a client who will be interested in you, a very powerful client who can solve all your problems, a client who can give you a name."

Q was overjoyed at this prospect. The Headhunter tempered his enthusiasm with mention of the daunting paperwork that would have to be handled, but Q begged to begin the process at the Headhunter's earliest convenience, so they set off at once for his office, Q so engrossed that he tripped over one of the naked beggars that lay on the sidewalk all around them.

The Headhunter's office was on the top floor of a skyscraper that rose as an island of opulence in the endless sea of privation. As they stepped over the last of the beggars into the lobby, the bright noise of the street was silenced and its odors of garbage, urine, sweat, feces and smoke faded into the clean, air-conditioned world of international finance. Smartly dressed men and women coursed the gleaming marble floor with briefcases and folders. They wore fedoras or turbans or keffiyehs over business suits or thawbs. There were burqas atop stylish pumps, colorful kaftans and dashikis, blue jeans and suits from Paris and New York. The place was a kind of Babel, the murmur in the lobby being comprised of snippets of Chinese, Arabic, English, Japanese, Flemish, Dutch, German, French, Spanish, Portuguese and Russian, along with smatterings of Wolof, Swahili and Fula.

They took the elevator to the top floor, fifty stories up, and exited directly into the Headhunter's posh office. Here the Headhunter took Q's picture with his digital camera and then bade Q wait in the conference room, where he could amuse himself with the panoramic view of the city. Anon the Headhunter returned with another gentleman whom he introduced simply as the Colonel. The

Colonel was dressed quite strangely, all in camouflage, and he was heavily armed, with pistols and knives on his waist and grenades hanging from snaps in various places about his person. Q looked for any insignia on this uniform but found none; there were various stripes, epaulets and decorations, but nothing that seemed to be the insignia of a nation.

The Colonel handed Q his card:

BROWNWATER™

Q examined this card for a moment but then was surprised to find himself under attack from this Colonel. The officer backed up a step and dropped into wide squat, waving his hands before him and making a high-pitched squealing sound. He then spun around, lifting one leg off the ground and aiming the heavy steel-reinforced boot at Q's head. Q, however, had by now become quite adept at dodging boots that were aimed at his head, and he avoided the blow easily with a miniscule dodge.

Now the Colonel came at him with arms and fists flailing. Q deflected every blow harmlessly with his hands. He had no desire to hurt this strange fellow, whom he suspected was a potential employer. Finally the officer, panting a little, leapt onto the conference table, got a running start, and dove in Q's direction, executing a perfect forward somersault in the air. Q didn't want to endanger the man—who, despite his obvious desire, was a ridiculous failure as a fighter—but at the last second he was forced to step aside, allowing the Colonel to land on his face on the marble floor, bloodying his nose.

"Sorry, sir," Q said.

"You're hired," said the Colonel, wiping the blood from his face.

Then the Headhunter sat them both down at the table and put a stack of forms in front of them. They each signed every one and then shook hands, and the Colonel informed Q that he was now officially an employee of Brownwater™ Security Services.

The Colonel inquired if Q had any affairs he needed to put in order before beginning work, to which Q replied that he had no affairs. Here the Headhunter intervened by handing Q a small valise which, upon inspection, was found to contain:

1.) A passport with Q's picture on it.

2.) A Social Security card.

3.) A Driver's License.

4.) A diploma and transcripts naming Q as a magna cum laude recipient of the degree of Master of Business Administration from Harvard University.

5.) Various other documents attesting to the veracity of those previously mentioned.

6.) An Android™ Smartphone.

7.) A Platinum debit card (Credit Suisse).

Q stared at this treasure trove of Identity in wonder. For how long now had he been pining for these simple papers? How easy his life would have been in the previous months if he had only had these documents. He began thanking the two gentlemen profusely, but stopped suddenly when he noticed one peculiar detail.

"Um," he stammered, "there is one detail I see that isn't correct, which is my name. All these documents have me listed as Q, but Q is only a marker I acquired by accident, arbitrarily, at the Shelter in my home city. Surely these documents should indicate my Real Name."

The Headhunter was flummoxed. "Q isn't your Real Name? But it said so on your van; it said 'The *Rap*ture, featuring Q.' It said so in every document I reviewed by which your reputation preceded you. How was I to know that wasn't your Real Name?"

The three of them conferred, then, for several hours on how this problem might be rectified, with both the Colonel and the Headhunter consulting various CEO's and Heads of State as to the efficacy and precise procedure of resolving Q's Real Name. In the end, however, it was decided that, since in the time they had been arguing Q's Identity and status had been logged in 6,660 databases with governments, law enforcement agencies, hospitals and universities world-wide, it was easier to change Q's Identity to fit the documents than vice versa. And Q became Q in fact.

With this matter settled, Q and the Colonel bade the Headhunter good-by and exited to the helipad on the roof. As they were strapping themselves into the UH-60 Blackhawk™ Q quietly said good-by, as well, to his former life; good-by to his Father and young Santo; good-by to the simple life on the rails, in the camps and in the shelters; good-by to Lucy, wherever she was; to the Troll under his bridge; to his Mother and Sister; and, finally, good-by to Provincial Oaks, the only subdivision he had ever called home, where he had first come to himself and learned his Real Name, which was… Well, what was it? Q furrowed his brow and tried to concentrate. His real name was…

Forgotten.

They lifted off the rooftop and into the first layer of brown smog. They headed out across the city, whose squalor, Q could now see, stretched to the horizon in all directions. But Q was distracted by his curiosity as to where they were going and what his first assignment would be, and he fired questions at the Colonel over the noise of the helicopter.

The Colonel informed Q, naturally, that his reputation preceded him, and that Brownwater™ had good use for a young man of his considerable talents. Their mission, he said, involved maintaining security for governmental and corporate clients. To Q's question about his compensation, the Colonel informed him that he would enter employment at level E17, which carried a salary of 36,000 USD per month.

Q mulled these details for a moment, then inquired: "Are we, then, mercenaries?"

"In a way," the Colonel replied, "but you must understand the importance of our role. When governments, because of political pressures from their constituencies, are forced to divert resources away from the military to fund social programs, infrastructural support, elections, etc., they sometimes find themselves suddenly at odds with their own best interests. That's where we come in. We help refocus the attentions of the public sector on primary goals by securing resource supply-chains and providing structural adjustments. And, as everyone knows, the private sector can provide these services more efficiently and economically than governments, because of their unwieldy bureaucracies, can provide for themselves.

"Here, Q, have one of these cigars. They're from Cuba, finest in the world."

He produced a cigar from the Blackhawk™'s humidor and handed it to Q along with a jeweled case which held a solid gold cutter and lighter. He then had to show Q how to use the cutter and, indeed, how to smoke a cigar. He then produced a bottle of Cristal™ from the cooler, popped it, and poured them each a refreshing draught in a pair of fine Austrian crystal champagne flutes.

Below them the landscape had changed from suburban slums to verdant jungle. They were following the path of a large river, flying low enough that Q could make out crocodiles and hippopotami on the river banks. Occasionally large flocks of colorful birds would pass under them. Rounding a bend, Q saw a small, primitive village on the riverbank ahead. Smoke rose from small fires in the huts. Children splashed at the water's edge.

Then Q saw a bright flash from a corner of the village and heard immediately an alarm going off inside the helicopter. The pilot made a hasty adjustment, sending cigars and champagne flutes flying about the cabin, and then flames rose up outside the windows, and Q thought they were done for. But the flame died away instantly and they continued on their path up the river. Q looked back and saw the village engulfed in flame.

"Here you go, Q," said the Colonel, handing him a fresh glass of champagne.

"What just happened?" asked Q.

"Well," said the Colonel, "I believe we came under enemy fire and were forced to take out a hostile position."

"But who fired at us?" Q was concerned to know.

"Hard to say," the Colonel replied. "What country are we in?" he asked the pilot over the radio. The pilot responded with a shrug. "Not sure," the Colonel continued. "They might have been genuine unfriendlies, or they might have thought we were Chinese or Russian or something. But villagers don't get to shoot at Blackhawks™; that's the only hard and fast rule. Shoot at a Blackhawk™ and you will be taken out."

They left the river's course then and headed out over the jungle. The terrain began gradually to rise and become more mountainous until finally they were flying in the clouds to pass over the peaks. From beyond a ridge in the distance Q could see smoke rising, and the Colonel indicated that this smoke was indeed their destination.

When they topped the ridge they dropped down into a great hole in the Earth, like a volcano. As they coursed down into the pit Q watched the geologic strata pass outside the window. Here and there veins of shiny ores shone in cross-section through the smoke, and Q began gradually to make out human figures on the cliff face. Women walked along narrow ledges balancing barrel-sized baskets on their heads while men flailed at the rock-face with picks and children dug into the crevices with hammer and chisel.

"What kind of volcano is this?" asked Q.

"It's a human volcano," said the Colonel, "a vent into the subterranean core of humanity. It is a volcano of coltan, of diamonds, of copper, of pure gold."

They settled down into the bottom of the hole, clearing a place on the ground with the wind from the rotor. What Q had mistaken for smoke was in fact dust, and instead of molten lava at the bottom of the pit they found a terra firma coursed with a maze of roads and tracks which were trafficked by a steady stream of enormous trucks, loaders, boring machinery and military vehicles carrying loads of soldiers and weaponry. They landed near some portable buildings. There were several other helicopters on the pad, sleek corporate models, very light-weight and sporty compared to the Blackhawk™.

At a signal from the Colonel he and Q leapt out of the craft and, covering their faces from the dust, ran to the nearest building and entered. The building was a simple metal container which, Q observed, still had cables attached to it so that it could be moved easily around the site by one of the great cranes that dotted the area. Inside, however, they found an air-conditioned, sound-proof room, finely appointed with wool carpets and chandeliers. Men in fine European suits (reminding Q of the lobby of the Headhunter's office building) lounged on white leather sofas attended by scantily clad Nubian maids with trays of martinis and hor d'oeuvres.

"Hello, Colonel," one of the Businessmen said, and rose from the couch to meet them. "Great to see you again." He was a middle-aged white man in a dark suit who would have looked more at home on Wall Street than in the jungle. "And you must be Q. Very pleased to meet you. Your reputation precedes you, of course. I'm very pleased to see the Colonel has drafted a man of your diverse talents. Very pleased indeed. Sit down, Q, and you too, Colonel. Have a martini. Perhaps you would like some caviar?" He clapped his hands and several of the maids sprang into action, easing Q and the Colonel onto the sofa, settling the cushions around them. They brought warm rags soaked in rose water for them to clean their hands, which were still grimy from their rough journey, and then tray after tray of food. Ice trays of oysters and shellfish complemented local delicacies such as wild birds, fish and various reptiles, along with the promised caviar.

Q ate ravenously, The Colonel picked, and their host watched them both with a pleased surmise. After a very few moments of idle chit-chat, the Colonel made a simple inquiry:

"And?" he said.

"Oh of course, of course. I apologize for keeping you waiting," the handsome young fellow entoned. He clapped his hands again and now five of the Nubian maids appeared, each carrying a large Luis Vuitton™ case, which they set in front of the Colonel He, in turn, got down on his knees and opened each case in turn, verifying that each was completely full of American $100 bills.

Q was interested in this and attempted—after all he was his Father's son—to calculate the number of bills in each case. As the Colonel opened them, Q saw that the bills were stacked neatly in rows and columns. Each held 10 stacks of bills along the x axis and 3 stacks along the y, for 30 stacks in all. There remained only to count the height of each stack to arrive at an accurate value for each case. Q estimated that the cases were 7.3 inches thick, net, and that the bills were approximately .0043 inches thick, so that each inch would contain 233 bills. Thus the calculation was simple: 233x7.3 x 30 stacks = 51,000 bills or 5.1 million dollars per case, 25.5 million total.

"OK," said the Colonel, snapping the last case closed. "Don't you want to see your merchandise?"

"Why Colonel," their host replied, "I've already seen the merchandise." The rest of the lounging businessmen laughed at this comment, and one of them aimed a remote control at the wall, which immediately became a video screen. On the screen was their Blackhawk™. One of the military trucks they had seen from the air was backed up to it and several young men were unloading crates whose labels indicated they contained rocket launchers, oozis and various types of explosives and chemical weapons.

The Colonel tipped his hat to the businessman's resourcefulness, then made a sign for the girls to pick the cases back up and take them out to the Blackhawk™, which they did, with remarkable agility considering their high-heeled footwear and tight evening gowns. They put the heavy cases on their heads to carry them, Q noticed, just like the head-bearers who were working on the ledges above them.

As the pilot lifted off and they began their climb out of the volcano, Q asked the Colonel if that businessman was one of their clients.

"Not exactly a client," said the Colonel. "In a way, in fact, he is a competitor, since he maintains his own militia, and if you asked me if there was a chance that one day those weapons we just sold him might be used against us—and I mean *us*, this very craft—I would have to answer that yes, there is a chance of that.

"However, these informal relationships are important to the working of the system as a whole. If our only business were legitimate business, we would in fact be out of business in a very short time. The capital generated by transactions such as these is necessary to keep valuable products, products that enhance the quality of our lives and the lives of our loved ones, in distribution. They allow us to negotiate the peaks and troughs of the business world while maintaining an even keel. Without this"—he pointed back to the steaming pit they were now leaving behind—"you can't have this." And he held up a cell phone. On each finger of the hand that held the phone was a ring of gold

"But now, Q, I think it's time you heard the whole story. You see, I've been on the Dark Continent a long time. I came here with a very different goal in mind, years ago. Right away I began developing the contacts that enable me to operate today. And I learned a lesson or two along the way. Listen to my story, now, so you don't have to relive it."

The Colonel's Story

My first assignment on the Continent was, preliminary to our setting up operations, to arrive at a figure, however approximate, for the total population of a certain tribe in a remote jungle, the very jungle that is passing under us now. All the indications I had collected along the line pointed to a rapid decline in population. Thirty years before, for instance, a known faction of the group comprised more than a thousand individuals; when that same group visited the local telegraph station recently it consisted of one hundred and twenty-seven men, plus their women and children. Soon after that, moreover, an influenza epidemic broke out. The disease turned into a form of pulmonary oedema, and three hundred natives died of it within forty-eight hours. The whole group disintegrated, leaving the sick and dying to fend for themselves. Of the thousand who had once been counted, only nineteen men and their families survived. The decline was due not only to the epidemic, but also to the fact that some years ago this group was at war with some of their easterly neighbours.

What was the position at the time of my arrival? Probably a bare two thousand natives were scattered about the territory. I could not hope to make a systematic count, because certain groups were always hostile, and because, during the nomadic season, all the bands were continually on the move. But I tried to persuade my friends to take me to their village at a time when a rendezvous had been arranged with other allied or related bands. Thus I hoped to estimate the present size of a gathering of this sort and to compare it with the reunions that had been scrutinized in earlier years. I promised to bring them presents, and effect some exchanges, but the leader of the band remained hesitant: he was not sure of his guests, and if my companions and I were to disappear in the region where no white men had penetrated since the disappearance of seven mining executives in 1955, then the precarious peace which existed there would be compromised for a long time to come.

In the end he agreed, on condition that we cut down the size of our party, and took only four oxen to carry our presents. Even so, he said, we should have to forswear the usual tracks, because our beasts would never get through the dense vegetation which abounded in the lower reaches of the valley. We should have to go by the plateau, improvising our route as we went along.

This was a very dangerous expedition, but it now seems to me largely grotesque. We had hardly set out when my colleague remarked to me on the absence of native women and children: only the men were with us, each armed with bow and arrows. All the literature of travel indicated this as a sign that an attack was imminent. Our feelings were mixed, therefore, as we went forward, verifying from time to time the position of our Ingram™ machine pistols and our rifles. These fears proved misplaced: towards the half-way point of the day's march we caught up with the remainder of the band, whom their provident chief had sent on ahead of us, the day before, knowing that our mules would make much better time than the women, laden as these were with their baskets and encumbered with little children.

Soon after this, however, the natives got lost. The new itinerary was not as straightforward as they had supposed. Towards evening we had to come to a halt in the bush. We had been promised that there would be game thereabouts and the natives, counting on our rifles, had brought no food with them. We, for our part, had brought only emergency rations which could not be shared out all round. A troop of deer which had been nibbling away at the edge of a spring fled at our approach. The next morning everybody was in a thoroughly bad humour: ostensibly, this took for its object the leader of the band, whom they considered to be responsible for the venture which he and I had devised between us. Instead of going off to hunt or collect wild food on their own account, they decided to spend the day lying in the shade, leaving it to their leader to find the solution to their problem.

Then he went off, accompanied by one of his wives: towards evening we saw them coming back with their baskets heavy-laden with grasshoppers that they had spent the entire day in collecting. Grasshopper pie is not one of their favourite dishes, but the entire party fell on it, none the less, with relish. Good humour broke out on all sides, and next morning we got under way again.

At last, we got to the rendezvous. This was a sandy terrace above a watercourse, bordered with trees between which the natives had laid out some little gardens. Incoming groups arrived at intervals during the day and by the evening there were seventy-five people in all: seventeen families, grouped under thirteen crude shelters hardly more solid than those which served in camp. I was told that when the rains began the whole company would take refuge in five round huts built for several months wear. Many of the natives seemed never to have seen a white man, and their more than dubious welcome combined with their leader's extreme nervousness seemed to suggest that he had forced their hand, somewhat, in the whole matter. Neither we nor the natives felt at all at our ease and, as there were no trees, we had to lie on the bare ground.

No one slept: we kept, all night long, a polite watch upon one another. It would have been rash to prolong the adventure, and I suggested to the leader that we should get down to our exchanges without further delay. It was then that there occurred an extraordinary incident which forces me to go back a little in time. That the tribe could not write goes without saying. But they were also unable to draw, except for a few dots and zigzags on their calabashes. I distributed pencils and paper among them, none the less. At first they made no use of them. Then, one day, I saw that they were all busy drawing wavy horizontal lines on the paper. What were they trying to do? I could only conclude that they were writing or, more exactly, that they were trying to do as I did with my pencils. As I had never tried to amuse them with drawings, they could not conceive of any other use for this implement. With most of them, that was as far as they got: but their leader saw further into the problem. Doubtless he was the only one among them to have understood what writing was for. So he asked me for one of my notepads; and when we were working together he did not give me his answers in words, but traced a wavy line or two on the paper and gave it to me, as if I could read what he had to say. He himself was all but deceived by his own play-acting. Each time he drew a line he would examine it with great care, as if its meaning must suddenly leap to the eye; and every time a look of disappointment came over his face. But he would never give up trying, and there was an unspoken agreement between us that his scribblings had a meaning that I did my best to decipher; his own verbal commentary was so prompt in coming that I had no need to ask him to explain what he had written.

And now, no sooner was everyone assembled than he drew forth from a basket a piece of paper covered with scribbled lines and pretended to read from it. With a show of hesitation he looked up and down his list for the objects to be given in exchange for his people's presents. So-and-so was to receive a machete in return for his bow and arrows, another a string of beads in return for his necklaces, and so on for two solid hours. What was he hoping for? To deceive himself perhaps: but, even more, to amaze his companions and persuade them that his intermediacy was responsible for the exchanges. He had allied himself with the white man, as equal with equal, and could now share in his secrets. We were in a hurry to get away, since there would obviously be a moment of real danger at which all the marvels I had brought would have been handed over. So I did not go further into the matter and we set off on the return journey, still guided by the natives. There had been something intensely irritating about our abortive meeting, and about the mystifications of which I had just been the unknowing instrument. Added to that, my mule was suffering from aphtha, and its mouth was causing it pain, so that by turns it hurried impatiently forward and stopped dead in its tracks. We got into a quarrel with one another and, quite suddenly, without realizing how it happened, I found myself alone, and lost, in the middle of the bush.

What was I to do? What people do in books: fire a shot in the air to let my companions know what had happened. I dismounted and did so. No reply. I fired again, and as there seemed to be an answer I fired a third shot. This scared my mule, who went off at a trot and pulled up some distance away.

I put weapons and photographic equipment ready at the foot of a tree, memorized its position, and ran off to recapture my mule, who seemed quite peaceably disposed. He let me get right up to him and then, just as I reached for the reins, he made off at full speed. This happened more than once until in despair I jumped at him and threw both my arms round his tail. This unusual proceeding took him by surprise, and he decided to give in. Back in the saddle, I made as if to collect my belongings, only to find that we had twisted and turned so often that I had no idea where they were.

Demoralized by this episode, I decided to rejoin our troop. Neither my mule nor I knew where they had gone. Sometimes I would head him in a direction that he refused to take; sometimes I would let him lead, only to find that he was simply turning in a circle. The sun was going down, I was no longer armed, and I expected at every moment to be the target of a volley of arrows. I was not, admittedly, the first white man to penetrate that hostile zone. But none of my predecessors had come back alive and, quite apart from myself, my mule was a tempting prey for people who rarely have anything very much to get their teeth into. These dark thoughts passed, one by one, through my mind as I waited for the sun to go down, thinking that since I at least had some matches with me I could start a bush-fire. Just as I was about to strike the first match I heard voices: two of the bearers had turned back, the moment my absence was noticed, and had been following me all afternoon. For them to recover my equipment was child's play and, at nightfall, they led me to the camp where our whole troop was waiting for me.

Tormented by this absurd incident, I slept badly. To pass the time

I went back, in my mind, to the scene of the previous morning. So the natives had learnt what it meant to write! But not at all, as one might have supposed, as the result of a laborious apprenticeship. The symbol had been borrowed, but the reality remained quite foreign to them. Even the borrowing had had a sociological, rather than an intellectual object: for it was not a question of knowing specific things, or understanding them, or keeping them in mind, but merely of enhancing the prestige and authority of one individual or one function at the expense of the rest of the party. A native, still in the period of the stone age, had realized that even if he could not himself understand the great instrument of understanding he could at least make it serve other ends. For thousands of years, after all, and still today in a great part of the world, writing has existed as an institution in societies in which the vast majority of people are quite unable to write. The villages where I stayed in Afghanistan are populated by illiterates; yet each village has a scribe who fulfils his function for the benefit both of individual citizens and of the village as a whole. They all know what writing is and, if need be, can write: but they do it from outside as if it were a mediator, foreign to themselves, with whom they communicate by an oral process. But the scribe is rarely a functionary or an employee of the group as a whole; his knowledge is a source of power so much so, in fact, that the functions of scribe and usurer are often united in the same human being. This is not merely because the usurer needs to be able to read and write to carry on his trade, but because he has thus a twofold empire over his fellows.

Writing is a strange thing. It would seem as if its appearance could not have failed to wreak profound changes in the living conditions of our race, and that these transformations must have been above all intellectual in character. Once men know how to write, they are enormously more able to keep in being a large body of knowledge. Writing might, that is to say, be regarded as a form of artificial memory, whose development should be accompanied by a deeper knowledge of the past and, therefore, by a greater ability to organize the present and the future. Of all the criteria by which people habitually distinguish civilization from barbarism, this should be the one most worth retaining: that certain peoples write and others do not. The first group can accumulate a body of knowledge that helps it to move ever faster towards the goal that it has assigned to itself; the second is confined within limits that the memory of individuals can never hope to extend, and it must remain the prisoner of a history worked out from day to day, with neither a clear knowledge of its own origins nor a consecutive idea of what its future should be.

Yet nothing of what we know of writing, or of its role in evolution, can be said to justify this conception. One of the most creative phases in human history took place with the onset of the neolithic era: agriculture and the domestication of animals are only two of the developments which may be traced to this period. It must have had behind it thousands of years during which small societies of human beings were noting, experimenting, and passing on to one another the fruits of their knowledge. The very success of this immense enterprise bears witness to the rigour and the continuity of its preparation, at a time when writing was quite unknown. If writing first made its appearance between the fourth and third millennium before our era, we must see it not, in any degree, as a conditioning factor in the Neolithic revolution, but rather as an already-distant and doubtless indirect result of that revolution. With what great innovation can it be linked? Where technique is concerned, architecture alone can be called into question. Yet the architecture of the Egyptians or the Sumerians was no better than the work of certain American Natives who, at the time America was discovered, were ignorant of writing. Conversely, between the invention of writing and the birth of modern science, the Western world has lived through some five thousand years, during which time the sum of its knowledge has rather gone up and down than known a steady increase. It has often been remarked that there was no great difference between the life of a Greek or Roman citizen and that of a member of the well-to-do European classes in the eighteenth century. In the Neolithic age, humanity made immense strides forward without any help from writing; and writing did not save the civilizations of the Western world from long periods of stagnation. Doubtless the scientific expansion of the nineteenth and twentieth centuries could hardly have occurred, had writing not existed. But this condition, however necessary, cannot in itself explain that expansion.

If we want to correlate the appearance of writing with certain other characteristics of civilization, we must look elsewhere. The one phenomenon which has invariably accompanied it is the formation of cities and empires: the integration into a political system, that is to say, of a considerable number of individuals, and the distribution of those individuals into a hierarchy of castes and classes. Such is, at any rate, the type of development which we find, from Egypt right across to China, at the moment when writing makes its debuts; it seems to favour rather the exploitation than the enlightenment of mankind. This exploitation made it possible to assemble workers by the thousand and set them tasks that taxed them to the limits of their strength: to this, surely, we must attribute the beginnings of architecture as we know it. If my hypothesis is correct, the primary function of writing, as a means of communication, is to facilitate the enslavement of other human beings. The use of writing for disinterested ends, and with a view to satisfactions of the mind in the fields either of science or the arts, is a secondary result of its invention and may even be no more than a way of reinforcing, justifying, or dissimulating its primary function.

There are, however, exceptions to this rule. In ancient times the Dark Continent included empires in which several hundred thousand subjects acknowledged a single rule; in pre-Colombian America, the Inca empire numbered several million subjects. But, alike on the Dark Continent and in America, these ventures were notably unstable: we know, for instance, that the Inca empire was established in the twelfth century or thereabouts. Pizarro's soldiers would never have conquered it so easily if it had not already, three centuries later, been largely decomposed. And, from the little we know of the ancient history of the Dark Continent, we can divine an analogous situation: massive political groups seem to have appeared and disappeared within the space of not many decades. It may be, therefore, that these instances confirm, instead of refuting, our hypothesis. Writing may not have sufficed to consolidate human knowledge, but it may well have been indispensable to the establishment of an enduring dominion. To bring the matter nearer to our own time: the European-wide movement towards compulsory education in the nineteenth century went hand in hand with the extension of military service and the systematization of the proletariat. The struggle against illiteracy is indistinguishable, at times, from the increased powers exerted over the individual citizen by the central authority. For it is only when everyone can read that Authority can decree that ignorance of the law is no defence.

All this moved rapidly from the national to the international, thanks to the mutual complicity which sprang up between new-born states confronted as these were with the problems that had been our own, a century or two ago and an international society of peoples long privileged. These latter recognize that their stability may well be endangered by nations whose knowledge of the written word has not, as yet, empowered them to think in formulae which can be modified at will. Such nations are not yet ready to be *edified*; and when they are first given the freedom of the library shelves they are perilously vulnerable to the ever more deliberately misleading effects of the printed word. Doubtless the die is already cast, in that respect. But in my native village people were not so easily taken in. Shortly after my visit the leader lost the confidence of most of his people. Those who moved away from him, after he had tried to play the civilized man, must have had a confused understanding of the fact that writing, on this its first appearance in their midst, had allied itself with falsehood, and so they had taken refuge, deeper in the bush, to win themselves a respite. And yet I could not but admire the genius of their leader, for he had divined in a flash that writing could redouble his hold upon the others and, in so doing, he had got, as it were, to the bottom of an institution which he did not as yet know how to work. The episode also drew my attention to a further aspect of tribal life: the political relations between individuals and groups.

At this point Q could restrain himself no longer and interrupted: "But Colonel," he cried, "it sounds like you came into the jungle as an anthropologist, or even a humanitarian. How is it that you changed your role so drastically, from scholar to mercenary?"

"That's a very good question, Q," the Colonel replied, "one that I will answer directly, as my story continues."

The story's continuation, however, was not forthcoming, for at that moment the Colonel's head exploded. There where the mouth that was telling the story had been was only a ragged stump from which gushed buckets of dark red blood. The Colonel's body seemed to be continuing the narration with simple gestures, as it mimed riding a horse, climbing a rope, and then hacking with a machete.

"Shit, I think we've been hit," Q heard the pilot say over the radio, and the Blackhawk™ again began to tumble chaotically. The cabin filled with smoke as more large caliber bullets penetrated the hull, leaving holes of daylight. Q saw the flash of the Blackhawk's™ weapons firing, too, but then he heard the pilot announce, as if it were business as usual: "Prepare for hard landing."

Q didn't know what to do to prepare for a hard landing, nor could he have done anything had he known what to do, since the craft was bucking and rotating so violently he had no choice but to remain strapped in his seat while bullets and champagne bottles orbited around him. At some point in the chaos one of the latter struck him in the head, and he was relieved of his consciousness.

When Q awoke he found himself hanging head down in his seat. The headless Colonel was still seated across from him, blood still dripping, though more slowly now, from his jugular. The pilot was in even worse condition, all but obliterated in the cockpit. The entire cabin was so riddled with bullet holes Q couldn't imagine how he himself had survived, and yet here he hung.

When he opened the buckle of his seat belt he fell straight forward onto the Colonel and spent a moment extracting himself from the ghastly embrace. They had come to rest in a tree, but Q couldn't tell how high up in the jungle canopy they were. The five Luis Vuitton™ suitcases were strapped to the floor in front of the side hatch, and he decided to cut them loose to get them out of his way. He pulled the combat knife from the Colonel's scabbard, cut the straps, gave the bundle a judicious kick, and heard the cases crash through the foliage, hitting the ground some long seconds later.

He climbed out the other side hatch, clambering over the ruined cockpit and the nose onto a limb of the huge tree they had come to rest in, and this none too soon, as he immediately heard machine gun fire from below and saw new bullet holes opening in the side of the chopper. After a few minutes came the sound of wood cracking, and the thing sank out of the tree and crashed to the ground far below.

Q remained on his limb at the top of the canopy all the rest of that day, fearing his fate at the hands of the rebels on the ground. But as darkness fell new fears arose, and the jungle came to life around him.

The sun fell, the full moon rose, and all around him nocturnal creatures began to stir. Even in the bright light of the moon, he never caught sight of a single, whole animal, but the shadows churned with vague shapes and thrashing leaves, and gradually a hellish cacophony of calls and screams and crashing brush rang out. He heard the deep growl of the panther and the horrid laugh of the hyena. Monkeys and baboons and cheetahs sounded out on all sides and underneath him. Sometimes he felt footsteps on the very limb he clung to, or felt fur or scales if he stretched out his hand too far. And yet he had no thought of climbing down, for at least here he had the moonlight, while beneath him was an abyss.

It seemed the night would never end, and yet it did, and was no longer than any other night, and as dawn made itself known on the horizon, Q began his descent. He was much higher than he had imagined, yet the tree provided an accommodating ladder to the ground, and he was soon and gratefully back on solid ground.

He was exhausted and ached all over from the long night of clutching his limb, but he knew he wouldn't live long if he remained here. He took a quick look around and gathered such weapons and supplies as he could from the wreckage of the Blackhawk™. One of the attackers had apparently been caught unaware as the chopper had fallen and had been crushed under it. He was pinned under the tail, dead, with his head sticking out and his Uzi™ beside him. Q estimated his age to be 11 or 12.

Outfitted, now, rather as the Colonel had been when they had first met, Q set off into the jungle. He consulted his compass, but quickly realized it had no meaning for him, since he had no idea where he was, where he was heading, or even where he had been. So he put the instrument away and began walking, only to be brought up short by the sight of something he had forgotten. There, miraculously—or perhaps simply as testament to their quality—unharmed, off to the side of the wreckage, lay the Five Bags.

Now when Q had done his careful calculation of the value of the money in each bag, he had failed to make a calculation that was about to become of great importance to him here in the jungle: their weight. Had he made that calculation, he would have known that the net weight of the 100 dollar bills in each bag was 112.33 pounds, which, added to the tare weight of 11.9 pounds for each bag, left him with a gross weight of 124.23 pounds per item, for a grand total of 621.15 pounds to be transported across the uncharted jungle.

Q silently made these calculations, in a rough way, now, and then went over and hefted one of the bags just to be sure. He was young and healthy and so could carry one bag quite handily, especially if he could strap it to his back. Two bags could even be managed, though it would be slow going, requiring frequent stops. But the thought of leaving 15.3 million dollars on the floor of the jungle, no matter its weight in pounds, was more than he could bear, so he put his able mind to finding a solution.

He reviewed many possible solutions, including building a dray or some sort of transport out of the wreckage of the helicopter. But the longer he stayed there the more anxious he became, as he was sure the rebels would be coming back to sack the wreck themselves, so in the end he decided he would just get the bags as far from the site as he could, simply to have more time to consider a course of action.

So he picked up two Bags and carried them approximately 100 meters into the jungle. There he set them down and returned to the wreck and took two more. Then he returned for the last one. This had only been his interim plan, but now, since no better option evinced itself, he had to continue on with it, so he kept moving the bags forward in short increments for the rest of the day. By evening he reckoned he had gone about two miles.

At this point he was quite exhausted and he sat down and reexamined the Bags. Whereas that morning they had had a sort of luster about them, now they were scratched up, beaten, muddy and dingy. When Q had looked upon them that morning he had felt something resembling hunger or thirst for those Bags. Now he felt only revulsion when he looked at them, and he wished with all his heart that he could leave them behind. But for some reason that he himself did not understand, he could not.

That night he built a sort of shelter around himself using the Bags and some tree limbs, and he was able to get a little rest. He awoke the next morning with renewed vigor and immediately set to moving the Bags again.

The renewal, however, was short-lived, for after only the third leg of the day's trek he was cursing and spitting on the Bags. After the fifth leg he began talking to them, in words far too indelicate to repeat here, calling them horrible names and sending down curses on their ancestors and progeny as if they were living things.

By mid-afternoon he was completely spent, and he collapsed on the ground in front of the Bags and sobbed. Then he got up in a rage, urinated on them and splattered them with mud. Then he fell on the ground again and begged their forgiveness. Then he moved some distance away and sat with his back to them while he collected his wits. He tried to reason his way out of the quandary.

He knew that just one bag contained enough wealth to support him—and probably the rest of his family too—for the rest of his life. So why not just leave four Bags behind, strap one to his back and press on? But then again, would it be enough? Look what had happened to his Father. Look what had happened to the Church of the Ostensible Jesus. Could one ever have enough money to be safe from destitution?

He thought back to his time on the street, a time when he would have been very excited to encounter 25 dollars, but now he had 25 million in his grasp, and all he felt was enormous anxiety. He looked back at the bags, and the sight of them, now filthy and stinking, made him nauseous. He was so disgusted he couldn't even think clearly, so he stood up and began to pace around the clearing with his chin in his hand. He pulled up short, though, at a break in the underbrush which afforded him a view of what lay ahead. He saw a river just a short distance from him, and on the bank of the river a boatman with a small dinghy stood waiting.

"Aha," thought Q, " if I can just get the Bags to the river, perhaps I can find a raft and my travel will be much easier." So he grabbed one of them and took it the riverbank. He set it down near the Boatman and made it known, by hand gestures and mime, that he would be returning with the others, which he did, each in turn, running from the riverbank to the clearing and back again and again until all Five Bags were stacked near the dinghy.

Unfortunately for Q, however, at this moment another traveler arrived at the landing. This man was a local on his way to the market with a fox, a chicken and a sack of grain. The Boatman greeted the Newcomer like a long lost friend, then directed him to board the boat. The man began to board with his livestock and feed, but the Boatman stopped him and indicated that the boat was too small to take them all; he could only carry the Newcomer and one of his charges on a single trip.

"This is unfortunate," said the Newcomer, "because I can't leave the Fox alone with the Chicken nor the Chicken alone with the Grain. This will make our trip across somewhat tricky. In fact, it will take a number of trips. How many?"

"Seven," the Boatman replied, and then he set about getting them across. How did he do it?

(Write your answer here)

____

____

____

____

When the Newcomer with his livestock and feed were safely across, the Boatman came back for Q. At the same time, another traveler arrived. This one was—one could tell from his shifty eyes and general disreputable appearance—a thief, and Q was not willing to leave any of the bags alone with this gentleman. So when Boatman arrived Q motioned that the Thief should go first. The Thief, however, would not hear of it, and signed that since Q had already been waiting some time, he must go first and he (the Thief) would wait his turn. But the boat, obviously, could not carry Q and his Five Bags at once.

"This is unfortunate," said Q, "because I can't leave any of the bags alone with the Thief. This will make our trip across somewhat tricky. In fact, it will take a number of trips. How many?"

The Boatman held up seven fingers, and then he set about getting them across. How did he do it?

(Write your answer here)

____

____

____

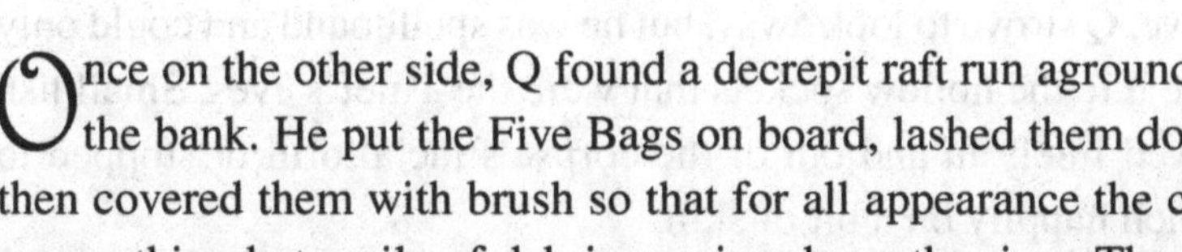

Once on the other side, Q found a decrepit raft run aground on the bank. He put the Five Bags on board, lashed them down, then covered them with brush so that for all appearance the craft was nothing but a pile of debris coming down the river. Then he pushed off and crawled into the pile and concealed himself.

He traveled in this manner for several weeks, sleeping concealed in the pile by day, poling and fishing by night. In the day he lay face down on the raft and peered into the water through a gap in the logs. Hippopotami, crocodiles and giant pythons coursed beneath the tranquil surface of the water. With his military issue fishing equipment he caught fish which he cooked with his solar cooker, and with the water purifier he had found among the Colonel's gear he was able to drink the river water.

As he lay motionless in hiding during the day, he mused on his life, and it was as though his memories floated among the aquatic life below. He saw, again, his Father hanging in the atrium, with the one Guchi™ loafer on the floor beneath him. He saw, again, his Mother and Sister pulling away in the Tennis Instructor's SUV, without looking back. And then, most painfully, he saw his Lucy, her dirt-tanned face and her butchered hair, sitting up shirtless in their rude bed in the boxcar, smoking and telling the fantastic story of her life.

By and by, however, the river began to run a little faster, and with it his memories seemed to fly by. His new Father, rediscovered in the rail camp, floated by in his dhoti. Santo and the Entropy™ Executive came and were gone in an instant. The Associate Pastor, his Turntablist and the rest of the crew from the Church of the Ostensible Jesus drifted past with no more fanfare than the rest, followed by the headless Colonel.

But then came one who became stuck just below him on the underside of the raft. It was the Thief, his body bloated and hideous from days in the river, having caught up with the raft and now entangled and riding it beneath the surface, mirroring Q's position above. Q strove to look away, but he was spellbound and could only stare into the hollow sockets that were the Thief's eyes. Small fish moved freely in and out of the corpse's facial orifi or stopped to munch happily on a bit of skin.

Q grew dizzy staring into the nightmarish face, until world and raft rotated so that the Thief rode on top and Q under the water, Q becoming Memory's fancy and the ghastly corpse the Real. And this condition proved to be more than fanciful as the river picked up speed and the raft began to be buffeted by violent rapids. Q bounced from side to side and was washed over and under by huge waves and should by all rights have lost his grip and been swept away, but even as he lost consciousness his fingers gripped the raft and held on like a bat to the ceiling of its cave.

And in the midst of that violent upheaval, awash among his
memories and his deeds, somehow, impossibly, Q slept.

He awoke on a soft bed in a sunlit, wood-panelled room. When
he sat up and looked around he found himself naked under
the sheets and saw he was in a stateroom on a large boat. Through
the window he could see the shoreline at some distance and so
deduced that he was now either at the mouth of the river or perhaps
already out to sea.

At the foot of the bed a young man in a porter's uniform was
sleeping in an armchair. When Q hailed him he awoke with a start,
gave Q a wild-eyed look, then leapt from the chair and ran out of
the room, returning a moment later with a bundle of clothing and
linen and a cart full of refreshments. He poured Q a glass of mineral
water and handed it to him, but Q was parched and ravenous and
unceremoniously grabbed the bottle from the boy and drank it down.
He then tore into the tray of hors d'oeuvres, quickly inhaling all
the exotic cheeses, fruit and caviar that were on it.

Only after he had sated himself for the moment did he notice
that he was feasting naked, and the boy was standing to one side,
embarrassed, holding up a silk robe. Q slipped it on, after which
the boy handed him an envelope on a silver tray. Q took the missal,
ripped it open, then sat on the edge of the bed to read:

My Dear Q:

Your reputation precedes you, and we are honored to
have a guest of your talents and accomplishment sailing
with us on our voyage.

We trust you will find everything you need in your
quarters; if anything is lacking, do let us know.

Please join us on deck for cocktails when you've had
a chance to freshen up. We will be having a small
reception in your honor.

With the very kindest personal regards, I remain
Sincerely yours,
The Richest Man in the World

When Q, now properly attired in white linen and yachting cap, joined his host on the boat's luxurious Lounge Deck, he was surprised to find that he recognized the man. He had met him at the mine when he and The Colonel had stopped by. He was of very ordinary appearance to have such an exalted title, so ordinary that Q had barely noticed him at the mine. Balding with a little paunch, he was dressed like Q in white linen and cap.

He greeted Q warmly. "Ah, Q," he said, "how glad I am to see you rested, conscious, and, by all appearance, none the worse for the experience. How fortunate you are that the pilot happened to see you floating on your raft and recognized the suitcases which we had given to you and The Colonel."

Here Q inquired as to the fate of his precious bags and was informed that they were safely on-board the yacht and accessible for Q's use at any time.

"Tell me, though," Q's wealthy host continued, "what has happened to our Colonel? I trust no harm has come to him."

Q then related, verbatim, the story The Colonel had told him on the helicopter, complete with its dramatic ending in which the storyteller was obliterated. Then he told the equally fantastic tale of his own escape and the harrowing adventure on the river.

"Well," replied The Richest Man in the World, "please accept our sincere condolences for your former employer. I wonder, though, if I might be so bold as to presume that, since you have worked so hard to salvage The Colonel's good name, as well as his assets, that you have inherited also his obligations? We would be honored to feel we could call upon you to perform the extremely valuable services The Colonel formerly provided for us."

Q assured him that, though he was still learning the trade, he would certainly give his very best effort to performing whatever tasks The Richest Man in the World might desire to be performed, and that if he did not accomplish them he would expend his life in the effort.

The Richest Man in the World seemed pleased with this response. "Q," he said, putting his hand on Q's shoulder, "I look forward to a long and productive relationship."

"So do I," said Q. "But, may I ask you a question?"

"Certainly, my friend."

"How did you get to be The Richest Man in the World? I have been, recently, in a rather reduced condition and would be most interested to learn the arts of self-betterment from so accomplished a teacher as you."

"Why Q, of course I would be happy to share any insights I have with you. However," he shook his head humbly, "my case is not one that presents lessons for the novice. Hard work, to be sure, played a part. I spent more hours than I care to remember in front of a computer. But beyond that, I'm afraid, there is nothing I can tell you, for there are certain details and techniques which are the exclusive property of the Very Rich, and I would be breaking a sacred trust if I were to divulge them."

"Ah, I see," said Q. "But—and please pardon my confusion—how does anyone except the Very Rich ever get to be Very Rich if there is no way to learn these techniques?"

The Richest Man in the World chuckled and patted Q on the head. "Ah, how you remind me of myself at your impetuous age. But wait, is that a helicopter I hear? I believe our guests are beginning to arrive. We must prepare to receive them."

The two of them took up their positions at the entry to the Lounge Deck and watched as guests began to arrive. Some came by helicopter, but some were apparently already staying on the yacht and merely appeared from below. The Richest Man in the World introduced Q to each of the tuxedoed men and the elegantly coifed women as they arrived, but Q was far too nervous to remember their names. The men all clasped his hand warmly and, naturally, praised his reputation, and their wives put forth delicate hands to be kissed, sometimes giving him a sly wink in the process.

When at last he was relieved of the receiving line, Q headed for the bar to refresh his martini, then walked among the crowd and made small talk, as his host had instructed. The men were all anxious to hear his advice on stocks and futures, but the women seemed determined to steer the conversation away from business with witty innuendo. The men, far from expressing jealousy, seemed in every case happy to leave their wives alone with Q, sometimes even nodding to Q as they walked away, leaving Q to extricate himself awkwardly from more than one too-intimate conversation.

Q was finally rescued by his host, who leaned into the middle of one of these painful conversations and whispered to Q: "There are two more guests for you to greet. I've just gotten word that The General and His Daughter will be joining us shortly. I think you will be glad to meet these two. The General is one of the world's greatest conversationalists, and his daughter… Well, what can I say? She is beautiful and a talented singer. It may be that we can persuade her to join our orchestra for a song or two."

Though less than enthusiastic concerning the General and his Daughter, Q was nonetheless grateful to be called away from the present conversation, and so he rejoined The Richest Man in the World at the door. The sun had set, and the crew had turned on the helipad lights to guide the General's helicopter in. All the guests came out on the veranda to greet the distinguished pair and applauded as the copter set down.

The General emerged, waving to the crowd, and the orchestra stopped their set and struck up a rousing military march that Q had heard before, though he couldn't remember where. After waving to the crowd from a distance, The General put out his elbow and his daughter appeared, gleaming with sequins, stunningly elegant in her strapless Jean Paul Gaultier™ gown. As the pair walked across the deck from the helipad, the crowd of guests spilled out of the Lounge to meet them, so that by the time they entered the reception they were quite surrounded.

Q, since he wasn't particularly anxious to meet yet another important guest, did not press his way forward but merely followed the crowd into the Lounge, and once there he concentrated his energies on refreshing his drink rather than attending to formalities. Finally, reasoning that he would let the excitement die down before he attempted to meet the obviously illustrious couple, he sat down at one of the tables in front of the orchestra with his martini.

But no sooner had Q settled himself than the Orchestra leader came to the front of the stage to announce that the General's Daughter had agreed to grace the proceedings with a song. This news was greeted with unanimous applause, which only increased when the diva took the stage. Now with an unobstructed view, Q was dumbstruck with her beauty. Her perfect features coupled with her elegance and grace to form such an image of feminine perfection as Q had never seen before, and yet there was something, also, oddly familiar about her.

She took the microphone offered by the conductor, had a brief word with him, then came to the front as he turned to the orchestra.

"Thank you," she said to the continuing applause. "Allow me to express, for my Father and myself, how grateful we are for this gracious welcome. However, we are embarrassed to have taken attention away from our guest of honor, and I wish now to correct this faux pas by dedicating this song to him." Now she looked directly at Q, taking his breath away. "Q, I hope you will accept this song as an expression of our fond esteem."

Q blushed at this outpouring, and his embarrassment was only heightened by the spotlight that was suddenly trained on him and the applause that ensued. But then the conductor raise his baton, the orchestra played a wistful opening bar, the spotlight moved back to the beautiful singer, and she began.

The General's Daughter's Song

Who knows why we go where we go
and wake up each day thinking of you?
I thought of you in Peking
and I thought of you in Regents,
and I'm thinking of you now
on the coast of this Dark Continent.

Oh who will it be this time?
Who will be my you?

Who knows when we live and when we don't
that wake up each day thinking of you?
I thought of you in the Pharoah's tomb,
I thought of you in Eleusis time,
and I thought of you in this future
when nothing is as it seems.

Oh who will it be this time?
Who will be my you?

And who knows what we're made of
who wake each day thinking of you?
I think of you as simple clay,
I think of you as wind-born dust,
and I imagine you in the water
that carries us and buries us.

Oh who will it be this time?
Who will be my... Q?

As she pronounced this last note and the applause began, Q found himself once again under the spotlight and mortified from all the attention. As the lovely singer demounted the stage and came over to his table, Q tried his best to appear calm and suave, but as he raised his glass in her honor his hand was shaking and he was blushing violently. The crowd seem to take this as a winning naivete and applauded all the more.

Q busied himself motioning to the waiter as she sat down across from him, and then he fumbled with cigarettes, drink, napkin, bread sticks, flowers, candle and everything else that was on the table, all merely to forestall that moment when he would look her in the eye. And this even though—and in an instant he knew it to be true—there was nothing in the world he wanted more than to look upon this lady's face. And so he pulled himself together, took a deep breath, held to the table-edge so she would not notice his trembling, and looked up.

"Hello, Q," she said, extending her hand.

"Hello, Lucy," he replied.

Two days later, Q awoke beside his true love on the Egyptian cotton sheets in his stateroom. Outside the window beside the bed porpoises breached and frolicked in the crystal-clear blue water. The northern coast of the Continent was just visible on the horizon.

Lucy was still asleep, and sunlight from the corner of the window fell upon the perfect skin of her bare shoulder and back. Silently, so as not to wake her, Q motioned to the maid and manservant who waited by the foot of the bed to bring their breakfast and to freshen up the room. This they did with remarkable efficiency, refreshing the flowers that were arrayed on almost every surface until the room smelled like an orange grove in full flower, then carrying in their breakfast on golden dishes and in baskets of wreathed silver. There were heaps of candied apple, quince, and plum, jellies soother than the creamy curd, and lucent syrops, tinct with cinnamon, manna and dates, in argosy transferr'd from Fez, and spiced dainties, every one, from silken Samarcand to cedar'd Lebanon, and beignets rolled in powdered sugar.

When everything was ready, he slipped his arm under her pillow and drank in the perfumed smell of her hair before whispering: "And now, my love, my seraph fair, awake!"

Lazily she rolled over and faced him, then put her arms around his neck and pulled him to her, and again he drank in her sweet breath, arousing such passion in him that the succulent meal had to be postponed.

When at last they were ready for their coffee, Q asked the manservant for a newspaper, which was promptly supplied. He then inquired of their present location and was told they would be passing the Straits that morning.

"Ah, my love," he chortled at this news, "it will be good to be back in civilization. For all of the Dark Continent's unspoiled beauty, its rustic conditions aren't suitable for people of leisure. Where shall we go? I'm sure we could dock in Barcelona. Or would you prefer the Riviera? I hear that Pula is lovely. They say the wharf there is three thousand years old. We could be there by tomorrow night."

"Ah Q," she whispered, running her fingers through his dark, thick hair, "my wild, impetuous Q. Who knows what the future will hold. One morning we'll wake up and this boat that now floats freely will be held fast, and that's where we shall take our leisure."

Q was not entirely satisfied with this reply, but he had learned to appreciate the enigmas that dwelt in the depths of Lucy's dark eyes, and so he did not question her further, just as he had not questioned the impossibly fortunate coincidence of their second encounter. The Richest Man in the World was an old friend of the General's, and that had seemed, to Lucy at any rate, a sufficient explanation of the miracle. To Q it all seemed a little overdetermined, but the pleasure of her company was more powerful than his scepticism, and he was content to enjoy the moment without understanding.

He had asked her, of course, why she had abandoned him so unceremoniously at the railyard, but she had only lit her cigarette and looked out over the rail at the night sky. "Look there," she had said, "it's Capricorn. Look how different the constellations are down here."

Considering the suddenness of their reunion, Q had been concerned that she might disappear just as suddenly, leaving with her father after the party, yet no one seemed the least surprised when she remained on board with Q. The General had made his rounds quickly, shaking Q's hand in a perfunctory manner, then heading back to his helicopter, waving good-by in the spotlight with his fake politician's smile affixed, departing just as he had come, but without his daughter, almost as if his mission had been precisely to deliver her.

Despite the luxury of Q's stateroom and their concupiscent preoccupations, the couple finally grew restless and decided to venture out on deck. Q ordered swimwear, and the servants brought Lucy a silver diNeila™ bikini along with a pair of olive-green Prada™ trunks for Q. The matching robes were custom-made for the yacht by Armani™. They lay on the deck beside the pool with cucumber slices on their eyes.

"Lucy," Q said, grasping her hand, "I won't ask you again why you left me at the railyard, but will you promise me, now, that you won't do it again?"

She squeezed his hand. "I won't leave you again, Q," she said. "I'm here to stay."

They lounged by the pool the rest of the day, then went down and dressed for dinner. They joined the Richest Man in the World on his private deck for a late supper. The threesome dined by candlelight while the full moon swam in the waves beneath them. Q commented on the strength of the breeze.

"Yes," his host replied, "we're cruising at almost 30 knots, round the clock. We'll be in Pula in less than a week."

"Ah, Pula," said Q. "I've always wanted to visit Pula." He gave Lucy a knowing look. "And there's a ferry to Venice, I believe, made famous in literature."

Their host, of course, objected that while in his company the two of them would never need cross a body of water in lesser circumstances than those they presently enjoyed. Q thanked him graciously but declined the offer as too generous, for though he was enjoying himself immensely, he was also anxious to be on his own again with his Lucy. In his mind's eye he saw the two of them in a gondola on the Giudecca Canal, fog and accordion music drifting to them from San Marco.

After dinner they sipped brandy and had warm but unmemorable conversation. Q had not been so long apart from her naked body since their reunion, and gradually he began to burn with Desire, and, if the urgency of her foot-play under the table were any indication, so did she.

Finally they feigned fatigue and excused themselves, taking off at a run the moment they were out of sight. Once in the room they tore off each other's clothes, fell into the bed and ravished each other until the sky began to brighten. They fell asleep with the first rays of dawn coming over the horizon.

A few hours later the sun fell full on Q's face, waking him. He stretched in indolent pleasure and rolled over to touch his love again, but she was gone.

He stared at the empty pillow beside him uncomprehendingly for a moment, then the distant sound of a helicopter rotor came to him, and he screamed. He leaped from the bed and ran down the hall naked, knocking aside servants as he went, sending their silver trays flying, all the while screaming her name like a madman.

He tore up the stairs and through the Lounge Deck toward the helipad. She was just stepping into the idling machine's cockpit beside the pilot. Q threw himself across the deck, but they lifted off just as he stepped onto the pad, and the last he saw of her, as he fell to his knees at the center of the bull's eye, was her looking out at the sea through her dark glasses, not even deigning to look down at the pitiful creature as he became but a mote in her wake.

The helicopter tilted itself to the north and was quickly out of sight, but Q remained on the helipad alternately calling her name and beating his breast, finally collapsing in a heap. He lay there for hours and would have been baked by the sun, but the Richest Man in the World had been watching the scene unfold from the bridge and sent down a man with a tray of food and drink and an umbrella. This faithful butler stood over Q the better part of the day, occasionally bending over to coax a little mineral water into his mouth, and shifting the umbrella when Q, in his writhing, moved into the subtropical sun.

Q lay in this pitiful state for some hours, sobbing and babbling incoherently, then fell into a state that most resembled sleep, except that his eyes were open. Then, suddenly, he sat up and, in the most calm and polite voice imaginable, called for an overcoat, which the tailor brought right away. It was, naturally, a lovely piece of work by Cole Haan™. Q, however, put it on directly over his nakedness. Then he took a knife from the hors d'oeuvre tray and stabbed and ripped until it quite resembled the coat he'd worked the streets in, so long ago, when a shopping cart full of cans had been sufficient

to bring him happiness. Then he motioned to his host, still watching
from his veranda, to put him ashore.

The Richest Man in the World, however, elected not to follow Q's
advice in this instance, and this much to Q's advantage, since
they were nowhere near any hospitable landing. Q rode the rest of
the way on the bowsprit, immobile as a figurehead, through day and
night, in the sun and wind and salty spray, till he looked as haggard
as he felt. He refused most of the libation the crew brought to him,
taking only the occasional Perrier™, draining the liter bottle in a
single draught and tossing it back to the waiter.

When they passed the Straits he motioned toward the White
Tower angrily, but no one paid any attention to him, and they
continued on their monotonous course through the calm waters
of the Mediterranean for another day, finally turning toward shore
along some white cliffs that became, on closer inspection, a row
of high-rise condos on the beach.

As they pulled into the yacht harbor Q prepared to disembark. He
gathered his meager personal effects into the pockets of his overcoat,
then requested five valets to carry his five bags. He explained to
his host, with exaggerated politeness, that he was only borrowing
the men and would send them back as soon as he had gotten the
bags safely to his hotel.

"Of course," said The Richest Man in the World, "but I'm afraid
I can only spare four at the moment, so I guess one of the bags will
have to remain here. Anyway, the 5.1 million dollars contained in
one case will only be a contribution toward the fuel, entertainment,
food and drink expended on this little journey."

"Certainly," said Q with scarcely restrained hostility. "Accept
it with my gratitude." He bowed to his host and strode down the
gangplank, followed by the four valets. They walked in single file

across the wharf to the hotel, in the front door and across the lobby toward the front desk. Q, however, noticed a sign on the other side of the lobby and diverted his little train toward it. They entered the casino.

Q went straight to the roulette table, took the bag from the first valet and placed it without hesitation at the center of the table, on the 17. The Croupier looked to the Floor Manager, who spoke into his lapel mike, waited a moment, and then nodded. The Croupier spun the wheel and set the ball in motion.

"An aggressive bet, Q," said the Player next to him. "Good luck."

Q nodded, eyeing the man suspiciously, then looked back at the spinning wheel.

"It's hypnotic, isn't it," continued the Player. "Like a spinning atom, or like the planets in their diurnal course. Did you know, Q, that the game was invented, by accident, by Pascal, when he was attempting to create perpetual motion? And indeed, its motion does seem perpetual, does it not? Pascal was also, if you hadn't heard, the first to wear a wristwatch. He must have needed it to verify that his wheel was not spinning indefinitely, an illusion that would have resulted had he allowed himself to become entranced."

"Interesting," said Q, without looking up.

"Pascal's interest in the perpetual motion machine sprang, oddly enough, from his attempt to build a mechanical calculator for the inordinately complicated French monetary system of the 17th century. In this system, there were 20 sols in a livre and 12 deniers in a sol. This made his task infinitely more difficult than it would have been in a decimal system like the Euro or the Dollar. The Pascaline, as the device was called, had eight dials and could accurately add and subtract in livres, sols, and deniers. Quite an accomplishment, don't you agree?"

Q nodded, again without looking up.

"Pascal's father, you see, was of reduced means after the Thirty Years' War, and in 1639 he took the job of tax commissioner in the district of Rouen. The tax records were, of course, a shambles in the wake of the war. Young Blaise, only 18 at the time, had already impressed Descartes with his mathematical prowess, and now he set his precocious talents to assisting his father in the complex arithmetic involved in the accounting."

Q looked up, suddenly interested. "My Father was similarly employed," he said, then quickly turned his attention back to the spinning wheel.

"An interesting parallel, to be sure," the Player continued. "And I'm sure you would have been more than excited at the notion of building a helpful machine for your Father." Q nodded wistfully, without looking up. "Tell me, Q, do you find it curious that Pascal's investigations led from the complex significations of monetary exchange, through perpetual motion, to gambling and probability theory, leading ultimately to his famous wager?"

"Interesting," said Q. "I'd never thought of it that way before." He looked quickly back to the wheel, though neither wheel nor ball were yet showing any signs of slowing down. Q could only imagine the quality of the wheel's mechanism, which must be all but frictionless. "But of course!" he suddenly added. "Even though the existence of God cannot be proven, a rational person should *wager* as if it could."

"Why, that's very good, Q. You've remembered Pascal's Gambit. And we can follow this curious progression from exchange or taxation to unending motion to the wager on God yet a little further, if we so choose, to Leibniz' addition of multiplication and division to the Pascaline, and thence to the *Theodicy*, in which he successfully proved that our world is optimal among all possible worlds, since it was created by an all-powerful and all-knowing God who would not choose to create an imperfect world if a better world were possible."

"Are you implying," said Q suspiciously, "that the best of all possible worlds would be a world in which taxes were levied? Because if you are, I'm afraid I can't support you. After all, what wealth I have I have earned for myself with my labor and my intelligence, and I am not willing to share my earnings with any institution or authority."

"Oh no, that's not my implication at all," the Player quickly interjected. "I am merely relating certain facts, not expressing my opinion. And indeed the fact that Pascal's father was a tax collector should not influence our investigations in the slightest. For the father's occupation has, for the purposes of this illustration, no absolute value but only a structural position. It is not tax collection, per se, we are concerned with, but rather the Father's Occupation. Let us indicate this occupation by the variable r. My point is that in this situation r is to the Father f as perpetual motion m to the Son s. Thus we have $f/r=m/s$, and it is easy to see how this could lead to Leibniz' famous conclusion."

"No," replied Q adamantly. "There can be no tax collection in the Best of All Possible Worlds. Period." Here he allowed his attention to be diverted from the wheel and stared menacingly at the Player.

"Well then, I suppose you're right," he responded coyly. "By the way, you might to return your attention to the wheel. I believe the ball is about to alight."

Q quickly looked back to the table and saw that the wheel was slowing and the ball bouncing chaotically along the pins. Soon the ball found its slot, and he was able to discern it was on a black square. Q held his breath. The wheel came finally to a stop, and at last the winning number was revealed: 17.

A cheer went up across the casino. Q had not been aware that almost everyone on the floor had stopped what they were doing to see the outcome of his extremely risky bet. Now the well-heeled crowd gathered around him for congratulatory handshakes and back-pats.

"How much do I win?" asked Q.

"A single number bet pays 35 to one," said the Croupier. However, instead of showering upon Q a large pile of chips, he removed the suitcase full of cash from the table and handed Q a single chip. "Let this chip represent 183.6 million dollars," he said.

"Good," said Q. "Let it ride."

Gasps of disbelief went around the casino, followed by some excited whispering, which was finally followed by utter silence. The Croupier again looked to the Floor Manager, who again spoke into his lapel mike and again nodded approval.

"Bravo," said the Player, "you'll take 6.4 billion if you win, but Q…" Q, however, held up his hand to indicate he could not be swayed. He then motioned to the Croupier to begin play.

"You'll see," said Q, turning toward the Player. "I know what I am doing."

"Yes, of course," said the Player, pointing toward the wheel. When Q looked, the wheel had already come to a stop; the ball was on the 16.

"But wait," cried Q. "I didn't see the wheel spin. Did anyone see the wheel spin?" He directed his question to everyone in earshot, looking anxiously from face to face, but no one would either confirm or deny that the wheel had already spun. The Croupier collected the single chip.

"This is unacceptable," said Q, fuming. "My wealth, that I earned by my wits and labor, has been taken from me by a rigged machine. I have been cheated, and I won't take it lying down. Bring me the *libro de reclamaciones*." He raised his voice and repeated: "Bring me the *libro de reclamaciones*."

Again, a hush fell over the floor and all eyes turned to Q, who stood with his head upturned and arms resolutely crossed. The

Floor Manager spoke into his microphone, and momentarily there appeared two valets carrying between them the huge book. They lay it on the table in front of Q and opened it to the first page. One of them handed him a Mont Blanc™ pen.

He looked down haughtily at the empty page, as if he would not, in the end, deign to sully the virgin surface. But finally he uncapped the pen, leaned over the table and began to write. His hand moved haltingly at first, with frequent caesuras during which he seemed lost in thought, but gradually a rhythm seemed to develop and the ink began to flow freely. He wrote a sentence, then a paragraph. He filled a page and then another and another. He wrote a large Roman numeral 2 at the top of the next page and continued on. He wrote so quickly that the valets had to quickly place blotter paper between the sheets as he turned them to keep the ink from bleeding.

Finally, at the end of chapter XXXI, which coincidentally ended on the last page of the book, Q drew an elaborate flourish, recapped the pen and stood up.

He turned away from the table, then, and made his way across the casino toward the lobby, stopping at the teller window to exchange his bulky suitcases for chips. The teller handed him three chips, each with "5.1" printed on it.

Now, since he had no further need of bearers, Q dismissed the four valets to return to their yacht. "Adios," he said and was turning to go when he remembered his manners. He took one of the chips from his pocket and flipped it to the dumbstruck attendants.

"Take me to my room," he said to no one in particular, then waited for the Bellman, who came up aflutter, looking this way and that for Q's bags, finally leading Q across the lobby with empty hands. They got on the elevator, and the Bellman inserted the key which took them to the Penthouse. They took positions against the back wall for the ride up.

"Are you enjoying your stay so far, sir?" the Bellman asked, making small talk.

"No," said Q. "The tables are rigged and the service shoddy. You may have had many a happy customer, but you will not be able to count me in those ranks. I think it safe to say that I am the Unhappiest Customer."

"Well," said the Bellman, "let us see if that could be true. Let us see if we can decide who the Unhappiest Customer might be."

"Very well," said Q, confident.

"Let us, first, use our imaginations to establish candidates for this lofty post.

"Imagine a Customer who himself had had no childhood, this age having passed him by without attaining essential significance for him, but who now, perhaps by becoming a teacher of youth, discovered all the beauty that there is in childhood, and who would now remember his own youth, constantly staring back at it. Too late he would have discovered the significance of that which was past for him but which he still desired to remember in its significance. If I imagined a Customer who had lived without real appreciation of the pleasures or joy of life, and who now on his deathbed has his eyes opened to these things, if I imagined that he did not die (which would be the most fortunate thing) but lived on, though without living his life over again—such a Customer would have to be considered in our quest for the Unhappiest Customer.

"The unhappiness of hope is never so painful as the unhappiness of memory. The Customer with hope always has a more tolerable disappointment to bear. It follows that the Unhappiest Customer will have to be sought among the unhappy individuals of memory.

"Let us imagine a combination of the two stricter types of unhappiness already described. The unhappy Customer of hope could not find himself present in his hope, just as the unhappy Customer of memory could not find himself present in his memory. There can be but one combination of these two types, and this happens when it is memory which prevents the unhappy individual from finding himself in his hope, and hope which prevents him from finding himself in his memory. When this happens, it is, on the one hand, due to the fact that he constantly hopes something that should be remembered; his hope constantly disappoints him and, in disappointing him, reveals to him that it is not because the realization of his hope is postponed, but because it is already past and gone, has already been experienced, or should have been experienced, and thus has passed over into memory. On the other hand, it is due to the fact that he always remembers that for which he ought to hope; for the future he has already anticipated in thought, in thought already experienced it, and this experience he now remembers, instead of hoping for it. Consequently, what he hopes for lies behind him, what he remembers lies before him. His life is not so much lived regressively as it suffers a two-fold reversal. He will soon notice his misfortune even if he is not able to understand the reason for it. To make sure, however, that he really shall have opportunity to feel it, misunderstanding puts in its appearance to mock him at each moment in a curious way.

"In the ordinary course of things, he enjoys the reputation of being in full possession of his five senses, and yet he knows that if he were to explain to a single person just how it is with him, he would be declared mad. This is quite enough to drive a Customer mad, and yet he does not become so, and this is precisely his misfortune. His misfortune is that he has come into the world too soon, and therefore he always comes too late. He is constantly quite near his goal, and in the same moment he is far away from it; he finds that what now makes him unhappy because he has it, or because he is this way, is just what a few years ago would have made him happy if he had had it then, while then he was unhappy because he did not have it. His life is empty, like that of Ancaeus, of whom it is customary to say that nothing is known about him except that he gave rise to the proverb: 'There's many a slip 'twixt the cup and the lip'—as if this was not more than enough. His life is restless and without content; he does not live in the present; he does not live in the future, for the future has already been experienced; he does not live in the past, for the past has not yet come. So like Latona, he is driven about in the Hyperborean darkness, or to the bright isles of the equator, and cannot bring to birth though he seems constantly on the verge. Alone by himself he stands in the wide world. He has no contemporary time to support him; he has no past to long for, since his past has not yet come; he has no future to hope for, since his future is already past. Alone, he has the whole world over against him as the *alter* with which he finds himself in conflict; for the rest of the world is to him only one person, and this person, this inseparable, importunate friend, is Misunderstanding. He cannot become old, for he has never been young; he cannot become young, for he is already old. In one sense of the word he cannot die, for he has not really lived; in another sense he cannot live, for he is already dead. He cannot love, for love is in the present, and he has no present, no future, and no past; and yet he has a sympathetic nature, and he hates the world only because he loves it. He has no passion, not because he is destitute of it, but because simultaneously he has the opposite passion. He has no time for anything, not because his time is taken up with something else, but because he has no time at all. He is impotent, not because he has no energy, but because his own energy makes him impotent.

"And now our hearts are indeed sufficiently steeled, our ears stopped, even if not closed. We have listened to the cool voice of deliberation; let us now hear the eloquence of passion—brief, pithy, as all passion is.

"There stands a young woman. She complains that her lover has been faithless. This we cannot take into consideration. But she loved him, and him alone, in all the world. She loved him with all her heart, and with all her soul, and with all her mind—then let her remember and grieve.

"Is this a real being, or is it an image, a living person who dies, or a corpse who lives? It is Niobe. She lost all at a single blow; she lost that to which she gave life, she lost that which gave her life.

Look up to her, dear Q, she stands a little higher than the world, on a burial mound, like a monument. No hope allures her, no future moves her, no prospect tempts her, no hope excites her—hopeless she stands, petrified in memory; for a single moment she was unhappy, in that same moment she became happy, and nothing can take her happiness from her; the world changes, but she knows no change; and time flows on, but for her there is no future time.

"See yonder, what a beautiful union! The one generation clasps hands with the next! Is it unto blessing, unto loyal fellowship, unto the joy of the dance? It is the outcast house of Oedipus, and the curse is transmitted from one generation to the next, until it crushes the last of the race—Antigone. Yet she is provided for; the sorrow of a family is enough for one human life. She has turned her back on hope, she has exchanged its instability for the faithfulness of memory. Be happy, dear Antigone! We wish you a long life, significant as a deep sigh. May no forgetfulness deprive you of aught, may the daily bitterness of grief be yours in fullest measure!

"A powerful figure appears, but he is not alone, he has friends, how comes he here then? It is Job, the patriarch of grief—and his friends. He lost all, but not at a single blow; for the Lord took, and the Lord took, and the Lord took. Friends taught him to feel the bitterness of his loss; for the Lord gave, and the Lord gave, and the Lord also gave him a foolish wife into the bargain. He lost all; for what he retained lies outside the scope of our interest. Respect him, dear Q, for his gray hairs and his unhappiness. He lost all; but he had possessed it.

"His hair is gray, his head bent low, his countenance downcast, his soul troubled. It is the father of the prodigal son. Like Job he lost his most precious possession. Yet it was not the Lord who took it, but the enemy. He did not lose it, but he is losing it; it is not taken away from him, but it vanishes. He does not sit by the hearth in sackcloth and ashes; he has left his home, forsaken everything to seek the lost. He reaches after him, but his arms do not clasp him; he cries out, but his cries do not overtake him. And yet he hopes even through tears; he sees him from afar, as through a mist; he overtakes him, if only in death. His hope makes him old, and nothing binds him to the world except the hope for which he lives. His feet are weary, his eyes dim, his body yearns for rest, his hope lives. His hair is white, his body decrepit, his feet stumble, his heart breaks, his hope lives. Raise him up, dear Q, he was unhappy.

"Who is this pale figure, unsubstantial as the shadow of the dead? His name has been forgotten, many centuries have passed since his day. He was a youth, he had enthusiasm. He sought martyrdom. In imagination he saw himself nailed to the cross, and the heavens open; but the reality was too heavy for him; enthusiasm vanished, he denied his Master and himself. He wished to lift a world, but he broke down under the strain; his soul was not crushed nor annihilated, but it was broken, and his spirit was enervated, his soul palsied. Congratulate him, dear Q, for he was unhappy. And yet did he not become happy? He became what he wished, a martyr, even if his martyrdom was not, as he had wished, to be nailed to the cross, nor to be thrown to wild beasts, but to be burned alive, to be slowly consumed by a slow fire.

"A young woman sits here of thoughtful mien. Her lover was faithless, but this we cannot take into consideration. Young woman, observe the serious countenances of this society; it has heard of more terrible misfortunes, its daring soul demands something greater still. —Yes, but I loved him and him only in all the world; I loved him with all my soul, and with all my heart, and with all my mind. —You merely repeat what we have already heard before, do not weary our impatient longing; you can remember, and grieve. —No, I cannot grieve, for he was perhaps not a deceiver, he was perhaps not faithless. —Why, then, can you not grieve? Come nearer, elect among women; forgive the strict censor who sought for a moment to exclude you. You cannot sorrow. Then why not hope? —No, I cannot hope; for he was a riddle. —Well, my girl, I understand you. You stand high in the ranks of the unhappy; behold her, dear Q, she stands almost at the pinnacle of unhappiness. But you must divide yourself, you must hope by day and grieve by night, or grieve by day and hope by night. Be proud; for happiness is no real ground for pride, but only unhappiness. You are not indeed the unhappiest of all; but it is your opinion, dear Q, is it not, that we ought to offer her an honorable accessit? The room we cannot offer her, but the place adjoining shall be hers.

"For there he stands, the ambassador from the kingdom of sighs, the chosen favorite of the realm of suffering, the apostle of grief, the silent friend of pain, the unhappy lover of memory, in his memories confounded by the light of hope, in his hope deceived by the shadows of memory. His head hangs heavy, his knees are weak; and yet he seeks no support save in himself. He is faint, and yet how powerful; his eyes seem not to have wept, but to have drunk many tears; and yet there is a fire in them strong enough to destroy a world, but not one splinter of the grief within his breast. He is bent, and yet his youth presages a long life; his lips smile at a world that misunderstands him. Stand up, dear Q, bow before him, ye witnesses of grief, in this most solemn hour! I hail thee, great unknown, whose name I do not know; I hail thee with thy title of honor: The Unhappiest Customer! Welcomed here to your home by the community of the unhappy, greeted here at the entrance to the low and humble dwelling, which is yet prouder than all the palaces of the world. Lo, the stone is rolled away, the grave's shade awaits you with its refreshing coolness. But perhaps your time has not yet come, perhaps the way is long before you; but we promise you to gather here often to envy you your good fortune. Accept then our wish, a good wish: May no one understand you, may all men envy you; may no friend bind himself to you, may no woman love you; may no secret sympathy suspect your lonely pain, may no eye pierce your distant grief; may no ear trace your secret sigh! But perhaps your proud soul spurns such sympathetic wishes, and despises the alleviation, so may the maidens love you; may the pregnant in their anguish seek your aid; may the mothers set their hopes on you, and the dying look to you for comfort; may the youth attach themselves to you; may men depend upon you; may the aged lean upon you as on a staff—may the entire world believe that you are able to make them happy. So live well, then, unhappiest of Customers! But what do I say: the unhappiest, the happiest, I ought to say, for this is indeed a gift of the gods which no one can give himself. Language fails, and thought is confounded; for who is the happiest, except the unhappiest, and who the unhappiest, except the happiest, and what is life but madness, and faith but folly, and hope but the briefest respite, and love but vinegar in the wound."

At this point the elevator slowed to a stop and the doors parted in the middle and opened onto the living room of Q's spacious suite.

"He vanishes, and again we stand before the empty room. Let us then wish him peace and rest and healing, and all possible happiness, and an early death, and an eternal forgetfulness, and no remembrance, lest even the memory of him should make another unhappy."

The Bellman held the doors open as Q stepped out of the elevator. "Thank you for that explanation," he said. "Your careful consideration of my comfort has gone a long way toward making me a happy Customer, perhaps even the Happiest Customer."

"I am pleased to be of service," the Bellman said. "Before I leave you, may I assist you with any of your needs?"

"No, thank you," Q replied. "I'm very tired and want only to rest until morning."

"Of course," he said. "I'll bid you good night then." The doors began to close, but he stopped them and added: "Excuse me, Q, I'm sure you know that the hotel offers a full range of services, including the finest in female and male escorts. I don't know the source of your Unhappiness, but if an evening of sensual relaxation might be desirable, I can certainly see to that for you."

Q stared at him for a moment. Certainly he would never consider cheating on his Lucy, and yet, as he considered, he realized they were doomed, and he would likely never see her again. The thought made him want to weep, but, steeling himself cynically, he replied with a sneer: "Very well then. Make the call. Of course make the call."

"Yes, sir," the Bellman replied. Q turned to go but then, noticing that the Bellman had not moved except to put out his hand, rummaged in his pocket for a tip. He had nothing but the two chips, so he gave him one of them. "Thank you, sir," the Bellman said, slipping the little coin into his pocket without looking at it. Then the doors closed and he was gone.

Q gave the room a cursory glance when he entered, then went to the bar and mixed himself a Hendricks™ and tonic with cucumber garnish. He then took his drink out onto the veranda. It was a clear night and moon and stars swam brightly both in the sea and in the sky above. The view was breathtaking, but he had no heart for it and gazed out as impassively as if he were staring at the blank face of a concrete wall.

He stood in this attitude of dejected torpor for a few minutes, then shuffled inside, undressed hastily, and lay himself down on the bed.

He settled in to the satin hotel sheets as into amniotic water, asleep the moment his cheek touched the pillow. In his dream he was back on the river, but now raftless, swimming in long and easy strokes, as at-home in the water as the hippopotami and anacondas below him.

He swam without effort and without need of breath. Fishes and crocodiles approached and then retreated in the murk. Up ahead he saw a flash of light like the glint from a mirror. He aimed for it, or at the place where it had been, pulling himself deeper and deeper. The water grew darker as he descended, until at last he was swimming in pitch black, and still he went deeper.

The water moving past his body became more and more palpable until he thought he might be swimming through some sort of leafy aquatic foliage. Even when he ceased all movement on his own, the current and the leaves stilled moved over him, and the lazy motion around and on and through him was most pleasurable. He surrendered himself to it.

Then, however, the water suddenly began to roil. A torrent of bubbles and silt plumed up around him. The leaves gripped him like hands. A flash of panic struck him, and he made frantically for the surface. Someone or something, he noticed, swam beside him, matching his motion stroke for stroke, rising with him toward the surface, like a shadow become corporeal.

He struggled, breathless, to break free, but just as he was about to do so was overcome by panic at being cut loose, and he thrashed and grabbed in an attempt to hold on to whatever had surrounded him. A cry escaped his lips, and he came back to consciousness on the bed where he and the nameless, naked woman were floundering. "Stop," he yelled, but as she moved away every pore of his body seemed to call for her return, and he reached out and pulled her back to him. With his mouth he found a breast and with his hand another breast, and other parts of him found their place in other parts of her.

He ravished her again and again, with scarcely any loss of vigor in the successive forays. She, for her part, responded with an animation that truly seemed more than thespian, and Q was impressed with her professionalism. And indeed when, after several hours, they finally sat up in bed and lit their cigarettes, she whispered, "Well, Q, you earned some bragging rights tonight; you made a whore come."

"Oh, sure," he replied with worldly sarcasm. "I'm so proud."

At this she got out of bed and went across the dark room to the bath to clean up while Q lay back, spent. He was just falling asleep again when she grabbed his shoulder. She stood over him, dressed now, silhouette in the darkness. "I have to leave," she whispered, "and was thinking you might want to tip me?"

Q reached down to his overcoat on the floor, took the last chip out of the pocket and gave it to her in the dark. "Good night," she said, tucking him in and kissing him on the forehead. "Don't let the bedbugs bite."

The next morning Q awoke missing Lucy, he was ashamed to admit, somewhat less than he had the day before. He was even on the verge of calling Room Service to arrange a reprise of his midnight feast, but he stopped himself, for he had a strange inkling that there were other fish in the sea and that they were swimming all around him.

He went downstairs to the dining room and had a poached egg with beluga caviar and smoked salmon, his head buried the while in a *Wall Street Journal*. Then he walked out onto the veranda to have his coffee. The sun was already high over the Mediterranean. The pristine beach stretched in front of him, ending at a frothy line where the blue water began. Off to the west the sandy beach was flanked by white cliffs, and it was toward these cliffs that Q decided he would make his way.

When he got to the water he took off his boots and his overcoat and waded in naked. He lay back in the buoyant sea and surveyed the clouds that passed in the brilliant sky. The white bulbous forms shape-shifted in the mild breeze, turning human and animal and back in subtle gradations, and Q began to imagine their movements as scenes from an epic struggle of man and beast, with rearing horses and clashing swords.

His fascination with this home-made entertainment, however, was soon interrupted by a human voice. Someone was calling his name. He lifted his head so he could hear better, but this upset his center of gravity and he had to sputter and flail to find his balance again. Once righted, he looked down the beach to see who was calling him. Some distance along, on an otherwise desolate patch of beach, he could just make out a beach umbrella with two people standing near it. They were waving and calling to him, jumping up and down and yelling incoherently.

Then Q had a notion that sent a chill up his spine: sharks! The bathers were yelling at him to get out because the waters were infested with man-eaters. He looked around quickly but saw no fins on the surface. He dipped his face in the water and looked down in the murk. He thought he saw something moving in the depths and went into utter panic, kicking furiously toward shore, with each stroke imagining a pair of horrible jaws closing onto his leg. When his feet finally touched bottom he scrambled out quickly, expecting to see that maw of death breaking the surface just behind him. But there was no sign of sharks anywhere.

Now the pair of bathers down the beach redoubled their effort to attract Q's attention. They were jumping up and down and screaming. "Q, Q," they yelled. "Down here. Come down here." So Q picked up his overcoat and his boots and began walking down the beach toward them. He was about to cover himself but decided not to when he got close enough to discern that they, too, were naked.

"Ah Q," the man said as Q approached, "great to see you. Please, won't you join us under our umbrella?" The woman, too, implored Q for his society, and so the three of them walked up the beach a little further to the couple's cozy encampment. Their umbrella was quite large and well appointed, with two chaise lounges equipped with special trays for laptops as well as drinks and a fine Moroccan rug covering the sand. The woman inquired if Q needed refreshment.

"Why yes," said Q, since he was suddenly quite thirsty. "What do you have?"

"Well, let's see," said the woman, digging into their huge cooler. After searching for some minutes she looked up. "We have ice water," she said, "and celery."

Q was somewhat surprised at the paucity of the offering relative to the opulence of the setting, but he took the water with gratitude. Then the three of them seated themselves on the carpet, Q and the man electing to sit in the shade and she in the sun. "I'm working on my tan line," she told Q. "We've been in the States for so long. I just hate having to wear a suit."

Q felt a stirring within him and for a moment was afraid he might embarrass himself in this public setting, but he directed his gaze at the blue water and the white sand rather than the woman's shapely figure and was quickly in a more philosophical mood. And soon, at any rate, the conversation required all his attention.

The couple, as it turned out, were novelists, both of them, of some renown. The Male Novelist had recently won a prestigious prize, and his current novel had already been translated into more than twenty languages and distributed around the globe. The Female Novelist, however—and it quickly became apparent that this was a source of some little contention between them—had only been translated into a dozen or fewer tongues. "Not that it matters," she added disingenuously. "Sri Lankans don't buy novels anyway."

The pair told Q that they had been following his eccentric, implausible story for some time now, through friends of friends and various anonymous reports, and were more than intrigued. When they heard he was coming ashore at one of their favorite vacation spots they immediately cancelled all engagements for the week and came here in the hopes of getting an interview.

Q stretched himself out comfortably on the rug, digging into the warm sand by the fringe with his toes. He couldn't imagine, he told them, what was so interesting about his life as to attract the attention of two such imminent writers, and then he proceeded to tell them his life's story to that point, just as you've heard it here. By the time he finished, the sun was setting over the cliffs.

"Incredible," said the Male Novelist. "It's as if you had lived a symbolic journey, like some Candide or Quixote or someone like that."

"Yes, Q, it's stunning," the Female Novelist added. "We have to get this down. And we have to get it right. Your life is too important to be allowed to fade away like a face drawn in the sand at the edge of the sea."

Q was flattered but also flummoxed by their enthusiasm. "But how?" he asked. "How should we proceed?"

"The first step," the Female Novelist replied, "will be to make an outline, prioritizing major events, plots and subplots, etc. And of course we'll need a character list, which we can then conflate to a manageable number."

"Well," said the Male Novelist, "I have to disagree with my wife here. What drives a novel is not the plot or the sequences of events but the characters. A novel comes to life when your characters start speaking for themselves."

"Yes, I see what you mean," said Q excitedly. "When they speak it's just like they are real. But..." He paused a moment, confused. "We're speaking, and for ourselves, right now."

"Oh Q, stop it." The Female Novelist gave him a playful kick on his leg.

"Very funny," said the Male Novelist, giving his wife a stern look. "But don't let the joke blind us to the very real issues we are facing here. The narrative—whether it is the narrative of a life or of a novel—is pre-existing. It awaits only the writing, and that's where we come in. We have to write it right."

"Yes," said the Female Novelist, "if we write it right, we right the wrong, but if we write it wrong all we write is the rite."

"Right," said the Male Novelist. "But say Q, while we're on this topic, there is something I want to address. Specifically, your friends and family have no names, only titles. You have 'the Competition' or 'the Turntablist' or something like that but you have no names. It's almost like they're just elements of an outline rather than real people."

"Aha! You see!" the Female Novelist interjected. "The outline is the first necessity. The list of structural positions, complete with sensoria. Then you just fill in the names."

"I didn't know the Turntablist had a name," Q remarked sadly. His toe touched something in the sand, and he bent over to examine it. It was a gray stone whose surface gave way when he put his finger on it, revealing a core of thick tar. Q pulled back his blackened finger. "What is this stone?" he asked.

"It's the stone that got us stoned," said the Male Novelist.

"It's the stone come down from the mountain a million years ago," said the Female Novelist. "It used to walk on four legs."

Q pulled his foot back out of the sand and was distressed to discover it coated with the tar. He tried to wipe it off, but the tar-balls were all over. He sat down and cleaned his feet as best he could, then put on his boots.

"It's very sticky," he said.

"Yes," said the Male Novelist. "That's why we had these rugs brought out. It would be best, I think, to go ahead and assign your characters names, whether they are real or fictional, so that they will begin to sound natural in the narration."

"I'll grant that," said the Female Novelist. "The name can be a marker, also, of certain traits like race, social class, nationality and, of course, accents."

Q mulled this over for a moment, then decided to try it. He would assign a name to his dear Turntablist. What should it be? John? Too common. How about Rudolfo? Very mellifluous, but did it connote the right nationality? This question was vexing because Q didn't know the Turntablist's nationality. He told the Novelists of his dilemma.

"Well," said the Female Novelist, pressing Q's leg, again, with her toe, "what nationality should he be? What feels right? I find myself picturing the Turntablist as Polish."

"Really?" said the Male Novelist. "I was thinking Argentine."

"I'm not sure," said Q. He furrowed his brow and thought very hard about what nationality felt right for the Turntablist, but try as he might he could not discover a national origin that seemed feasible for his rhythmic collaborator. Then he had an idea.

"Perhaps the nationality, the past, even the name, of the Turntablist could be a mystery, about which we only hint until the very end, when his true Identity is revealed."

This idea met with some approval from the Novelists, but it did nothing to solve the problem with the other characters. Finally the three agreed that firm decisions need not be made that day and that they would meet again in the near future, giving each of them time to reflect upon the problem in tranquility. There remained, however, one more issue the Male Novelist wished to address.

"Q," he said thoughtfully, "another narrative problem we have encountered is consistency of characterization. Most of your characters, despite lack of name, are quite consistently themselves, but there is one character who is not, one who is one day a spoiled middle-class brat and the next a hardened street punk. One day he's a naive child and the next a wordly savant. In fact, he seems to be a different person every time we meet him."

"But who could that be?" said Q, concerned.

"Alas, it is yourself," said the Male Novelist.

Q's jaw dropped in disbelief. "Me?" he said. "But I'm always the same. I'm always me. I'm…" But here Q stammered, for he realized the truth of what the Male Novelist was saying.

"Well," said the Female novelist, after an awkward silence, "how fortuitous, our meeting today. Through coincidence and serendipity, a new project is born. Here's to it."

They clinked their water glasses together in solidarity.

Q bade his good-by then, despite the Novelists' protestations. The Male Novelist implored him to stay the night, and the Female Novelist begged him to apply Moroccan oil to her back. But Q had been a long time, now, in close society, and he had a desire to be alone for a time, despite the pleasing ambiance of the couple's company. So they all three promised to stay in touch, and Q put on his overcoat and went off toward the setting sun.

He walked pensively, staring at the ground, on the alert for tar-balls, but at the same time not really caring when he saw one, and he sometimes stepped on them in his boots, and sometimes he stepped over them.

The further he went, though, the more his conversation with the Novelists haunted him. He had never considered it before, but now his life seemed barren and empty, with all its details swept away and only an abstract sketch remaining, as if someone had replaced an actual thing with a line drawing of that thing. He tried to focus on specific, sensory details of his past, yet when he did so he could not find any. His life, it seemed, was composed only of an interplay of nebulous concepts, each of which inspired in him a certain curiosity, but not the emotional tie of a real-life connection.

The more he thought about it, the less his life seemed suitable for recording in literature, and he eventually resigned himself to living out his days and disappearing without leaving his trace on paper. And though he had never before thought about the possibility of obtaining immortality through print, the sudden realization that such was not to be his fate filled him with melancholy.

In this mood he shuffled down the beach, hands in his pockets and head down, as the full moon rose over the sea. When he got to the cliffs he followed the path which led along a narrow ledge up the sheer face. The waves broke in a white moonlit froth on the rocks far below him, but Q was lost in his thoughts and oblivious to the scene's majesty.

"If I were to cry out," he thought, "who would hear me among the Angels? And even if one did decide to take me to its heart, I would disappear into its more powerful presence."

He lifted his eyes from the ledge to the heavens. The great sky full of stars stretched over him.

"Beauty," he continued in his reverie, "is nothing but the beginning of terror. We revere it because we can just barely survive it, and yet our survival is nothing but its calm disdaining to destroy us. Every Angel is terror."

Tears welled inside him, but he held himself back and stifled the dark sobbing.

"Ah, who then can we make use of?" his monologue continued. "Not Angels, not men, and the resourceful creatures see clearly that we are not really at home in our interpreted world. Perhaps there remains some tree on a slope, that we can see again each day, yesterday's street, and the thin loyalty of a habit that liked us, and so stayed, and never departed.

"And oh, the night, this night, when the wind from space wears out our faces…. Who would she not stay for, the longed-for, gentle, disappointing one, whom my faltering, solitary heart stands before? Is she less heavy for lovers? No, they merely hide their fate from themselves.

"Don't you get it yet? Throw the emptiness out of your arms; add it to the space we are breathing; maybe the birds will feel the expansion in the atmosphere and fly toward us."

In like fashion his subvocalization continued for several hours along the promontory, finally to be interrupted only by sign of further human habitation ahead. Down the other side of the rock face, far ahead where the sandy beach resumed, Q could see the small glow of a fire. As he got closer he began to see the shadows of people dancing around the flame, and he could hear the rhythmic twang of a guitar over the rumbling of a drum.

He didn't really want to join them. He had come seeking solitude, but some unknown drive kept him from changing his course, and he continued toward the camp against his own will, like a puppet under the direction of some God.

As he drew closer to the fire and the music became more distinct, Q found his feet moving faster and his blood quickening, and when he joined the perimeter of the crowd he fell straightaway into the dance. A bare-breasted woman holding a wineskin grabbed him as he leapt by and held the bota aloft for him to drink from.

The Guitar Player stood in the middle near the fire, elevated on an oil drum, reminding Q of the player at the railyard. What was burning in the roaring fire was the root-ball of a great oak that had washed up on the beach after what appeared to be centuries in the ocean. The upper end of the huge bole was hollow and serving as the drum, with several of the enthralled dancers beating on it with sticks. The sticks smoldered and sent up showers of sparks as they played.

The crowd danced and spun with their eyes rolled back. Many of them were naked; some were smeared with paint or decorated with strange lettering drawn in soot. A group of women threaded through the crowd with a long diaphanous scarf. Q asked one of his dance partners who they were and was told they were maenads and not to let them look at him.

Q fell into the trance of the music, feet moving faster and faster, feeling no fatigue as he wheeled and spun and leapt into the air with the rest. Then he saw something very strange; one of the dancers in front of him suddenly pitched forward as if collapsing. Q bent down to help her, but as he did she leapt away on all fours looking for all the world like a leopard. Then he began to notice others doing the same; just as their dance was reaching a fever pitch, they would fall forward, land on all fours, and leap away through the crowd in feline form, then stand back up and become human again.

Q himself was becoming dizzy from the heat and exertion and could feel himself falling forward. He saw the beach sands rising to meet him and put out his hands to prevent the fall, but what touched the ground in front of him were the black paws of a panther, and he watched them ply the ground through the crowd until he regained his strength and was able to stand again. He saw those around him standing up and resuming human form also.

The woman with the bota found him again. This time he lay on the ground as she stood over him and aimed the stream of pungent liquor into his waiting mouth. He reached up toward her, but she danced away laughing. He got up and gave chase, and they bounded through the crowd in their feline aspects.

Now the Guitar Player, as if all that had come before had been mere introit, began to sing:

> Well Q you're going home now—
> Tra-la: you've come full circle.
> A man of no fortune with a name to come.
> Come back and see us when there's nothing to be won.
>
> Q, you're going home now,
> back home to make a name.
>
> Just remember these little lessons.
> We've seeded you for a reason,
> a little something to remember us by
> through those morning-after blues.
>
> Q, you're going home now,
> back home to deserve a name.
>
> Now good king Pentheus you will recall
> riding home in his best faux-fur
> found himself in a desert, and then torn open.
> Remember not to bite the nape that fed you.
>
> Q, you're going home now,
> back home to fall into a name.

And that fool the Don, whose name everyone knows,
when in his last gasp turns homeward
does so naked, and his armor falls to the ground.
You've been lucky, Q, but luck wears out like shoes.

Q, you're going home now,
back home to borrow a name.

Do you have a home to go to?
You who have come full circle?
Man of no fortune with a name to come.
Let's see what happens when the battle's won.

Q, you're going home now,
back home to speak your name.

And the crowd danced and danced, maenads moving in and out.
Q threw himself on the ground and rolled on his back in ecstacy.
The bota woman, now completely naked like the rest of the crowd,
stood over him again and again aimed her stream at his waiting
mouth. And then Q and she went dancing, leaping up, throwing
themselves into the night sky like brilliant shards of the flame.

The gentle surf woke him, licking at his wrist. He found himself
just at the edge of the foam, the sun already high above him
and warming his naked skin. He got up and went straight into the
water to clear his head, which was reeling with dreams, memories
and fantastic inventions.

He went looking, then, for his clothes, meager as they were, and
he quickly found them, the overcoat folded neatly and laid on a log
beside his boots. He recognized the log and its tangle of roots, half
submerged in the sand, from the night before, but the wood was
polished by the wind and the sea and bore no trace of having burned.

The sand around the log, likewise, was smooth and undisturbed. When Q walked across, his footprints made the only trail to be read in it. This caused Q to wonder if he had merely dreamed the events of the night before, the dance and subsequent orgy, but the thought made his fragile head hurt, so he hurried on down the beach and left the scene behind.

He walked 20 miles along the water's edge, sandy beaches broken by the occasional promontory of white stone, coming finally to a small port with a rotten wharf and a rusting crane for handling containers. There was a freighter loading when Q arrived, and he had no trouble stealing aboard and making himself a den among the maze of containers. He searched out a bill of lading and satisfied himself that the ship was bound for home, then settled in for what he knew would be a long ride.

He stayed in his hiding place by day and roamed the ship by night. He located a bathroom that was mostly unused and was able to sneak into the galley in the wee hours to gather food from the fridge. He lived like this for almost a week and barely caught sight of the crew, but on the sixth night a storm blew up which caused the giant boat to pitch and yaw. Though Q was safe in his container during the episode, he did not know it, and he threw himself out onto the deck and made for the cabin, where he was quickly apprehended by two of the crew.

The brawny sailors grabbed him, each by an arm, and dragged him roughly up to the bridge, where a dozen more mates had gathered to watch and wait out the storm. They all stopped what they were doing and looked up when Q was thrust into the room. "Stowaway, eh?" one of them said, as they threw him face-down on the table and began to queue up. "We'll see who's stowed away."

Luckily, this scene was truncated by the entry of the Captain, who warned everyone to obey norms of decorum and further ordered Q up from his ignominious pose.

"Who are you?" the Captain demanded of Q. "May I see your passport?"

Q was flummoxed, for he did not have a passport.

"If you do not have Identification," the Captain continued, "we will have to assume you are a pirate, and you will be jettisoned."

Q sputtered but could not speak, for he did not have a passport. "It seems wrong, somehow," he finally managed to speak, "that until now my reputation has preceded me at every turn. Each new acquaintance comes with prior knowledge. But here, with you, and the only place it seems to really matter, I am a stranger. Who am I? I am a traveler, like yourselves. Who are you?"

"Thank you for your thoughtful answer," the Captain said. Then, turning to the crew, he added: "You may finish your interrogation, then throw him into the propeller."

A cheer went up, and they grabbed him and took him back to the table. The Captain took his leave and the rest gathered eagerly around, but again the festivities were stopped, this time by the entrance of the First Mate, who announced that Q was indeed who he said he was, and that he was in possession of his passport.

"But how?" the crew wanted to know. "How can it be that one moment he has no Identity and the next he does?"

"Well," said the First Mate, "to answer this question a brief story must needs be told."

The Story of Q's Identity

Now, Reader, you may have noticed that the once all-important issue of Q's Identity has been ignored by this narrative for the past several chapters. We apologize for this careless omission, pleading only that in any narrative certain details must be omitted for the sake of brevity and focus. In this case, however, present events have rendered our decision to exclude certain information obsolete, and we must now return to augment earlier events in order to explain the curious situation in which we now find ourselves.

You see, at the moment the Colonel's face exploded on board the helicopter, we failed, in the chaos that ensued, to mention that Q's attention had turned only secondarily to saving his skin, because his first thought was to protect the precious documentation he had acquired from Brownwater™. He had, even as the helicopter descended, secreted the documents in a Tyvek™ pouch which he then put down his waist, cinching his ammunition belt tight around it.

Likewise, throughout the long ordeal of dragging the five suitcases through the jungle, he always kept track of his papers, never allowing them to leave his person even for a moment. Throughout the protracted negotiations with the boatman he kept one finger touching the documents at all times, not out of suspicion but merely in an abundance of caution. And when he was floating down the river on his raft he kept constant track of the packet, using it for a pillow when he slept and keeping it on his person when he was awake.

But despite all the care he took, the river finally took his Identity from him, for when he was pulled onto the yacht by the Richest Man in the World's crew, he was naked, and though his fingers retained their clutching posture, there was nothing in them.

What had happened to the pouch containing Q's papers remained a mystery for some time after that, but the story can now be told, having been deduced by the First Mate from evidence obtained on board the freighter. The pouch had been ripped from Q's grasp in the rapids and had travelled down the river on a parallel course to his own, but once the current had slowed to a normal pace the pouch had sunk to the bottom. Here it was chanced upon by a foraging elephantfish. This curious fellow encountered the pouch while probing the bottom with his trunk and became instantly entangled in its Velcro™ straps.

This panicked the poor fish, and he made off down river at the fastest speed his fins could propel him, only to swim right into the waiting maw of a lungfish. This morose creature swallowed the morsel without a second thought, but quickly regretted making his meal in this way, as the elephantfish gave it a series of electrical shocks. The lungfish, agitated by this activity inside it, bestirred itself from the bottom and made for open water, only to run, itself, into the mouth of an even larger species—one of the many as yet unnamed fishes that inhabit this part of the world.

Now this process of each fish being eaten by a larger one continued, with each one in turn being stimulated by the electrical shock from the elephantfish at the core, until Q's Identity reached the top of the aquatic food chain and was carried out into the ocean in the gullet of a tuna. The tuna, in turn, seeking to ease the indigestion that seemed to be coming from deep inside its core, took the bait that the crew of a freighter had thrown out. It was hooked instantly and hauled up onto the deck.

There, in front of the astonished crew, the great fish, overcome by anxiety and indigestion, vomited up its latest meal, which in turn spat out its own, which did the same, until there lay on the deck a succession of smaller and smaller fishes, the very last one being the still-sparking elephantfish, from the tip of whose trunk yet dangled Q's Identity. This the crew, using rubber gloves, removed and presented to the First Mate, who examined its contents with little interest and put it away. When Q was apprehended, however, he recognized the face from the passport and retrieved the documents for a full review.

Now the Captain, who had returned to the proceedings to hear the story, took the passport and other documents from the Mate and examined them carefully. Then he ordered the passport tied around Q's neck on a lanyard, so that, at least on shipboard, his Identity would be plain to see. He gave the rest of the documents back to Q and then spoke:

"Sir Q, your Papers are a gift bestowed on you by a nation-state.

You've probably heard the popular saying, 'ship of state,' for the state is, like a ship, an island, a floating agglomeration of people and materials. And here, on board this freighter, we can even carry the metaphor a step further, for this ship is a state, a state that contains naught but this ship. Here we are on the state of the ship, and we govern ourselves as we see fit.

"Handle your Papers with care, Q, because without them you are but a piece of flotsam on the waves. Without these documents you are adrift; with them, you may join the rest of us aboard this ship and within this state. Wear this badge for all to see, so we all know you are fit to serve, and proceed to swabbing our decks and cleaning our latrines."

Here the Captain took his leave with a nod to the First Mate, who, rubbing his hands in anticipation, announced to the crew the order of events. Q would be escorted to the dirtiest facilities on the boat, to work his way up to the cleanest ones. There was some debate, then, on which lavatory was actually the dirtiest, but all finally agreed that he should start in the machinists' lounge, deep in the bowels of the boat. Everyone laughed with glee when the decision was made, and every member of the crew volunteered to escort Q to his assignment.

"But wait," the First Mate held up his hand. "Before we can send this man off to his workplace on this soon-to-be spotless ship, I think—and I believe I can speak for the Captain in this matter, as well—that we need to complete the hazing process." He winked, and scarcely had his eye reopened than Q found himself, once again, bent over the table, and this time, rather than saving him at the last minute, the First Mate led the charge.

Q spent the rest of the voyage below, in the darkest and most foul recesses of this ship of state. And yet the work, while unpleasant enough, was not the worst of it. The worst was the treatment by the crew, who not only acted as if he were invisible when in his presence, but also went out of their way to foul the bathrooms, making Q's work both more difficult and less sanitary.

The last straw, however, was laid on when Q overheard the following conversation between two crew members:

A: "Well, it looks like bad news for old Q."

B: "Really? How's that?"

A: "It seems that the amount of his fare is more than can be covered by working the few days we have left in this trip."

B: "I see. And what will be the remedy?"

A: "The Captain has said he'll just have to work the return journey also."

B: "But will he submit to this indenture?"

A: "The Captain suspects he will not, and so he is prepared to lock him in the hold when we make landfall, to assure his cooperation."

B: "Ah."

Now Q was not sure if this conversation was indeed candid or if it had in fact been manufactured for him to overhear. Similar cruelties were de riguer among the crew. But at this point Q decided he could not take the risk, and he hatched a plan to debark as soon as he possibly could.

That moment came quicker than he had imagined it would, for it was only the next day when land showed itself on the horizon. Viewing its distance and the roughness of the sea between them, Q had second thoughts, but he was committed by the vow he'd sworn to himself and so, without delay, leapt rashly over the rail to the sea below.

He had underestimated, of course, the length of time it would take one to fall the fifty feet to the water, and he had grossly underestimated the force with which he would hit the surface from that height. The landing didn't quite render him unconscious, but put a ringing in his ears that the roar of the nearby propellers on the giant boat could barely drown out. When his breath began to fail he began to swim, making it to the surface in the nick of time, casting off his overcoat and boots to make swimming easier.

Once free of the vicinity of the boat, he breathed a sign of relief and set out for land. The shore came in and out of view as the waves rose and fell, but did not seem to move closer with successive waves. Though Q prided himself on his swimming ability, he quickly tired against the churning sea, and thirty minutes into his long journey he was reduced to a dead-man's float just to keep his soul within his body.

24 hours he floated thus, lifting his nose out of the water to breathe as each wave peaked, tossed along like a piece of bark. When he finally washed onto the shore he came to rest in a pile of seaweed and old hawser. There he rested until the next day, when hunger and thirst roused him even against the exhaustion of his battered body, and he set out, famished, naked and alone, but on his native soil again.

He went off down the beach and luckily immediately encountered his overcoat and boots, half-buried in the sand and considerably the worse for the wear, but, after some rinsing, still quite functional. The fact that his Identity papers were no longer among them didn't even trouble him, but he continued on, clothed, and began gradually to come upon strewn Styrofoam™ and other plastic litter that told him civilization was at hand. And then, a ways off down the beach, he saw a small building with people milling around and, in the back, a dumpster.

A little sustenance drawn from this first horn of plenty gave him strength to make it to the next, and that to the next, and so on, until he was sated and ready to be off. He found the railroad without difficulty but, not knowing which way he should turn, spent his first few hours walking down a blind spur. He had to retrace his steps, then, but this was soon accomplished, and he proceeded then at a good clip and made it to the main line before nightfall.

He watched the first train go by at terrible speed—no hope of getting on there. Then he hit on the idea to build a false barrier. He searched in the vicinity until he found a pile of discarded books and magazines, apparently dumped in the course of cleaning house at a library or school. He gathered a considerable volume of the reading matter and piled it in the middle of the interchange. Then he concealed himself a little way down the track as he heard a train approaching.

His plan worked perfectly. The Engineer, mistaking the pile of books on the tracks for a solid obstacle, immediately applied the brakes and prepared to stop, lest the expensive engine be damaged in a collision. As the train slowed to a jogger's pace, Q leapt aboard and situated himself on the end of a hopper car. By then they were close enough to the pile that the Engineer was able to discern its content. Seeing that it was only literature, he again applied the throttle, and the juggernaut roared on into the night.

Q let the train take him where it would, and his car wound its way toward the beating heart of the system, where it was inducted and sent out again, refilled, along the arteries. He rode patiently, keeping an eye out for any familiar landscape, remaining on the train except for occasional forays for food or a period of rest off of his hard iron floor.

He found the tracks somewhat busier than they had been in his previous journeys. There were more camps, and they were larger than the ones he had encountered before. And though sometimes he craved solitude when deboarding, he found no berth of easy exit and reentry, near food and water and urban waste containers, that was not already crowded with destitute wanderers. Whole cities of squalid tents and lean-tos had sprung up, some with small shops and markets where meager goods were traded. In some areas there was even rudimentary mail service from camp to camp.

Q avoided these knots of society when he could, preferring to sleep under the stars and alone, and further out of simple caution, since he had heard that these encampments were routinely raided by police and vigilantes from nearby cities, the tents torn down or burned and the inhabitants beaten and evicted. Sometimes it happened that young women or men would follow Q out of these camps and seek to become his disciples, for even when he was silent he emanated a charisma that many found irresistible. But he had no heart for this and would chase them away or ditch them at first opportunity.

Less often, he happened upon other solitaries like himself, though usually older, and with these sometimes he would wile away an evening talking about the signs they'd seen and what the future might hold. The following conversation is typical of many he had.

"The world is in decline, Q, perpetual decline," said the old fellow as they sat beside Q's fire.

"In my experience," replied Q, "this is actually not the case. Also, physics itself would seem to contradict your view: since energy cannot be created or destroyed, any decline must be followed by improvement. Perhaps it is not, as the Exceptionalists maintain, that our progress is ever toward improvement, but surely the currents of the world ebb and flow."

"No," said the old gentleman, rolling a cigarette, "you misunderstand me. It doesn't matter what the currents of the world do; for what happens happens to you alone. The world you are born into is perfect, joyous, pregnant with possibility. The child born to crippling poverty opens its eyes for the first time in wonder. It wants nothing but its mother's breast to suck. As long as that warm nipple is in its mouth, it looks out on the world like a little emperor, pleased with all it surveys.

"But this world can only decline because we can only decline. Once the bloom of youth has fallen away, no windfall of riches, no lover, no great accomplishment can please us. The world we see is sere and bare no matter how much we have progressed. The rich man, surrounded by his possessions, longs only for his first, worthless bauble. The artist, laurelled for her brilliance, sees only darkness and pretense in her ouvre. The writer, hailed as a genius, with his tomes collecting dust, remembers fondly the time before language conquered his senses.

"The first time I saw a campfire like this one it was a miraculous thing of beauty. I was in awe of its light and warmth. Now to my fading eyes the light is but a blur, and the heat does little to placate the perpetual cold, for this perpetual cold is caused by poor circulation in my extremities, not the weather."

"I see your point," said Q, "but as yet I still refuse to believe there can be no succor. Even taking what you say at its face (which I am not necessarily prepared to do,) even allowing that our perception of our world must follow the inevitable decline of our bodies and minds, even then there remains the indomitable strength and idealism of Youth to guide us."

"Certainly," said the fellow, "strength and idealism Youth has in abundance; reason less so. What does the child do when she sees the lovely flower but pluck it and put it in her pocket, so that what emerges after an hour is but a ball of lint and dirt? Look at this world around you. What does it resemble more than a wadded-up flower, its petals crumpled, its perfume discharged, its nectar spilt? All the possibility that lay dormant in that flower is thus lost, squandered by that bumbling child, Humanity."

This conversation haunted Q for some time. Though he spent long nights in sleepless rumination attempting to reason his way out of it, he was unable to arrive at a satisfactory rebuttal. The sad truth and irrefutable logic of the stranger's philosophy colored his entire world. He saw it, now, in every pile of rubbish, in every landscape ruined by a strip mine or refinery, in every river choked with debris and fouled with chemicals and sewage. After a while he even began to see it in human countenance, in the curl of a lip as it enunciated a curse or a cruel joke, or the lines of a face contorted in laughter.

Nor was this fellow his only unnerving encounter. One day he chanced upon a man of great age hobbling along the tracks. He was dressed in the customary rags, but on every visible surface of his clothing and upon his skin too he had drawn or tattooed the insignia of his nation, over and over again. Q found it odd that this old man should display such adamant patriotism from the depths of his squalor, and he told him so.

"Oh, you misunderstand," said the old gentleman. "I'm not feeling the least bit patriotic; I just want to make sure I'm buried with some dignity when I croak and not tossed into some mass grave with the rest of the railroad trash."

"You're right that I don't understand," said Q, "for surely there is no politics of mourning. In death our nationalities are forgotten and we weep for our common fate. We are all equal in death."

"Ah, isn't it pretty to think so, Q?" he replied. "But in point of fact the first question we ask of a corse is its nationality, and if it belongs to us we treat it with reverence and respect; we lower it to its final rest with solemn music and quivering cheeks. But the body of a stranger we shove into a ditch, only bothering to cover when the stench becomes unpleasant. I'm just making sure my cold remains are treated better than these warm ones have been."

This lesson, too, cut to the quick, for it reminded Q that he himself was nationless, and it pained him to think that at the end of his sojourn his earthly countenance might lie uncovered on the plain. Some time later, though, while on a forage for food, Q came upon an old woman sitting beside the tracks, and this encounter soon overshadowed every other.

"Old Woman," he said to her, "why do you sit here on the hard stones? Who or what are you waiting for? Surely you would be more comfortable in an encampment. I have just passed a group, back there, and would be happy to take you."

"I have no need for your charity, Q, nor for the company of fools. Save your pity for yourself, who is more pitiful than the flea that sucks at my bum." She lifted her head as she spoke, and Q could see by the milky emptiness of her eyes that she was blind. He was offended by her rude response to his offer of assistance, but he felt pity and attempted again to reason with her.

"I can well understand your Desire for solitude," he began, "but how can you, in your condition, survive the hardships of the road? How do you compensate for your lack of sight?"

"How do you compensate for yours?" she replied.

"But how do you live out here, alone? Who brings you food?"

"I've no need of scraps. If I need to eat, the Hawk will bring me a Snake to roast, or the Hare will crawl into my lap and offer up its throat. You take me for a beggar, but it is you who have come begging."

"What?" Q replied, blushing. "I ask for nothing from you. What do you have that I might beg for?"

"Why, exactly what you ask for," she replied. "Nothing. I have the emptiness you crave, the abyss that is your certain end and toward which you steer unerringly."

"No, it's not true," Q stammered. "My effort is always toward progress and improving my situation. I strive only to better myself. Anyway, what can you tell me about such things? You are blind. You can't even see what effect your words have on me."

To this the Old Woman laughed long and loud, and then replied sarcastically: "Oh, you have me there, Q. How can I argue with such reason?" She guffawed and slapped her thigh, then abruptly stopped laughing and grabbed the hem of Q's coat. "You'll know how blind I am in the end," she hissed. "You'll pluck out your own eyes to know it."

After this strange incident Q endeavored to avoid the solitaries he saw along the rails. He began, in fact, to frequent the camps, as he found the degree of intimate interaction forced upon him in these crowded quarters to be significantly less than when he encountered a single human on the road. He still preferred solitude, but losing himself in the crowd appeared to be the next best condition.

Now it happened that on these occasional forays into society, however meager the interaction, that Q needed to supply a few facts about his life, to satisfy the curiosity of casual acquaintances. Where did he hail from? The Dark Continent, he told them, preferring to give his most recent residence rather than the original. And where was he going? To this he answered Provincial Oaks, not because he had any desire to return to his old home, but simply because this answer was so neutral and uninteresting that the conversation was normally brought to a halt by it.

But this prevarication, which became habitual, had an unexpected consequence, for when Q would awaken alone in the night, on the hard floor of a rail car or in a field under the stars, he was often confused and would have to ask himself certain questions to remember where he was. "Who am I?" he would whisper to himself. And then he would remember. "Q," he mouthed in the darkness. "Where am I going?" And by and by he began to answer this second question to himself with the answer he had grown accustomed to giving to others. And so he would whisper "Provincial Oaks" to himself, over and over again, to quell that feeling of being lost and empty inside him.

And then it came to be that in the daytime, when he was wide awake and staring at the scenery along the rail, he found himself becoming attentive when passing through suburban environments, and his heart quickened when he saw an entry gate or guardhouse that reminded him of his old home. And so what had been conversational pretense became his journey in truth, and the angst that woke him at night found its restless object in a longing for home.

All that long cold winter Q rode the rails in search of his home. Spring came and with it warm days, flowers and budding fruit. Q was returning to the tracks from a very productive visit to a shopping mall. Pleasantly full from the pizzeria's dumpster, he was stepping down from an overpass when he saw something familiar in the shadows. A human figure squatted in the gloom under the bridge. It was the Troll.

Q could scarcely contain his joy and threw himself on the reclusive fellow, hugging him and kissing him through his grisly beard. The Troll tolerated this unpleasant display of affection for a moment, then sidled away to a more comfortable talking distance.

"Ah, Troll," said Q, "you can't imagine how good it is to see you after all this time and having traveled so far."

"Yes, Q," said the Troll, "we enjoy seeing things we've seen before."

"Well," said Q, "certain things we enjoy. Certain things we don't. But to see you again is pure pleasure."

The Troll grunted and sat back in his squatting posture as Q fired questions at him. Had he seen any of the old gang? Where were the Tall-Bikers? And the Singer? And... he caught himself before asking about Lucy. The Troll answered his questions with noncommittal musings. "They're fine, I'm sure."

Then the great coincidence of their meeting finally came home to Q, and he inquired of the Troll how he happened to be here, under this bridge, so very far from where they had first met. To this inquiry the Troll chuckled, then laughed deeply, for he had gone nowhere. "It is you who have traveled, not me," he said. "This is the very same bridge under which we first met."

Q was flabbergasted. "But the rails, the trees along the siding," he said, "and there's a mall up on the road. This can't be the same place."

"Things change," the Troll informed him. "Humans are a restless bunch, always building, digging, demolishing and rearranging. And things, also, change themselves. But this is the same place. I have not been anywhere."

"Do you mean," cried Q, "that we are just down the tracks from the Switchyard where you introduced me to the crew, to the Singer and to… to everyone. And the boxcar where… where I heard the story. Where I first…."

"Yes, Q," the Troll replied. "Had you ridden your train another five minutes you would have been there. You have returned."

Q could not contain his excitement at this news and leapt around under the bridge admonishing the Troll to accompany him immediately to the Switchyard. But the Troll would not be moved from his substratal perch, saying that he'd been to the Switchyard recently and that he had business to attend to under the bridge.

Vowing to return, then, shortly, Q set off hurriedly down the track. He had not gone but a few paces when a whistle from the Troll informed him he was going the wrong direction. He turned around undaunted and set off at a trot, reaching the Switchyard in just a few minutes.

The place was still populated by ruffians, as Q remembered, but the atmosphere was far less festive than Q's first visit. There were no tall bikes nor any of the other odd contraptions that had been operable before, except for a few rusting remnants that lay in the weeds. There seemed to be more people inhabiting the place, now, and yet Q found no familiar face among them, and he was not greeted with enthusiasm. In fact, the first thing he was told was

that there were no more sleeping berths available and that all good
forage routes were assigned, so that if he wanted to eat and sleep,
he would need to do that elsewhere.

He wandered around, forlorn, for a few minutes. And though
he knew he was not welcome in them, he examined the boxcars
where he had spent his first week with Lucy, merely making himself
more unhappy in the process, as he looked inside and saw the
tarps arranged for bedding. He finally walked on down the tracks,
crestfallen, unwilling even to wait for the next train to escape the
hostile stares of the residents.

He was walking with his head down, paying no attention to where
he was, when he suddenly stopped and looked up. At the top of the
embankment on his right was the Sound Barrier he had climbed so
long—or not so long—ago and seen Provincial Oaks for the last
time. And though he did not want to climb it again, did not want to
see the old home he had taught himself to be nostalgic for, since
he knew he could never go there again, in the end he decided he
must scale the wall once more, if only because if he didn't he was
not going to be able to move from the spot where he was presently
planted.

And so he went up the embankment again, and again he climbed
the Sound Barrier. It seemed somewhat more difficult, this time, but
at last he got a hand on the top edge and managed to throw a leg
over. He pulled himself up and sat on the top edge of the concrete
parapet. He looked down, then, into the valley at his old home, and
was amazed at what he saw.

He looked first for the house he grew up in, and he soon found
it. It seemed relatively unchanged, still with its manicured
lawn, only now with only one car in the driveway. While he watched
someone came out of the front door and began walking down the

street. But… walking? This is very strange, he thought, since no one ever walked anywhere in Provincial Oaks.

He followed the walker (apparently, judging by apparel, female) on her way down the street, and as he did so gradually became aware that much had changed in the subdivision. In fact, only his house had remained the same, while everything else seemed to have deteriorated drastically. As the walker passed in front of houses they came gradually into focus, and Q saw that the lawns were not only not manicured, they were overgrown with weeds. Cars were parked curbside, but when he looked closely he saw they rested on flat tires. On many of the cars and houses too the doors stood open. Houses had dark, open holes where their windows had been, and some of them had sheets of plastic hanging in tatters from the roofs. Garage doors hung crookedly, off their tracks.

But Q was most distressed when the walker got to the gate of their gated community, for the gate was gone. The way stood open for anyone to enter. The guardhouse, where formerly the Private Police Force had checked the credentials of everyone who went in or out of Provincial Oaks, appeared to have been rammed by a vehicle and flattened. It lay in a heap, half-blocking the exit lane.

In short, all of Provincial Oaks lay in ruins, houses and cars abandoned, streets cracking with weeds and small trees beginning to take them over. Everywhere in the subdivision, except Q's old house, the dilapidation was rampant. Q stared at this improbable scene for a long time but finally made up his mind to investigate and leapt to the ground on the quiet side of the Sound Barrier. He proceeded with caution, for the memory of his beating(s) at the hands of the Private Police Force had mellowed little with age, but the fact that the guardhouse was in ruins gave him heart, so he walked down the road and in through the entrance where the gate had been. As he passed through he saw the gate itself, rotting in the weeds at the side of the road, broken from the post at the hinge.

He passed slowly by the empty houses, aghast at the destruction. Up close it was even worse than he had imagined. Broken glass and rusting appliances littered the streets and yards. He went up to one of the open doors and looked in. The front room of this particular house was a whorled mass of mildewed furniture. The ceiling had caved in from the leaking roof, leaving long trails of dirty insulation trailing in the breeze.

As Q neared his old home, both his curiosity and trepidation increased, but the former finally won out. He turned the corner onto his own street, he saw the walker he had seen from the Sound Barrier, returning now with an armload of something. She stopped when she saw him, and he did too, and they confronted each other like gunslingers from a distance of a hundred yards.

Q lifted up a hand and waved to her. She remained motionless for a moment, then did the same. Now Q started forward again, as did she. They met at the driveway and looked at each other warily. She was dressed from head to toe in Adidas™ gear, her hair like a rat's nest, with tangles dangling in front of her face.

"What do you want?" she said.

"Nothing," Q replied. "I used to live here."

She squinted at him. "Are you my Brother?"

"Are you my Sister?"

"I guess so," she said. They stared at each other in silence a moment. "We didn't think you'd be back."

"'We?'" said Q.

"Yeah," she said, "we. Mom and Dad are inside."

And she turned and walked up the driveway to the front door.

She went in the door without waiting for her brother, and this made Q wistful for the old days in the family, when the two of them were so close there was no need to be polite. He followed her through the familiar opening into the house he had lived in for so many years so long ago.

Inside, the house was quite different than he remembered. He supposed the architecture of the rooms had not changed, but in truth he would not have recognized the place had he seen a photograph of the interior. The den, which he recognized by its size and the high ceiling, now held neither the giant flat-screen TV he had spent so many hours in front of, nor the plush sectional couch he had spent those hours on. In their place was now a hodgepodge of mismatched, well-worn furniture upon which rested, equally mismatched, his Mother and Father.

His Father sat cross-legged on a cushion on the floor, wearing nothing but his dhoti, plucking at his guitar. He smiled and nodded a greeting, engrossed in his instrument. His Mother, however, leapt up from her sewing to embrace him. Q had never seen his Mother sewing before, nor could he remember her ever embracing him, so he was somewhat taken aback by her greeting. He was further confused by her apparel, as she was dressed in denim overalls, whereas he had never seen her wear anything but fashionable athletic wear.

He quickly warmed, however, to her new, affectionate self. She kissed him repeatedly and wet his face with her tears, then bade him sit down with her and tell his story, where he had been, what he had seen, etc., all of which he told her in a rush, sparing minor details to give the bigger picture, coming to the conclusion in only a few hours. Then he hastened to ask about her own adventure, which she told in a perfunctory fashion.

To no one's surprise but her own, the relationship with the Tennis Instructor did not last long. He lost his job as soon as the Club began losing membership to the economic crisis, and though he was quite adept at socializing (and more) with the Rich, as it turned out he had no riches of his own. Besides that, Q's Mother had caught him, once, being indiscreet with her Daughter, and that, together with his lack of financial resources, had prompted her to leave him.

She and Q's Sister had then wandered and made their way as best they could (she seemed reticent to provide details, here), sometimes coming near to destitution but always managing, by the barest margin, to survive. Their luck had changed, though, when they found employment in the gambling industry. Their employer had sent the two of them to one of their remote locations, and there, in the course of her duties Q's Mother had received a large tip from an extremely well-off patron. The tip had been large enough, actually, for them to retire from the gambling business, return to Provincial Oaks and buy back their house. Not only that, but as the downturn had affected so many of their neighbors, and so many of the neighboring houses were foreclosed upon, they were, in the end, able to buy the entire subdivision.

"We," she said proudly, "are the new owners of Provincial Oaks."

At this news Q's jaw dropped. "It can't be," he said. "We now own all of Provincial Oaks? But… it does seem to have deteriorated somewhat since last I saw it."

"Well," she said, "that's the reason I could afford it. I mean, my 5.1 million could only go so far. Since Provincial Oaks had privatized all their services, such as water, electricity and sewer, as well as our famous Private Police Force," (Q winced) "these services were discontinued as soon as the Property Owner's Association became insolvent."

"Oh, that's no problem," said Q without thinking, for he had lived so long without such amenities he had forgotten they were necessities to some. "Everything we need is right here inside the Subdivision."

"Yes," she replied, "your Father calculated that we can live for about 5 years on just the contents of all the abandoned pantries. Why, just look at this." She opened the door to their own pantry, revealing shelves solidly stocked with canned vegetables and boxes of cereal.

Q was overjoyed at the sight, but the mention of his Father caused him to raise an eyebrow. "But," he said, "Dad, how did you find him?"

"Oh he just appeared one day, like you," she said.

"And was he alone?" Q asked.

"Yes," she said, then quickly recanted, "I mean no, he wasn't. There was a dark-skinned fellow with him, Santo. He's out back working in the garden."

Q turned then to his Father and attempted to engage him in conversation, but the old gentleman merely smiled and continued noodling on his guitar, so he went to the back yard to say hello to his old friend. He was somewhat taken aback at the condition of the yard. The pool, which formerly had gleamed with clear blue imitation seawater, was now, in the absence of the pool boy, a bowl of stagnant green sludge, with lily pads and even a few frogs breaking the surface here and there. The yard, too, was quite different. The fences had been removed so that the back yard now stretched to the adjacent houses in all directions. Arrayed along this expanse were several raised gardens built from the demolished fence boards. On one of these Santo was working with a hoe.

As Q approached he stopped his arduous work and leaned on the hoe. "Hola Q," he said. "¿Tu vives?"

Q concurred that his mortal frame still walked the Earth. They sat, then, and told each other of the intervening adventures. Q thanked Santo profusely for looking after his near-helpless Father while he had been on his mission to the Dark Continent. It seems that when the Church of the Ostensible Jesus had discovered the source of the accounting irregularities that had led to its demise, they had immediately, of course, given Q's Father the boot, but they had thrown Santo out with him, even though he was a loyal servant of Christ and had nothing to do with the debacle. "You came in with him; you're going out with him," they had said.

At first Santo resented the burden of Q's Father. He was anxious to get on with his life and with his campaign for Governor and for Esperanza's hand. But, despite several attempts, his conscience would not allow him to abandon the old man, and in the end he brought him back to Provincial Oaks (which he had some difficulty in finding, given the addled descriptions of the place he had from Q's Father) in the hopes of finding some relative or acquaintance he might be able to leave him with. They were both quite surprised to discover Q's Mother and Sister living in the old house, and these two, to be sure, were surprised to find their Husband and Father resurrected, or rather reincarnated, in this bearded holy man who, after perusing the environs, nodded sagely and declared it the same old house with different furniture.

At first Q found the whole notion of gardening odd, since they were surrounded by houses with pantries full of canned and packaged food products, but under Santo's tutelage he quickly warmed to the task and began to help out with hoeing, sowing, fertilizing and watering. He found instruction books on the topic in one of the nearby houses and soon became something of an expert himself. Their beds flourished.

The five of them were quite comfortable in the old house. Days they worked in the garden or foraged in the neighboring houses for food and fuel, and at night they cooked over an open fire and told stories, or Q's Father entertained them with his songs. One night he announced he had written a new one he was excited to share:

My New Life

Oh my old life was so eggy
It hatched me like a sprite
And when I jumped out of the nest
A settling hawk saved me like air.

Oh my old life was filled and risky
Now I drink whatever I want
I'm back with my egg girl
A settling hawk saved me like air.

They all cheered and congratulated the minstrel, though, if truth be told, neither his guitar playing nor his voice nor, indeed, his lyrics, were of professional caliber.

Over the course of time others came to the gate wanting to stay in Provincial Oaks, and a few of them, after being judged to be compatible with the core group of Q's family, were allowed to take up residence in the empty houses. One of these was a man they came to call the Philosopher.

This fellow occupied himself by studying the subdivision in minute detail. Q often saw him pacing about with a ruler and a note pad, taking measurements and making annotations. Finally Q's curiosity got the better of him, and he asked the Philosopher what he was doing.

"I'm looking for points of structural congruence," he replied. "You see," and here he held out his notebook for Q's inspection, "I am superimposing over Provincial Oaks a grid of dotted lines which will provide the basis for a map, or rather maps."

Q looked at the sheet and puzzled over the apparently chaotic assembly of lines, vectors and angles, with notations concerning dimensions and elevations. "I see," said Q. "But tell me this: Provincial Oaks Avenue does not run straight. It curves and then bifurcates and then bifurcates again, finally ending in a host of small cul-de-sacs. It would seem that such a structure would not be amenable to the imposition of a grid."

"Oh, you're quite wrong there," the Philosopher replied. "It is in fact the grid that allows us to see the curvature of the space. If there were no grid, there would be no way to determine that each cul-de-sac was not a separate universe. Notice, here, the parabolic section formed by this stretch of Provincial Oaks Boulevard, as compared to this stretch of Provincial Oaks Lane."

He pointed to a cluster of marks on the drawing. Q examined them closely, but could not determine what point the Philosopher was trying to make. "You see," he continued, "the one is merely an enlargement and rotation of the other. All the ratios remain constant. Why even the angle of this driveway's intersection with the sidewalk on Provincial Oaks Lane matches the vector of this rear fence on Provincial Oaks Way."

On hearing this explanation, the drawing seemed to come into focus for Q, and he saw the resemblance the Philosopher had indicated. Another question occurred to him. "But how can you know," he asked, "if the parallelism you point out is inherent in the structure of Provincial Oaks and not merely a product of imperfections in your drawing? Perhaps drawing the one instance predisposed you to draw the second instance in like fashion."

"Perhaps," the Philosopher replied, his interest piqued. "It may not be possible to separate, with empirical certainty, effects that are in the world from effects that we have merely drawn on our map. And yet is not the world itself our drawing? What is Provincial Oaks but the illustration of a concept? What is a concrete truck but a calligrapher's pen, making lines thick and thin, all according to the skill—or lack thereof—of the particular artist?"

"Do you mean," said Q, "that the world is but a blank page and all these things we build in it but signs, glyphs on the surface?"

"Precisely," the Wise One replied. "Think of the child in her room, building houses, farms, even small cities, on the floor. But the point, unbeknownst to her, is not the construction of an edifice but the learning of the letters and numbers on the blocks. The Builder, Q, is but a Writer, and the Writer merely a Builder."

They walked in silence a little way, then seated themselves on the grass beneath a Plane Tree behind one of the ruined houses. For a while they did not speak, with Q knitting his brow in consternation and the Philosopher scribbling in his notebook. Finally, though, Q could contain himself no longer and blurted out: "But your endeavor is backward, upside-down. Here around us is the World. We make notes, draw parallels, make analogies, all to better understand that World. You seem to be saying that the World is here to illuminate the Writing."

"Of course you are right, Q," he replied. "And yet, if we are out to understand the World, who is to understand our understanding? There is an end to the chain of reasons. Let me illustrate with an analogy. Some years ago, many in my profession concerned themselves with the question 'where does time go?' They knew that time came and went, so they wanted to know *where* it went. But this question is fundamentally flawed, for it confuses, just as you have, the writing and the world. They have imagined time 'going' in the way that, say, a log 'goes' when it floats down a river and disappears around a bend. They imagine that time 'flies' in the same way that a bird flies, but this sameness is only in the Word."

"I see," said Q skeptically.

"You do not sound convinced," the Philosopher said with a smile. "Let me see if I can illustrate the concept with a more telling metaphor. The two arcs I showed you on the map a moment ago did not coincide in name, for one was on Provincial Oaks Boulevard and the other on Provincial Oaks Lane. Neither did they coincide in direction or scale. And yet their paths were of perfectly congruent arcs. On the other hand, the Bird's flight does indeed correspond to Time's flight in name, yet in no other way, which leads us to infer that since linguistic homonymy is no assurance of a conceptual analog, likewise conceptual analogy need not imply homonymy."

Q was getting confused but tried to hide this fact by nodding and saying, "yes, I see."

"Time's flight, then, does not find its representation in the Bird's flight but rather in, say, the Dew's evaporation or, perhaps more pertinently, the arc of your Desire for Lucy. Parallelism, then, the analog itself, fundament of both linguistic and non-linguistic discourse, finds its meaning in neither Word nor World."

One day not long after his encounter with the Philosopher, Q was tending his garden and stopped for a moment, leaning on his hoe to rest. As he looked off absently toward the horizon his eye was caught by a lone figure seated atop the Sound Barrier, just at the point where he had once looked over with Lucy and, more recently, where he crossed the wall to return to Provincial Oaks.

The distance was too great for Q to make out who this figure might be, but something in its posture suggested to him that its gender might be female. He watched a long time without moving, then decided to wave. She didn't wave back.

Now came that time of the year when they were to make their harvest, and—thanks to Santo and, to a lesser degree, Q—their baskets were overflowing, so it was decided that there should be a gathering.

They set up long tables in the back yard and covered them with bounty. Bushels of tomatoes; barrows of bearded corn; buckets of beans red, black and green; great piles of loamy potatoes; yucca and yams in heaps; toe sacks spilling brown and yellow rice; chicken-wire hoppers full of spinach, collards, arugula, curly kale and mustard greens; gnarly carrots with green tops still crisp; radishes of every size and shape; celery stalks in flower; beetroot and turnips with their variegated leaves; piles of purple-stalked rhubarb; mushrooms in great variety, round caps and oysters and the lung-like morels; heaping jars of spice, oregano, tarragon, pots of basil and chives, parsley and sage; piles of shallots and onions; pyramids of red cabbage and white cabbage, radicchio and endive; great pumpkins and gourds; cucumbers, yellow squash and green zucchini; green and white asparagus. Of late a few cows and goats had begun to appear around the subdivision, and so were added to the table pitchers of milk and crocks of butter along with great wheels of pungent cheese. Chickens and ducks, too, had taken up residence and contributed baskets full of eggs along with the many preparations eggs make possible, creamy custards, puddings, cakes and pies. There were fruits and nuts in abundance: peaches and nectarines dripping with juice; apples and pears in red, green and yellow; bushels of pecans; salty almonds and pumpkin seeds; currants and red plums; quarts of green and purple muscadines; blood-red cherries; strawberries and blueberries and blackberries; bunches of bananas yellow and red, and plantains just turning. From lattices above the tables hung bunches of green and purple grapes, and the tables were garnished with clay pots of pickles, black and green olives, bowls of honey and jams, as well as great loaves of seedy breads made from wheat and rye. To quench the harvesters' thirst were barrels of beer made from their fields of grain, as well as steaming vats of sweet mead. The bees whose honey had made that mead joined the celebration themselves, swarming drunkenly around the vats, many of them falling in, so that those who filled their cups were obliged to drink with caution.

(Now, some of the guests would later complain that, in all this sumptuous feast, there was not one gram of meat or fowl. There were several who turned up their noses at what they took to be a facile vegetarianism in a world where the vast hordes of humanity ate whatever they could in their relentless struggle for mere survival. This, however, was not the case. The reason there was no meat on the menu was not out of any consideration of ethics or even fashion, but rather of expediency. For if you have a thousand cows it is no great loss to slaughter one or two for your feast, but if you have only one, and you have, beyond that, named her Bessie and carried on a conversation with her every morning while milking her, you'll not be in a hurry to kill your only source of milk, much less your pleasant morning company. Likewise, if you have ten thousand chickens, plucking fifty out of the flock for roasting is no great matter, but if you have five, named Doris, Squishy, Rachel, Ninny and Val, and a single rooster named Jim, you'll have a hard time killing even one, for who would feel good gnawing on a thigh bone and having their host say, "How do you like old Val?")

They sent word to the neighboring encampments so that everyone might come to the celebration. Q was surprised to see many of his old acquaintances, including some whom he greeted less than enthusiastically, such as the two Policemen who had originally removed him from the Garden, and his former Best Friend from high school, who had treated him so rudely on his first night in the Shelter. These were considerably reduced from last sighting, dressed in rags and grown very thin, as apparently neither the extorted insurance money of the Policemen nor the Best Friend's MBA from Harvard had been enough to save them from *La condition humaine*.

Likewise, the Competition showed up, arriving in a chauffeur-driven limousine, still babbling his incoherent monetary policy and ignoring everything anyone else said. Q recognized others from the Shelter too, but he was delighted to see some of the tall-bikers from his initiation at the Railyard. Even the Troll was there, looking extremely uncomfortable in the bright daylight and vociferous crowd. One whom Q remembered from the Railyard, obviously, was not in attendance, but he kept his mind in the present and refused to ruminate upon the painful lessons of the past.

Then there came the friendly Campers who had been displaced from their flooded city. They had, coincidentally, parked their Airstream™ nearby. Tagging along behind them, still in his business attire though somewhat more ragged than before, the Entropy™ Executive came up to shake Q's hand. "This is lovely," he told Q, "just lovely. So good to see you again. Thank you so much."

Now came a group that Q did not recognize, a beautiful young girl with her parents. She walked up to Q and introduced herself. "I am Esperanza," she said, and these"—indicating the elderly couple behind her—"are my parents."

"Ah, Esperanza. Your reputation precedes you," said Q, bowing deeply. He expressed his great joy at finally meeting and then took them to the back to find Santo. He found the loyal Gardener tending, as always, to the beds. When he saw Esperanza he stood up, at first simply staring at her, transfixed, then came forward and took her hand.

Q turned to go back to greeting the arrivals, but Esperanza stopped him. "Q," she said, "I thought you would want to know that we were able to get the law changed. Santo can run for Governor now."

"Great news," replied Q. "So now aliens may run for Governor?"

"Yes," she said, "in fact the law now says that only aliens may run for Governor; citizens are not allowed. Thus Santo's election is all but assured." Q was enormously interested in this strange twist of fate, and had a thousand questions about the implications for citizens and for government in general, but, social duties taking precedence, he was forced to resume his station in the vestibule, promising this lovely, competent, politically-engaged young girl to return to the topic later.

He never suspected that he might get to see any of his dear friends from the Church, for only incredible coincidence could have resulted in their being near Provincial Oaks on that day, and yet now the Turntablist, the Associate Pastor and the Secretary appeared at the door, along with a fourth whom Q did not recognize. After greeting his friends, he turned to the newcomer and extended his hand.

"Q," said the Turntablist, "allow me to introduce our new rapper, Little A."

"Very happy to meet you," said Q, shaking Little A's hand. This new rapper was an odd character with incongruous and confusing features. Q was unable to determine whether his replacement was tall or short or fat or thin, nor could he discern the skin color or even gender of this enigmatic artist. He gave a questioning glance to the Turntablist and the Associate Pastor, but they were smiling as if nothing were wrong, so he decided the problem must be with his own perception and politely bade them enter.

Now Q was confronted by another surprise: all those he had met on the Dark Continent. The Headhunter was there, along with the entire gang of Entrepreneurs from the Strip Mine, complete with the five beautiful head-bearers. And in what may have been the greatest surprise of all, the Colonel himself arrived, still in combat gear, draped with weapons, his ruined head covered by a bloody sack. When Q expressed his amazement at seeing the Colonel alive, or at least ambulatory, he merely nodded and joined the others in the yard.

Now came the Ferryman, still bearing his insoluble riddles, and after him the Richest Man in the World with his entire consort of valets and serving people. Q expressed his surprise that someone so well-heeled was joining them in their humble subdivision, but the Richest Man in the World just said how glad he was to be there. Then he winked and announced his own special guest, upon which the door opened and the General appeared. Q stammered and blushed when he shook the General's hand, and he couldn't stop himself from asking after his daughter, but the General merely grasped Q's hand a little harder and moved on.

Now came his friends from the Casino. The Player, of course, who managed to get in one more anecdote about a mathematician as he passed, the Croupier, who tried to smile but seemed not to know how, and the Floor Manager, who still had a microphone on his lapel, though its signal now went nowhere. The Bellman also appeared, and this reminded Q of something, which he whispered in the boy's ear. "But I think she's already here," he replied.

Next came the Novelists, clothed now in stylish but comfortable linen, she winking her greeting and he nodding his head suggestively. Behind them Q saw the Captain of the freighter and his insolent crew. These Q refused admittance, blocking the door and threatening to notify the Policemen if they tried to enter.

The First Mate, however, drew Q aside and handed him a packet from under his coat. "I wonder if you would be interested in having these back," he said, winking slyly. Q examined the battered Tyvek™ wrapper which, he recalled, contained the various pieces of his Identity.

"But how?" he queried.

"I saw you jump," said the Mate, "and then the packet floated to the surface. I scooped it out with a net, thinking it might come in handy sometime. And indeed it did. In fact, I became you for awhile, used your papers and took on your life. And seeing things from your point of view like that... well, it gave me a new perspective, that's for sure. I have a new appreciation for your struggle. We're brothers, now, Q."

Q ended by letting them in, but only on the stipulation that the Mate keep his Identity and his papers, for the time being, and then dispose of them in some remote area of the ocean on his next voyage. He handed the packet back and showed them to the yard.

Last of all came the Singer and his motley tribe, arriving en masse on tall-bikes, skates and scooters. Several of these immediately set about building a bonfire, stoking it with lumber ripped from nearby houses, while the others set up a stage for the performance, and the Singer occupied himself tuning his strange instruments.

While they were setting up, the rest of the crowd mingled, talked, ate and drank happily. Q joined his Father, Mother and Sister in front of the stage. They lay on the grass and admired the pleasant weather, a jar of mead between them. The warm liquor went quickly to their heads as the moon rose over them in the still-daylit sky.

When the Singer finally climbed up on his soapbox to begin, the sun was setting behind him, and the first clear tongues of the flame were lapping up the sides of the bonfire. Everyone was ready. He struck the first chord and, after a short, stumbling introduction, began to sing, once again, in his ruined voice.

Garden of Sleep

This world's a sleepy place,
Everyone walking around logy
Shall we take advantage
Of their inattention?

Wake up Robber
It's time to tend your garden

And in your dreamed of dreams
Who'll be your Eve or your Adam?
Who walks the route with you
But disappears when you turn your head?

Wake up Lover
It's time to tend your garden

Odd finitude makes the stars to
Shine and unwind
Do you find your friends among them?
We'll be together soon

Wake up Aristocrat
It's time to tend your garden

People like to leave
A bit of sign in their wake
A little trail of bread-crumbs
For the sparrows to enjoy

Wake up Worker
It's time to tend your garden

These things you mind the least
Are the things you'll think of last
That's my Moral I think
That… and the kitchen sink

Wake up Reader
It's time to tend your garden

Tend your garden.

Little A

XIX

His Lady sad to see his sore constraint,
Cride out, Now now Sir knight, shew what ye bee,
Add faith unto your force, and be not faint:
Strangle her, else she sure will strangle thee.
That when he heard, in great perplexitie,
His gall did grate for griefe and high disdaine,
And knitting all his force got one hand free,
Wherewith he grypt her gorge with so great paine,
That soone to loose her wicked bands did her constraine.

XX

Therewith she spewd out of her filthy maw
A floud of poyson horrible and blacke,
Full of great lumpes of flesh and gobbets raw,
Which stunck so vildly, that it forst him slacke
His grasping hold, and from her turne him backe:
Her vomit full of bookes and papers was,
With loathly frogs and toades, which eyes did lacke,
And creeping sought way in the weedy gras:
Her filthy parbreake all the place defiled has.

—Edmund Spenser, *The Faerie Queene*

It's sad, the shipwreck of a civilization, it's sad to see its most beautiful minds sink without a trace—one begins to feel slightly ill at ease in life, and one ends up wanting to establish an Islamic republic. Ah well, let's just say it's *slightly sad*…

—Michel Houellebecq, *The Possibility of an Island*

A dying culture destroys everything it touches. Language is one of the first things to go.

—Jerry Rubin

ααα

The Crowd was restless, insistent, voicing its demand in rhythmic codes of clapping hands and stomping feet, vibrations of which penetrated even through the great deadening mass of concrete that was the Dome, even into the ostensibly sound-proof Green Room, causing the Turntablist to pace the room and work his tongue inside his mouth, hands twitching rapidly back and forth at his sides, as if practicing his Art accidentally, spinning in muscle memory. He wasn't nervous, he would have claimed, just limbering up. He never had stage fright even in front of the largest crowds, he maintained to himself, because his hands could never fail him so long as he let the Spirit guide. Problems only arose when he allowed Faith itelf to flag and attempted to control the performance with his conscious mind, counting beats and such.

To quiet this apprehension he did not feel, his habit was to think back to the moment of his conversion, that fateful Sunday morning so many years ago. He had attended the service at the Church of the Ostensible Jesus at the behest of a friend, and his blasé "Sure, why not?" had seemed anything but portentous at the time. He had come prepared to be bored, to sit in his pew and scribble on the Bulletin as he tried to stay awake through a monotonous sermon. But when he arrived he found, to his surprise, that there was no Bulletin, and there was no sermon. Why, there were not even pews, this venerable but painful seating tradition having given way to comfortable Theater Seating.

The service itself bore little resemblance to the Spartan affairs he had occasionally attended as a child; this one grabbed his attention from the very beginning. The lights dimmed until nothing lit the Great Hall but a projected image of Christ on the giant screen. Then a tympani roll began, low and quiet, as if rising from the primordial silence and darkness, and smoke began to rise around them. Suddenly, the air was pierced by lasers. One, two, and then

213

a thousand needle-thin colored beams coursed through the room, enmeshing the worshippers in a dense weave of light. Then the tympanis reached the apex of their crescendo and were joined by a fanfare of trumpets.

Then the Turntablist saw that the lasers were not moving randomly, but were projecting scenes from the Holy Book on the screens and walls and even the smoke above them. He saw Adam and Eve expelled from the Garden. He saw the parting of the seas. He saw the Pharoah's dream of the kine; he saw the thin ones eat the fat ones. He saw Jesus born in the manger. He saw the Good Samaritan, the money-lenders cast out of the Temple. He saw the walk in the garden, the Last Supper, and he saw the Christ crucified, blood from his wounds spreading through the room. And then he saw the stone rolled away, the Resurrection, Pronouncement and Ascension.

And then, as times mingled and the narrative flowed seamlessly from past to future, he saw John's Revelation, the Second Coming with all its attendant glories and horrors, the Believers swept up to Paradise as the Others writhed in the thousand agonies of Armageddon.

Yet all this was but prologue to what happened next, when the lights suddenly came up and the band on stage struck the first chords on their electric guitars. "Make a joyful noise unto the Lord," the Pastor proclaimed, as the infectious rock-'n'-roll beat brought the Congregation to its feet. Dancers moved to the front of the stage, clapping their hands over their heads, as the Singer began the first hymn, and Everyone, the Turntablist included, joined in. There was no need for hymnals, of course, as the Words were projected, karoake-style, on the screen behind the stage.

The rest, as they say, was History. He'd gone down to the front with a hundred others who heeded the call that morning. Hands were laid upon him. Through the ineffable spiritual draw of the music he came into the Church, though he did not know at the time that the current would pull the other way, too, that the Church would lead him into the music.

It was shortly after his conversion when Q appeared on the scene.

The Turntablist had been in the Congregation that day when the ragged, road-weary gutter-punk came forward and inspired everyone with his rhythmic tongues, and the genre of glossolalic rap was born. The Turntablist found in Q, at first, an image of utter fascination. This fetid ruffian was an irrepressible font of pure Spirit, with his words which did not describe but rather evoked the pulses behind the scenes of Everything. And so when the Call came out for musicians to support Q in his Traveling Ministry and on the album, *Rappin' in Tongues*, the Turntablist had gone to the Associate Pastor for Music and confessed that he felt himself being called to Turntablism, and that furthermore he had, from his misspent youth, some little knowledge of hip-hop.

Q and the Turntablist had gone on to do great work, taking their ministry not only across the Country but the World, converting tens of thousands from among the poor and struggling masses with their concerts in the Third World. But that had come to an abrupt end, he remembered, with the financial collapse of the Church. The Associate Pastor and the rest of the Group had been called back home, leaving Q to fend for himself in a remote and hostile land, ending his career and even his association with the Church.

And even though the Turntablist spent many a night, after that, tossing in his bed and worrying over his own (and indeed the Church's) role in Q's rude abandonment, there had been no time to be lost in such navel-gazing preoccupations, since all hands were needed to save the Church from Oblivion. Everyone was called on, day after day, to help raise funds to keep the massive organization afloat. And it was at this propitious moment that Little A appeared.

When the Turntablist thought back on it, he could not remember his first meeting with Little A. He could remember a time when there was no Little A, when he had never heard of Little A, and then there was a time when Little A was already a central part of his and the Church's life, but the time of first meeting and even the period of getting-to-know seemed lost in a lacuna in his mind, a sort of blind spot that, come to think of it, resembled the featureless image that seemed Little A's primary attribute, both in memory and in presence.

Such considerations of origin aside, there was no question that Little A was the savior of the Church. The phenomenal success of the Group under Little A's tutelage had first paid off the Church's Debt, then refilled its coffers and then overflowed them with financial bounty. The Church, now, was rich beyond anything It could have imagined in the past. Now, suddenly and with the direct assistance of Little A (and—if he might allow himself this little bit of pride— himself), the Church of the Ostensible Jesus was becoming the most powerful and far-reaching denomination on Earth.

$$\partial$$

The rest of the Group had all the appearance of calm or even boredom as they lay about playing with their smart phones and slouching in the armchairs of the well-appointed Green Room, but their suppressed tension was revealed by the fact that they all (except, of course, Little A) jumped when they heard the knock on the door. This harsh alarm was followed instantly by the door's opening to reveal the full figure of the Stage Manager, clipboard in hand, holding his cellphone to his side to address the room.

"Look," he said, "we are at five minutes. Hear that Crowd? Let's bring them to the Lord tonight." He went back out the door without bothering to close it.

After this interruption, the timbre of the room seemed to reverse itself, with all the formerly calm members of the Group suddenly rising and looking around and chattering nervously, and the Turntablist becoming still, quietly coming into Mountain Pose, inhaling, exhaling. The Linguist made a note in his notebook, then folded it, stood, placed it under his arm like a schoolbook and looked anxiously toward the door. Mirror and the other two dancers stood up, shaking hands and feet to get the blood flowing.

Now the A2 came to the door, dressed as if for combat, with his camouflage pants tucked neatly into his boots, long chains of keys and pliers and colored tapes and other tools of his trade dangling from hooks and zippers distributed about his person, so that he jangled when he walked, and he walked with a certain rhythm, giving him the air of a ritual dancer. The A2 was the one who did the last check of the stage and then came to the Green Room to announce it ready and lead the Group to the surface, and he always did this with a simple announcement. "Ladies, gentlemen, and the rest of you… would you follow me please?" Without another word he turned and walked off down the hall, and the Group came after, scrambling to keep up. The Dancers went first, then the Turntablist, then the Linguist, with Little A bringing up the rear, for this was the order in which they would take the stage.

They walked quickly through the basement, where dim bulbs and dripping pipes coursed the ceilings. The halls were lined with police and the army of workers employed to put the huge event together, but the Group kept their heads down and moved quickly, following the A2 with utter trust. Their way twisted circuitously through the under-structure of the Dome, past turn-offs and bifurcations and doors open and closed, and the Turntablist was amazed that the A2 had already memorized the complex path, when he had memorized another, just as complex, the night before.

They passed control rooms full of monitors and computer stations where the Police monitored the Crowd; a great kitchen where butchers in blood-splattered aprons chopped meat and prepared the food for the masses; rooms full of ducts and wiring where white-jacketed technicians monitored dials and gauges; and carpeted rooms where tuxedo'd Patrons sipped martinis, looking up curiously as the troupe passed.

Above them, the Crowd was speaking again, stomping its myriad feet and chanting in time. The chant was coherent and rhythmic at first but soon fell apart into the vocal equivalent of applause, a generalized rumble of desire and malcontent, from which gradually emerged another dominant tone and a new beat, rising from the background until it reached unison again, and again fell apart. The Turntablist felt the beat and felt his heart rate syncing to it as his hands spun automatically. The Dancers, too, were moving to the rhythm.

As they approached the surface the hallway widened and also became more populous. Cameras flashed and microphones were thrust in front of them as the gaggle of reporters fought with each other and the Police for a precious photo or quotation. A pair of groupies who had managed to sneak through the line dropped to their knees in front of the Turntablist and folded their hands in prayer, a gesture he'd seen many times, and he stepped around them without a second glance.

The Crowd's volume increased exponentially as they turned the last corner and ascended toward the entrance to the stage. The opening at the top of the stairs shone with rays of white light as they climbed in proper order. First the dancers, Black (they were named for their monochromatic body suits), then White, then Mirror in her signature chrome, disappeared into the light, and the sudden roar of the Crowd told the Turntablist that they were bounding across the stage with somersaults and pirouettes. He moved to the doorway in time to see the followspot picking up Mirror, despite her rapid flight, and the rays of blue and red and yellow light reflecting off of her perfect body, for the suit was designed, like a prism, to not only reflect the light but split it into spectra. This vision was so stunning it silenced the Crowd for a moment, as if taking its breath away, and in that silent moment the Turntablist stepped out into the light.

ааа

Q walked out the patio doors of his childhood home at the Provincial Oaks Commune and strolled among the gardens and along the irrigation canal, and with him the Chief Gardener and the soft spoken Singer.

"It's true we are unknown," said Q, "so will you take up auto racing? Then you will become known, or perhaps I should take up auto racing, or wrestling? Or perhaps I should become a politician,

218

which is to say a comedian?"

And one of the newcomers said, "I would put our defences in order."

And another one said, "If I were leader of a commune, I would put it in better order than this is."

And one of the older ones said, "I personally would prefer a small mountain hermitage, with natural order in the observances and suitable respect for the ritual."

And the Singer said, with his hand on the strings of his instrument, the low sounds continuing after his hand left the strings, and the sound went up like smoke, under the leaves, and he looked after the sound: "The old swimming hole, and the boys flopping off the planks, or sitting in the underbrush playing mandolins."

And Q smiled upon all of them equally. And one desired to know which had answered correctly.

And Q said, "They have all answered correctly, that is to say, each in his nature."

And Q raised his stick against the Philosopher, even though the Philosopher was his elder, for the Philosopher sat by the roadside pretending to be receiving wisdom. And Q said, "You old fool, snap out of it. Get up and do something useful."

And Q said, "Respect a child's faculties from the moment it inhales the clear air, but a man of fifty who knows nothing is worthy of no respect." And, "When the Leader has gathered around all the savants and artists, his riches will be fully employed."

And Q said, and wrote in the minutes: If we have not order within us we can not spread order about us; and if we have not order within us our Commune will not act with due order; and if the Leader has not order within, there will be no order without. And Q gave the words "order" and "deference" and said nothing of "life after death."

And he said, "Anyone can run to excesses; it is easy to shoot past the mark; it is hard to stand firm in the middle."

And they asked if a man commit murder, should his father protect him and hide him? And Q said he should hide him.

And Q said anyone could live with whom they wanted and that the prisons should be torn down by the politicians who built them.

And Q said, "My Mother ruled with moderation. In her day the Commune was well kept. And even I can remember a day when the historians left blanks in their writings—I mean, for things they didn't know—but that time seems to be passing."

And Q said, "Without character you will be unable to play on that instrument or to execute the music fit for the Codes. The blossoms of the apricot blow from the east to the west, and I have tried to keep them from falling."

ə

This bit of poetry signalling the end of the Master's Discourse, the crowd dispersed, some going down by the canal to meditate on what they had just heard, some back toward the House, and the rest on to various duties around the Commune. A few remained behind and sought a private word, and Q entertained their questions for a time under the Plane Tree on the canal bank, and then each of them went along to their respective chores, until only one remained.

"Q," this one said when they were finally alone, "you might not remember me." But Q did remember his old friend and embraced him with unfeigned affection.

"Of course I remember you," he said. "How could I forget my dear friend and Turntablist, fellow pioneer in the genre of Christian rap and the real reason—for surely it was not my own glossolalic gruntings—for the great success of my album, *Rappin' in Tongues*? Fellow traveler, who haunted the jungles of the Dark Continent with me to spread God's Word, only to be called back just as we were starting to do some Good, what a joy to see you and to see—by your dress and your healthy appearance—that you are thriving. But tell me, what brings you to Provincial Oaks? Surely your duties serving the Lord and Little A—yes, I've been following your career from afar—don't leave time for purely recreational travel. To what do I owe the pleasure of your company?"

Though the Turntablist strenuously objected that his affection for Q would be ample justification for an Odyssey of any length or complexity, in the end he did admit that he had come for a specific reason, or actually two specific reasons, one of which being to seek advice on an issue regarding Little A and the Group.

"Ah," said Q, "of course I am aware of the complex interactions of Group members and of the myriad delicate negotiations involved in keeping them all happy, productive and… together."

"Oh," said the Turntablist, in a halting voice, "though we have, of course, encountered our share of difficulties along those lines, what I wish to discuss with you if of a very different nature. Our shows, of late, they've been… well, it's hard to describe."

"Have they not been well-received?" asked Q. "For what I've been hearing is that the Group is enjoying unprecedented success, both financially and spiritually, that you are commanding larger and larger venues and receiving hordes of converts at every show."

"Oh, yes," said the Turntablist, "what you are hearing is certainly true. Since Little A came on board, the ranks of the faithful have steadily expanded, until now there doesn't seem to be a venue large enough to hold them. We're turning fans away from even the largest Domes these days."

"What a marvelous problem to have," said Q. "I look forward to the time when I can finally hear Little A and the group for myself. I wonder if you have brought a recording with you?"

"I regret to say that I have not," said the Turntablist, "and that the only way you will ever be able to hear Little A and the Group will be to attend one of our performances, for Little A insisted on a contractual stipulation that our work never be recorded."

Q furrowed his brow at this strange news. "How odd," he said, "that Little A would want such a stipulation, since recording is precisely what most performers desire."

"Strange, yes, strange," said the Turntablist. He was silent for a moment then, seemingly lost in contemplation of some distant vista. Suddenly he came back to himself. "But everything about Little

A is strange. That's why I'm here, Q, not for the big mysteries but for all the little strangenesses, all the minute oddities that, taken separately, seem like nothing at all but, taken together, form an overarching, almost overwhelming question."

"I see," said Q. "I see that the situation is more involved than I had imagined. Perhaps you'd better start from the beginning and tell me the entire story, leaving out not the smallest detail."

"Yes," replied the Turntablist, "perhaps I'd better start from the beginning. It will make for a long story, but that's what I'll do. I'll start from the beginning."

ꝗ

The Turntablist took a deep breath and closed his eyes as if to settle himself before a performance, then looked directly at Q and opened his mouth to begin. At this point, however, Q thought it best to interrupt, and did so, suggesting that they retire to the patio of the Main House where they could take some refreshment and be more comfortable during the telling of the Turntablist's story.

As they walked through the gardens toward the Main House they spoke of the weather and other matters unrelated to the business at hand. Many of the trainees were still walking the grounds, singly or in pairs, ruminating on the day's lesson or on the beauties of nature all around them. And Q saw his Mother among them, going from one to the next with her notebook and a small satchel.

When they reached the patio Q seated his friend at one of the pool-side tables and went inside to fetch drinks and something to nibble on. He returned with two glasses of raw cider, made from apples grown on the Commune, and a small plate of the local olives, both of which met with the Turntablist's unqualified approval. Q explained that one of the earliest pilgrims to the Commune had been a Spaniard who had shown them the techniques of brining olives and fermenting apples, as well as other tricks of Spanish cuisine, such as salting hams. "Well," said the Turntablist with a smile, "the recruits are worth something, then, aren't they?" to which they both chuckled knowingly.

After a few sips of the heady *sidra*, however, Q folded his hands together and sat back in his chair, signifying to the Turntablist that it was time to begin his story, which he prepared to do, sitting back in his own chair and putting his finger to his chin as he contemplated how to start. He looked up suddenly, as if the Word had just come to him, and opened his mouth to speak.

Just then, however, they were interrupted by Q's Father, who was coming out the patio door laden with his guitar and a clattering tangle of other instruments—tambourines and maracas, castanets, bongos and bells. The Turntablist leapt up to help but sat back down, somewhat offended, when the old fellow objected that he would have an easier time without his help than with it.

"Don't mind Dad," said Q to his ruffled friend. "The recent influx of pilgrims has upset his routine, and even though his only duty is the daily Music Circle, his mood is sometimes tenuous."

"Why, I haven't seen your Dad in some years," said the Turntablist, "but he doesn't appear to have aged a day, nor does his temper seem to have improved."

The two of them watched as he crossed the field in his *dhoti*. A cluster of pilgrims waited for him around the arbor, hungry to begin the Music. Q returned them to the matter at hand.

"But you were about to begin your story," he said. "Please do continue."

"Yes," said the Turntablist, "yes, let me begin." He paused and looked away as if searching, again, for the right word. "I have wanted to tell this story so many times," he went on, "but now I find myself at a loss, so to speak, tongue-tied, my thoughts a jumble, unable to…"

"Are you comfortable?" asked Q. "Perhaps another glass of *sidra*?"

"No, no, it isn't sustenance that I lack. What I need is… is… time, I think, time to think, to consider…"

Here they were interrupted yet again, this time by Q's Mother and Sister, who came out the patio door and walked up to the Turntablist.

"I don't believe I've collected your tuition," Q's Mother said.

The Turntablist stared at her uncomprehendingly for a moment, then leapt from his seat and began digging for his wallet before Q could calm him.

"Oh no, certainly not," said Q, rising also. "Mother, this is my Turntablist, an old and dear friend, not simply another pilgrim."

"Oh no, I insist," said the Turntablist, handing Q's Mother his card, which she took and prepared to swipe on her Smartphone. Q, however, reached out quickly and took it back from her, saying:

"Not a chance. Your money is no good here." He handed him back his card.

"But I'm happy to contribute, for the health of the Commune," the Turntablist said. "Please let me…"

But Q was adamant, and his Mother, after a moment's hesitation, also graciously relented. She then begged their pardon as she set off to catch the new recruits while they were still assembled. Q's Sister, however, remained behind to greet the Turntablist. She put out her hand and introduced herself.

"I know you," she said, "though you may not remember me." She emphasized this statement with a wink, to which the Turntablist responded by blushing. He shook her hand weakly. "You see I was at the Little A show last week at ________," she continued, "so I've seen you spin. You're… an extremely talented individual. That show was… Well, I can't even describe…."

The Turntablist mumbled a thank you, and Q was surprised to see his friend, who must have been well used to receiving such compliments, tongue-tied and embarrassed in front of his Sister. He stammered and blushed, and sweat beaded on his forehead as he tried, with no success, to reply.

"Well," said Q, "like many devoted artists, my friend and former collaborator doesn't take praise lightly. But say, Sis', I know you're anxious to rejoin our Mother to assist in the Collection, so don't let us keep you."

"Yes," she said, glancing at Q harshly, then turning back to the

Turntablist. "It was nice to meet you in the… flesh… so to speak. I hope we have opportunity to do so again."

"The pleasure is… um… mine…" the Turntablist managed to stammer as Q's Sister turned and followed her Mother across the field.

ə

"Why, I didn't know that my Sister had gone to a Little A show. She must have done it secretly," Q said, as he and the Turntablist reseated themselves on the patio. Q begged his friend, then, to pardon the interruptions and to please continue with his narrative. So the Turntablist again prepared to discourse his novel. Again he drew a deep breath, looked off into the distance, brought his finger to his chin. Again he opened his mouth to speak. And again he was silent.

"I'm sorry," said Q, hoping to break the strange ice that seemed to have settled over them. "The continuous non-sequitors and distractions of the Commune, and my own Family not least of all, have broken your concentration. But we're alone now and without danger of further intrusions. You're among friends, at any rate, so I hope that you can feel free of anxiety and be comfortable enough to speak."

"Oh no, please," said the Turntablist, "it has been a pleasure to meet your Mother and Sister and to see your Father again, and further to experience the workings of the Commune and indeed to commune with its members and initiates. These entertaining delectations have nothing to do with my difficulties in beginning my story. The difficulties stem, I have to say, from an internal reticence and no small degree of confusion on my own part, for while my memories of that night seem to remain within me with what I might call an overly-insistent clarity, yet I find the images unwilling to coalesce into words. For example, there were… or I should say there are… Well, perhaps I should… um…"

They sat for a moment in silence while the Turntablist's lips trembled in his effort to continue. They could hear, distantly, the tambourines and bells of the Music Circle coming from the arbor across the field, and finally, almost in desperation, the Turntablist looked in that direction and once again found his tongue.

"So they have a musical session each evening?" he asked with utter eloquence. And Q responded with like chit-chat, sensing now that his friend was so troubled by some memory that he was unable to put it into speech and the best way to get to the matter of this discourse would be by indirect means, waiting for details to surface in accidental and desultory remarks. Sometimes the best way to approach a Subject is to steer clear of it.

With this in mind Q attempted to make a fresh start by refilling their *sidra* glasses and suggesting that they take a stroll, in this pleasant hour of the evening, across the gardens in the direction of the arbor and the Music Circle. "Of course," Q apologized, "the music you will hear there will be primitive by your standards, and indeed by my own, but I am often uplifted by such direct communion with the Spirit—or Spirits—of the rhythm."

"Thank you for that qualification," said the Turntablist, "for as you know in my Faith there can be only one Spirit." He assented to the stroll, more, really, for the exercise than for the music, and they took up their glasses and began to walk in that direction. They walked through the maze of gardens; raised beds of cabbage, squash, tomatoes and various greens; long rows of corn, string beans and lentils; and wide fields of turnips and potatoes. Further on, the fruit orchards began, and it was at their threshold that the Music Circle was held, in a hollow naturally festooned with peach blossoms and grape vines.

As they drew closer, they began to hear the twanging of Q's Father's guitar behind the cacophony of percussion instruments in the hands of the recruits. The Circle opened for them when they arrived, almost as if they had been expected, and they saw the old man seated on the grass in the center. The percussion ceased as if on cue; he strummed one pregnant, introductory chord and, looking directly at them, began to sing.

> Spin, spin, spin,
> the world she is a'turning.
> Oh it's time to plow the earth again
> Though the city's still a'burning.

At this point some of the recruits rejoined the song with finger cymbals and bells, and the Circle began to slowly turn.

> Turn, turn, turn,
> the seasons pull up brusquely.
> Remember there'll be graves to dig
> if we treat our gardens roughly.

Now the tambourines and maracas faded in and began to crescendo, and the old man's voice rose also, becoming much stronger than his pitiful physique would suggest was possible, and the rhythm became more compelling as well, until everyone, Q and the Turntablist included, were turning in the Circle.

> Yes, spin, spin, spin;
> till like a child you're dizzy.
> It all goes by you in a blur
> and your memory's gotten fizzy.

Now the sticks and drums joined in, tempo and volume rising. Many of the recruits seemed to be in a trance.

> So burn, burn, burn,
> fires turn up in the gloaming.
> Turn earth again before the table's turned
> and again you're set to roaming.

Q and the Turntablist, Q's Mother and Sister and all the recruits danced clockwise around the ring as Q's Father flailed his guitar. The percussion rose in volume and speed until it reached a fever pitch, and then went beyond the beat into a frenzy.

The Turntablist, ecstatic in the dance, caught Q's ear in passing and yelled, "Your Father's gotten really good."

"Yes," said Q, "he's like a fire."

"How odd," the Turntablist responded. "I was just thinking that."

ა

As distracting as the Music Circle was, Q did not forget the matter at hand, which was discovering the inarticulate cry, the plot that lay dormant behind his old friend's silence. And so even as the music seemed to be reaching its peak, he leaned to the Turntablist and suggested with a nod that they quit the Circle, and they made their way through the crowd and started back across the fields.

"Now that, that was something," the Turntablist said, breathless, as the noise began to fade behind them. "So earthy and basic, primordial almost. If only we, with our truckloads of equipment, our enormous amplifiers and banks of samplers, with our road crew and dancers and laser show… if only we could capture something that pure, that irresistible, that wholesome…"

"Wholesome?" said Q, pricking up his ears.

"Yes," his friend replied, "out here among the gardens, under the arbor, among the apples plump and ready to harvest, the vines heavy with dangling grapes, how unlike… so very different from… from…"

"Yes…" Q said, trying not to appear too anxious. He restrained his curiosity and waited for his friend to finish, but he waited in vain. They walked back toward the house in silence, ellipses hanging between them like an expectation that was never to be met.

When they reached the back yard again, the Turntablist made to seat himself, again, at the patio table, but Q stopped him and insisted that their visit should end there, citing the lateness of the hour, the coming darkness, and the length of the drive his friend had in front of him. The Turntablist looked confused, even hurt, for a moment, but then assented to the wishes of his Host.

They walked around the house to the front, where the Turntablist's limousine sat idling at the curb. As soon as they came into view the chauffeur hopped out of the driver's seat and came around to open the door. Q was somewhat taken aback by this extravagant mode of transportation, and told his friend as much. "Of course you're right," he answered, "but Security has deemed this the only way safe way for me to travel. I guess I don't even think about it anymore."

"Ah," said Q, "I wasn't thinking in terms of security. Of course the Turntablist for Little A shouldn't be left to travel in a Toyota™ or a Nissan™, with no bullet protection or chauffuer who can double as a bodyguard."

"An unfortunate truth," agreed the Turntablist sadly. He stepped into the car and sat down. The Chauffeur closed the door and immediately the opaque black window lowered itself. Q leaned in and surveyed the luxurious interior, which was done in black leather and mahogany, noting, to his surprise, that the Turntablist was not alone. An attractive young woman was seated near the front, her feet drawn up beneath her, fingernail file in hand. "Q, may I present my Secretary." They shook hands through the window. "And Q," he went on, "to be sure you understand… any assistance you can give me in solving this… mystery… I would be eternally grateful. And if there is anything you need…" —he indicated with a sweep of his arm the limousine with its Secretary and Chauffeur—"…just ask. As Little A's Turntablist, I do have access to… certain resources. In fact, please take this."

"Of course, I am always at your service," Q replied, taking the Card the Turntablist put into his hand. As a gesture of trust in his friend, Q didn't even look at what he now held in his palm.

They said their good-byes, and the limo started to pull away. It had barely begun to move, though, when it abruptly stopped and the window came back down. The Turntablist leaned out the window. "Q," he said, "I almost forgot. At our last show, the one that I have been having such trouble speaking about…" Q leaned in… "Anyway, after the show a certain gentleman came down to the Green Room and was asking a lot of questions, about the show and about the Church and about our converts. I asked him who he was and why he wanted to know all this, and it turns out he's a Deprogrammer, on assignment."

"What?" cried Q. "Surely he did not think your followers in the Church of the Ostensible Jesus were members of a Cult? This is an outrage."

"Oh no, of course not," the Turntablist replied, "he wasn't inquiring after our present operations but our past ones. In fact, the greater part of his questioning concerned you. He wanted to know what you'd been doing since you left the Group, where you were, etc. I told him nothing, of course, but I believe that one of the others let something slip about Provincial Oaks. I think he may be coming here. So you may want to take more care in your credential checks for the new recruits, one of which, I assume, would be his target. And you wouldn't want him snooping around incognito."

"But…" was all that Q managed to say before the window raised itself and the car pulled away.

ᴣᴣᴣ

Esperanza Pilar Dolores Jerez Delacruz pressed the Pause button on her Dictaphone™ and stared at the blinking light on the interoffice phone. She didn't pick it up because she knew, as if it were blinking in code, what her Secretary was going to tell her. In her mind's eye she saw the Lobbyist sitting on the couch in front of her Secretary's desk, studying his fingernails. There would be a briefcase at his side, a briefcase that would not be leaving the office when he did.

She and the Governor had spoken about this Lobbyist over breakfast that morning. It was to be their first case of outright bribery, and it pained both of them to know that they had been maneuvered into a position which demanded this sort of overt action. *"Es un mal necesario,"* Santo said between bites of migas. "We can't continue our Work—and we both know how important the Work is—if we lose the Office, and we both know I won't be elected if that money goes to *Furhoncle's* campaign rather than ours."

"Furhoncle" was Santo's nickname, gleaned from an obscure book he had read in his youth, for their arch-enemy, the rabidly ambitious Speaker of the House. *Furhoncle* had stabbed Santo in the back early in his career, when the naive new Governor was still exhilarated from his first victory. The experienced and unscrupulous Speaker had smelled blood immediately when the diminutive Santo came before the House and had to be given a stool to stand on so that he could be seen over the podium, for Santo was only 4'9".

The Speaker had seized upon this fluke of nature and turned it into an ideological push-button. The Governor's own team had tried to spin his shortness back toward an endearing cuteness, rather like a munchkin governor, but realized quickly that this was not going to work and made a complete turn-around toward a tough, short-guy-syndrome, he'll-take-on-anyone image. But no matter what strategy they embraced it seemed to work to the Speaker's advantage, for the Speaker spun their "cute" campaign as weakness and the "tough" campaign as laughable, never missing a chance to slip in a crack about size. "Can our Governor see over the podium into the future?" he once remarked. "Perhaps size *does* matter." And he would pepper his comments with double entendres and subliminal emphases. "The Governor's job program has fallen *short*," he might say, or "To what should we attribute these budget *short*falls but the Governor's regressive economic policy?" Etc.

Which might go a long way toward explaining why, still over that self-same breakfast of *migas y huevos*, Espe argued that she should be allowed to keep the appointment with the Lobbyist that afternoon. "Espe, I don't want your hands dirtied with that money. It should be me," Santo countered. But she was not, to his and indeed to her own surprise, to be dissuaded.

"No, mi vida," she replied. "I think this situation calls for a señora's touch. You attend to your affairs of state, today, and I'll take care of our Lobbyist."

And yet—she mused from her chair behind the desk where the intercom light was still blinking—did this explain anything, or did it simply raise more questions? She shifted in her seat, uncomfortable in the new clothes she had purchased barely two hours ago. And why had she done that? She'd never set foot in such a shop before, yet this morning as she left for work she had driven straight there, then parked and walked in as if she'd done it a hundred times before. She had walked directly to the aisle, found what she was looking for, put it on in the dressing room, paid cash at the register for that and a small bag of accessories—in and out in 15 minutes. But now she shifted in her seat.

And then, of its own accord, her hand went out and picked up the handset. "Yes," she said into it. She heard what she knew she was going to hear. "Of course. Yes, send him in."

He came in, smiling warmly, briefcase in his left hand so that he could shake her hand with his right. "Oh, Miss Esperanza, what an unexpected pleasure."

She did not rise but shook his hand demurely over her desk. She motioned to the leather chair. "Well, the pleasure is all mine, I assure you," she said quietly.

"Of course," he went on as he settled into the chair, "Of course, I'm very happy to meet with you, but I had understood that this meeting was to be with the Governor."

"Yes," she said, "and the Governor has asked me to convey his regrets that he is otherwise occupied this afternoon and will not be able to join us. We have conferred concerning your and your client's situation, and I am authorized to negotiate with you."

He looked at his hands in his lap for a moment, then continued. "Well… it is a matter of some… um, delicacy."

"At the risk, then, of seeming indelicate," Esperanza went on haughtily, "may I examine the contents of your briefcase?"

Both of them were taken aback by the crude forwardness of this statement. The Lobbyist once again directed his attention to his hands in his lap while Esperanza sat staring at him with her best poker face, determined not to reveal her shock and embarrassment at her own words. After an awkward pause, he picked up the case without a word and then got up and placed it on the desk in front of her. She undid the brass buckles with a loud snap and opened it.

"How much is here?" she asked as she randomly checked some of the stacks.

"A quarter mil," he said softly.

"A quarter mil," she repeated calmly. "Two hundred and fifty thousand." Now her lip curled and rage hardened her face. "And what are we supposed to do with that? Hire bums to pass out handbills?"

"It's only the first traunch," he said. "There will be more."

"Yes, there will," she said decisively, "there will be many more."

"I can bring another tomorrow," he said, beginning to look concerned.

"And does your client wish us to look after his interests a quarter at a time also? Shall we dribble out the incentives in twenty-five cent increments? I hardly think so. We are on the verge of giving your client and yourself quite a windfall, and we expect a windfall, not wages, in return."

"Well, my client," he went on, "has sent this good-faith deposit, and is willing to send that much again, prior to any legislation being enacted. However, given the uncertainty of the situation, he has respectfully requested that final payment be forestalled until such time as the Act has passed on both floors." He looked at her, now, to emphasize the get-tough stance, but she noticed that his hands were trembling slightly. She reached down into her bottom drawer, took something out and put it on her desk, then she got up, walked around the desk and stood in front of him. He looked up at her with something like terror in his eyes.

"Take off your jacket and shirt," she said.

"Wha…?" he mumbled nervously.

"Take them off." And then, as if leading by example, she began to unbutton her own blazer. She took it off, revealing the leather corset underneath, then folded and lay the jacket neatly on her chair. She unzipped her skirt, dropped it to the floor and stepped out of it, then picked it up and placed it neatly on the chair also. Now she stood in heels and stockings, garters, g-string and cruel leather bustier. She picked up the cat o' nine tails from the desk and approached him. "Take them off," she repeated.

"Oh, Miss Esperanza," he whimpered, but began to comply. His hands were shaking violently, and he began to cry. "I'm sorry," he said. "I'll bring all of it next time. I'm sorry."

His skin was pasty white under his shirt, and his jelly roll, formerly obscured by the jacket, hung over his belt. He was weeping outright now. "Get on your knees," she said.

He slumped onto the floor and pitched forward, grabbing her feet and kissing them, all the while blubbering apologies and pleas for mercy.

"You're getting tears and snot on my pumps, you snivelling pig," she said. "How dare you touch me." She punctuated this with a lash from the whip, leaving nine light-red welts across his back. Then she drew it back and lashed him again, and then again, and again. "You come in here and insult me with this chump change, and then you blubber all over my shoes. Look at you, crawling on the floor like a little baby, like a little baby pig, a squealing little pink baby pig."

At this he grunted and whimpered and gasped the more, his obsequious tone still connoting apology but without actual words, as if language itself were being whipped out of him. Espe stepped back and let the cat o' nine tails rest. She put one shapely foot on her desk, then took one of the hundred-dollar bills from the briefcase and wiped her nether regions with it. She threw it in front of him. "Take this back to your Clients," she said, "—after you've licked it clean, of course—and tell them we can't remember their names.

Tell them their briefcase was so small I lost it among the papers on my desk, but they'll be receiving a nice photo of Santo and myself for their contribution." She sat on her desk, crossed her legs and lit a cigarette as he cowed below her. Despite his quivering condition, he managed to crawl forward a few inches to put his face on the bill. "Now stop your blubbering, get dressed and go out there and get me the rest of my money."

"Yes, ma'am," he sputtered.

She punched a button on the interoffice phone, told her secretary to have her carpet vacuumed as soon as the Lobbyist left, then hung up, picked up her skirt, blazer and briefcase and left the office via her dressing room door at the rear. She deposited the contents of the briefcase in her safe, then caught sight of herself in the mirror. She couldn't help striking a haughty pose in her new costume. She watched her face change its look of curiosity and concern for a leering grin. "Who are you?" she said to her Reflection.

"Who are *you*?" her Reflection said to her.

She went to the dresser and took out a bra and panties. Then she took off the corset and hung it in the closet with her office collection of business suits and evening wear.

ⱥⱥⱥ

Lucy stepped out onto the terrace and closed the triple-insulated, Large Missile Impact rated glass door behind her, instantly converting the World's Most Boring Party into a refreshingly mute pantomime. Through the glass partition her Father's living room looked like the showroom at Viver hosting a reception for a group of Generals and Admirals, peopled as it was by slender mannequins in evening gowns and men in formal military regalia, with stars on their shoulders speaking their rank and the bars on their chests telling their histories in the strange semaphore. There also were, among the crowd, certain men in civilian garb, who, despite their apparent lack of rank, seemed to speak and move with an air of authority.

On the marble table outside was a jade box from which Lucy took an unfiltered Galoise. She lit it with the small propane torch left there for that purpose, then leaned on the railing and looked down toward the street 870 feet (265 meters) below. The mêlée of traffic and lights down there evidenced itself to her as a faint glow, with only the occasional siren making itself heard.

As she picked up the cigarette and lit it, viewed from her left profile, she was stunningly beautiful, her natural grace and perfect Aryan features accentuated by the elegant coif, tasteful jewelry and simple dress by Elie Saab. But as she turned to the railing she let the cigarette dangle from her lip and curled the corner of her mouth downward, so that, leaning on her elbows and lifting her foot to the bottom rail, she looked rather like a longshoreman in an evening gown.

The lights of the city dotted the space around her, blending seamlessly with the stars. The skin of this building she and her family had called home for the past few months, a warped surface of polished steel, reflected the light in geometric arcs and streams, like a funhouse mirror. This had been the intention of the Famous Architect who designed the place.

The irritating noise of the party guests' facile speech found her again, briefly, when the door opened and closed behind her. She didn't turn around but stood motionless as her Father came and stood beside her. The brass buttons on the cuffs of his uniform clinked lightly as he leaned onto the chromium rail, standing now beside his daughter in identical attitude. They stood without looking at each other for a few moments, parallel gazes into the void, before he broke the silence.

"Our guests are beginning to leave," he said into the night, "you should be near the door to say good-by with your mother and myself."

"There are so many to say good-by to," she said. "Couldn't I just wave from out here?" She took the cigarette from her mouth and spat a grain of tobacco into the abyss. "I believe they would consider it a 'delightful informality,' as opposed to me acting as your puppet."

He sighed. "You don't yet know the meaning of 'puppet.' In that room behind us, among those Officers and their Wives, each star on each epaulet guides the fate of millions. As they blather over their gin, they pronounce the destiny of the planet, indeed, the solar system. They are like gods and this place Olympus."

She giggled. "Gods are they? It seems to me they are but vessels for the power that is deployed through them. If someone were to do me the favor of machine-gunning the entire bunch of them, it would cause not the slightest stutter in the corporate war-machine they dream they control. Each star that is added to a shoulder, each medal pinned to a breast, decreases the importance of the body beneath, making it ever more subservient to the signs that cover it. A medal is a brand identifier, like the tag on a shirt or the owner's name on a dog's collar."

"You are young and brash. You will come, eventually, to respect this world that created you and that now supports and nurtures you."

By way of response she bent down and pulled off her Jimmy Choo jeweled pumps. "These things are giving me blisters," she said. She tossed the shoes casually over the side, and they both watched as they careened toward the street, bouncing off the side of the building, their faceted surfaces occasionally catching the light, until they disappeared into the general city.

"One day," he said, "you will learn what such things are worth. One's symbols are not shed so lightly but persist and return, even as you return, to me, no matter how many times you leave."

"I know," she said, "that it is not possible for you to imagine a world that does not repeat the patterns you learned in your childhood. If your obsessions were not so oppressive to me—and to the entire World—I might pity you. But even if I am bound to you by blood and money, even if I must return again and again, I must also leave, again and again, to breathe, if only for a moment, an air that is not permeated by your ambition." She spat once more into the night and flicked her cigarette after, then turned and walked back to the door. She glanced back, briefly, at her Father, then opened the door and reentered the crowd.

He watched as she was assimilated, moving through the crush with easy grace, politely accepting a peck on the cheek or laughing naughtily at something whispered in her ear.

While she appeared to be wandering aimlessly through the crowd, she was in fact taking the shortest route to her room, and when she got to the door she slipped inside and closed it without ceremony or adieu. A couple was rutting and grunting on her bed, the Officer's jacket draped over the footboard and a sequined gown on the floor, but she gave them scarcely a glance as she disappeared into her dressing room. She emerged dressed in grimy fatigues, boots, and a torn t-shirt. Then she left the apartment via the back elevator.

In the lobby she paused and opened her handbag. She took out a small wad of cash and put it in her pocket, then dropped the bag, with its contents of credit cards, licenses and passport, into the trash and left the building. She turned toward the subway station and walked quickly through the street, muttering to herself. "Q," she whispered. "I think you are there, and I'm coming."

aaa

At that precise moment, a thousand miles away, Q woke out of a deep but troubled slumber and rose from his bed. He opened the window and stood looking over Provincial Oaks, the idyllic subdivision he and his Mother and Father had turned into an off-grid paradise, harmonious and beautiful, where each contributed according to ability and received according to need. As he looked out over the crops, lit only by the Harvest Moon, a gust of wind struck, sending ripples across the acres of corn and barley.

He remembered, suddenly, that he had been dreaming, that it was the dream, in fact, that had roused him. But just as he realized the source of his wakefulness, however, he felt it slipping away, and he attempted to concentrate and remember, moving his lips to the whispered narrative. He began to set his memory to words and felt the broad expanse of the dream contracting, the panorama of sensation and emotion dissipating into the single thread of a sentence.

He was walking across a vast desert at night. The moon cast an eerie glow, and the sand blew around his feet and up and down the dunes in snake-like patterns. Somehow the Turntablist was with him, though invisible, as if he were just behind, over his shoulder, telling the story as it unfolded.

"Don't listen, Q, don't listen," he said, "to the soft susurration of the sand. Think outside the sound, look away, lest the shadow steal over you like a great sigh. Don't listen. Don't think."

With the dream thus crystallized into this single image and single phrase, Q filed it, unanalyzed, in memory and proceeded with his awakening, lifting his head with a burgeoning sense of purpose. He knew that something was to be done, and he knew that he was about to do it, but he didn't yet know exactly what it was.

He found himself dressing in his field clothes and heading out to the crops before the sun had even come over the horizon. He labored for several hours, checking and re-setting the irrigation weirs, clearing the troughs and checking for signs of insects and worms. He spoke briefly to the Field Foreman, letting her know by implication and innuendo that he would be leaving and would be gone for some time. She leaned dully on her hoe as the news gradually dawned on her. Then Q looked out to the fields one last time and headed back to the house.

He worked steadily all afternoon putting his things in order, giving instructions to his Family on how to handle the chores he normally took care of. There were chickens to be fed, eggs to be collected and goats to be milked. Q's Father nodded happily and strummed his guitar the harder when Q gave him his assignments. His Mother was sure his Sister would take care of everything, and his Sister just smiled and nodded when he told her.

Finally, as dusk was approaching, Q went into his room and closed the door. He emptied his pockets onto the dresser then set about dressing for the road. In a corner of his closet lay, in a heap, his boots and overcoat, and he put them on for the first time since he had come back to Provincial Oaks, so many years ago. He took the case off of his pillow and put a few meager provisions in it, then tied it to his walking stick.

He went to the dresser and picked through the detritus from his pockets, taking the little bit of cash and coin that was there and sweeping the rest into the drawer. As he was about to turn away, though, something in the pile caught his eye. It was a Card, a simple card like any other, nondescript, and yet so nondescript as to be striking, dark gray, utterly uniform, the entire card being the same color as the magnetic strip on the back, and on the front, where one would expect to see an account number, only this, in raised text:

LITTLE A

Q ran his thumb over the letters as if they were braille. Then he opened his coat and felt inside until he found a small slit in the lining. Here he stowed the card and sewed it in securely with the needle and thread from his travel kit. He threw his bag over his shoulder and went downstairs.

His Father was playing guitar in the Living Room for his Mother and Sister and a few of the Recruits. There was a new one there, one that Q didn't recognize, dressed somewhat better than the rest; his shoes were especially fine, well-polished oxfords. Q stood in the door for a moment, but no one looked up, and he elected to make his exit without disturbing them.

He went out the door and turned toward the subdivision gate. The ruined hulks of the houses that had once made Provincial Oaks so desirable and were now used for nothing but stables and firewood, loomed in the shadows on either side of him. Q passed by them without nostalgia, though, and he was glad when he was out the gate and his boots on the road again.

a

He didn't travel far that night, going only as far as the railyard. He climbed up into the superstructure of the overpass where there was a level perch he was familiar with, and he made his bed there that night. From here he had a clear view of the entire yard, and he lay there looking out all that night while the trains moved forward and back.

And all the next day he lazed there, and all the next night, and the next, but on the third morning, when he opened his eyes after falling asleep momentarily, she was there, standing at the end of the dock, looking down into the weeds. When he joined her he saw what had drawn her eye: a heap of bent and rusted bicycle parts, frames and handlebars and wheels, with other rubbish thrown in, including a crushed, acid-eaten drum and an oil-soaked canvas tarp. It was, albeit much the worse for the years that had intervened, the setting of their first meeting.

"Must we always begin here?" she said without looking at him, "Must we always replicate the past?"

"I don't understand," he said. "I came because… because there is something I have to find out, something I have to get to the bottom of. And because, somehow, I knew you would be here."

She grunted in response, and then they stood silent. Q put his hand on her shoulder, but she turned away from him. "Look," she said, "we can catch the west-bound now if we hurry."

They were lucky and found an open boxcar as the train eased out of the yard. They left the door open for the breeze and sat back in the shadows as they moved through the city's industrial back side, but when they reached the outskirts they moved into the doorway, dangling their legs and breathing the mild country air. All day they rode thus, and the nation passed before, pine forests and trestles, bluffs and valleys and muddy rivers.

That night the temperature dropped, and they huddled together for warmth, but this, to Q's chagrin, proved to be the limit of their intimacy. Even as well as he knew her, and much as he had longed, these past years, to be with her again, Q now found himself reverting into a flustered, stammering teen-ager in Lucy's presence. He tried, in a voice quaking with emotion, to ask her what was wrong, but she rebuffed him. "Nothing. Don't worry about it," she said, turning away. "I've been living too long with my Father. I need time to decompress."

ƨ

By the third day they had exhausted their provisions, and their bones ached from the hard boxcar floor, so they decided to de-board. When the train slowed for a curve they were able to jump off without injury and continue their way on foot, grateful for the exercise and for relief from the incessant rocking and noise of the car.

They began to forage along the highway that ran adjacent to the track, and they soon began to find bits of road manna—scraps of burgers, bags yet a quarter full of stale chips, half-eaten bagels, etc.—which they were able to wrest from the crows. But Q soon discovered that his years at the Commune, during which he had eaten only the most wholesome, home-grown fayre, had ruined him for this humble aliment, glad as he would have been to have it in leaner times. Lucy, too, had fallen quite out of the habit of dumpster-diving while living with the General these past years. And so, as they looked down the road and saw the smoke of an urban center rising in the distance, they elected to try the other direction, heading cross-country into a valley below, where they could see what appeared to be large fields covered with crops.

They walked through weeds and brush until they came to the edge of a vast cornfield, the healthy green plants, ripe and remarkably uniform, arranged neatly in rows which stretched as far as the eye could see. They entered the field and harvested a few of the ripe ears but then had to run for their lives when an irrigation robot suddenly appeared over them. They dodged the enormous wheels and ran to the center of the span where they were drenched with the spray but otherwise unharmed, then ran out of the field once the irrigator had passed.

They skirted the edge of the planted ground until the cornfield ended and soybeans began. The thought of some fresh edamame made Q's mouth water, so, warily this time, he ventured among the vines long enough to gather a double handful of bean pods. Then, with a sumptuous supper now assured, they quit the fields and went off in search of a suitable spot to build a fire and camp for the night.

They found it in a stand of trees, beneath the wide canopy of an oak, beside a small stream which ran plashing over moss-covered rocks. Here Q set about building a fire while Lucy fashioned their blanket into a lean-to. Once the fire was tindered and stoked, Q took the unshucked ears of corn down to the water and dipped them in, holding them under to soak through, then lay them beside the fire to steam in their husks. Then he put some water in his camping pan, added the edamame pods and set them to steam.

Lucy now suggested, since they were already wet from the cornfield, and since they had a convenient source of clean water, that they do their laundry now, as well as bathing themselves. Q assented, trying his best not to appear too eager, and they went down to the stream-side and stripped off their clothes. They washed their bodies and their clothing with their backs to each other, each stealing a peek now and then, but when they went back to the fire to hang the clothes and dry themselves, Q's impatience was revealed in all its glory.

"Happy to see me, are you Q?" Lucy quipped. Q blushed and stammered. "Oh, let me see," she went on, holding up a pair of her dainties, "where can I hang these? Oh… I see the perfect place." And she hung them on Q's outcropping.

"Lucy…" he said, blushing the more, and he removed her panties from himself and hung them on a limb near the rest of their clothes.

"What!" she exclaimed, "you can't even hold up these light little things? Well I think it's time we got you in shape. I have some exercises I can show you."

And so there under the spreading oak, beside the murmuring stream, they were at last reunited, enacting and confessing their love over and over again. After a time a popping sound was heard. This was the corn drying out and beginning to burn. And later there came a violent hissing as the water in the edamame pot boiled away.

ᘔ

Q awoke famished—and yet rejuvenated—the next morning. He eased himself from the blanket where he had slept, entwined with his love, when exhaustion had finally stilled them both, and set about rebuilding the fire. The charred remains of the corn and edamame he simply added to the kindling, realizing as he did so that his first order of business would have to be harvesting some breakfast.

He had noticed, as they were making camp, an Apple tree nearby, and he went there now and picked two ripe and perfect fruit from a low-hanging limb. He brought them back to the lean-to and handed one to Lucy, who was just beginning to stir. She too was ravenous and devoured it without a word, tossing the core toward the fire when she was done.

Q, having finished his also, stepped, still naked, discreetly behind the tree to relieve himself. He stood looking out toward the sunrise, musing happily on the previous night's adventures, when a little movement in the air caught his eye. At first he thought it was a bird of some sort but as he brought it into focus began to comprehend that it was in fact a Drone, hovering about twenty feet above the ground a short distance away. When he listened he could hear the soft purling of the four rotors, and he could see the leaves kicking up below it, and then he saw the glint of its camera eye aimed toward him. While Q was watching it, however, seemingly in response to his attention, it repositioned itself directly between Q and the Sun, so that Q had to avert his eyes. He moved to one side and shaded his eyes with his hand, but this enabled him only to catch the briefest glimpse of the thing as it moved back into the Sun.

244

Suddenly conscious of his nakedness, Q went back to the lean-to and slipped on his clothes, apprising Lucy of the surveillance as he did so. She held the blanket in front of her and dressed hurriedly, with an occasional furtive glance toward the Sun, and they both commented, then, that however unabashed they were in the society of humans, however accustomed they were to living in close proximity to Others and all the daily familiarity such a life might entail, here under the unblinking eye of a machine they knew that they were naked.

Now the Drone came closer, and Q and Lucy hid themselves behind the tree. "Where are you?" the Drone said.

And Q said, "We were afraid, because we were naked; and we hid ourselves."

And the Drone said, "Who cares if you're naked? You're camping on private property."

And Q said, "I'm sorry. I had thought to camp here with my woman, and she liked the spot."

And the Drone said to Lucy, "You like the spot, do you? And your friend, the serpent, likes your spot too." They both blushed at such crude talk. "Let's hope you're not pregnant; that would be no fun. And remember, you pass your debts on to your Children. Pray that they can pick fast enough to stay ahead of the interest. Thus you may eat of the fruits of this ground until you return unto it."

"Lucy," Q said, at a loss for words. Then he said to the Drone, "I'm a farmer myself, you know."

"Then get out of here," said the Drone, "and go till your own earth. Don't come back. I don't like competition. At this gate where you stand will be an electric fence tomorrow."

And so Q and Lucy put on their rags, picked up their few possessions and set off once again.

They went back to the tracks and were able to get themselves into a boxcar very like the one that had brought them. They found a tarp which they spread out to make a bed, and they lay down with the intention of getting some of the rest that their night of passion had robbed them of, for they were famished and exhausted.

And yet not completely, as after only a couple of hours of sleep Q found himself slipping closer to his love under the tarpaulin, and she to him, and they quickly found themselves indulging in the same excess that had worn them out the night before. Now, however, Q was distracted by a movement in the shadows; it was another person in the car. Q stopped and sat upright as Lucy moaned disapproval.

"Who's there?" Q said into the darkness.

"Oh, thank you. I can't thank you enough," came the reply. A diminutive figure came forward from the shadows.

"Thank you for what?" Q said.

"For that…" he raised his nose… "that smell. It's been a long time since I smelled that smell."

"Is that right?" said Lucy, lifting herself to one elbow, gazing unabashedly at the Stranger, whom she quickly recognized was not. "Q," she went on, "you remember our friend, the Troll?"

And of course Q did remember the Troll, one of the gurus of his early years, who had lived under a certain bridge for a certain period of time and had became a kind of gatekeeper between the realms of the Haves and the Have-nots, and the stories of his encounters with denizens of both sides were legion.

"In fact," the Troll went on, ignoring Lucy's question, "the last time I smelled that smell was in a car very like this one, on a tarp very much like that one, and the smell very much like… well…"— he looked at the floor, at his feet, then up at Lucy—"…like you."

"But tell me this," Q said, as oblivious to his interlocutor's discourse as the listener to his, "how have you come to leave the bridge that is your home? What a marvelous mansion it was! I cannot imagine that bridge without you, nor you without it. Look, you still walk stooped over, though the ceiling here towers above you."

"Yes," the Troll replied, "and I'll stay down here, if it's all right with you; it makes it easier to duck, should some random thing come flying at me."

Lucy sat up without bothering to keep the tarp around her and lit a cigarette. "You've changed, Troll," she said. "Something has happened. Tell us. Tell us what has happened."

ɔ

The Troll looked at her for a moment with his head atilt, then settled himself cross-legged on the floor. The car rocked gently on the aging tracks as the train began to pick up speed over the karst. He looked out the door at the dim landscape passing in the dusk. "Coming into desert soon," he said.

He paused for a long moment, staring into space, until Q began to fidget with impatience. And Q was about to complain until he remembered that the Troll was under no real compulsion to speak, that he was merely responding, politely, to Lucy's question, and had no obligation to entertain his audience. So Q kept silent, and in the end this proved prudent, as the Troll soon looked back at them and began his story in earnest.

"Ugh, how long has it been?" he said, slumping in resignation. "The years take their toll, even on Trolls. Ah, we didn't know how good we had it, how easy everything was then. I had my mansion under the bridge, you" —he nodded toward Lucy—"were on the rails with the tall-bikers, and you" —he looked at Q—"were just coming down from the surface to join us.

"Ah, you were a quick study, Q. The very first night, at your very first party on the rails, in a car just like this one, on a tarp just like this one, you bedded the one, this one, whom everyone else had been wanting." Q blushed at the Troll's guileless and disinterested familiarity. "That was the last time I smelled that smell. And tonight again, and that puts me in a mind…. It makes me wonder…."

He trailed off again but quickly recovered himself.

"In those days," he went on, "I was a go-between, a guardian at the gate. Just as I helped you, Q, to step down from the streets to the rails, I assisted many an Other. They would come to me in such states of worry and/or fatigue. Just like you, they collapsed at my threshold.

"What I did for them was nothing extraordinary, unless simply listening and being patient are extraordinary; I sat by them and waited while they regained consciousness, then pointed the way down the track. There was nothing heroic in it, but there was nothing cowardly or dishonest in it either. Not many people realize what a saintly thing it is to listen. It isn't just paying attention to the Other, it is also suppressing your own story, not allowing it to circulate into the culture where it may vie with the rest of them. Thus you are relegated to a permanent unfashionability, which results finally in invisibility. Such is the cost of one's true attention.

"Perhaps all this is but a human's usual share of bitterness, a 'normal life,' so to speak. And perhaps I was even, at the moment in question, relatively content, placid in my place, with my hard-packed and dry dirt floor, my cardboard walls to protect me from the wind, and my fire pit in the winter. Who knows what I was feeling, for I never spoke."

Now Q sat up; something had been bothering him about the Troll, and he now realized it was, indeed, that the Troll was speaking. He had never before heard him speak more than a couple of words at a time.

"But there came a time," he went on quickly, as if sensing Q's epiphany and making sure he did not have to stop his own story to hear it related, "when things began to slow down. I don't know what I was feeling then any more than the time before, but I do know that we all gradually succumbed to a torpor. For one thing, business started to die down. For a while there I was seeing two or three of you newbies per day, but something began to happen, up top, and then it was one per day, and then two per week, and then one every two weeks.

"I would sit under my bridge and watch the pigeons and bats come and go for days at a time, reviving only briefly when someone new stumbled down the slope. Then they quit coming altogether. I lay on my blanket and watched an ant crawl along a stick near my pillow. A mouse came into view, stopping to sniff my fingers. A beetle was crawling up my sleeve. I had reached my nadir. My mind hung by a grass blade.

"Then something encroached on my vision, settling down right in front of me and blocking my view of everything else. It was a foot. A bare and filthy foot, of indeterminate race and gender, but obviously a foot of some distinction, rail-hardened, tough as leather, adapted to its environment, of the same dust it stood in.

"I stared at that foot a long time before I comprehended its meaning, its natural implication of a ragged knee above, and then some thighs and hips, covered with rags, and then a torso, clothed or no, arms, and finally, *pièce de résistance*, pinnacle of the body, the face, smiling or sneering, grinning or smug, eyes alight or half-closed, hanging over me like the moon over a lake, staring down.

"And so I looked up.

"And it was just what's-his-name. You remember him. Just a kid. A good kid. Nothing special, but a good kid. You remember. His name started with K. Anyway it doesn't matter who exactly he was, just that someone was there, and that someone wanted something new of me.

"'I need to ask you something,' he said to me. I just stared up at him. It would be a while before I found my voice. 'I hear there's something called an Employment Office. How does that work?'

"So I told him how the system works, how one can be remunerated for living in obeisance on the surface. He mulled the information over for some time, pacing back and forth in my Great Room. Once or twice he climbed up the railing and peeked over at the racing traffic and hurly-burly of the city. Finally he came back and told me:

"'I want to try. I want to try it on top. I know I'll be living in domination up there, but I've been living in domination down here. I get nothing here but seconds and thirds. I was in love with one of the girls, and I thought she liked me too. Then some new guy swaggers in, drinks some moonshine and dances a bit, and next thing you know he's banging her in the boxcar. And it wasn't any quickie, either. I had to listen to them (we all slept in the one car) going at it day and night for a week. Then I wake up one morning and they're gone. So now I'm ready to go. I'm going topside again.'

"I tried to dissuade him, of course. In fact, I used all my powers to steer him back home. I didn't oppose him directly but began by agreeing with him, in order to gain his confidence. With the ostensible purpose of gaining background so as better to advise him, I asked him simple questions, all with very obvious or even innocuous answers, but which, taken together, in sequence, had the logical consequence of causing him to question the efficacy of the entire endeavor.

"Still, despite the subtle insidiousness of my strategy, which had brought him to the point of questioning himself, indeed of arguing with himself, he refused to heed his own cautions and remained adamant in his decision to quit the rails. 'I'll be back in a bit and let you all know where I get to,' he said. And I just said OK, good luck.

"He was the first. He was the beginning of the contra-flow. A few days later another came, and then the next week another, and then there was one a day, and then two per day. And then the yard dried up. The Tall Bikes lay rusting in the weeds. The straw beds in the boxcar lay empty. All alone I lay, and I who had been the hermit, the patiently waiting one, began to realize that even the infrequent human contact I had while living in my reclusive mansion under the bridge was something, and necessary for my continued survival. In short, I was lonely.

"And so I left my home of so many years and set out on the long road that has brought me here. There were certain detours along the way, of course…. Certain decisions were made…."

Here, despite the pregnancy of the pause, the Troll ceased speaking
and turned away from them. He seated himself in the doorway with
his short legs dangling over the side. A three-quarter moon was
rising and cast his gnarled figure in stark silhouette. His hair, woven
into dreadlocks some many years previous, stood around him like
an illustrator's scribble, with the occasional star shining through
it. Q watched him thus framed by the Universe as Lucy drifted off
and he felt his own eyes getting heavy. They would remember the
Troll in this somewhat mystical pose for some time thereafter, for
when they awoke the next morning he was gone.

ааа

Espe pulled the Lexus™ over to the curb and stopped. She was
driving, talking on the phone and battling the clear, plastic-
like but ostensibly biodegradable wrapper on a pack of American
Spirits™ at once, and something had to go, so she chose the Driving.
Phone gripped tightly between shoulder and ear, she put the SUV
in park and set both her hands against the ridiculously well-sealed
Nicotine Delivery System. During a particularly heated moment in
her conversation, she managed to get a purchase with one perfectly
manicured nail, then ripped violently and threw the wrapper on the
floor. She took out a cigarette and put it in her mouth. It bobbed
and dangled as she attempted to light it and yell at her secretary at
the same time.

And what, exactly, was she doing here? How had it come to this?
She felt like one of those neurotic bimbos in a Woody Allen™
movie. It seemed that every day she was less and less in control,
closer and closer to the edge of something, though she was unsure
what that something was. Sometimes she got lost, the familiar street
she was driving down suddenly becoming unfamiliar. She forgot
things. She forgot the words for things, and she forgot what things
her words stood for. Sometimes it seemed the words were just
bouncing around in her head like the dead seeds inside a maraca,

sounding, one had to admit, with a certain rhythm, yet signifying nothing, standing for nothing.

She stared at the Dashboard while the incessant litany of schedule conflicts continued in her ear. The screen scrolled inanely through rear views, safety advice, routing suggestions, and complex graphs of engine performance. Occasionally the Dashboard, too, spoke to her, adding news of vehicles passing on the left or pedestrians on the curb ahead to the information her secretary was imparting.

Somehow through the noise a memory of her childhood came to her, and her face softened. Who would have ever thought that this cute little *campesina* would one day be a Governor's wife, and with a political career of her own, someone whose favor was courted by the most powerful politicians in the State, someone who could call in six-figure favors with a three-minute phone call. She who had worn unbleached cotton to her *Quinceañera* now had designers sending her clothes. Why, she didn't even think in her own language any more.

But yet (and she thought this even in the utter confusion of the moment, with her Secretary, her Cigarette, her Car, and her Memories of Childhood all vying for her attention) in what sense was that original language her "own"? In what way, really, did she possess it, now or even then? Granted, it was given, gifted, in a way, to her in early childhood, almost at birth, and yet so was her pacifier, her binky, and so were her toys and rattles. So was the tricycle that now lay rusting in a ditch somewhere. Her heart sank as she thought about that Trike that she had loved and prized for a fleeting moment, and then sank again when it occurred to her that all this that presently surrounded her, her shiny new Lexus™ and her shiny new Language, would one day be abandoned just like that Trike.

She finished with her Secretary, dropped the phone in the passenger seat and pulled back into traffic. Her Constituents crowded in around her, lost in their rush-hour rituals, phones in their ears, cigarettes hanging from their mouths, slapping their steering wheels when some inconsiderate fellow citizen cut them off. At least, behind her smoked glass, Espe felt safe from their prying, hungry eyes.

The Robot that guarded the rear gate to the Capitol raised its arm obsequiously when she approached. She drove up the ramp to the fifth level and pulled into her place, then gathered her briefcase and her phone. She pushed the button to open the rear gate and got out. Leaning in to the back, she lifted the tire cover, and then the spare itself, revealing a small box marked only with a barcode. This she took in with her.

Inside that box were a few accoutrements to add to her growing collection. She thought of Santo and how he might react if he learned the contents of this box and of the locked drawer in her dressing room. She knew that his tough politician facade would fall away in a single breath, that he would whimper and cry and be utterly crushed, for he prized his Espe more even than his Office. Though a sad look softened her face for a moment, she only held tighter to the box and the secret it contained, for if truth be told she hated feeling pity for her husband. In a way she had more tender feelings for the lobbyists and congressmen who bowed under her whip than she did for Santo, for they were pitiful and deserved to be treated that way. But the Governor was her husband and should be standing beside her, in solidarity and strength. And she had a sudden vision of him doing exactly that, standing beside her, his diminutive but muscular frame cinched in leather, like a Centurian, whip in one hand and a briefcase full of cash in the other, matching her stroke for stroke on the bloodied back of the corporate whore at their feet.

This fantasy actually put a smile on her face as she walked the short distance down the hallway to her office, and she went in the back door in a rather elated mood. She went first to her dressing room, where she unlocked the drawer and deposited the contents of the box. She then cut the tape off the box with a knife she kept there for precisely this purpose, then stomped it flat and put it in the trash by her desk. She seated herself in front of the neat but substantial stacks of paper on her desk and picked up the first folder.

She leaned over the draft text of the new Bill the Speaker was putting forward, pen in hand, intent on ferreting out every flaw in the argument, any possible phrase that might be spun or quoted out of context to make him look as idiotic as he was. And where his language was strong, she began to formulate her rebuttals in her mind.

She noticed at the bottom of the first page that a drop of water seemed to have fallen on the text, smearing the ink. She touched it with her finger and found that it was still wet. She looked around in consternation. She looked up at the ceiling, down at the floor, on her desktop. Then she put her fingers to her face and discovered she was crying.

ᚪᚪᚪ

The lovers worried, some, over the Troll's disappearance. There was the sobering possibility that he had nodded off during the night and fallen from his tenuous perch on the threshold, but Q found it hard to imagine the road-savvy Troll making such a mistake. It seemed far more likely, really, that after his uncharacteristic hour of loquacious sharing he had come to himself and sought more solitary surroundings, even if that meant abandoning this particular train for another, later one.

Q and Lucy, however, found themselves affected by their old friend's disappearance in quite the opposite way, wishing now, despite the vast satisfaction each felt to be in the Other's sole company, for a bit more Human Society. Thus it was that they rode that day in the doorway, surveying the passing landscape for Signs of something, though neither was sure exactly what.

They rode most of the day at high speed, covering untold miles through all types of terrain, both urban and rural. They waved to farmers in their gardens and children in their tenements. They saw great cranes towering over buildings, and squadrons of mechanized reapers moving across the fields. And then with dusk approaching Q began to feel there was something familiar about the landscape, that he had been here before.

"I think we're getting close," he told Lucy, and then, as if on cue, the train began to slow. They debarked on a curve, rolling in the soft grass to break their fall, and as they were getting up and dusting themselves off, Q said, "Yes, this is it. This is the very place."

"Which place is that, Q?" Lucy said, looking around at the nondescript surroundings.

"Why, it's the very place where Santo and my Father and I jumped down, so many years ago, when my Father sprained his ankle. Look, there's the tree, now stunted, from which he cut his crutch. We went off that way, down through that valley, and came to the offices of the Church of the Ostensible Jesus within a day.

"Ugh," replied Lucy. "Look, it's almost dark, I'm tired and hungry and in a generally foul mood. I need food and rest before we start our detective work."

Q voiced his agreement with her sentiment, adding, however, that since there was no food to be had in this remote place, they would have to move on if sustenance was on her mind. And yet even as he spoke Q lifted his head and sniffed, for he had caught a whiff of smoke and then, yes he was sure of it, roasting meat in the air. Lucy sat up too when she noticed it, and then the two of them set off with noses uplifted, following the scent trail into the woods.

The smell grew progressively stronger and more succulent, causing each of them to practically howl with longing and to quicken their pace until they were travelling at a lope, jumping over logs and ducking under the lower limbs. They burst noisily into a clearing, surprising a group of about twenty motley Campers seated around a fire over which there was roasting, on a primitive spit, what appeared to be an entire lamb.

Q and Lucy stopped in their tracks and surveyed the scene with mouths watering involuntarily as the Campers stared at them. One of the Campers moved slightly and Q turned quickly to face him, his lip curling into a snarl. Then suddenly the Clearing erupted in a din of yelling, Q and Lucy and each Camper trying to outdo each other in ferocity. Then, as the disadvantage of numbers began to dawn on them, Q and Lucy's tone subdued to a whimper, and they sat down in the grass submissively as the Campers circled around them, sniffing and prodding the newcomers with unabashed curiosity.

And then the scene, which had seemed on the brink of violence, turned quickly into unbridled revelry, everyone whooping and dancing around happily as they all began to recognize each other as long lost friends, for these were fellow travelers that Q and Lucy had met many years ago when their paths had crossed on the road.

"Dear Friends," Q attempted weakly to declaim, "what a happy coincidence that we should encounter you today, when we are near starvation and you are roasting a delectable meal. Well met, well met…"

"Of course," said the Campers, "we are ecstatic to see our old Friends again, and you are welcome to share in our repast."

The scene quieted somewhat then, as all settled down to quell their hunger on the delicious meat, which was cooked to perfection. Q and Lucy were each given a succulent hind-quarter, and they gorged themselves while the rest ate more politely. A wine-skin, which turned out to be filled with thirst-quenching cider, was produced and passed from hand to hand. Q turned it up and drank long and deep from the ambrosial stream, then aimed it at Lucy who did the same.

Darkness fell. All that remained of the Animal that had given itself to their sustenance was a pile of bones turning to ash in the Fire. One of the Campers stoked the flame with heavy branches, sending a whirlwind of bright embers into the air. Then they took turns telling stories of the intervening years, and each story was a retelling of events very like the one they had just experienced, chance encounters with old friends that began with reticence and ended with happiness and abandon. Everyone was quite interested in Q's history of the Provincial Oaks Commune, which they had all heard about but none had visited.

When it came Lucy's turn to speak, she at first refused, and Q realized this was because she was ashamed of the life of wealth and privilege she had been living since any of them had seen her last. But when Q leaned over and whispered something in her ear, she suddenly came alive and began telling them about the Troll.

The mention of the Troll and his close proximity in both space and time caused the Crowd to hang on her every word, for there was no one on the rails who did not know the Troll. There was some speculation as to what had happened to him when he had disappeared from the boxcar, but in the end everyone agreed with Q that it was quite unthinkable the Troll might have come to some sort of accidental harm during the night, since his competence at the traveling life was unparalleled. But though agreement on what had *not* happened to the Troll was unanimous, there was no consensus on what *had*, for no one could recall the Troll ever telling a story, especially about himself and his psychological condition, and all agreed that the idea of the Troll seeking out companionship, moving among what we call Society, was not consistent with what anyone knew about the Troll, nor anything else.

"This is an Omen," said one Camper. "Great change is afoot."

●

The wine-skin lay empty, but now a bottle of something stronger than the delicate cider was circulating through the Group. One of the women, whom Q recognized from the Old Days (though she seemed to have aged a bit more than the few years which had intervened), got up and began slowly to walk around the fire in the center of the Circle. She was clad only in filthy blue jeans and a tattered brassiere, and her withered belly hung over her belt.

As she passed Q she took the bottle from him and drank deeply, then handed it to someone else and continued her circuit until the bottle was passed to her again and again she drank, this time spitting into the fire, causing it to flare up. Then someone asked if she would tell a story, and the motion was seconded by another, and then the whole Crowd joined in the supplication. She demurred coyly at first, then demanded payment in the form a cigarette before she would begin. This caused a bit of a bustle as everyone searched their pockets for scraps of tobacco, but eventually the critical mass was reached and a rude smoke rolled up in a scrap of newsprint. Now the Storyteller moved a bucket to the center of the circle and sat on it. She lit the cigarette with an ember from the fire, took a long drag, spat a bit of loose tobacco at her feet, then gathered her breath, looked up, and began.

The Old Bawd's Story

Nothing is known of the origin of Anna Weatherman, save that she was an orphan and was adopted, when approximately six years old, by Mr. Antoine Weatherman, of M______. She was, for all practical purposes, raised by a maid, one Sarah Jameson, who has since disappeared, and who had appeared, rather mysteriously, at the Weatherman home in the early Spring of 1970, the very year of Anna's adoption. The little girl was sent to a good private school and did moderately well in her studies, but she preferred spending her time in the woods and fields. Those who remember her tell of strange tastes: her preference for moonlight, for example, over daylight; and they also tell of her habit of talking constantly to unseen companions. Sarah Jameson spoiled her charge by giving way to her whims, and frequently the two would disappear from their gated subdivision for a whole day at a time, going deep into the woods and swamps across the highway to "study nature." What really went on in the woods, no one knows, and no one can safely conjecture, but there were stories of the child riding a goat through the fields; once she was nearly shot by a hunter who mistook her for game.

Sarah was in sole charge of the child after the death of Mrs. Weatherman in 1995, when Anna was 11; and, in the years following, their intimacy grew. The maid spoke to the girl in

French and read her stories from Mythology. Mr. Weatherman humored his adopted daughter, giving her expensive presents, among others a synthesizer, upon which the girl played eerie melodies which sounded, say those who listened, like nothing they had ever heard before. In so far as is known, Sarah was her only teacher in music, but the young girl soon out-stripped her instructress in the art of keyboard manipulation.

Anna grew to womanhood in that lonely gated community, with few friends but with many books. Her favorite copy of Burton's "Anatomy of Melancholy" is in my backpack as I speak, the margin covered with hieroglyphs that I am unable to decipher. Upon the flyleaf, there is a creditable drawing of a Centaur, possessing a handsome man's head with pointed beard and wild eyes. The lower portion of the figure is that of a horse, with four well-shaped legs and flowing tail. Oddly enough, in the drawing, the Centaur is shown holding a lady's high-heeled slipper in one hand.

When Anna was 20, she married John Wesley Collins of M______, a good provider with many good qualities. He was a lawyer and speculator in Real Estate, considerably older than Anna, whom he idolized. They were married in February, 2002, in the home of the bride's father, and went afterward to New Orleans for Mardi Gras, staying at the Ritz.

A photo of the young bride, taken in New Orleans at that time, shows her a slim, dark-eyed young woman with a high-bred, oval-shaped face, wearing her hair parted Madonna fashion. The eyes are limpid and beautiful, and the full lips are richly red. There is one peculiarity about this portrait: although the face is unsmiling, almost grave in expression, it is, at the same time, full of secret laughter. The longer one studies the picture, the more puzzled one becomes.

During the brief honeymoon, Anna met many friends of her husband's; among them Amy Boudier. Boudier praises Anna's beauty and wit, but hesitates to comment upon the quality of her conversation, which she found "advanced" (to use her own term). She (Anna Collins, for she took her husband's name) appeared rather dreamy, Boudier testifies, but enjoyed the Mardi Gras parades and costuming, appearing to enjoy particularly the mythological quality of the festivities. Among the nymphs, mermaids, satyrs and fauns of the French Quarter costume contests, she was radiantly happy, and even had her husband buy her own costumes and masks, including a plastic horse's head and winged slippers from the shop called Madame Alabau's on Bourbon Street. What became of these gaudy trifles afterward can only be conjectured, but, according to the proprietor of the shop, they were shipped to the gated community at M______.

News of the death of Mr. Weatherman cut short their revelry in New Orleans. Ms. Boudier found Anna Collins in tears in her room at the Hilton one afternoon and was told of Mr. Weatherman's sudden demise (caused by a fall from a horse). The Collinses left that night for M______ and Amy did not see Anna again for three years.

Anna Collins was Weatherman's sole heir; she received the house and various other properties and investments. She turned the management of the Real Estate over to her husband, but kept to herself the liquid investments and a considerable quantity of actual Cash which Weatherman had kept in a wall safe at the house. Collins, it should be said, managed his wife's Real Estate well. Throughout this history, one never doubts the devotion of this sterling man for his wife, but one is often amazed at the strange tests to which she put his affection.

So they lived, these two, in that lonely place, seeing few people and entertaining visitors but rarely. True, he drove into the town of M______ daily, to his office in the Business District, but Anna resumed her life in the woods, taking daily strolls, sometimes eight hours in length, through dell and glade of the woods across the highway from the subdivision. It was during this time that she published (in *Harper's* no less) her first poem, "The Wolfman," which became widely known for its mysterious air.

Other poems followed shortly: "Pan" in 2003; "Phantom Lovers" and "Europa" in the same year. In 2004, she published "Leda," in January, followed almost immediately by "Una and the

Lion" and "The Bride of the Faun." These poems, it was considered, were too realistic for the taste of the period, and *Harper's* refused to publish her later effusions, which are said to have bordered on the pornographic. One of these prose poems will be quoted in its proper place, as it throws considerable light upon her ultimate downfall. She did not write at all after November, 2004.

One shudders to think of the humiliation of Mr. Collins at this trying period; but despite the busy tongues of M______, he remained loyal to his wife, passing the neighbors' comments with a smile and a shrug. Like Caesar's wife, Anna was above suspicion—although, to be quite accurate, the Bard of Avon says that "Caesar's wife should be above suspicion," if I remember Shakespeare correctly.

In June, 2004, when Anna Collins was 20 years old, she brought a strange pet home with her—a Centaur, according to the testimony of Charity Jimmeson, who declares that Gaius (for thus Anna called him) was a very handsome fellow, half-man, half-beast. It is impossible to shake her testimony; she declared that she helped take care of Mr. Gaius and knew him well; she refused absolutely to believe the theory that the Centaur was nothing more than an unusually intelligent horse which the perverse and unhappy woman had disguised to resemble a man.

Now this Centaur was very timid about entering the house, but by careful coaxing Mrs. Collins induced him to enter the den, where he stood, restless and wild-eyed and switching his tail, while she played for him upon her synthesizer.

Here we present the prose poem called "The Centaur Plays Croquet," written by Anna Collins at this time (approximately). Needless to say, this effusion was never printed, but was found among her papers, after her death:

The Centaur Plays Croquet

Come, my Centaur, let us have a game of croquet! The colored balls lie like painted flowers on the lawn and the wickets stand in order as do the events of my life. It amuses me to have you play so prim a game—you who remember Pan and who have cavorted with nymphs. Sadly you stand, slowly swaying your tail, and holding the mallet poised; while I, with tiny black lace parasol tilted against the sun, lift mincingly my skirt and strike the ball with an affected scream of excitement—strike daintily, for fear of splitting my polonaise of striped silk.

Your body, tanned by the sun, is like creamy ivory, and the texture of your flesh has the humid quality of a magnolia petal. You stand before me, my simple, sinewy fellow, with shoulders drooping —shoulders strong and hairless like those of the men of Castile. Your black curls shine sleekly; your teeth are of snowy whiteness and your lips are vivid beneath your beard. At the loins, where your man's body melts into that of the stallion, you become wholly animal; there your hide has the sheen of satin and is mottled like moonlight under trees.

...

At this point several of the Campers, who had been fidgeting uncomfortably and murmuring under their breath for the past few minutes, stood up in protest. The Old Bawd protested, in her own turn, saying that no real impropriety had occurred in the story thus far. But the Campers retorted that they could see what was coming, and that no decent person could allow the story to continue with such portent emanating from it.

The Story's Teller scoffed, calling the Campers prudish and old-fashioned. She attempted to continue:

What a Godlike brute you are, my Centaur! Still, you
gaze at me with wistful eyes. Is it a soul you seek? Perhaps,
who knows? For you have no soul, you fabulous man, you
glorious beast, born two thousand years too late... Or is it I
who have mislaid my era?

If it is a soul you long for, you may have mine. See, I
will tear it from my breast and offer it to you, glowing, in
my pink-tipped fingers! (But the striped silk is stronger than
I thought, and my stays resist my tugging.)

...

"This is more than we can bear," said one of the Campers, rising
and shaking his fist. "This is pernicious and indecent. Stop the
narrative at this instant." Still the Bawd attempted to continue:

In the following year, Anna's dreaminess increased and she
seemed to suffer from melancholy. She hardly allowed her husband to touch her hand, nowadays, and aside from playing her
synthesizer, she did little. She never read or studied now—save to
read French poems to Gaius, who did not appear to understand.
Sometimes they played at croquet upon the lawn, or tossed
quoits; or, reclining under a tree, played at chess or at cards.

...

Now several more people stood up and began to decry loudly
for the unholy narration to stop. The Woman, finally getting the
message, cackled and wandered away from the fire, continuing
her story, by all appearance, but now out of earshot of the Group,
who made haste to apologize for the Crone's behavior and distance
themselves from her, saying that, though she was a regular Member
of the Group, she often kept to herself on the Fringe, occasionally
stepping forward with her Discourse, which bordered on the Hysteric.

Q stood up, however, to quiet his Friends' anxieties. "My dear
and gracious Hosts," he began, "please don't think that Lucy and I
identify this Woman's inappropriate, misguided or inchoate Speech
with the Group as a Whole. We know well..."—and here he gave

Lucy, sitting at his feet, a quick nod and a wry smile, which she returned—"…both the trials of Living on the Edge, being critiqued from the Middle, and Living in the Middle and being critiqued from the Edge. We know, as well as you, that the Group is not Responsible for the Individual, and Individual is not Responsible for the Group."

"Here, here," the Group replied in Unison.

"And please, also, Dear Friends," Q continued, "accept our heartfelt thanks for the delicious Lamb you sacrificed for us this evening. For we were hungry, and you gave us food."

No one replied to Q's thanks, however, and many seemed to look at the ground or busy themselves with small tasks. Finally One said: "You are very welcome, my dear Q and Lucy, to our humble fayre. Any time we have 'Railroad Lamb,' as we call it, you may consider it part yours."

"'Railroad Lamb'?" replied Q. "I've never heard that term before. Does it denote a special breed?"

For some reason, the entire Group laughed heartily at this question, yet no one made answer to it.

❧

The evening's activities now drew to a close and everyone prepared for bed, which, for some in the Group, meant nothing more than reclining where they sat and arranging a backpack or whatever was at hand for a pillow. Q and Lucy, however, elected to move a discreet distance away from their Hosts to make their bed, for they both realized they would not last the night without giving in to their Desires, and they did not wish to further embarrass their strangely modest Friends.

"Isn't it odd," Q whispered to his Love as they lay down and entwined in the forest glade, "how sensitive they are? For while the Old Bawd's story had a certain prurience to it, yet it seemed rather tame, prudish even, by Today's Standards."

"Yes, I noticed that too," Lucy agreed, her breath quickening as

they began to move in concert with each other. "One would think
that such road-hardened veterans would have witnessed scenes from
Real Life far more explicit than the delicately implied quasi-bestial
yearnings of this…" —she paused her narration to take a few quick
breaths, and to bite Q on his ear—"…this …this Victorian damsel."
They both left off speaking now as their passion demanded better
uses of their mouths.

A few minutes later they lay beside each other, panting and spent.
As their breathing gradually subsided, they began to notice that
the night was not entirely quiet around them. Indeed, the sound of
amorous respiration continued even as Q and Lucy began to cool.
Q rolled over and pushed aside the drapery of vines that formed
their arbor so they got a view of the Campers. The fire had burned
down to coals but still cast a dim glow over the scene. All of them
had retired, it seemed, for no one was upright, and yet none were
sleeping, for no one was still. Hips rose and fell in rhythm or in
unison around the circle, and the heavy breathing was occasionally
punctuated with little yelps and screams. Why, it was not even
possible to distinguish couples in the general orgy that was ensuing.

"Why did we bother to move?" Q asked himself.

"Why indeed," Lucy answered, shifting her legs, rubbing Q's
calf with her foot. "Why indeed."

ॐ

The morning rose quite splendidly upon them, with a fingernail
moon hanging just over Venus in a cloudless lake of blue. And yet
no one seemed to notice as they nursed their "railroad hangovers,"
the price one pays for a night of revelry on the road. The Fire was
resurrected and some water brought to boil in a gallon can. The Old
Bawd then added a handful of roots and grasses she had gathered
for the occasion, producing a bitter but therapeutic tisane which
everyone sipped morosely, some squatting by the fire, some standing
wrapped in tattered blankets.

Though the stuff tasted like a mixture of vinegar and quinine, Q noted that after forcing down a small cup of it the throbbing in his forehead diminished considerably. Lucy agreed, and thus refreshed she and Q put on their boots and prepared to continue their journey. They said their good-byes and heartfelt thank-yous and gathered their belongings into Q's sack. The Campers were surprised to see their Guests heading away from the railroad, cross-country, but Q explained that he knew the area and knew where he was going; they need not be concerned.

Before they quit the campground, Q made a point of saying a word to the Old Bawd. He was afraid she was feeling ostracized and wanted to tell her how much he had enjoyed her story the night before, and how he hoped he might hear the rest of it one day.

"Ah, Q," she said, in a tone Q could not quite read, "how you make an Old Woman feel welcome. And you shall certainly hear the end of this story one day, and I pray it won't be too long, my Gaius." She smiled at him then, a crooked, leering smile that showed off her rotten teeth, and put her face close to his, showing him, as well, her malodorous breath. She also, in a subtle gesture that no one except Q noticed, touched him gently on the thigh, causing him, to his great surprise, to become instantly tumescent. He blushed and stammered with embarrassment, but no one else, not even Lucy standing beside him, saw his humiliation.

"Q, are you OK?" Lucy asked him as they left the Group and started out through the woods. "Your face is quite flushed. And are you limping?"

Q blushed the more, mumbling that he was simply hung over. He tried to walk normally, doing his best to ignore the pain his tight jeans were causing him. He said to Lucy:

"You know, when I'm hung over like this, there is only one cure."

"Really?" She said. "And what is it?" He opened his mouth to reply but instead fell on her with mouth and hands, tearing at her clothing and kissing every bare patch of skin. "Oh," she said. "I see."

They were barely out of sight of the campers when she let him take her, bending over a log, with her boots on, (it would have taken far too long to unlace them), Q biting his tongue to keep from crying out.

Afterwards, they sat on the log and put themselves back together. "I have to admit," Lucy said, "I'm a little sore. Out of shape, I guess."

Q blushed yet again. "I'm sorry," he said. "I just… I had to… I had no choice."

"I know," Lucy smiled. She got up, buckling her belt, and started walking. Q scrambled to keep up with her.

ᴧ

They walked the better part of the day across pastures and woodlands in the gently rolling hills, following cattle trails or rutted farm roads, but they saw only a few cattle here and there. Once, as they were crossing a barbed-wire fence, they had to jump back quickly to avoid a bull that came charging across the field. The great beast huffed right up to the fence and stood there glaring at them, steam blowing from the flared nostrils. Q could feel the heat of the powerful body. But then his two cows lowed seductively from the other side of the field, and the Bull returned to his duties.

By afternoon they were both tired, and Lucy was complaining of chafing. Q, although he made every effort to appear confident, was actually beginning to worry that he might have lost his way. It had been, after all, several years since he'd walked this route. Perhaps his Memory was not as crystalline as it seemed. Indeed, perhaps the seeming clarity of the remembrance was exactly what should make him suspicious. Had his vision abandoned the complex murk of reality for the clear simplicity of dream?

Finally they crested yet another hill and saw, still at quite some distance, the great mirror-covered structure that was the corporate offices of the Church of the Ostensible Jesus. "Ah, good," said Q, relieved that they were on the right track, and yet dismayed that they had yet such a distance to travel. His dismay was only increased when, with a belligerent toot of its horn, a freight train came into view, snaking across the valley, passing within a football field's length of the Church, slowing to a crawl at just that point, a perfect spot to debark. In other words, they had walked all this way and could just as easily have ridden. "But how?" said Q.

The Dialogue of Q and His Memory

Q: I remembered where we leapt off the train, those many years ago, quite clearly when we passed it yesterday. It was this memory that prompted me to jump. And there I saw the tree from which Santo cut the crutch that enabled my lame Father to get to the Church with us.

Q's Memory: Yes but perhaps I—I mean You—were mistaken about the spot and the tree. Perhaps someone else at some other time cut a crutch from that tree. In fact, perhaps a cow broke a limb off as it was passing, or perhaps it was struck by lightning. There are many ways to account for a tree with a missing branch. And don't all railroad sidings, running through woods, look the same?

Q: I remember a long journey, yet not *this* long, and yet considerably longer than the way from the train, down there, to the Building. So perhaps we left the train at yet a third point, somewhere between here and there, down in the valley, at a place that resembled (to the point of identity) the place where we got off yesterday.

Q's Memory: Keep in mind that resemblance is sensory, sensitive, defined by a certain feeling. But this feeling, this *dejà vu*, can be induced by other means than the physical congruity of the object. Half the experience is context, shall we say, and the other half is chemical, the chemistry of the brain.

Q: Perhaps between context and chemistry lies a third point, the point that is neither One nor an Other. Perhaps it is not pos- sible to debark the train twice in the same place.

Q's Memory: I'll keep track of this insight for you, filed under Sylvan Meadows. When the train of consciousness passes this meadow, or rather this file, debark to experience your Memory.

This argument, despite its profound metaphysics, having moved Q and Lucy not one step closer to their destination, they left it in abeyance and bent actual legs to continue on their way. Q's Memory lingered a moment at the crest, looking around and taking notes on a little pad, mumbling the names of plants and verifying the positions of the clouds. But then Q whistled, and the Construct hurried to catch up.

ঽ

The Church of the Ostensible Jesus had expanded its facilities since Q's initial visit. Where there had been a single mirror-covered building, there was now an entire complex, with some of the towers reaching high above the original single skyscraper. The cluster of commercial buildings stood in stark contrast to the uninhabited forest that surrounded it. "The Church seems to have fallen on good times," said Q, as much to himself as to Lucy.

The Astute Reader will recall that upon Q's first visit to the Church of the Ostensible Jesus he and his Companions had been immediately attracted to the dumpster at the back door. They had found it full of quite delicious finger sandwiches and other snacks, still fresh in their plastic containers, "vagrant bait," as it were, to lure hungry Travelers within earshot of the ministry. Q and his Father and Santo had fallen happily into the trap. It was in this very building that Q had realized his Calling, and the genre of Christian Glossolalic Rap was born.

Now, after a full day's march, and despite the feast of "railroad lamb" they'd had the previous night, Q and Lucy were again famished, and Q's mouth began, again, to water involuntarily when he spotted that selfsame dumpster by the selfsame back door of the main building, as they, like the rest of us, were quite willing to be ministered to if there were food in the bargain.

The dumpster turned out to be, to Q's surprise, not simply *a* dumpster in the same location, but *the* very dumpster from years before, and rather showing its age, rusting at the corners, its orange paint fading and beginning to peel. The side gate, in fact, proved to be rusted shut and quite immoveable. The top cover, however, did yield to Q's effort, creaking on its hinges, and they peaked over the rim anxious for the bounty inside.

And what they found there: Nothing. In stark contrast to the feast they expected, Q and Lucy found only a pile of filthy rubble, rotten cardboard and pieces of plastic which Q realized in shock were the blister forms that had covered the very sandwiches he and Santo and his Father had sated themselves on, so many years ago. How could it be that the dumpster had not been serviced in all that time?

"What has happened here?" said Q. "Where is the Church of the Ostensible Jesus?"

"Very little, apparently," Lucy replied. "And elsewhere."

Lucy also pointed out that the building itself appeared to be in poor repair. One of the windows above them was broken; a bird roosted on the sill. Upon examining the door to the building Q found it not only unlocked but ajar and the carpet inside rotten from long exposure to the weather. There was no light in the hallway but from the open door, but their curiosity was piqued now so they entered. Most of the office doors stood open revealing the abandoned desks and computers within. In one they surprised a pair of squirrels cavorting among the scattered papers. In the large meeting halls and gymnasia, pigeons roosted in the rafters, flying in and out the broken windows.

The hallway ended at a large pair of doors. "The Sanctuary," Q gasped, almost afraid to open them. When he did they found the enormous room in the same state as the rest, only on a grander scale. The great stained-glass window on the North wall was in pieces—clouds, sky and woodland showing through a fragmented Christ—with the landscape actually entering the room at the bottom, where grasses and small trees had taken root in the rubble on the stage. A Hart was grazing there. When they approached it looked up, snorted once, and bounded away out the window, followed by a pair of long-eared Hares.

Though the front of the Sanctuary was well lit from the sunlight streaming in the enormous window, its far reaches were in darkness. Q stepped into the room to investigate further, but Lucy stopped him. "Look, I saw something there," she said, pointing into the murk. And when Q looked closely he did see something moving in the shadows, something rather large. "Let's go," she said, and they did.

They decided to try exploring some of the upper floors, a task that was somewhat daunting due to the lack of elevators and lighting. Most of the stairways were in utter darkness, and neither of them were inclined to venture in when they heard fluttering and rustling sounds from above. But the front atrium had a stair that reached up to the fourth mezzanine, and they went up that far, finding nothing but more wildlife and vegetation. Vines hung, out of control, from the planters that lined the balcony rails, and where orderly rubber trees had stood in pots tall pines now grew, their roots having burst the containers and spread across the room. The great wall of glass that had been the building's architectural focus was mostly open to the heavens now, the mullions wrapped in honeysuckle and jasmine, bees coursing among the fragrant blossoms. Mosses, ferns and other forest-bottom flora had taken root in the fertile humus where the floor had been. Birds and small ground mammals were plentiful, and Q even noticed a hawk perched up high in a window frame, keen-eyed, on the lookout for shrews and mice moving in the grasses below. And near the top of the third stairwell they disturbed a banded King Snake sunning on a step.

Having seen enough to convince themselves that further investigation would reveal only more of the Same, the couple quit the atrium and the building in favor of the outdoors, though, once *al fresco*, they noticed there really wasn't much difference between Interior and Exterior in this place. The great courtyard between the buildings resembled nothing so much as the atrium they had just left, which itself was indistinguishable from the forest around. The Forest, in fact, seemed to flow without interruption into and through the Structures, as if the Buildings were nothing more than oddly linear and symmetric Sedimentary Formations. Q was reminded of Roraima or Montserrat.

Midway through the Courtyard a small stream widened to a tranquil pool, the water so clear it almost appeared empty to its gravel bottom. A small school of Trout looked up warily at Q and Lucy through their reflections. Our Travellers were thirsty and dropped to all fours to drink, like a pair of Narcissi kissing themselves. Then they moved to a shady knoll to rest and reconsider their position, for they were, if thoroughly enthralled, also completely confused. They lay down on cool moss and stared up through the trees and overgrowth at the tops of the buildings and a patchwork of blue sky and perfect cumulous clouds. Small birds darted between the buildings, slipping in and out of the upper windows, while larger ones—raptors, apparently—glided lazily from rooftop to rooftop or hovered further up.

"Something isn't right, Q," Lucy offered. "I mean, it's strange enough that these buildings appear relatively new and yet are overrun with vegetation, but other anachronisms haunt this place too. How long has it been since you were here last? One year? Five? Ten? These accretions of humus, a veritable forest floor, do not accumulate in a mere decade."

To emphasize her point, Lucy patted the ground beside her, then tore into the moss with her fingernails to expose the damp earth beneath. To their surprise, however, when the moss was peeled away it revealed not Earth but a rotting bit of text:

> ＿ ve agreed. Yusimí will ＿
> nen while Ámbar entertains Filo Doug＿
> ＿ns leaning her head back in the big armch＿
> at the living room ceiling which is als＿
> ＿memade loft, all the while making ar＿
> ＿mments about the nutritional value of ſ＿
> ＿d how expensive it is to put togethe＿
> ＿discerning guest.
> ＿ (nicknames vary) doesn't pa＿

And when Lucy tore this bit of page from its position, they discovered yet another beneath:

          part of the drama

     ...tacks.

   ρ down, aren't you looking for the same tl

    ɔdy else: sex, pleasure, a bite of flaky Filo Dou

   ad. Eat. Though truth be told, it's paradoxical

   ou want to sink your tooth into a dentist, I me

   n't make fun of me, Ámbar. So smart and profes

   tolerant to the core. Why does she always have to

   everybody else were an imbecile and only she had hi

   lties? If Filo hasn't got much protein, what's it to Ám

   Yusimí who's going to swallow him. It's up to her

   ody else to choose one diet over another.

   Brilliant, a genius. At the peak of her imagination Y

   erves not one treat but a whole shipping container fu

   ek delights. Ámbar seems sincere in her enthusiasm be

   ts up from the chair, gives Yusimí a good strong

"Whaaa…? Someone buried a book here?" Q tore away this top page to reveal another. He began to widen the hole in an attempt to get hold of the entire book, but at the limit of one sheet he merely found another. The two of them fell to peeling away the moss, eventually discovering that the entire knoll on which they had hoped to take their leisure was but a pile of discarded books overgrown with a thin skin of vegetation. "How deep do they go?" Q inquired, and they began tearing their way through the matt in an attempt to discern its bottom, looking a bit like a pair of dogs digging up buried bones.

It was tough going, for all manner of texts had coalesced here into a kind of Papier-mâché, dense and sticky, clumps of half-congealed paper coming out in handfuls indiscreetly and incoherently. They excavated Plato, ridden with worms, in the same handful as Dear Abby; Kierkegaard, and centipede, with Raymond Chandler; Houellebecq, with dung beetles, next to Chef John Besh. Two feet, three, four feet deep they dug and still did not reach the bottom of the stratum, nor did they find the pages layered in any particular order. At first they imagined they might find the literature arranged chronologically, like strata of glacial ice, but even four feet down they were as likely to run across a page of E.L. James as Aristophanes.

After several hours work, and nearing exhaustion, they climbed out of their hole and began to explore horizontally, digging just a few inches deep in a wide arc in an attempt to reach the edge of the formation. They dug near the boles of trees to verify that they were, as they appeared, rooted firmly and solely in the textual mass. They did not reach the limit of the text and concluded, finally, that the entire complex was composted with this same material.

"And who would have thought," mused Q, climbing out of their hole and patting the solidity of a trunk, "that real trees might root in conceptual soil. From tree to mulch to tree again, the eternal circle of life."

"We have no time for your Romanticism, Q," Lucy grunted, wiping sweat from her brow. "There's something not right about this place. I have a feeling we're about to be in serious trouble here, and we need to figure out what we're up against."

"Trouble?" said Q. And at that moment an arrow pierced his breast and transfixed him to the tree.

ааа

Outside the house Mr. Simpson announced that Sally couldn't go to the meeting. He went on cleaning his blue Rolls Royce, a relic now, though still the apple of his eye, and indeed only for the eye, as it hadn't run in years. But it was a lovely place to sit and wile away the day, listening to music and polishing the burled wood dash.

Sally didn't care about the Rolls, one way or another. She'd never seen one actually roll, and so as accustomed as she was to talking to her father inside his, she considered it merely outdoor furniture, a skeuomorph in the shape of a car, and at this moment one would have to say it disgusted her. Upon her Father's pronouncement she bolted from the leather seat, slammed the door in his face, and ran into the house, less as an expression of rage than shame, for she couldn't bear him seeing her tears and thus confirming the power he had over her. She ran into the house and straight upstairs, without a glance at her bewildered Mother, and threw herself on the bed to sob into her pillow while she clenched the covers with her fists.

Why wouldn't he let her go? It made no sense. All her friends were going. They were home now putting on their make-up and deciding what to wear, not salting the Earth with their tears because of their crazy parents. It was so unfair. What objection could he possibly have to her attending a concert that was so akin to a Church Service? Wasn't Little A a minister who spread God's Word through sacred rap?

Oh, she wanted to go so bad.

Little A was just so cool, so perfect, so beautiful in every way. Who would not be enthralled, captivated even? She stopped crying a moment to swoon in her fantasies, letting her wildest dreams run rampant, indulging herself even as her movement had been restricted. For there was one secret she had never told anyone—not her friends (not even Brittany!), not the Boyfriend (or whatever He was), not her Therapist (though she had been tempted). Why, this secret was such that she barely knew it herself. It was like an impulse that was buried inside her, impossible to vocalize, yet it motivated her every word and action, and now, despite the impossibility, she felt it turning inside her, demanding concrete expression, and she raised up her head and said, to the empty room, the only thing she knew to say:

"I love you."

Having said it, a feeling of relief and resignation came over her. Yes, she was in love with Little A. She was in Love and nothing could stand in her way: not her Father, not her Mother, not Brittany's cynical doubt, not the lack of a ride to the concert, nothing. She would get there, one way or another; she would walk if she had to; she would sneak out after dinner, climb down the tree from her bedroom window. She was going to see Little A.

She was exhilarated by her decision, and her heart raced. She clutched the pillow to her and kissed it. Ah—dare she think it?—what might it be like to kiss Little A? The Thought was irresistible, despite her inexperience; the phantasy seemed the more compelling for being vague, with promises of pleasures beyond compare with any previously known. Whatever it might be like to embrace, indeed to lie with, Little A, one could only assume it would be quite beyond those casual, exploratory dalliances with Brittany or those messy evenings with the Boyfriend.

And would it truly be too much to hope that Little A might have some bit of feeling for her? How would Little A even know she existed? Well, stranger things had happened. When you really think about it, how does anyone know anything? How did she, for example, know that Little A was even performing tonight? There had been no publicity, no radio announcements, no TV ads, no Tweets or blog posts or email campaigns. It was just that, quite suddenly, Everyone was going. And I mean *Everyone*. All of her friends and schoolmates. Even some Parents! It was like news of 5rthe performance had travelled through the air on some kind of radiowaves that went straight into Everyone's head. And if that was possible—and it obviously was—it was certainly possible—indeed, probable, certain, even—that Little A knew about her in the same way, knew that she was in love, knew the constancy of her heart, and—could one dare say it, despite all evidence and probability?… and yet it must, *must*, be true—reciprocated.

She rolled over in the bed, still clutching the pillow, tears now dry, in an almost religious ecstacy. What was it that was so special about Little A? She smirked at the internal question, so inane to an initiate, though one could understand the consternation of those not in the know. Was it physical attractiveness? Well, not exactly (and the irony that she was rubbing her thighs together even as she thought this was not lost on her) since she actually had no idea what Little A even looked like, for, as everyone knew, Little A allowed no photos or videos of the performances. Was it the music, then, the hypnotic rhythms and pure visceral power of the glossolalic rap? Well, again, not exactly, since Little A did not allow audio recordings of the performances either. Was it the Words, then (or should one say "Words")? And again Sally had to answer No, for what she felt, she had to admit, despite its inexplicability, was not the spiritual attraction of language, but something more sensual, more physical (she began to squirm on the bed), shouldn't she just say it? (her lips parted to actually do so), *lust*.

Her hand, as it travelled down her abdomen, seemed curiously not-her-own, as if it really were someone else's, a little small, perhaps, to be Little A's own—but then again who could say with certainty that Little A's hand was fat and clumsy like the Boyfriend's, not diminutive, gentle and sensual, like Brittany's? Expertly now it sought her core—and found it. "Oh, Little A," she whispered, "your skills aren't limited to music, I see."

Later, as she lay in luxurious afterglow, she began to consider the more practical aspects of their relationship. Of course, Sally couldn't be just another groupie. There would have to be some sort of formal arrangement, a contract, as it were, not marriage per se (although she would consider the possibility, were the subject to arise), but an agreement as to duties and responsibilities and also, of course, disposition of the vast wealth accumulated by Little A's operations. A role within that operation was the obvious answer. What role? Well, hadn't Sally's Mother told her over and over again that she had a natural ear for music? Why, one need only give her a pitch on a piano and she could find it, or at least get very close, instantly with her voice. Perhaps the Sound Booth, then. She pictured herself in headphones, bending over the Great Board, checking levels and making slight adjustments to the brightly lit buttons.

Yes, a Future in the Church. That was obviously her calling. That settled, she turned her attention to the evening in front of her. She picked up her phone and called Brittany.

"I'm going," she said, then waited in silence as Brittany fired back questions.

"He said No," she went on. "But I can't obey him tonight. I have my own responsibilities to the Church, and that must come first. Can you pick me up? I still have to decide what to wear."

They agreed to a rendezvous, and Sally set about preparing for the evening. She laid out her outfit then went downstairs to dinner. Her Father had come in from the Rolls and was preparing to say Grace. Sally sat down and bowed her head. Her Dad's blessing seemed quaint, compared to Little A's raw inspiration, and she had to smile. In fact, giddy as she was with anticipation, she almost sputtered with laughter during the solemn moment.

After dinner she ran back upstairs, ostensibly to study. She rationalized the lie by telling herself she was indeed going to study the Word that evening. She put on the dress previously selected, then climbed out her window and down the tree that leaned to her dormer. She crossed the yard and walked down the dimly lit street to the first corner, where she spotted Britanny's Volvo. The back door opened for her. Years later, this is the last thing she will remember.

ααα

Upon being impaled by the arrow, Q reacted with all the anguish and surprise you might expect of one so cruelly treated. He let out a yelp of mere amazement, then began howling with the pain. He flailed violently but quickly stopped and held himself fast and trembling when he felt the effect of his exertions on his wound.

Lucy screamed in horror at Q's suddenly wretched visage, then, as the implication dawned upon her, dropped into the foxhole she had conveniently been digging, cowering behind its cover and peeking out in anguish to find the source of the missile.

In spite of the violence and cruelty that now seemed present in their vicinity, the Woods presented a face of utter calm, with a light spring wind just ruffling the leaves and small birds twittering in the brush. She searched the sylvan scene in vain for the source of their agony, but then she heard a musical whistling, as if from some country lad taking a stroll, and a young man sporting a bow and quiver stepped into the clearing in front of her.

He was dressed all in green, from his pointed woodsman's hat to the curled-up toes of his forest boots. A pheasant, its throat freshly cut, hung at his belt, and its blood stained the suede of his breeches along the thigh. Upon his lapel he wore an insignia, large enough for Lucy to make out even from her lowly vantage:

CUSTOS
SCRIPTI

When his eyes fell upon Q—pinned and wriggling to the tree, now lapsing into a pitiful state, trembling and pale, bloody drool stringing from his chin—he let out a little cheer. "Woo hoo, we've nailed him, Harpin. Professor, come up. Our quarry's here."

Thereupon appeared a limping hunchback, drug into the glen by three bull mastiffs on heavy leather leashes. Using all his strength to control the great, huffing beasts, he managed to get them tied to a tree safely away from the others. He then approached, bent over, ape-like, and surveyed the scene with the Archer.

"Can you imagine?" he said proudly, "a shot like that, more than 100 meters, through the brush. I lined up the shot with that tree so as not to have to chase It down wounded. We'll put It out of its misery, of course, but what a shot, eh? We could have left It behind while we pursued other game, with no danger of it wandering off and getting lost in some thicket."

Harpin slapped his thigh with glee. "Oh, Master, you're right. What a shot! You pinned him perfectly!"

These two went on happily congratulating themselves for some few minutes, until Q managed to gather his breath and speak up, hoarse behind the blood welling in his throat. "Who are you? Why did you shoot me?" he sputtered.

The Archer looked at him with surprise, as if amazed that his quarry spoke like a human, then indicated with a sweep of his arm all of the woods around them, from the canopy of the larger trees above to the dense cover on the ground. Then he pointed to his insignia and said simply, "I am the Guardian of the Text, the protector of this Wood. You are trespassing here and pose a threat to our fragile ecosystem."

Something about the way he said this made Q even more apprehensive, and yet he was still compelled to implore the "Guardian" to remove the arrow from his chest. The Guardian furrowed his brow and put a finger to his chin as if considering some complex philosophical conundrum. He ruminated for some time, twice opening his mouth as if to speak and then thinking better of it and returning to his meditation.

Then Harpin limped forward and tugged on his Master's coat-tail. He pointed down at Lucy, cowering below him in her pit. Lucy had been keeping still in the vain hope they would not see her, but now caught directly under their gaze she made haste to escape. Unfortunately, the pages of moldy text that lined the pit were shifting and slippery and her effort to extricate herself was in vain. The Guardian pulled another arrow from his quiver and nocked it into the bow. He drew back, ready to pin Lucy just as he had her lover, but Harpin stopped him and again whispered in his ear.

As the Guardian listened his face went from impassive to ecstatic, and then he jumped up eagerly. "Oh, yes, how perfect! Oh my Professor, that's it. Why what a wonderful idea," he gushed. "What a perfect scene. We have the dogs. We have our Therese. We'll recreate… No!… We'll *realize* the scene. "

Now Harpin took from his knapsack a length of rope and fashioned a loop and slip-knot in one end. He twirled the loop over his head for a moment like a cowboy, then threw it expertly over Lucy and lassoed her. With a jerk he took up the slack, pinning her arms to her sides. Then he pulled her, kicking and spitting, out of the pit and over near (just out of reach) the dogs, where he tied her to another tree. Now Harpin and the Guardian (and it took both of them) set about stripping Lucy of her clothes and resetting the rope so that her hands and feet were free though the tether remained tight around her torso, allowing her some small range of movement. Then they cruelly loosed the dogs upon her.

As Lucy began fighting for her life against the hounds, the Guardian and Harpin returned to Q's side to commiserate. "Remember, Q?" the Guardian asked excitedly. "From *Justine*? Sade's *Justine*? Remember? They tie her to a tree and set the dogs upon her? I had always pictured that scene just as we see it here. Except, of course, your Lucy is putting up a much better fight than did that delicate, spoiled Therese."

And, indeed, Lucy's knowledge of martial arts was standing her in good stead. She had managed to severely hinder at least one of the dogs—its leg seemed to be broken—and she had poked out another's eye. But even wounded the great beasts were formidable opponents, and the blood that covered the ground around them was not solely of canine origin.

Q struggled as best he could to come to her defense, wiggling and straining, at the cost of great suffering to himself, in an attempt to break the arrow and free himself from his impalement. But it quickly became clear that his situation was hopeless; there was no way that he could extricate himself from the transfixion without someone else's aid, and he settled into a forlorn and hopeless whimpering.

"Why are you doing this to us?" he blubbered tearfully. "Please stop. Call off your dogs. I'll give you whatever you want. But I pray you please please please stop this punishment."

The Guardian took a green handkerchief from his vest pocket and gently daubed at the blood that had splattered on his waistcoat and shirt-sleeves from the force of Q's anguished plosives. Then he moved to one side and put his arm around Q in the attitude of a dear friend, leaned in and said, close to Q's ear:

"And what, prithee tell me, is it that I want?"

"In truth I do not know," Q gasped, "what lack has prompted you to inflict these cruelties upon us, yet if you tell me what it is, I will endeavor to fill it, even if I die in the attempt."

"Oh, very good. The very thing. Oh, this is excellent." The Guardian clapped his hands in delight and began to dance about. "What I lack, you shall provide, and in so doing save your damsel. Oh, how appropriate, how perfectly perfect." He leapt up light as a fairy and tapped his toes together, but then he came suddenly to his serious pose again, with his finger to his chin. "But herein, dear Q, lies a problem, a certain dilemma, even a paradox, for what I lack is precisely the ability to tell you what I lack. I lack that inward look, and I lack the words to tell you what that inward look might reveal. So, if you will tell me what I lack you will in that selfsame gesture have remedied that lack. And yet this lack is of such a nature that were it once possible for it to exist—and I…" he indicated, with an ouroboric gesture, himself "…am living proof of that possibility—it should henceforth be impossible for it not to exist. I want, shall we say, what I want."

Here Lucy interrupted the conversation, effectively putting her proposition across with vigorous screaming. The dogs, too, seemed to chime in, growling their gutturals as best they could around mouthfuls of Lucy's flesh. Harpin laughed with glee at the scene, turning his attention from Q to Lucy and back like a tennis fan. "I think you've got them where you want them now, Master," he said, rubbing his hands together. "What a Brilliant Argument you've made!"

"Elementary, my dear Harpin," said the Guardian of the Text. "Do not be so easy with your praise, for just look at my Opponent." Q was now slumping on the arrow, head lolling on his chest, blood dripping from mouth and nose. "I seem to be losing him." He grabbed Q by the hair, lifting his head, then took from his pouch a roll of silver tape with which he secured Q's forehead to the tree, fixing him in an attitude of attention, however wretched. "Now Q," he went on, "if you can manage it before you slip away, I propose to offer you the exact wager you have wished for, which is, quite simply: You give me what I want, and I will spare your Lucy, and perhaps even yourself. Do you agree to the terms?"

"Yes, yes," Q managed to spit out. "Tell me what you want, and I will provide it."

"Oh Q, Q, Q," the Guardian scolded. "Have you not been listening? What I want is for you to know. I want you to tell me what I want. Tell me what I want and I shall no longer be wanting. Go ahead. I'll give you three attempts, but we are, as you can see," —he indicated Lucy—"running out of time." (Harpin gave a loud guffaw to this last statement.)

Q glanced hopelessly toward Lucy and the Dogs. She was not actually in sight any more; all he could see were the three dogs standing over something, feeding. He racked his brain for the answer to the conundrum, but he had by now lost a good deal of blood and that organ was suffering from a lack of oxygen. He tried to analyze the grammar. The Guardian had said that what he lacked was the ability to say what he lacked, and that merely to say it would be to solve it. So there was nothing required in the way of actual performance, a mere statement. But even as the glimmer of an idea formed in Q's mind, he found himself, physically, barely able to speak, as he was laboring horribly merely to breathe. To make it even worse, the Guardian began to lose patience and started prodding Q to hurry up, which of course made him even more tongue-tied. Finally, from the edge of consciousness and the depths of excruciating pain, Q managed to say:

"Have you no Pity? Do you lack all Pity?"

"What? Why, that's wonderful, Q. Brilliant," the Guardian gushed.

"Not the correct answer, mind you, but I'm going to give you partial credit for a good attempt, and, actually, doesn't that in itself prove your answer wrong?" He pulled an arrow from his quiver, then, and with barely a glance in the direction of his target shot it quite precisely into the chest of one of the dogs, which fell instantly dead. The other two beasts seemed not to notice and went on feeding. "Care to venture another response, Q? I know you can do it. Tell me, prithee, what do I lack? Get to the Heart, Q…"

Even though Q had felt some measure of vengeful satisfaction when he saw the first dog felled, the fact that the other two were now continuing unabated, and that Lucy no longer seemed to be fighting back, caused him to despair utterly. He attuned his mind once more to the riddle, but he was too weak and addled to even remember the problem, much less pose a solution, so that all he could do was mutter to himself, spitting blood:

"No Hope; there is no Hope…"

The Guardian had to lean close to hear him, but when he did he again clapped his hands together in glee. "Oh, very good, Q, you're so close you're on fire. And for such a good try I think I can call off one more dog." He pulled another arrow from the quiver, nocked it in and sent it on its way instantly toward the dogs, another of which now fell dead. "And you see, there is Hope—the tiniest glimmer, I agree—but Hope nonetheless, Hope in the abstract, the remotest empirical possibility. So, Q, give us another one. Before darkness overtakes you, answer my riddle and you shall be Free."

Q's knees gave out from under him, and he slumped in utter weakness and despair. Pain ripped through his body as the arrow further abraded his wound, but he had not the strength to respond, and so he hung there in agon and pathos, ready for the Earth to swallow him up.

"Come along Q," the offensively upbeat Guardian continued, "give us one more guess before you give up the ghost. Come on, what do you say?"

The day was growing dark. All Q could mutter was the emptiness inside and out. "Nothing," he whispered. "You lack Nothing."

The Guardian bent down, again, to hear him, and then stood up without a word and killed the remaining dog. Then, for good measure, he took out another arrow and killed a very surprised Harpin. Then he walked over to Q and unsheathed his knife.

ααα

On a dark night, full of longing, inflamed with love, the Linguist was experiencing one of those passages of the soul which he seemed to be having so often, these days. And though he knew, rationally, from experience, that these intervals of uncertainty to the point of despair almost always ended happily, the knowledge was little comfort as he sat, once again, over the reams of his notes, smoking cigarette after cigarette, head in hand, trying to make sense of it, trying to believe that all this work was, in the end, going to be worth it, that it was, finally, going to be published and that it was going to make his name. On nights like this the scribbled hieroglyphs of his transcriptions seemed to make no more "sense" than the utterances they documented, and the highly evolved graphemes of the phonetic alphabet began to resemble grapholalia.

And beyond the intellectual struggle, beyond the search for patterns, repetition, productivity and stereotypy, beyond the minute, moment by moment struggle to discern divisions that one might call words, beyond, in short, Linguistics itself, there was this loneliness, a feeling that the work stood outside the continuity of discourse, outside the system of reference and rebuttal of the academic community that was the closest thing he had to a home. It seemed he had nothing to rebut, nothing to refer to, no textual anchor whatsoever for his work. It was like standing in the middle of an enormous empty room, talking.

How had he come into this state of existential despair? Who had forced him into this untenable position? No one but himself. Yes, he was here by choice. Actually, by dint of dogged effort. He had looked at the Little A phenomenon and seen (imagined?) an opportunity to take Linguistics to a new level (and, while he was at it, see his own name up there beside Chomsky, or even—dare to dream—Saussure!).

And beyond this interest in engaging the contemporary, sectarian discourse in his field, he was interested in working, again, with the Church. The Christian Church was, of course, the originator of his discipline. Wasn't Augustine the first real linguist? Weren't the medieval monks the carriers of the torch through the millennia, with their detailed studies of biblical texts leading to their translations, transcriptions and textual analyses setting the standard for modern semiotics and Linguistics itself? Didn't Linguistics, in fact, originate as a defense of the Bible? He felt, in his own rather pagan way, that he was being *called* to a monastic life, in the service of transcribing, preserving, studying, translating Little A's unique text.

In preparation for the Grant Application he had thrown himself into background research, searching out every book, every paper he could find on the topic of glossolalia. He'd spent long hours at the library, searching the databases and reading articles; he'd carried home stacks of books. But then he quickly found that most of the literature he was reading was exactly that: fiction, fantasy, free-form interpretation, or the enthusiastic endorsements of the faithful. And once he had eliminated this dross and culled his bibliography down to true case studies with real objective data, he could have read it all in a day. There was, astoundingly, only one book on the topic, Goodman (1973), and only a handful of articles, most of which were replies to Goodman, with no original field work. And even the Goodman, for all its rigor, remained mostly anecdotal, as it studied only three congregations over the course of only a few years. Two of those congregations were Spanish-speaking, the third Mayan, so it had the great benefit of a non-Indo-European Control, and yet little is made of this seemingly very important data, with very few transcriptions from the Mayan group, and nothing really inferred from the cross-cultural continuities.

This made writing the Statement of Merit relatively simple, of course: the field was simply under-studied. Despite the viral rise in popularity, beginning with the Q era, almost nothing was known, scientifically speaking, about glossolalia. This was explicable, partially, by the very nature of the beast, as an inability of subjects to remember the experience was a common denominator across all the extant sample-sets. Goodman noted that subjects who crossed over into the dissociation and began speaking in tongues almost never remembered anything of the event, and that when they were played recordings of their own utterances they could not identify the speaker. Goodman herself slipped into the trance on more than one occasion; she knew this by reports from members of the congregations, but also by the blank spaces in her memory.

He had sent off the Application with little hope, thinking it sketchy and incomplete and himself not truly qualified. To convince himself to finally put the stamp on the envelope he had cultivated a "who cares?" attitude, thinking it a one in a million chance, like a lottery, sick of the research and his feeling of inadequacy in the face of it, wanting simply to have it off his desk. And then, with greater expedition than he'd ever heard of, the Grant had come through. An acceptance packet, along with an initial check and a plane ticket, had arrived almost by return mail. There was no informal correspondence, only tax and automatic deposit forms to fill out and return and a single page of instructions from Little A's group, giving only the name of the hotel where he was to meet them and the time and place of the first performance he was to document. And there was one further instruction, at the very bottom of the page: "No recording equipment is allowed at any Little A performance nor anywhere near the performer at any time."

He was flummoxed at first. How could he possibly do field work without recording? But then he thought he understood. "Aha," he murmured to himself, "copyright issues. They don't want anyone bootlegging recordings of the performances." This would be easy enough to get around. A digital recorder in his pocket, a tiny microphone in his lapel, the staple of bootleggers everywhere, would be sufficient for a performance. It was one of those rules that was designed from the outset to be broken. He was familiar with those, for they are the backbone of Academia.

He got off the plane still a little befuddled, but the first thing he saw outside security was a sign with his name on it, held up by a formally attired, enthusiastically waving chauffeur. He was whisked downtown in a limousine and dropped at the hotel, where the bellhops greeted him by name and brought him to his suite on the top floor without even stopping at the desk. The room was bigger than his apartment and far better appointed. There was a welcome basket of fruit and cheeses and a fully-stocked bar. There was even a carton of cigarettes, his brand.

Unused, as a poor academic, to such luxury, the Linguist was immediately suspicious that there had been an error, some kind of mistaken identity, but then, almost as if in response to his sheer anxiety, the bell rang and his Assistant entered. She, too, seemed rather too good to be true, articulate and beautiful, rather what the jaded academic might have called up in a phantasy of the perfect object of his desire. Yet as they sat on the sofa and talked, mapping out the evening's schedule, it quickly became apparent that she had read everything he had written, including his dissertation, and was herself an accomplished linguist, fluent in Romance languages, Russian, and Mandarin Chinese, passing familiar with Arabic and, most surprisingly, conversant in the Yoruba dialect of Lucumí. She was also well versed in, though not necessarily convinced by, Chomsky's Transformational Grammar, as she found much there to be pondered, but she also found herself generally sympathetic to the Foucauldian critique. She was quite familiar, of course, with Structuralism, with a focus on the linguists (Saussure, Humboldt, Husserl, Barthes, etc.) but was surprisingly engaged, also, by Poststructuralism, with an adept's command of literary theory (Derridá, Jameson, the de Man controversy), though she confessed to being baffled by Lacan.

And yet she grew most animated when engaged on the subject of Goodman, glossolalia and the pressing—indeed urgent—need for further field work on the topic. Indeed, before the two of them had been talking for half an hour, they were already making plans to visit churches in the deep South, Cuba, Mexico and Uruguay to write what would essentially be a continuation of Goodman's work, to develop a sufficient data-set to begin running digital queries that might be able to discern the deep structures of glossolalia utterances and see, once and for all, if Transformational Grammar could be seen to be operational outside of any semantic grounding. Further field work would be necessary in Africa, they both decided, as they both intuited the Dark Continent to be where the origin, the beating heart of the dissociation might be found. Surely, the Linguist added, the work they would be doing with Little A would be the first step into a secret history that would encompass the entire World and reveal the very fundament of Language.

The mention of Little A, however, reminded his Assistant of the time, for they would be leaving for the Dome shortly, and the Linguist still needed to bathe and dress, which she discreetly helped him do. She unpacked his modest suitcase while he was showering and laid out his clothes on the bed. He was concerned that he had nothing really appropriate to wear, but she assured him it would be best if he appeared as he was. "There is no reason," she told him, "to be ashamed of being a linguist. Wear your wrinkled clothes proudly." Then she ushered him to the door and, much to his surprise, wished him good night.

"But… I thought…? I'll be needing your help," he stammered.

"Oh, I know, and I would love to," she said, "but you're the Linguist here. I'll be around when you need me for research or, well, whatever you might need, but the Group has made it very clear that only you are allowed backstage." And with that she handed him off to the security guard who had appeared in the hallway, and he never saw her again. Though quite stunned by this initial introduction, he quickly grew accustomed to such apparitions.

While in the elevator the guard politely searched him and removed the recorder from his pocket. This was the first time the Linguist felt the uncanny feeling of being a prisoner in Little A's machine, another situation he grew used to over time. For while this gig would prove to be as *comfortable* as any that one could possibly imagine having, he also constantly had the feeling that there was only one option at any given turn in the maze. It was as if, at every moment, there was a genie standing next to you with a silent question always on his lips,—*what do you wish?*—and when you told him, it was immediately granted, and yet you were never quite satisfied, never quite fulfilled, until you finally wanted to say something like "stop granting my wishes," and then….

He'd met the Group—the gregarious Turntablist, the beautiful dancers and the A2 (Little A rode alone that night, and every night)—in the limo outside the hotel. Introductions were gracious. Despite the Group's star status and the Linguist's rather nondescript role in it, he was greeted with casual warmth and made to feel immediately at home. The limo was equipped as would befit a superstar, with food and drink and pretty much anything else one might hunger for, yet no one really partook. The Turntablist took a tiny spoonful of the Beluga caviar on a toast, saying that he liked a little salty snack before a show, but the open bottle of Dom Pérignon was left to go flat, and the aromatic box of Cohibas was untouched. The Group expressed polite interest in the Linguist's work, and politely nodded when he attempted to explain the necessity for extended data-sets to map cross-cultural and dissociative productivity as the first real test of Transformational Grammar.

"Wow," said the Turntablist. "Sounds like Einstein."

At the Dome the Linguist sat nervously with them in the Green Room, wondering what was to happen next, which turned out that he was added unceremoniously—by means of the A2 silently crooking his finger—to the entourage as they took the stage. He followed them up through the scaffolding, cowering from the lasers and spotlights that pierced the rigging and the smoke. His heart pounded when the dancers hit the stage and went bounding off. Their impossible antics reminded him, strangely, of Goodman's report of Mayan glossolalists, kneeling, dissociated, ecstatic, at the altar, jumping up and down, "jumping from their knees, to a height of several feet," she reported.

And that, next morning, was the last thing he remembered. On the bedside table he found his notebook, with some fifty pages filled with his scribbling. He'd borrowed, apparently, Goodman's method of notation, except that he'd used the International Phonetic Alphabet instead of simple English phonemes. This surprised him somewhat since, while he was familiar, as all linguists are, with the IPA, he was far from "fluent" in it, and had someone asked him if he were capable of transcribing in it in real time, he would have answered, flatly, no.

He had also recorded, a la Goodman, the rise and fall of stress, intonation, pitch and volume, with a wavy line above the text. There were other marks, too, rather like hash marks or accents, at regular intervals, which, after some study, he decided were beats, with every fourth one of these slightly elongated, indicating a measure. The total effect of the notation, then, was of a kind of hymnal, with the "music" above and the "words" below. At first he was aghast at the complexity of it, but as he read along, moving his lips silently, struggling to remember the symbology, he quickly adapted and began to actually hear the sounds. He turned his attention to the rhythm, then. He tapped his finger to a regular beat, approximately eighty beats per minute, and tried to pace his reading to the beat marks, and suddenly it was there. Just as a page of English, to a native speaker, is transparent to its Concepts, the page became transparent to its raw sound. He began to hear the half-rhymes and alliteration, the forced iambs and bacchic emphases, the masculine and feminine repetitions, the repeated particles and the almost-repeated declensions.

He'd never seen—or heard—anything like it. After reading the first page he had a sense of the stunning syllable inventory. Most—

really all—of Goodman's field recordings indicate a fairly small phonemic repertoire which descends into stereotypy and chanted repetition very quickly—essentially, baby talk. But this—this was glossolalia that could rival semantic language in both complexity and regularity. One could sense, if not exactly follow, the poetry attempting to erupt from it, the compulsion toward rhyme reigned in by a craft that sought to avoid the easy choice in every instance, yet relaxed into refrain in intervals, like the troughs and peaks of wave motion.

He sat up in the bed and began to tear through the notebook, pounding his knee with his thumb harder and harder, beginning to vocalize rather than whisper, when he suddenly stopped and stared into space. Something had come to him. Not exactly something but the shade of something, an Image—was it a Memory? He struggled to bring it into focus, to remember it outright, yet even as he did a chill ran through him and the hair stood up on his arms.

He got up and began to pace the room, holding his head, trying to remember and yet even in the thrall of that effort realizing that he really didn't want to remember. This latter wish was now granted by distraction as he suddenly began to notice his surroundings. The plush bedroom was a wreck, with clothes—and not all of them did he recognize—strewn all around. The overfull ashtray had fallen from the side table to the carpet. There were several glasses, either half-full of amber liquid or lying on their sides in puddles. The bed was completely stripped; he'd been sleeping on a bare mattress.

He then turned his attention to his person, which he found completely naked and quite the worse for wear, with a scrape on his shin and a large bruise on his forearm. As dirty as the room was, so was his body, with his hair matted in places and nameless substances stuck to him in blotches. He put his hand over his mouth in a gesture of awe and disbelief, but he quickly removed it as he caught a whiff of something unmentionable, and then caught sight of it too, a dirty stain on his index finger.

He stumbled into the shower, which was itself no island of

cleanliness, with two wet towels dumped on the floor and long black hairs (whose could they be?) around the drain. Kicking the filth aside, he turned on the shower and stood under it, closing his eyes under the spray and feeling the flood run down. The soap was a scummy mess on the floor so he took the micro-bottle of hotel shampoo and washed himself with that, water swirling at his feet, first gray, then clear. The mirror was fogged when he got out because he hadn't turned on the exhaust fan, and he left it that way, his head and torso a blur as he dried himself, genitalia visible in the small strip of clear glass just above the sink.

He dressed and then stood looking at the chaos of the bedroom, uncertain how to proceed. And then he noticed the Driver standing in the doorway. They looked at each other in silence for a moment. The Linguist indicated the mess scattered around the room with a silent gesture, and the Driver responded with a shrug of his shoulders and by walking over to the side of the bed, picking up the Linguist's notebook and handing it to him. The Linguist understood, somehow, the meaning of this gesture, understood, in that moment, the futility of gathering up his rags, and they left the room as it was, open suitcase and all.

When they arrived at the next hotel, of course, there were new clothes waiting for him, and a new Assistant, and he knew then that he was in the service of something he could never truly know, an event at the core of Language that could never be described because it was the ground of possibility for description itself. His Waking Life, henceforth, would be at the service of this unremembered world.

He lit another cigarette and leaned back in his chair. He was struck, suddenly, by the resemblance of Little A's performances to Todorov's conception of the Signified. Todorov defines the sign as an "entity that (1) can become perceptible and (2) for a particular group of users, marks a lack in itself…. The aspect of the sign that can become perceptible [we call] the signifier; the absent aspect, the signified; and the relationship between them, that of signification." Thus for Saussure's "sound-image" we now have a potential perception, applicable equally to any of the senses. The problem arises, as Todorov freely admits, with the signified:

> [The signified] has been defined here as a lack, an absence in the perceptible object, which thus becomes a signifier.... The signified, let us say tautologically, does not exist outside of its relation with the signifier—before, after, or elsewhere. The same gesture creates both the signifier and the signified, concepts that are inconceivable apart from each other: a signifier without a signified is simply an object; it is, but it does not signify. A signified without a signifier is the inexpressible, the unthinkable, the nonexistent itself. The relationship of signification is, in a certain sense, the opposite of identity with self; the sign is at once mark and lack, originally double.

Todorov's analysis reminded him now of an old argument he had once heard in Buddhist circles: Words are an expression of desire. Every fact is a wish. But since what one desires must, by definition, be absent, words may only refer to what is not and can only indicate conditions that are, in practical terms, the opposite of reality. Language, then, is a (grossly inadequate) system for plugging holes, bolstering insecurities, theatrical pretense, mask rather than revelation, obfuscation rather than discovery. The old cliché of the homosexual man who attempts to hide his proclivity under a costume of virility and overstated machismo is the model for the speaking human. Like a boxer who psyches himself up before a fight by sparring in a mirror, muttering "you're the greatest; no one can touch you," we speak to convince ourselves we are immune to Death, which is, or course, the Thing that is defined by our lack of immunity to it. "The Cretans, always liars…" said Epimenides, forgetting, for that moment, that he himself was a Cretan.

But now there appears Little A, like the Zeus the Cretans thought they could entomb. Try as he might, the Linguist could not but think of Little A as the sole exception to the paradox, the single moment of Truth, avoiding the lie, looking Death in the eye, by refusing to signify. For wasn't Little A precisely Todorov's "inexpressible… unthinkable… nonexistent"? Little A as signified to the Waking Life's signifier, the Sleep that drives the Action.

These resemblances haunted the Linguist, and yet they didn't. For once he realized the impregnability of the problem, the reflexive, irreconcilable Gordian knot formed in the relationship of the specific course of study he had now undertaken and the great unspoken world that Little A represented, he relaxed into it. There was no solving the problem; you might as well live in it and simply do the best you can. And though it was becoming more difficult to determine exactly what one might mean by "best," or "can," or indeed by "you," as he became more intimately involved with the Object of his Research, it really wasn't that different from Regular Life.

He understood, now, Goodman's blackouts, those periods of time indicated by lacunae in her notes and in her memory, periods of time during which she assumed she went into trance and spoke in tongues herself. Did he himself speak in tongues during the shows that were blanked from his memory? What he understood now was the banality of the question. What, in fact, was the distinction? Did Little A's phonemes mark their own lack? What was the difference between Little A's "words" and, for example, the words of Epimenides, or Todorov?

And suddenly, in this moment, this Night Before the Morning After, the Linguist saw his path before him, and saw as well the enormous significance of the work. Used to being a perpetual adjunct, a nerdy bystander to any group he associated with, always recording, futzing with his equipment or with his notes, he realized now his integral role in Little A's operation. There might be some projects to which a linguist would be an extraneous appendage, a student at the periphery, outside the real activity, but this was not one. As the Signified needs a Signifier to bring itself into existence, so Little A needed the Linguist. And henceforth the One would be servant to the Other.

When this self-aggrandizing thought finally coursed through his troubled mind he at last felt the purpose he craved, and a smile came to his lips. He stubbed out his cigarette, stood up and stretched. Leaving his notebooks spread open on the table—there was no need to tidy up; someone would do it in the morning—he walked into the bedroom, unbuttoning his shirt. Through the hotel window, high above the city, Moonlight fell upon the bed, illuminating in ghostly white the perfect, naked bodies of the three dancers entwined upon his bed.

"I remain; I have forgotten," he whispered as he got undressed. "I lean my face on my Beloved. Everything stops. I abandon myself, leaving my caution forgotten among the lilies."

ᴀᴀᴀ

Morphine drip, phosphorescent, one droplet per pulse, with each drop a dulling weight like ballast entering the body. LED readouts, the figure-eight grids refusing to gestalt into actual numbers. Drool hanging off the lip, motionless, feeble light matched by the rhythmic beeping of the EKG. A dark world that, when one's eyes first open on it, offers no easy answer to the question of up and down or inner and outer. Q, thus, whether looking in or out, not much caring to exert influence on the scene. "Means return," he mouths dreamily, centered, not bound but intubated, integrated into the process, the whole giant spaceship World pumping fuel and fluids through him. Q, a node in the circulation, unpowered filter, kidney of the culture, straining the toxins and passing them out, through yet another tube, to a reservoir of last resort, a place beyond both body and mind, the poisoned lake of our hereafter. "Luc…" he begins painfully, but cannot finish either the word or the thought, the name's image yet refusing to form in the tongue's phantasy. The slight wiggle of a pinky finger reveals the Dream's heroic struggle, fending off dragons, jujitsu and rockets, strange betrayals and even stranger misrecognitions. All of it happening on

296

the conceptual level first, then fading down into the actual. Is he dreaming or reporting a dream to an Analyst? That too, of course, imminently to be dreamt. Dreaming that One dreams. Morphine drip, phosphorescent, one droplet per pulse, with each drop a dulling weight like ballast entering the body. LED readouts, the figure-eight grids refusing to gestalt into actual numbers.

ꝛ

Upon the next waking, Difference. Daylight, first and foremost, but also the soft texture of the sheets, the mild pinching stricture of tape on various parts of the body, the small spot of coolness beneath his cheek, remnant of somnolent drivel. Without moving, Q let one eye drift over the room as he could see it, the sterile white walls chaotically festooned with gadgets and draping cables and tubes, with a television at the center. On the screen was a chart:

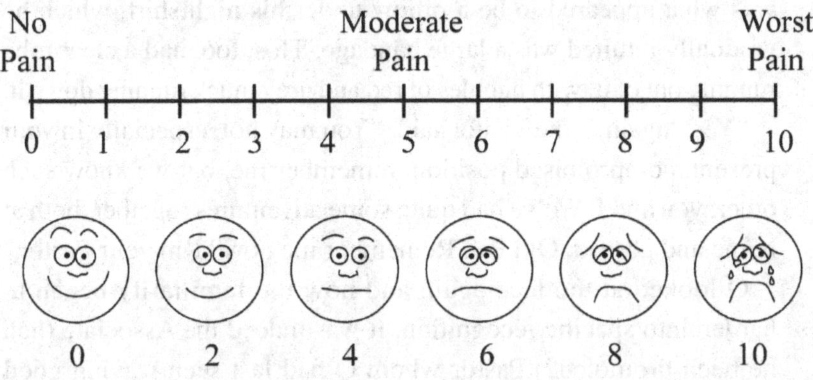

And below the sign an admonition:

"Q," it read, "please use your keypad to enter the number that corresponds to how you are feeling right now."

Though his fingers twitched automatically at the command, there was no keypad under them and the instruction went unheeded as Q's eye continued its circuit of the room. His attention stopped, finally, on what appeared to be a grey-suited male torso, quite close to the edge of the bed, inches, in fact, from his face. He rolled his eyes but was unable to shift his vision far enough upward to make out the face. He tested his neck muscles with a slight jerk, then gradually turned his head until he could see the face beaming above him. The face was familiar, he thought, without being able to precisely place it.

"By gosh, Q," it spoke, "I believe you've decided to rejoin us. I can't tell you how great it is to see you again."

"Again?" Q attempted to say, though all that came out was a rasping noise. He shifted his shoulders and lay back so as to look at his visitor directly, but in so doing his attention was caught by the image of his own body curled up in foetal position under the bedclothes below him. There were tubes running out of him in all directions, from each arm and also from between his legs. There was what appeared to be a pillow under his nightshirt, which he gradually intuited was a large bandage. This, too, had a clear tube running out of it, with bubbles of red and grey muck running down it.

"Yes, 'again,'" the Visitor said. "You may not, especially in your present, compromised position, remember me, but we know each other, you and I. We've had quite some adventures together, both at home and abroad, Old Pal. Remember me now? I'm your Pastor."

Q looked at the face again and now the familiarity began to harden into specific recognition. It was indeed the Associate (had he been promoted?) Pastor whom Q had last seen waving good bye as he boarded a plane, leaving Q, destitute and befuddled, to fend for himself on the Dark Continent, an abandonment that had necessitated Q's taking temporary (but wasn't it all temporary?) employment as a mercenary, thus instigating that period of his life of which Q was least proud. And so when, after a brief test of his vocal chords, Q began to speak, his voice was tinged with bitterness.

"Pardon my *méconnaissance*," Q began, politely. "I have no

excuse since, as I look at you now, I realize you haven't changed one iota in the intervening years. I'm glad to see that the Church of the Ostensible Jesus has, at least in this one instance, taken care of its own."

"Ah… touché, Q," the Pastor replied. "You always were a clever lad, and your irony cuts me to the quick now as ever. I can only pray that you have the grace to accept, here, this most sincere apology that I proffer you, both from Myself, a mortal like any Other, and from the immutable and perfect Church of the Ostensible Jesus, whose Holy Tongue, I flatter myself to say, now speaks through me."

"Think nothing of it. It wasn't the first time—nor even the most trying—I was abandoned unto death and yet survived," Q retorted. Then he thought, though he wasn't sure why, it would be best to defuse the conversation by silencing the more obvious recriminations. "But I'm not the only who has suffered; the Church itself seems to have weathered quite a serious downturn since it saw fit to curtail my ministry. I trust the finances are back in order."

"Oh yes," the Pastor replied with a wan smile, "we were fortunately able to sequester the source of our accounting irregularities and move beyond that chapter. Little A, of course, has been something of a shot in the arm for the ministry, both in terms of recruits and receipts. It is Little A, for example, who is responsible for this…" he indicated with a sweep of his arm the room in which Q was convalescing as well as the hospital that surrounded it… "and several others like it, as well as our new and ongoing programs of medical and pharmaceutical research. The latter has, in its own right, proved to be a bastion against pecuniary exigencies, allowing us to carry on and expand our many and various ministries without concern that our resources might again be overburdened, or that any necessity for drastic and unplanned action might, yet again, suddenly overtake us."

"Yes," said Q. "I—along with everyone else, apparently—have of course been following the track of Little A's unprecedented successes."

"Yes," the Pastor went on, seemingly somewhat ruffled by the interruption, "and I trust you will take our hospitality..." and he again indicated the medical facility with a sweeping gesture of his arm... "as being somewhat more determined than pure Charity, as we offer you succor, now, partly in gratitude for your ministries of the past, and partly in the hope that they might, one day, resume. Please understand that when the *Custos Texti* brought you to us, that day so long ago, we gave thanks and also prayed for the future..."

Here Q left off listening and retreated into his own Memory, which faculty had, with the mention of the Guardian, quite suddenly reconstituted itself and the vision of his and Lucy's (Lucy!) ill-treatment in the sylvan glade came back to him with full sensory force. Again he felt the horrid arrow through his chest. Again he heard the wretched laughter in the throat of the Guardian and his diabolical assistant. Again he saw Lucy fallen to the brutish appetites of the three beasts. And as the memories welled up from his Unconscious they seemed to spew forth in his speech. He cried and blubbered and swore and cursed his tormentors; he wailed and screamed Lucy's name. He fought with the bedclothes and struggled to rise.

The Pastor stepped quickly to the door and called to the nurse, who came running in, drawing a syringe from her pocket. Q was knocking at the bedside table, straining at his tubes, but she managed to get the needle into the shunt and quickly depressed the plunger, and Q lay back, eyes still wild but face softening and screams fading to a whisper, until his body seemed to sink into the bed, and he felt himself slipping under and then going back down, deeper and deeper, light fading and body and mind cooling as he sank through thermoclines of deepening green.

And upon the next waking, Difference, again. Daylight and the soft texture of the sheets, the mild pinching stricture of tape on various parts of the body, the small spot of coolness beneath his cheek. And, once again, the grey-suited male torso, close to the edge of the bed. Q attempted to look up, back into that face, but found himself unable to move, gradually becoming aware that he was restrained.

"Yes," the Pastor said, "I apologize for the ignominious treatment, Q, but we can't have you hurting yourself further. Your condition is still Guarded, but we need to get you started on your Physical Therapy before the muscle deterioration becomes irreversible. So I wonder if we can agree to certain ground-rules, the first being that you'll be civil and show restraint, no matter what surprises your Memory may have in store. Your placid cooperation is a necessary element of your Recovery, and, as I'm sure you realize, the absolute control over the Patient by all Doctors, Nurses and Other Staff is essential to the efficient operation of any Hospital."

While Q fuzzily attempted to parse this complex argument, his Memory was returning, again, with the horrors of his and Lucy's treatment in the forest. He attempted to turn his head and look at the Pastor, but not even this simple motion could be accomplished without, apparently, the intervention of Hospital Staff, and so, even as rage and grief were boiling, again, inside him, he opted to cooperate, and agreed to the terms. The Pastor expressed his great joy at Q's willingness to comply and immediately called for the Nurse and an aide to release Q from his restraints. He then took his leave, promising to return when Q was feeling better to continue their conversation.

And though it was Q's initial plan to deceive the Pastor and, immediately upon being released from his bonds, strike out with a vengeance upon the first scrub-suited flunky who came within reach, in the end he responded only with the exact placidity the Pastor and the rest of the hospital staff desired. There were two reasons for this failure of his Will, the first being that he quickly discovered that he was quite incapable of lashing out even when he was untied, as he was so weak he could barely make a fist, much less use one, and the second being that, the more he thought about it, the more his Memory returned to him, the sadder and more despondent he became, until pure Hopelessness overcame him.

His Love was gone. The one true object of his desire was now dead, torn to pieces and devoured by loathsome beasts and their even more loathsome masters. He wept at the suffering she must have endured in her final minutes. And he wept, too, at the happy memories of their brief reunion on the rails. He remembered the soft touch of her lovely body, the gracefulness of her small movements, the utter ecstacy of their perfectly reciprocated passion. He remembered her as he often had, longing for reunion, but this time Death cast a pall over his phantasies, as he realized that there was no hope of ever experiencing that vision, that touch, that smell again. There was no reason to hope; there was nothing left to hope for. There was no reason to travel; there was nothing to look for. There was no reason, in fact, to continue at all, for there was nothing to be continued.

In such attitude he lay for some weeks, as pliable as clay to the hands of the various Specialists, Nurses, Physical Therapists and other Staff that continuously orbited around him. They lifted food and drink to his mouth, and he ate and drank automatically, without tasting anything. They removed the drain from his chest wound, and each day when they changed the bandage they replaced it with another, slightly smaller. They picked up his limbs and moved them for him, returning flexibility to his joints. Later, they stood him up and commanded him to walk, which he did, faltering at first, with the short but very muscular Physical Therapist's arm around his waist to keep him from falling. His organs began to return to normal function, and he graduated from the catheter to the bedpan, and then one day he was able to walk to the bathroom, and the Physical Therapist, whom he was getting to know quite well, announced that it was time for him to begin exercising in earnest.

ℒ

They put him in a wheelchair for the long journey to the gym and took him down the hall, which was thronging with Medical Professionals and patients, many of them in wheelchairs like Q. The workers, Q noticed, all seemed in good spirits, moving rapidly from room to room, with smiles on their faces and purpose in their step. The patients, on the other hand, all seemed to resemble himself, blankly staring with mouths half open and drool hanging down, and Q wondered if perhaps this ward were reserved exclusively for those like him who had suffered great emotional loss along with physical infirmity.

In the gym the PT put him on a bench or a bicycle, strapped little weights to his feet or his hands, or cinched him into hydraulically pressurized gear that added a slight amount of resistance to most any movement a body could make. He swam, halfheartedly, in the pool, and he received reluctant massages and, despite himself, slowly began to improve.

Now through all this Q's Physical Therapist worked constantly beside him, timing and gauging the various therapeutic activities, but for several weeks Q gave the short, stout, ruggedly handsome man scarcely a glance, as if he were just another hospital appliance. Then one day Q happened to catch sight of him at just the right angle, in just the right light, and had a sudden jolt of recognition.

"I say," said Q, "don't I know you from somewhere?"

"Of course you do," the PT replied blandly. "I'm your physical therapist." He went on strapping Q into the Unweighing System Anti-Gravity Treadmill.

Q stood flummoxed a moment, for he now realized that the voice was familiar, too. In all the time he had been working with Q, he had scarcely uttered a word for Q to notice, but now, hearing the voice plainly, even the silence seemed familiar. Q was positive he had heard and not heard this man before. "No, from before. I know you from before all this… all my… trouble."

303

The PT cinched tight the last of the velcro straps on the diaper-like harness and turned the treadmill on to the slowest possible speed. But Q forced the question as his feet began to move under him.

"Yes, Q, we know each other," the PT finally admitted. "You knew me in different attire, different coiffure, different coloring, different smell. You knew me as the Troll."

"What? No…" Q stammered, but knew it was true even as he did. Though the clean-shaven young man before him bore little resemblance to his mentor of the rails, Q realized sadly that the dreadlocks, beard, dirt-tan and rags of the Troll had been his most prominent feature, and that now, bare-faced and in scrubs, only the eyes and nose gave him away.

They stared at each other in silence, a silence that Q recognized, but which now seemed imbued with a different meaning, and what Q had formerly interpreted as a deep, epigraphic wisdom now implied only timidity. Q's lips shook as he searched for right words to address the changeling before him. He even reached out to give his old friend a hug, but the PT stepped back just far enough to dodge the embrace, and Q could not follow, being caught up in his harness with his legs in involuntary ambulation.

"You've changed a bit yourself," the PT said, turning away to attend to another patient.

Over the coming months Q and the PT worked closely together, but it seemed neither wished to bring up the fact of the PT's true, or former, Identity, and the secret passed between them only in questioning glances.

ᘔ

This state of affairs grew increasingly uncomfortable for Q, and he began to dread their encounters. One day, after some months of the incrementally staged workouts, and now agile enough to walk to the elevator under his own power, Q elected to stroll to the gym on his own and somewhat earlier than his normal time, in the hopes of upsetting the routine.

He seated himself on the curl machine, as it was the most comfortable, set it to its lowest setting, and worked at it lazily while watching his fellow patients gazing out from their own lazy efforts. He noticed, however, one who did not fit the pattern, a very thin woman working on the Extension Machine next to him. Unlike anyone else in the gym, this woman was putting real effort into the exercise, puffing and sweating, gritting her teeth and grunting with each lift of the weights against her ankles. After an interminable time at this grueling work, she dropped the weights and went over to the Arm Curl Machine, and Q noticed that she walked with a marked limp. He also saw several large scars along her legs and arms.

There was something familiar about this woman. Q almost thought… but no, when he saw her face he saw nothing he recognized. Her face, too, was scarred, and red and raw in places. Her mouth hung open crookedly and was set in what seemed a permanent scowl, and when the urge struck her she simply spat on the floor. She did two or three curls, then stopped and increased the weight to the point that she trembled and strained with all her might for each lift, causing the veins to stand out on her forehead and neck.

Overcome by a strangely compelling curiosity, Q went over to the struggling woman and stood beside her as she worked. She paid no attention to him. Finally he said, "Not to interrupt you while you're working out, but I can't help noticing…."

"Just a minute, Q," she gasped. "Just one more sequence."

Q stood, mouth agape, as she finished her curls, for the voice that had come out of this woman's mouth was Lucy's.

~

"Can't help noticing…?" she reminded him as she wiped the sweat from her brow. Q, however, had forgotten his original inquiry and could only stare, with tears streaming down his cheeks, at the mangled face looking back at him. It gradually dawned on him that the unfamiliar face he was seeing was still in the healing phase of plastic surgery. She dabbed at it, gingerly, with her towel. "Can't help noticing that I remind you of someone? Maybe like a cut up and sewn back together version of your girlfriend? Or like a collage of the torn-apart pieces of everyone you ever knew? An ugly reality giving the lie to an idealized memory, reminding you that such memories are always fantasies, that life is only ugliness, and that only Death awaits us at the end?"

Even as accustomed as he was to his Lover's caustic humor, the level of cynicism expressed in this ostensibly playful ribbing, especially after their long separation, left Q speechless, and his only reply was to weep the more, finally collapsing in front of her in a kind of fit.

"Oh for Christ's sake, Q," she admonished, "get up and stop blubbering." She grabbed him by the collar of his hospital gown and stood him rudely erect. "Come on, let's go chill in the whirlpool and catch up. I think I've got some Oxies in my locker. Good for what ails you." She winked at him.

Like a sad, punished puppy, Q followed his Love as she limped across the gym to the women's locker room. He stood at the door, halted by the sign, until she returned with the promised medication. "Here you go," she said, handing him four small pills. "Choke 'em down." Q complied, as he had lost all desire to face reality without armor, that day.

She led him over to the whirlpool, then, where she unceremoniously shed her gym clothes and climbed in. The sight of her naked body moved Q, again, to tears, for her formerly perfect skin was now a patchwork of stitch-marks and grafts in varying colors, a crazy quilt of living flesh.

"Oh, yeah, sorry about that, Q," she said as she settled into the warm, frothing water, "must have been a bit of a shock. Never mind, though. It all comes out in the wash. Come on in and relax. Let the water run over you."

Still sniffling, Q dropped his gown and joined her in the pool. Luckily, they were alone in this section of PT. Q was concerned that the staff might object to this sort of mixed bathing, but she assured him she had the situation under control, and she gave the pill bottle a shake.

She told him, then, of her long recovery, the months in traction and the long succession of surgeries. They had been lucky enough, apparently, to be brutalized outside one of the most advanced hospitals in the world. All the best surgeons were here, practicing cutting-edge medicine with the most sophisticated equipment available, including robotic monitoring and "nano-divers" that performed micro-excisions and aided healing at the cellular level. There were several thousand of these, she told him, still coursing through her body, though most would be expiring in the very near future.

Her injuries had been classified as Severe, with one arm and one leg having been completely removed, and the other knee pulverized by a pair of massive jaws and having to be rebuilt practically from scratch, these being only the worst of a long list of wounds, most any of which would have been fatal had she been brought to a lesser facility. She lifted her left knee, still slightly swollen, out of the water and flexed it for Q's perusal.

Q was beginning to feel a bit better, beginning to feel glad to be talking to his Lucy once again. A lightness seemed to fill his chest, and in his arms and legs he was feeling a pleasant fatigue. When she was showing him her knee he nodded approvingly, and once he even caught himself chuckling at her descriptions of the Staff's ineptitude. The warm, frothing concoction of the whirlpool felt much better to him than he expected, and he found himself sinking lower and lower into the cauldron, until his ears were just out of the water, so he could still hear her speech but could also blow bubbles with his mouth.

He even, in this giddy mood, and so happy to hear his favorite voice again, started playing footsie with Lucy under the surface. "Watch out, Q," she cautioned. "I should warn you my plumbing's been rearranged a bit, which may require some readjustment on your part."

"That's OK," Q bubbled. "I'm just happy to have my Lucy back."

"Lucy?" she said, with a critical look. "Oh no, no. You mistake me. My name's Gwen."

℘

"Gwen?" Q repeated automatically, in a state of profound confusion. "But you are my Lucy. You look different, and you act different. It is as if your psyche had been rent asunder like your body, and reassembled in like fashion, but you have the same voice; I would know you anywhere. You're Lucy…."

" Q began to sputter a reply, but she went on. "Ask yourself," she said, "where you might find, now, your Lucy, who, when last you saw her, was but a pile of bloody bones in a dog's plate. Ask yourself how much a thing may change in form and quality and still claim Identity with Itself. I mean, given that there are differences of nature between things of the same genus, how can we even say that Identity is ever primary? Take, even, an iterative value such as a Word; is not Identity, here, merely a specialized instance of rhyme?"

Q pondered for a moment, feeling, as he did, the euphoria beginning to drain from his body. The lightness in his chest turned heavy; his arms and legs, so relaxed before, began to feel restless, and he sat up in the water. It was as if the weight of the conversation and the difficult metaphysical concepts coming from his Lover's mouth had killed his buzz, but it was more than that. Philosophers introduce new concepts, they explain them, but they don't tell us the problems to which those concepts are a response, what must have been taken for granted, what is not said but is nonetheless present. As Q thought about it, unconsciously moving his tongue inside his mouth, he became slightly nauseous. The name, Gwen, wasn't simply wrong; it was unbearable. Like some hideously warped, propagandized version of History being forced down his throat, it was awful not only because it was a Lie, but also because it obscured the Truth, erasing a Past that was dear to Q, a Past that formed an important part of his own Identity. He concentrated with all his might to craft his reply. "But your voice…" he said.

"Yes," she said, "my voice. With univocity, you should understand, it is not the differences which are and must be: it is being which is Difference, in the sense that it is said of difference. Moreover, it is not we who are univocal in a Being which is not; it is (if I may say, inverting Spinoza) we and our individuality which remain equivocal in and for a univocal Being. All this, however, presupposes codes or axioms which do not result by chance, but which do not have an intrinsic rationality either. It's just like theology: everything about it is quite rational if you accept sin, the immaculate conception, and the incarnation. Reason is always a region carved out of the irrational—not sheltered from the irrational at all, but traversed by it and only defined by a particular kind of relationship among irrational factors. Underneath all reason lies delirium, and drift."

Q let out an anguished cry. "Oh," he moaned, "it is as if you are telling me that my Past which I remember is some faulty Text that I have been taking for Gospel, and now nothing remains for me to attach my Identity to. 'Gwen,' you say, and how do I respond? Do I say 'Gwen,' or 'of course Gwen, my friend,' or do I say 'my lover, Gwen,' or should I say 'Gwen, yes, I remember Gwen when…'?"

"Q," she said (and did the corners of her mouth soften slightly in response to his plaintive appeal?), "herein lies the secret: to bring into existence and not to judge. If it is so disgusting to judge, it is not because everything is of equal value, but on the contrary because what has value can be made or distinguished only by defying judgment. What judgment, in art, could ever bear on the work to come? Gwen, at your service."

"Do you have any more of those pills?" Q asked.

The coming weeks were not easy ones for Q, for he had not only to cure his physical infirmity but also diseases of his mind and soul. Though he saw Gwen almost every day, either in the gym or in the constantly bustling hallways, and though he continued to treat her, in general, as his Lover-at-a-distance, time did not allay his initial confusion over her identity and her name. As the grafts on her face began to heal her visage seemed to solidify into something less and less familiar, and yet her very strangeness drew his attention toward her. He had difficulty, now, reading her emotions from her expression, but this prompted him to try harder, to study intently each little curl of the lip or twitch of an eyebrow, to search out hidden meanings in the smallest punctuation of her attitude.

In the rigidly controlled—one might say "sterile"—environment of the hospital, with video surveillance literally everywhere, conjugal visits were not possible, of course, but in truth this was something of a relief to Q. For though he felt the occasional twinge of randiness, usually when in the thrall of the pain-killers (to which he grew more and more attached each day), Gwen's off-hand comment remained in the back of his mind and engendered a deep anxiety, no less powerful for being unspoken, and the thought which kept occurring to him despite his best efforts to push it away: Were the changes to her face and name indicative of equivalent changes to Other Parts of her anatomy? The question lodged itself within him and refused to be dismissed.

He found himself, while exercising beside her on the Extension Bench or the Knee Raise, staring at her profile in wonder, for he found her both familiar and strange, like an image from a dream, something which has been very close for a very long time but whose remarkable qualities are only now being noticed.

The rooms in this ultra-modern facility were not sequestered by gender, but they were divided by pathology, and since Gwen's problems were mostly orthopedic and Q's entirely soft-tissue, the Lovers found themselves housed in quite disparate wings of the facility. Q had pled—with nurses, with the Pastor, with the PT, with anyone who would listen—that his Love be moved to a room closer, if not entirely adjacent, to his own, or vice versa, and his requests had been, according to all his sources, taken under advisement at the highest level of Hospital Management. And yet weeks went by with no Word on the matter, and Q was beginning to despair of ever getting anyone's attention in the vast bureaucracy where he and Gwen were, however benevolently, imprisoned.

This monastic life didn't seem to bother Gwen in the same way; in fact, she seemed almost happy, some days, to be going back to her quarters after PT. Once Q suggested that he sneak back to her room with her, or she to his, but she quickly dismissed this idea as impracticable in this controlled environment.

The day did come when Q's anxiety finally got the better of him, and he resolved to resort to dishonesty. He said good bye to her, as he always did, outside the gym door, but as soon as he turned the first corner he turned around and began to follow her in stealth mode. It was not easy to keep her in view, and he often had to jump to keep her in sight in the crowded hallways. When she got to the elevator in her wing he thought, at first, that all was lost, but it turned out that he easily concealed himself among the thirty other passengers who were crowding at the door, and he was able to slip into the very car with her without being detected.

This elevator, it turned out, was not just a conveyance but a popular Hospital Attraction, for it had a glass wall and rode along the outside of the building, offering breathtaking views from its hundred-story vantage, quite a change from the elevators in Q's wing, which were sanitary white boxes. Though Q could not get close enough to the glass wall at the rear to see the entire landscape, he could see the snow-capped, purple mountains in the distance. Their view was blocked by fog for a moment and then it opened again to a clear blue sky, and Q realized they had passed through a cloud. Birds darted by outside, and then Q saw what appeared to be an aircraft coming toward them. He was almost to the point of panic when he realized it was a miniature, a drone not unlike the one that had evicted Lucy and himself from the Garden, so many moons ago.

Gwen stood right at the window railing, looking out impassively, for the entire way up, making Q's job of avoiding her gaze while keeping her in his own exceedingly easy. He himself stood at the door, watching her carefully in case she would turn around at any of the car's numerous stops, but she did not, until the view out the window had turned into a veritable cloud-scape and the car announced that it had reached the top floor and all must exit, whereupon Q ducked quickly down and removed himself ahead of the other passengers. There was a rubber tree potted near the door, and he secreted himself behind its foliage and waited for Gwen to come out.

She came out virtually last, strolling in leisurely fashion, as if still in a reverie from the stunning view she had just taken in, while the rest of the passengers bustled off around her. Q watched her slow progress carefully, darting from plant to column to plant to keep himself unobtrusive and herself in his sight, but gradually he became distracted by his surroundings, for he now found himself on a large floor, surrounded by shops, offices and other structures that looked like small buildings in their own right, all surmounted by a vast transparent dome ceiling. Another Drone flew overhead, and then another, and then Q saw that the sky was in fact congested with them, coming and going from a central platform. The number of them was quite astounding, like a swarm of flies around a carcass, weaving among each other with reckless speed, and indeed two of them did collide while Q was watching, and fell onto the Dome, an occurrence which caused, apparently, no concern whatsoever among the humans coursing on the floor below.

His attention was caught, just then, by a policeman on a Segway™ scooter passing by at his elbow. He ducked instinctively, but the Officer was apparently engaged elsewhere and went on without a second look. The encounter did serve to bring Q back to his present mission, however, and he left off his Drone watching to search out Gwen on the floor, a task which proved dauntingly complex, as she had apparently entered one of the main concourses and was now just one head among the hundreds that were coming and going there. Miraculously, Q spotted her turning a corner outside an ice cream shop and was able to make his way through the crowd and pick up her trail before she turned again. Having lost the dreamy attitude in which she had debarked the elevator, she was now walking at a brisk clip, without a trace of a limp, and it was all that Q could do to keep up without making himself too obvious, and he practically had to trot behind her as she made her way down the rows of shops (for the place resembled nothing so much as an upscale shopping mall here) and then turned down a large but less populated concourse that was lined with offices.

There was very little traffic here and she would have spotted him, certainly, if she merely turned around, but she did not, and he was able to track her undetected until she turned at last into a pair of large doors that had the scene of the crucifixion carved into them. As Q came up to the doors he noticed that they were quite striking, having been carved and gold-leafed in imitation of Leonard Limousin's Crucifixion of c. 1510, and in partial relief, with certain of the "clear" portions of the scene having been done in glass, which gave Q peep-holes through which he could see Gwen as she made her way across the large ante-chamber. Q watched from under Christ's arm as she passed by the Receptionist, to whom she gave only a quick wave, and pushed open another set of doors almost as ornate as the first at the back of the room. Then he pushed in himself and approached the Receptionist at her desk.

"May I help you?" she asked in a way that sounded truly concerned for Q's well-being but at the same time conveyed the sense that he was indeed helpless without her, the truth of which he then proved by standing in front of her, lips trembling and at an utter loss for words. "Did you need to see the Pastor?" she ventured, making it very easy for him to nod in the affirmative. She picked up the phone. "Reverend, Q is here."

The second set of doors were somewhat more austere than the first, being done in imitation of the Rubens of 1610, yet they were still elaborate enough to give Q excuse to comment upon them and to step up and examine them closely while waiting for his audience. These doors, also, had vision panels worked skillfully into the carved and painted design, and it was these panes of stained glass that Q examined most closely, in the hope that he might catch sight of Gwen on the other side to determine where she had gone. He thought he saw her just disappearing around a corner, but he couldn't be certain. It could have been most anyone.

❧

The Pastor's office seemed designed to stop, rather than promote, conversation, as one could not enter it without a feeling of awe and, by comparison, the triviality of an individual's small spiritual concerns. The Pastor himself sat at a small desk with his back to a great window. In this window Christ was yet again depicted, this time, however, in Ascension, in a stained-glass rendering of the Garofalo of c. 1510. The effect was quite stunning, with Christ standing almost fifty feet tall and rising into the clear sky over a vista of mountaintops protruding through a bed of white clouds. Had angels been floating by instead of the ubiquitous Drones outside, it would have seemed quite natural.

"Ah, Q," the Pastor said warmly, rising from his desk and opening his arms. "I'm so glad to see you up and around, and I'm pleased at this impromptu visit. Take a moment to get your breath; most everyone has to upon first encounter with Our Office."

And indeed Q was standing, mouth agape, in wonder at the scene. It was as if Christ had been captured not in that moment when he was captured by the Old Masters, as he rose just above the heads of his followers, but later, higher up, above the clouds, at the very gates of Heaven.

The Pastor came out from behind his desk and directed Q to join him in a coign of vantage where a pair of armchairs had been set up, ostensibly for just such an occasion. Q walked in slowly, gripping the back of the armchair, for the alcove seemed to jut out into empty space, and he was, despite all Reason, filled with Vertigo. And then, just as he sat down, a Drone struck the glass just in front of him. It bounced off without a sound and careened wildly with two of its four rotors destroyed. The small box it had been carrying plummeted down through the clouds, followed shortly by the Drone itself.

"Yes," the Pastor said in response to Q's anxious look, "their guidance systems still occasionally fail, and yet they've become such an important part of our ministry that we simply must keep them in service. Our Programmers, however, are making them safer every day."

"How high are we, exactly?" Q queried, bending forward and looking down onto the clouds.

"Well, that depends on what you mean by 'How high?'. In absolute terms, I believe we are roughly 5276 meters above sea level. It is harder to measure the building's height relative to the ground, since the ground level, here, is in constant flux, but it normally ranges between 15 and 18 hundred meters."

"But how is it possible for the ground level to fluctuate so drastically?" Q wondered.

"Frankly, we don't know. It's hard to say what the laser is hitting, down there. We don't visit the ground much these days, as too much of our time is taken up with duties on high, so to speak."

"You never leave the Building, then?" Q inquired.

"Oh, Our duties often take us away from the Building and indeed from the Nation, but since we installed the rooftop airports there is little need for Us to descend to accomplish our travels."

"Well," Q volunteered, "you should know that the bottom floors of the building are in rather serious disrepair, having practically been reclaimed by the Wilderness. And there are some rather disreputable characters wandering the grounds, including that low creature who wears a badge labelled *Custos Scripti* and who is responsible for my and my Lucy—pardon me, Gwen—'s injuries."

"Yes, the bottom floors have, for all practical purposes, been abandoned. As to the Guardian, his eccentricities are well-known, but he remains a Necessary Evil, as our gateways must be monitored, one way or another. Excuse me." He held a finger to his ear and spoke into space: "Could you bring Q and myself some refreshment?" He turned back to Q. "Tell me, do you have any further questions about Our Facilities? I'm anxious for you to become familiar and feel comfortable with every aspect of the Church's Operations, for I am here to recruit you, Q. I think you could be an excellent addition to our humble fold, even more valuable now than when God originally brought you to us."

"I'm afraid I have my own duties at Provincial Oaks, these days, and I'm not looking to make a move. I'm here solely on a fact-finding mission, an investigation, of sorts. I've heard so much about Little A…."

"Ah, here we are," the Pastor interrupted. A prim young woman in a stylish but conservative business suit placed a tray of drinks and *hors-d'oeuvres* on the coffee table between them. Q paid no attention at first, but sat up suddenly when he realized that the woman was in fact his Gwen. He barely recognized her for she was now trimmed and coifed, made-up and immaculately dressed in suit and pumps.

"Hello, Q," she said with a wan smile, noticing the shocked look on his face. Q, too stunned to say a word, could only stare in disbelief.

"Yes, Q," the Pastor said, "we've been meaning to mention to you that Gwen has taken the position as Our own right hand and become, in a very short time, indispensable to the Ministry." He took her hand and gazed up respectfully into her eyes.

"Oh," she replied, somewhat embarrassed at the praise, "all I do is try to keep him from working so hard." She moved around behind him and began massaging his shoulders. "He would never sleep if someone didn't remind him to every night." As she noticed the color draining from Q's face, she went on in a more conciliatory tone. "I'm sorry about the suddenness of this. We've been planning to tell you for some time now, but everyone is always so busy. I only hope we can still be close, as I value your friendship, Q, above all else."

a

At this point Q leaned forward to the table, selected a bottle of spring water, and used it to wash down a small handful of Oxycodone pills which he took from his pocket. He then directed his attention out the window at the Drones, up into the face of Christ, around the room, anywhere he could find to look that was not in the direction of the idyllic power-couple that now stood before him. As he waited for the pills to take effect he tried desperately to retain his composure, but suddenly a little cry escaped him and he began to sob. The Pastor handed him a handkerchief. Gwen came and put her hand on his shoulder.

"I'm sorry, Q," she said. "I hope you can understand, one day, and forgive me. I loved you for your rustic, boyish charm, for your love of the rails, for your honesty. But in the end I guess I just wasn't ready to give up the life of luxury and power I was raised in. I've found that, again, here in the Church, and I've given myself to God."

Q sobbed the harder at these words of comfort, eventually becoming so despondent that Gwen and the Pastor left him in his chair and returned to the Pastor's desk to confer over some paperwork that had to be gotten out in short order. When they returned to him they found him, though still lachrymose, giggling now and then between his tears.

At a whispered direction from Gwen, the Pastor suggested that the three of them take a tour of the facilities. Q immediately agreed and stood up, somewhat wobbly but obviously game for an excursion.

They went out of the Church office into the main concourse, strolling at a leisurely pace, but they had not gone more than a few yards before the rather large dose of oxycodone began to evidence itself in Q's gait. At first they attempted to control his reeling by holding onto his arms, but in the end the Pastor whispered into his lapel mic and a wheelchair was brought to them. Q sank into it, head dangling onto his chest. The Attendant who had brought the chair stayed with them, now, to attend to Q's face, which was emitting a slight but constant flow of tears and drool.

Gwen and the Pastor politely ignored Q's saturnine despondency and happily pointed out the various features of the Mall to him, the skylights, the remarkable passive ventilation system, and of course the artwork that was everywhere. Q's attention was drawn to an enormous but strangely-shaped column some distance ahead of them.

"Ah, you've noticed our sculpture," the Pastor said, following his gaze. "Q, please meet The Custodian of the Heights." He pointed toward the strange column and then, with his finger, directed Q's gaze upward. Q lifted his eyes, higher and higher, until he was finally able to make out the great figure that stood over them. The column was, in fact, only the shaft of the axe on which he was leaning, his feet being planted some distance hence. Far above them, in the dizzying heights, his bearded face stared down, as if to say, "What have we here?"

Gwen and the Pastor chuckled approvingly at Q's awestruck look. "Don't worry, Q," Gwen reassured him. "He's not going to squash us. He's our friend. And a really great guy." Everyone had a good laugh over this one, except, of course, Q, who continued to look up and around in confusion and terror.

"Q," the Pastor said in sympathy, "I think you might be interested in something over here." He led the troupe over to a simple door that opened into the blank wall. He put his fingertip on the security pad, and they were suddenly overwhelmed by a great din, like a waterfall, as the door swung open. They entered and stood on a tiny observation platform above what appeared to be a factory floor, except that there were no people in sight, only great machines which seemed veined together by a network of conveyors along which travelled, at great speed, a panoply of product, a cornucopia of goods spilling forth at such a rate they went by in a blur; it was impossible to pick out any single item.

"Look, Q," the Pastor pointed with pride, "over here is our Publishing Arm." And "arm" it did appear to be, like a branch off of the main stream, rows of machines spitting out books at an amazing rate, hundreds per second, speeding them down the conveyors.

"With this operation," Q commented through a rather thick tongue, "it's hard to imagine anyone competing with the Church of the Ostensible Jesus in the Arena of Books."

"Ah, it's not about competition, Q," the Pastor said kindly. "It's about bringing the Word to all those hungry minds out there. It's about the Gift of Language and how it can be used to the benefit of our Congregation and, dare I say it, the Whole Earth."

❧

At this point Q began to feel, in the depths of his drug-addled consciousness, something like a déjà vu, for, unknown to anyone save himself (and, if truth be known, not even he was entirely aware…), for some time now he had felt himself being called to Write. Now, in the sudden, noisy proximity of the actual Means of Production of the Written Word, he felt obligated to learn all he could about the process, so that when his Time came he would be ready for the concrete contingencies that would confront him as he prepared to launch his Work into the World.

"May I ask," he said, "—and please don't hesitate to speak honestly here, as I have quite a thick skin in such matters—if you accept Submissions of secular works along with the important texts you disseminate as part of the Church's Ministry?"

Gwen leaned forward enthusiastically and opened her mouth to answer, but the Pastor stopped her with an upraised index finger. She smiled deferentially and said, "Oh yes, you tell him. You're so much more familiar with the process than I." Then she stepped back and proffered the Pastor her full attention.

"Our Gwen has been of immeasurable assistance in publishing operations," he said. "This cannot be denied. However, in this special case—for you, Q, are nothing if not a Special Case—I would like to respond to your question in proper person, not only because of our long history together, but also with an eye to what We hope will be our dealings in the future and beyond. 'In the beginning was the Word,' Q, and in the End also, and it is our professed goal—it's actually in our Mission Statement—that the Church of the Ostensible Jesus's brand be imprinted on every vehicle—every book, every ebook, every recording, every sign, placard, card, etc.—that carries the Word through the World, so that All may know the Glory of His Name."

"I see," said Q. "So you do accept Submissions from secular novelists, memoirists, etc. Interesting. But may I ask, further, out of my own simple curiosity and without any hint of accusation, how the Church might handle the more, shall we say, libertine Submissions you might receive? I cannot imagine that there are not some Texts in this World—for am I not here, myself, in your presence in this compromised, intoxicated and utterly humiliated position, by virtue of one wretched man's (dear God, the mere thought of him nauseates me) obsession with an even more wretched man's (that certain Marquis whose name I may not pronounce but which has become synonymous with lascivious cruelty) lewd and immoral Writing?—some Texts, I say, for which the proper, indeed the only plausible, reaction of any employee of the Church of the Ostensible Jesus would be to blush and then to say with me, '*hoc horrendum est*,' and condemn it to the fire."

"My dear Q," said the Pastor, smiling courteously to the young innocent, "such matters are of course taken quite seriously by Our Editors, and I'm sure that more than one manuscript has hit our recycle bin with more force than simple rejection required, and yet We must keep pace with the times and meet the ever-growing demands of the reading public. These days the submission process is entirely digitized. Submit your writing from your Laptop, anywhere in the world, to one of our servers, and only a few minutes later, after payment of a modest processing fee, it will be among those Texts you see below you, speeding their way to the millions of Readers We proudly call our Congregation."

Q mused on this development for a moment, until this occurred to him: "Do you mean to say, then, that your texts undergo no Editorial Review? That there is no Gatekeeper? Neither scholars checking facts nor clerks checking grammar? No Editors struggling to help their Authors find *le mot juste?*"

"Well," the Pastor replied, with just a hint of defensiveness, "our Servers do an excellent job with these matters. And while they may lack the human touch, I like to think that Our Work bears more than a passing resemblance to that of the great Johannes Gutenberg, who in 1439 introduced moveable type and enabled the dissemination of the Word to large numbers of parishioners simultaneously. We, in our modern, digital way, have enabled the circulation of millions of books to millions of readers."

"But it seems," Q replied, indicating with his eyes the factory floor beneath them, "that the entire process is automated, from Laptop to Server to…. Could not one imagine a Reader scanning books she hasn't time to actually read, storing the text on a Laptop for future consumption, or indeed for simple searchability in the event she might one day need a bit of the knowledge contained there, thus acquiring knowledge to be accessed without being, shall we say, known? It's almost as if we were seeing Language produced, distributed, consumed, answered—in short, the entire Discursive Circle—without Human Intervention."

"Ah, Q," said the Pastor, "your understanding of the deep philosophical implications of the Digital Revolution is, not surprisingly, considerably more advanced than My own. I might only add this caveat for your further ruminations: Do not we—you, your Gwen, Myself, even the Church of the Ostensible Jesus—owe our very existence to the Mechanism we are observing here? Are we not in its employ? Does it not sustain, feed and clothe us, even as we work within? Are we not just three more unhappy workers in that long History of Workers' unhappiness?"

ə

At this moment Q's discourse with the Pastor was interrupted by a commotion on the floor. One book apparently hadn't made a connection through the sorter and flown out of the line, in the process knocking another book askew, and it another, initiating a massive pile-up that was growing larger every second as books continued to careen down the track. Q pointed at the mess with concern, but the Pastor and Gwen only smiled wanly. "Watch," the Pastor said.

As Q looked the conveyors began to change configuration, shifting routes until the area of congestion had been bypassed so that the flow of goods could continue unabated. Then, to Q's astonishment, with a rush of wind a great door opened in the side of factory and the pile of disorderly books were swept out into the sky by a rotating arm. Q watched as the trove of literature fell down through the clouds, like a library raining.

The Pastor chuckled. "Though I've never seen it," he said, "I've heard that we've started our own little ecosystem down on the ground with our overruns. Books, of course, are completely recyclable. But come see this, Q."

They walked a little further on the platform and looked where the Pastor pointed, at what appeared to be storm clouds brewing above the floor. Perhaps a half-mile from them, the dark mass blocked the rest of the theater from view. "What?" said Q. "The factory has its own weather?"

"No," the Pastor said, "that's the Drone Port, Shipping Department." Now the view coalesced for Q, and he realized the black cloud was a swarm of Drones in the distance. "Yes," said the Pastor in response to Q's amazed expression, "We're getting the Word out."

They continued their tour of the Mall with the Pastor calmly explaining its marvels and Gwen gesturing and nodding enthusiastically. Finally the Pastor remarked that Q, now fairly well oozing in his chair, might do with a bit of refreshment, so they entered a Coffee Shop. "All our facilities are entirely Accessible," the Pastor quipped, smiling wryly, as the doors swung open in front of them and the Attendant pushed Q toward an open table near a window.

The Shop was abuzz with activity, with hundreds of Patrons at the tables bent over spreadsheets in business meetings or sitting alone, rapt in front of their Laptops or Tablets, earbuds installed and Lattés near at hand. "Let's sit over here, for the view," said the Pastor, and they wheeled Q onto a glass-enclosed balcony that looked down, distantly, onto the factory floor they had recently left, but more immediately onto the cloud-bank and snow-capped mountain peaks that protruded through it. The billowing cumulous clouds were in motion, apparently roiled by Winds, and Q could not but be entranced as he saw in them now a lamb, now an angel, now a jolly old man with great white beard. They placed his chair, however, directly next to the glass, which went to the floor and was also curved outward, so that Q was again breathless with Vertigo.

"You should see when it Storms," said Gwen enthusiastically. "The lightning…. And Master… oh…" —she brought her hand to her mouth, giggling with embarrassment—"I mean 'Pastor'… tell Q about our Digital Weather Management System. Oh Q, wait till you hear. It's just amazing."

The Pastor then, somewhat grudgingly, began telling Q about the above-referenced System which, among many other Wonders, was actually producing those visions in the Clouds Q was assuming were pure hallucination, for aesthetic effect and the enlightenment of the Congregation.

Q, however, was too distracted by his immediate surroundings—

including the cloud bank itself, which was just now forming itself into Tintoretto's *Coronation of the Virgin*—to pay much attention to the Pastor's descriptions. All around him, it seemed, things were in minute motion. He had, at first, attributed these movements at the periphery of his vision to the Oxies, but after being dispelled of this illusion concerning the cloud formations, he now began to pay closer attention and found that what he had been mistaking for bugs on the walls and floor were, in fact, bugs on the wall and floor. Ranging in size from a tick to a palmetto bug, they darted across the floors and up the walls. They coursed into and out of small holes in the baseboards and under the tables, up the table legs, even onto the tables. If someone dropped a crumb from their Raspberry Chocolate Chip Scone onto the table or the floor, one of these bugs would immediately run over, pick it up and scurry away with it.

Q, somewhat horrified, interrupted the Pastor to remark about this unsanitary state of the establishment. The Pastor stopped, seemingly flummoxed, and looked around. Gwen offered the explanation.

"It's the nanoworkers," she said to her Pastor. "He's confused by them as I was at first." And both she and the Pastor broke into loud laughter.

"Oh Q," he said, wiping his eyes. "You had me worried, since we don't allow any sort of vermin in the Complex. But what you are seeing are our Nanoworkers, tiny robots that work diligently and constantly to keep our environment perfectly clean. They perform other repetitive tasks for us, also. Take these for example." He directed Q's attention to a line of what appeared to be tarantulas coursing up a column in the center of the room. "These are Nanobuilders." Q looked at these closely and saw that each eight-legged robot was carrying some small item, a screw or nut or washer, and that some were fitted with drivers and drill bits. "These take care of all the construction and maintenance activities that are a constant travail in a structure such as this one. Ah, but look, here's our coffee."

A human barista, apparently employed for nostalgia's sake, complete with 2020s outfit, put their order on the table in front of them. "We took the liberty, Q," the Pastor said, as he and Gwen exchanged knowing looks, "of ordering an extra shot in your Latté."

The tall glass of nut brown liquid the waitress put in front of him was swirled with pink and white, and when he tasted it he found it as sweet and thick as syrup. "This is delicious," he said between gulps, emptying the great mug in a few famished draughts. The Attendant wiped his mouth as Q leaned back, smiled a little sadly, and vomited into his lap.

ααα

The Speaker has won out. After all that work and all those words, all the promises and demands, secret signals and coded evasions, all that sinking to His own despicable level… After all the lies and heartfelt confessions, all the grunts of unwilling assent, all the whining pleas and arrogant commands, whimpering solecisms under the lash, proud refusals to submit… After all those works and money, all the semen and tears, all the sweat of labor and sweat of childish terror… After all that literal and figurative blood…The Speaker has won out.

That loathsome, lowest form of politician (which is the lowest form of life), whose ends are as base as his means and whose means make perverts proud… The Speaker has won out.

Pedazo de mierda, who has his whores dress him in diapers so he can soil them (yes… she has her sources), *el orador gana más de esperanza...* The Speaker has won out.

Seething with bitterness and bile, Espe gripped the edge of her desk in an effort to control her trembling hands. Now all they'd fought for, all their dreams of making a better world for immigrants and citizens alike, all the noble causes they'd struggled so ignobly to defend, all are lost, and she and Santo are left with nothing to show but the blood on their hands.

But she, and then she and Santo? Were they even a Thing any more? It caused her immeasurable grief to realize that her own and her husband's interests no longer coincided. Now she must manage her private affairs, many of which had become rather extensive and time-consuming, privately. And, she supposed, so did he. She could only assume as much, given the days and weeks that campaign duties had kept them apart for the past year, and she had always known Santo to be… proactive.

So, what price had she paid for this all-out campaign that had netted her nothing, unless one could count those wriggling fish, her informants and sycophants, petty crooks, embarrassed, sniveling perverts, as something? Her little secret army had its value, she told herself, for they would do anything for her… or at least anything *they could*. And there, of course, was the rub, since they were universally inept, if sometimes specifically useful.

Yes, she realized fatalistically, victories won within the game remain in the game, even if the ostensible goal were to change the game itself. For one can "change the game" with clever playing, but the change remains on the board, remains within quotes, surrounded and subsumed by the System. There is no out, no larger world that one can seek recourse into. Neither winning nor losing brings the game to a close. Drawn in, now, by her very resistance, she has no choice but to continue.

While she had visualized herself as a kind of warrior before, swinging her sword through the Gordian knot of the bureaucracy, bringing the xenophobes to their knees and marching through with her banner of Truth, she now begins to see the continuum, how she was caught up in it too, how her whip belonged on the podium, how naturally her Boys had progressed from the floor of the House to the floor of her Office.

And what about that "Office"? What sort of Office was it? Oh surely it was a very nice room with nice—well, somewhat the worse for wear, now—carpet and a nice desk, a big picture window looking out over the Capitol grounds, its own full bath and dressing area with lockable cabinets for her—ahem—dainties. And yet this was, in fact, no Office at all. She had neither been elected to it nor had she wrested it by means of a coup. It had been neither bought nor stolen. No, Espe had acquired her Office through sleight of hand, through an almost accidental adjacency. That big leather Chair had scooted under her shapely ass, and she had granted its wish.

Not an Office at all, but the seamy underside of an Office. She looked down at her desk of burled Cherry and imagined, underneath, inverted below her floor, another desk just like it, but constructed of cheap deal, dirty and worm-eaten, stained with spilled ink, with smoke and ash and whiskey and blood, bullet-holes in the face. And from behind that desk in the flip side of her world, a *bandida* arose, lit a cigar, walked over to the big window and gazed out upon—far from pristine green lawns and rose gardens—heaps of smoking rubble with dogs and buzzards fighting over the bodies of horses and men and women.

Espe flicked her cigarette onto the carpet as her reverie faded and the Capitol grounds came back into view. It was time, now, to begin destroying the evidence, wiping hard drives and bagging up belongings, but she was having a hard time getting motivated. She realized—and was that the ghost of a smile on her lips?—that part of her wanted to be found out, wanted to leave it all to be found by the next First Lady or Press Secretary. She imagined her, the Speaker's Wife, that officious little anoxeric slut, fresh from the Inauguration prayer, with the help of the Capitol locksmith, coming upon Espe's gear in the closet, picking up the bustier and fingering the laces, sniffing the perfume, trying it on, mingling, as she did so, Espe's residue, tiny crumbs of skin and hair, with her own, perhaps secreting one of the collection away before calling the Press.

ᴀᴀᴀ

"Q ... Q, wake up."

He felt as much as heard the whisper, so close was Lucy's voice to his ear, felt the warmth of her breath, felt her lip brush the auricle, and felt that tiny sensation echo through his being, almost—oh, almost—cutting through the cacaphonic orchestra of pain that immediately surged to horrific volume. His head felt like a block of wood into which an ax had just been driven. His skin crawled as if covered with nanoworkers. His bones were trying to walk out of his flesh. All the cells of his body opened their mouths to declare their need, like the vast population of some impoverished state clamoring for opioids. A little cry—inarticulate, forsaken prayer—escaped him.

"Ssshhh..." she hissed quietly, "I've turned off the cameras so we could have a moment alone. Let's not alert the nurses. I have such great news. Oh, it is so wonderful, Q, a dream come true."

"Oh, God," Q whispered as he extracted his arms from her embrace and began to flail wildly in a blind search for his pills. He found the bedside tray and urgently searched it with his hand, knocking over the styrofoam water pitcher and scattering the rest of the tray's contents with his most unsubtle motor responses.

She responded with more admonitions to silence and by embracing him more tightly, finally crawling into the bed with him and using her entire body to hold him down. "It's OK, Q," she said in a voice so calm and soft it seemed unconnected to the great physical force she was using to wrestle him into submission, "I have Good News, news so wonderful, news of pure Joy. Oh Q, please be still so I can tell you."

She lay full length on top of him, gradually adjusting herself until she had him immobile and then, to silence his cries of terror, covered his mouth with her own. This sensation, delicious communion so longed for and so long withheld, quieted him for a moment, pressing even his urgent bodily needs into submission, until he surrendered and embraced her. "Oh Lucy," he wept.

"Gwen," she said with sudden coldness. "But whatever," she went on between kisses. "Names don't matter. Nothing matters now except that—oh Q you won't believe how lucky we are, how blessed, blessed beyond measure—we're going to meet Little A."

"Wha..." Q grunted, his interest now piqued despite the distractions of his continued agony and rising desire. He relaxed, slightly, as he began to realize that the goal of his enigmatic quest might actually be within reach, and she took advantage of the softened moment to bring one hand under the bedclothes and under Q's hospital gown to embrace that part of him that she herself lacked.

"Wow," she said as he lay, dormant and spent, after the prolonged tussle, "it's been a while for you, eh? I better clean up. Don't want the Pastor getting a taste of that Stuff running down my leg." She climbed down from her dominant position on the bed and began ablutions with a corner of the sheet. Her body, he saw now, was healing nicely, the stitch marks fading and the skin coloration of the various grafts becoming more uniform, like the map of a World from which the borders between nations were beginning to disappear.

"When?" was all he said, as the News still hung silently between them and had no need of specific reference.

"No one seems to know the exact date, but soon," she said. "Very soon." She had picked up her clothes from the heap on the floor and put them on the bed to sort through, and she paused from pulling her panty-hose right-side out to clutch them to her breast and gaze up at the ceiling. Q could see goose-bumps rising on her arms and belly. "God, can you imagine?" she said breathlessly. "Backstage with Little A. What a privilege!"

She finished dressing and stood in front of the mirror, straightening her blouse and the jacket of her business suit. Then she slipped on her pumps and left, turning back briefly at the door to give him a quick wink, whispering "I'll be in touch" before closing it behind her.

Q lay for a moment, confused and exhausted, before his corporeal hunger commanded him to rise. He ransacked the room for his prescriptions, and when he found nothing rang the nurse, who told him that his prescription had been revised and that she would be by in four hours with his next dose. "Of what?" he demanded.

"Aspirin," she said, and hung up.

Q's body itself seemed to respond to this Word, and he trembled and his teeth chattered as he struggled to control the panic rising inside him. Suddenly nauseous, he fell into the bathroom to retch for a moment, finally expelling barely a spoon-full of white bile. He lay in a heap for a few minutes with his cheek against the cool porcelain before becoming aware that he was not alone. A pair of white-clad short legs, standing near the sink gradually came into focus, and he raised his head to see the Physical Therapist—that one formerly known as the Troll—standing over him. Q sat back with a start.

"I seem destined to bear Witness," the PT said. "And yet perhaps I have borne enough. Please refer to me as the Troll from now on."

The Troll then exited the bathroom and left Q to his dry heaves, but he returned momentarily with a wheelchair into which, with some effort, he helped the Patient. He then placed a duffel bag in Q's submissive lap and wheeled him out into the hallway. They got on the patient elevator with several others and proceeded up toward the Gym, but when they arrived at the floor above the Troll held back as the others debarked and allowed the doors to close behind them. Then he pushed the button at the very bottom, so low on the console that he pushed it with his toe rather than bending over to reach it, and the car began a rapid descent.

They descended thus, alone in the car, with Q's stomach fluttering painfully, for several minutes until they heard a loud rattle, like a ratchet engaging, and Q felt the inertia inside him as the car began to slow. It came to a full stop with a sound of screeching metal, and the doors began to vibrate as they tried to open. The Troll, however, pushed the Close Door button to silence them and then began jumping up and down. When that failed to have any effect, he held to the railing and began jerking from side to side violently until finally Q felt the car subside a bit, and then a bit more, and then with no further warning they were in free fall, with Q screaming in terror and the Troll holding on to the railing for dear life as his feet lifted toward the ceiling.

They fell for an interminable couple of seconds before the car stopped once again, this time rather suddenly, slamming both of them to the floor. The electricity seemed to fail at that moment, also, with even the console lights going off. After a moment the battery powered emergency light kicked on dimly, and they took stock of the situation, which in truth seemed somewhat dire. Q went to great mental machinations to avoid the words "entombed alive" entering his thought chain, but as they tried the available options—the Open Door button, the Emergency Phone, the Manual Door Release—and found them all inoperable, the notion of Slow Death gradually began to settle in his bowels. And then as the emergency light began to flicker, panic hit him.

It turned out, though, that the Troll was more resourceful than communicative, and he opened the duffel he had given to Q to carry and removed from it a small pry bar. This he inserted between the inner doors and wiggled until he had opened up a half-inch gap. Then between brute force and the advantage of the lever they managed to expand this gap to a few inches, and then to two feet. They were stuck between floors, with only a small opening at the bottom where they might squeeze through, but lacking room, to Q's chagrin, for the wheelchair. Despite his whimpering and lack of cooperation, the Troll managed to get him out of the chair and through the portal, where he fell to the floor. The Troll then climbed through easily and lowered himself down, and they found themselves in what felt to be merely a larger tomb.

They had only the residual light from the car illuminating the space, which appeared to be a hallway that disappeared into utter dark in either direction. They stayed in the little ball of light for some time, pretending to discuss their options but in actuality merely delaying against the time when they would have to set out, blind and alone, into the darkness that surrounded them.

Q was of the opinion, and argued the point with all the rhetorical force the situation demanded, that they should go to the Right. Since the right side, he argued, was dominant in the vast majority of humans, and that the written and unwritten rule, for all but a few nonconforming oddballs, was that traffic always stayed to the right, the Architect would have designed the Building so that the flow from the Elevator would tend to turn in that direction, rather than having to cross the lane, causing confusion and disorder among the pedestrians who would have been, at such a time when lights were available, coursing the hallway.

The Troll, on the other hand, argued that any Architect in his right mind would avoid placing an elevator at the center of a traffic pattern and would opt, rationally, to place it at one end, and on the right side of the hallway traffic, so that those entering could do so with a minimum of fuss while those exiting could stay to the natural right, even while turning Left. The turn to the Right, then, would almost certainly come to a dead end, some electrical service closet or storage room, which could make for a rather complex, and useless, spatial readjustment in the dark.

At this point the emergency light made a slight clicking sound and then extinguished altogether.

This development caught them unawares, even though the entire purpose of their discourse had been to prepare for it, as they were so caught up in their argument they failed to notice the light's disappearance immediately and went on pacing back and forth, spinning around and pointing in either direction to emphasize their reasoning, until they suddenly came back to consciousness of their immediate surroundings only when they were completely blind and could no longer remember on which side of the elevator door they stood, so that Right and Left lost their relative reference, and they were forced to set off in utter ignorance, choosing the way at random.

They tapped their way along, the Troll keeping one hand on a wall and feeling with his feet before placing them, and Q on hands and knees behind him, and they kept talking so that they would not lose each other. Upon Q's noting that he felt they had been placed in a maze by some Scientist performing an experiment to see how anxiety affected an Animal's ability to negotiate complex situations, the Troll responded thus:

"In truth, this was not a technique that was unknown to the Ancients. Herodotus records that the greatest architectural achievement of the Egyptians was not the Pyramids but rather their Labyrinth, which has never been located, but which was a palace that put the mythical Cretan structure to shame. In the second book of the *Histories*, Herodotus claims to have actually visited the structure, remarking:

"'It has twelve courts covered in, with gates facing one another, six upon the North side and six upon the South, joining on one to another, and the same wall surrounds them all outside; and there are in it two kinds of chambers, the one kind below the ground and the other above upon these, three thousand in number, of each kind fifteen hundred. The upper set of chambers we ourselves saw;… but the chambers underground we heard about only…. For the passages through the chambers, and the goings this way and that way through the courts, which were admirably adorned, afforded endless matter for marvel, as we went through from a court to the chambers beyond it, and from the chambers to colonnades, and from the colonnades to other rooms, and then from the chambers again to other courts. Over the whole of these is a roof made of stone like the walls; and the walls are covered with figures carved upon them, each court being surrounded with pillars of white stone fitted together most perfectly; and at the end of the labyrinth, by the corner of it, there is a pyramid of forty fathoms, upon which large figures are carved, and to this there is a way made under ground. Such is this labyrinth.'

"The structure," the Troll continued, "is designed to be specifically unfriendly, to ward off guests rather than invite them in. As Strabo described this same Egyptian palace: 'Before the entrances there lie what might be called hidden chambers which are long and many in number and have paths running through one another which twist and turn, so that no one can enter or leave any court without a guide.' Thus the complexity is by design. It was what today we call Security. As we must have guides to take us through the fluid, changing maze of Bureaucracy, the Ancients designed physical premises with the same features."

"Are you implying," Q asked, "that we are presently entombed in such a structure, a structure from which we may never emerge without the assistance of a Guide, and yet for which no Guide exists?"

The Troll grunted non-committally. "I am merely stating," he said, "the fact of History, the fact that Humanity ties itself in knots and then attempts to extricate Itself by pulling the knots tighter. We think we have improved upon the Ancients, but in fact we have only complicated them."

"I'm not sure I follow you," Q said, though in truth his statement was motivated less by a lack of understanding than by his desire that his Teacher's voice continue in the overwhelming Darkness.

"Take another example," the Troll went on. "Heraclitus, in the fifth century BCE, told us that 'all things are exchangeable for fire, as gold for goods and goods for gold.' This metaphysical statement was then complicated, two millennia later, by Einstein, who gave the precise formula so that the most monstrous weapon ever conceived could be built. But the problem is that Einstein ignored, in his passion for the complex knot of the formula, the other half of Heraclitus' analogy, the 'gold for goods and goods for gold' part. And this is the part that actually cuts through the knot, not solving the problem, exactly, but rendering it irrelevant. Everyone thought that Heraclitus' insight concerned fire, but actually it concerned gold. That gold could burn, that was the point."

"I see," said Q, "the obvious wisdom in what you say, and yet I wonder if your logic is not slightly flawed."

"The point is not," the Troll continued, "to use perfect logic. The point is to talk our way through the Darkness, to move forward in distraction so that when the time comes to act we are not to be debilitated with sheer terror."

"I see," said Q. "A knot indeed." And in fact a knot had formed in the pit of his stomach, making his knees weak to the point that he was not certain he could continue on. Yet continue they did, slowly but doggedly, with the Troll feeling along the wall and Q on hands and knees following behind.

Though they might as well have been searching with eyes closed, they proceeded with lids and pupils opened wide and straining to open wider, so hungry they were for the slightest source of light. And this very straining for illumination actually created it, and Q was constantly distracted by flashes and brief glows, each of which brought a glimmer of hope that was immediately dashed by the realization that it was only his desperate imagining coalescing into hallucination, until finally hope ceased entirely, and he began to ignore his visions.

Thus it was that neither of them noticed the change in tone of the darkness, from pitch black to dark gray and then to a lighter gray, and when a speck of actual light did finally appear in the distance, they both treated it with suspicion and neither mentioned it until after several minutes of persistence they both, simultaneously, declared it to be real and redoubled their effort to reach it. Then Q became aware of a ghostly blur moving in front of him and realized this was the movement of the white legs of the Troll's PT scrubs, and he fairly wept with joy.

The speck gradually increased in size, expanding to the status of a dot, and then to a small rectangle. There was now enough light around them that they could make out the doorways they were passing, and the Troll urged Q to rise to his feet so that they could pick up their pace. This Q did, with the Troll's assistance, fighting his weakness and nausea with force of will, so that when they finally reached the light of the opening they were walking like normal, ambulatory humans and emerged triumphant onto the fourth mezzanine of the Great Atrium.

Q recognized the place by the tattered image of Christ that loomed over it, but if he had not had the symbol to refer to he was certain he would not have known where he was, so greatly had the room changed in the months he had been hospitalized. Whereas before it had been quite overrun with vegetation, it was now a veritable forest, the room itself scarcely visible for the proliferation of trees and scrub. The stairways had become sloping glades, covered with small pines and grasses, making for tough going as they sought, with increasing urgency, their exit of the building, and it took them yet another hour to descend.

а

They left the building by the same portal that Q and Lucy had used, so many months previous, and Q began to rejoice. "Surely," he said, "it is Heaven to be out of this place."

"We're not out of the woods yet," the Troll responded. "There are miles to traverse before we are out of the thrall of the Church of the Ostensible Jesus."

They proceeded through the forest cautiously, the Troll leading the way and cautioning Q to silence as he did so. They stopped to drink from the same pool that Q and Lucy had drunk from, and Q noted that it was no longer crystal clear as it had been but murky enough to cause him to worry about its potability. They had no choice but to drink it, however, for Q's withdrawals were still in full swing and the Troll was concerned that he might become dehydrated.

As they went on they were reminded of where they were by a sudden commotion in the tree-tops above them. It seemed at first to be a flock of large birds suddenly taking flight, but then something hit Q on the head and a shower of books and torn pages began to rain down around them. They took cover beneath some heavy limbs until the shower subsided, and were fortunate to have done so, as a mangled drone crashed to the ground where they had been standing.

"Sometimes they have to sacrifice a drone or two in the book showers," the Troll explained. "It's worth it to them to keep the lines moving."

Falling sky having abated, they continued on, but were soon forced to take cover again, this time by actual precipitation, as a sudden cloudburst of torrential rain, accompanied by thunder and lightning, bore down upon them. The storm was intense enough to be terrifying, yet as quickly as it came it went, and in five minutes time the sun was shining again on the dripping woods. Q expressed dismay at this fluke of nature, but the Troll reassured him that the rain had simply been called up to assist the composting process, and that it was all quite normal.

They went along, occasionally slipping on the wet mash the freshly fallen books had become, until they came to a depression in the ground that Q recognized, with horror, as the site of his and Lucy's torture at the hands of the Guardian and his cruel henchman. He looked around, trembling with fear and recollection (as well as withdrawals), and his worst fears were realized when, once again, an arrow pierced his breast and transfixed him to a tree, the very same tree as before, in fact.

∂

Q froze in terror for a moment, and then swooned unconscious, but not before noticing a familiar insignia stamped near the feathers on the arrow. He slumped on his impalement as the Troll, in seeming imitation of Lucy in the previous scene, took cover in the depression that was the remnant of the hole she had previously dug. Now, again, the *Custos Scripti* appeared with his quiver and bow, still dressed in his green suede forest suit, and quite as upbeat as ever. He paid no attention to the Troll cowering below him but went straight up to Q. He took a small vial from his pocket, cracked it open, and waved it under Q's nose to awaken him. Then he called out, "Mary, he's here. Come up Maria."

Q awoke to the happy face of the Guardian in front of him and the added vision of a young girl coming into the glade, guiding three small, yapping puppies on ropes. Catching wind of the scene, the puppies broke free from the small girl's control, ran up to Q and began joyfully licking his ankles.

"Ah, sorry Q," the Guardian said, "she's still in training, you see. I've been trying to teach her her knots—the bowline, half hitch, versatackle, etc.—but she hasn't really got it yet. Come along, pups, don't pester Q in his misery."

Upon this command the puppies turned their attention from Q and leapt into the pitkin with the Troll, who sat down with a chuckle and began playing with them. The girl stood where the pups had left her, looking sadly at the limp ropes in her hand.

"Calm yourself, Q," the Guardian responded to Q's terrified grimace, "and please pardon the off-color nature of my little joke. I saw you pass in front of your Tree and couldn't resist a little ribbing (no pun intended)." He then removed the arrow, painlessly, and Q realized that he was not even wounded, for the arrow had merely passed beneath his armpit, impaling nothing but a corner of his hospital gown, which ripped on the arrow's barb when the Guardian jerked it free. The flimsy gown fell off of him, then, and he stood naked in front of them. He attempted to cover himself when he noticed young Mary staring at him wide-eyed. "Ah, don't worry yourself, Q," the Guardian said. "She's seen worse. And here, too, is something you might appreciate."

He waved a hand overhead, then, and a drone appeared among the trees. It dropped a bundle at their feet. The Guardian picked it up and ceremoniously unwrapped Q's tramp coat and boots. He handed them to Q then turned around discreetly so that Q could dress in privacy. "We wouldn't want to send you *back* into the World naked, now would we?" he inquired, as Q quickly put them on. Though still, certainly, somewhat shaken, Q felt better in his old clothes, almost like his Old Self, and he began to breathe easier.

Now the Guardian led them, chattering all the way, out of the Woods. As they emerged at the rim of the valley, with the railroad now visible in the near distance, another drone descended on them and dropped a backpack which turned out to contain several days worth of food, water and supplies. The Troll donned the pack, in light of Q's still weakened condition, but as he did Q responded to a sudden thought and put his hand to his breast, feeling through his coat for the card he had, some time ago, sewn into the lining. The Guardian noticed the gesture and remarked: "Yes, it's still there, Q, and it is the reason you are, also. Use it wisely."

The Guardian pointed the way for them, then, noting that a train would be passing within the hour. Then he set about gathering up the happy puppies, who had fallen quite in love with our Q and his Troll and would have followed them anywhere, had they been allowed. He tied them up expertly, carefully explaining to Mary, as he did so, that essential difference between a Bowline and a Constrictor.

⊃

Q and the Troll walked down to the tracks, where a train uncannily materialized and slowed to such a degree that they simply stepped on. The boxcar they landed in seemed to have been prepared for them, with blankets and a mattress, scarcely used. They sat in the doorway and watched the country roll by while feasting on their tins and packets of survival food, which was tasteless but filling. The food seemed to lift their spirits, too, and they chatted happily for a while as darkness fell, saying over and over how good it felt to be away from that church or hospital or whatever it was, how like a dream the experience now seemed. They would, of course, be coming back, in force, as soon as they could regroup, to wrest Lucy from its tentacles, too.

At the mention of that name, however, the conversation paused, and the bliss that had come over them when they had started eating suddenly lifted, leaving only the hard reality of the barren boxcar, their tenuous perch on its ledge, and the cold fact that they both were thinking but neither would speak, though Q did speak it, finally, muttering under his breath so the Troll would not hear: "There is no Lucy."

339

Now Q's bones began to ache again, and he shook with fever. He soon found himself lying down with his head out the door, watching the gravel and the railroad ties pass beneath in a blur, puking up his entire half-knapsack of protein-enriched mash. He felt a little spray on his cheek and, looking to his left, found the Troll was doing the same. "What kind of poison have they given us?" he gasped between retches.

Q managed to roll himself away from the precipitous edge into the middle of the car. The train was picking up speed, and the car was now rocking violently and leaning vertiginously with the curves. The walls bent and creaked with the strain. He could see the night sky though the boxcar door, and it was thick with stars that wheeled and spun with the violent rocking of the car and of his spinning head. He rolled over onto his stomach, lay his cheek against the filthy, gritty floor, and tried to hold on.

ƧƧƧ

Espe sat smoking on one of the barstools in the kitchen of the house she had lived in, "owned," you could say, for the past four years. She could hear Santo crashing around in the next room, kicking holes in the walls, ripping down paintings, breaking glass and generally decimating everything he had stood for in what now seemed his very brief tenure as Governor, as well as doing the best he could to make the next tenants as uncomfortable as possible.

The morning—well, she thought it was still morning, though time, at least that normal time of getting up and starting one's day, of having one's coffee in one's stunning La Perla peignoir and scanning the internet for the latest gossip and polls, of listening to NPR in the shower and checking one's beautiful body in the mirror, turning front and then profile, leaning in close to examine the shadows, each day slightly more pronounced, under one's lovely hazel eyes, that regular, orderly, professional woman's time, the clock on the radio or on the wall always in the corner of one's view as the countdown to the first appointment ticked away, seeming to speed up as it closed in, until in its final moments it became frantic, with the quick dab of rouge over the light foundation, the rolling of the sensual full lips on a tissue, finishing touches on an artwork, an image that men (those weak, sniveling creatures) would, no matter how hard they tried to resist, look up from their newspapers or laptops, from their cabs and coffee shops and desks and security stations, and follow with looks of hypnotized longing, with looks that said they would give anything, any of the wealth, power, prestige or pride they'd sweated and saved and sacrificed to earn, for a mere moment in its proximity, for a whiff of its perfume or (better) its secret funk, for a fleeting glimpse of just another inch of its skin, as it glided haughtily along the sidewalk, into the door of the capitol building and down the hallways of state power… well, that time had crashed out the window with the first queen anne chair, had been stabbed and ripped with a steak knife like the Frida Kahlo in the living room, shattered into a thousand shards like the pre-Columbian vase in the hallway—the morning, or whatever time it was, wasn't going that well.

Santo, red faced and grinning madly, stuck his head in the door at the far end of the enormous kitchen, like that chilling vision of Jack Nicholson in *The Shining*. He still had on his Ralph Lauren pajamas, though they were now torn and drenched with sweat. "Mierde," he yelled.

"Si, mierde," she answered softly, without looking up.

He had found a few of her toys and outfits, naturally, when they were just starting to pack up, two days ago. But these had been no problem. "Ah, do you have a secret life, mi amor?" he had said with a wink. "I would love to see you in this." And she had blushed and laughed it off, saying that she would be far too embarrassed to put on these leather accoutrements, that a friend had given her as a joke, in front of him. "Ah come on," he had teased, "put them on. Show your daddy who's boss. Hey, you know, one good thing has come of all this. Now we'll have some time to lay about and, well, you know, like we used to. Why don't we go to the beach? Or to Xilitla? The Jungle is so beautiful this time of year. ¿Recuerdes tu español, eh?" She had nodded.

"Mierde mierde mierde," he screamed, bursting into the kitchen and heading in her direction. "Eres mierde. Tu! Tu eres mierde!"

"Si, soy mierde," she said, and took a drag of her cigarette.

But then, this morning, or sometime in the night, the photos had arrived. And why had he even picked up his tablet from the bedside table? Had he not proclaimed loudly, in one of those early fits of manic, phoney euphoria where he tried to pretend he was happy he had lost, happy to be out from under the burden of Power, happy to be free again, to have time again for all the little pleasures of the common man, the leisurely breakfasts and indolent afternoons… had he not said then that of all the advantages losing the election brought him, not having to pick up that Thing as his first gesture every morning was his favorite? Of all the onerous responsibilities he was so happy to be rid of, none ranked higher than that disgusting feeling that he had to check his email before he even got out of bed. For that particular duty never failed to ruin his day. Even when the news was good—which it had been, once upon a time, for such a brief (and yet long enough for the habit to form; he was like a rat who had learned to push a lever to receive a delicious morsel, but the reward, for the purpose of some cruel sociological experiment, gradually evolved into bitter poison) interval—even when the news was that his bill had passed or one of his opponents had been humiliated by the exposure of the bribes he had taken or the putas he kept, even then the news distracted his attention from the woman who lay beside him, his one true love, the most beautiful thing he'd ever seen. Her body always made him think of García Lorca:

Verte desnuda es recordar la tierra.
La tierra lisa, limpia de caballos.

Sometimes he would say it to her in English:

To see you naked is to remember the Earth.
The smooth Earth, swept clean of horses.

But this poetry of her body he would forsake for the transfixing screen, crawling with little characters that made him happy or sad or enraged him or consoled him but in any case drew him away from her softly breathing beside him, and the temptation he had felt, on first waking, to rouse her with the touch of his fingers or his tongue or his auroral tumescence, would be forgotten as the dreams that spawned it.

"¿Qué? he yelled, now in her face. "¿Qué digas? ¿Qué digas, mi amor? Mi *amor*," he repeated, drawing out the syllables. "¿Qué digas, mi puta? ¿Qué digas, mi mierde? ¿Qué digas? What do you say?"

But the habit had proved harder to break than to wish broken, and instead of reaching for her this morning he had reached for the Ipad™, just like any other morning, and the photos had come up. And why? And wherefore and from whence had they come? *Furhoncle* had already won the election. Had he sent them, it would not have been out of self-interest (a motivation which, one had to admit if one were not to be a total hypocrite, had a certain nobility), seeking to ruin their campaign so he could win. And even if it had been, even if the election had still been up for grabs, the photos would still have been worthless because they would have been censored even from the laissez faire world of the internet. For these photos went beyond scandal to the actionable. No social media site would allow this sort of thing to circulate. Even porn sites would give them a second thought or at least hide them away in some encrypted, pay-per-view only, secret corner of the secret world. No, whoever sent them sent them out of pure malice, pure evil, not for gain but simply to destroy them, to destroy Espe but really (for Espe, like the election, was already quite lost) to destroy Santo. To make sure that he lost not only the election but his will to ever, ever run again. And that campaign, so the polls were beginning to show, had been successful.

"Stop," she said. "Please stop."

And *how* had they done it? Who could have taken the photos? What sort of bug had they gotten into her office? Had it been, literally, a fly on the wall, some speck of a drone she had swatted with her shoe and then forgotten, but which had already emailed the irrevocable pixels? The shots were framed quite carefully, professionally, she thought. All that showed of the Representative was the crown of his white bald head, so that he could have been almost anyone in the government or its shadow world of lobbyists and operators. Espe, on the other hand, squatting over him, was looking back over her shoulder straight into the camera, hair pulled aside, smirking proudly, almost as if she were posing.

"Oh, my love," he crooned viciously, "how I love it when you tell me what to do. But please be more forceful. Look at me with contempt. Look at me with condescension, like a woman who looks down on every man and every thing. And don't just say it, say it with strength. Digalo con fuerza, mi vida. Don't just say it, proclaim it, as only a ruler can. Make it so with just your saying. Say 'STOP!'"

There was, of course, nothing to say to this, and the irony of the disgusting situation flashed in her mind (and did the ghost of a smile curl her lip, even as the tears rolled down her cheek?) causing her to bow her head even lower and finally to lay it on her arm on the counter, sobbing.

ᘒᘒᘒ

Q awoke, if one could call it that, in full daylight. He was staring up into a cloudless blue sky through a skein of vines and scrub which appeared to have grown over him as he slept and bound him so tightly, even weaving through his hair, that he was not able to move. In a little time he felt something alive moving on his left leg, which advancing gently forward over his breast, came almost up to his chin; then, bending his eyes downwards as much as he could, he perceived it to be a small rat. In the meantime, he felt at least forty more of the same kind (as he conjectured) following the first. He was in the utmost astonishment, and terrified, and roared so loud, that they all ran back in a fright, though this did not settle his own panic.

At length, struggling to get loose, he managed to break some of the vines and uproot the ones that fastened his left arm to the ground. Then, with a violent pull, which gave him excessive pain, he a little loosened the fronds that tied down his hair on the left side, so that he was just able to turn his head about two inches. At this point, he felt the creatures crawling on him again and tore himself out of the entanglement. He stood upright, swatting the last of them from his person, and made to get away from them.

It was tough going, though, as he soon discovered that the low vegetation he was struggling through had grown up through a field of rubble and detritus, and with every step he stumbled over a rotten pallet or a toy house or caught his foot in a tangle of rusty bed springs or a broken baby carriage, and he surmised finally that the vegetation he was stumbling through, comprised mostly of certain broad-leafed vine, had overgrown some sort of trash dump, which also explained, perhaps, the presence of the rodents, whose recent contact was still causing his skin to crawl.

There was a tree line some distance ahead of him and he made for that, hoping it signalled the limit of this lush green landscape that concealed just beneath it a hellish field of broken glass, tin scraps, nail-studded boards and vermin: all the poisonous slough of civilization. He struggled through the tangle for an hour before he made it into the trees and was able to sit down on a bare patch of earth. He was a bit bloodied, with a few rat bites and cuts around the ankles, but basically intact. The nail that had pierced his boot had gone, coincidentally, between his toes, and he breathed a sigh of relief at that good luck.

Looking back over the field of leaves, which was waving gently and beautifully in the light breeze, he realized that it was kudzu, which gave him the vaguest hint as to the region of the planet he had landed in. Beyond it, on the other shore, as it were, elevated on a berm, he saw a rail glint in the sun, which likewise gave him a clue as to how he'd gotten here. Beyond that, he had not much idea of anything, as his memory seemed to have been all but erased, with nothing showing on his internal cinema but a pastiche of snippets, too surreal to be trusted, like some collage taped together by an avant-garde artist.

The thing about memory, though, is that when it is gone one does not know that anything has gone, since it is memory itself that would supply that knowledge, so he was left only with a sort of premonition that something was missing, but he did not know what it was. The Thing he was missing had not only departed but erased all record of itself in the going, so it could not even be longed for. But he longed for that longing.

This emptiness was somewhat ameliorated by the relief he felt from his escape from the dump, but it quickly resurfaced in the form of a horrific thirst, a thirst so desperate he felt compelled to satisfy it immediately, and he walked on into the woods in search of water. He came presently upon a stream, but this served only to whet his appetite the more, as the orange water, slicked with oily rainbows and carrying along a dead rat, did not in the least tempt him to drink from it. In fact, his tongue thickened at the mere sight of it, so he continued on.

It wasn't long before he encountered a road of sorts, two worn ruts a car's width apart snaking between the trees, and he followed it with great expectation, praying that it might lead to someplace habitable, and potable, and not simply dwindle away, as roads in the woods sometimes do. He imagined, at the end of it, a quaint but well-tended country house with a garden hose coiled neatly by the back door, or lawn sprinklers broadcasting the blessed stuff wantonly; he imagined lying down in the wet grass and catching the spray on his tongue or putting the hose to his face and gulping. He prayed to have back all the clean water he had wasted in his life, all that he'd sent whirling down the drain after rinsing his coffee cup or rice bowl, all the beautiful clear stuff he'd fouled and flushed away, all that he'd washed his fetid mouth with and foolishly spat out.

Finally, just as he thought his strength was at an end, he did indeed come to the house the ruts were there to serve. It wasn't quite as imagined (though what, ever, is?), with its peeling clapboards and sagging roof, with a screen door hanging aslant on one hinge and no yard but an irregular area of bare ground, spotted with tall weeds, around which were scattered perhaps a dozen pickups, vans and autos in various stages of rust, on blocks or sitting flat on rotten tires. One side of the clearing seemed to have been designated as the Washing Machine Depository, as a half-dozen of these labor-savers lay on their sides in the weeds. With the tree canopy hanging over the scene, letting through only the occasional dapple of sunlight, the place seemed to Q to be a larger scale version of the dump he'd just walked through, and he half expected the foot of some giant to come down on the house or one of the junked cars, causing its owner to whimper in pain.

But such considerations are more for us, really, than our Hero, and He paid it all scant attention as he searched the outside of the house for a faucet. He walked around the outside until he spotted a rusty spigot sticking out of the ground, secured to the wall with a twisted wire. He knelt before it and turned it on, and, blessed be his luck, it ran, filthy and sputtering at first, then turning clear, and Q cupped his two hands under it and put his face in the little pool that formed there and drank until he felt human again.

ə

Having slaked his raging thirst, he sat back on the ground panting and took stock of his surroundings. Behind the house was the remnant of an out-building which might once have been a barn but was now was little more than a pile of rotten timbers collapsed upon an ancient, rusting tractor. The yard was strewn with all manner of junk—engine parts, ruined tools, rusted out buckets and tubs—all of which showed signs, being half sunk into the ground or with weeds growing through, of having not been touched in many years, so at first he thought the place uninhabited, but this notion was soon dispelled when a tenant came around the corner of the house.

The first thing Q noticed about this fellow was how extraordinarily well he fit in with his surroundings. Emaciated and filthy, he was clad in a rotten pair of farmer's overalls, one broken strap replaced by a length of rope. He was the thinnest person Q had ever seen, with spindly arms scarcely any bigger than a broom handle, face gaunt and stretched tight over his skull causing the bloodshot eyes to bulge from their sockets.

Q made haste to assure this vision of Death Itself that he meant no harm or aggression but was merely lost, in desperate need of water, and would happily be on his way now that he was sufficiently hydrated to do so. To this and Q's further entreaties the Apparition made no reply but merely cocked his head as if he did not understand, then suddenly said:

"I knew it. I told Kali. I told the boys. Told the copperheads under the house. I said sun comes up when the door's closed don't it. I said does a sparrow pester a crow. I said anything I wanted. Just like the old days. Everybody got the itch. Everybody got the run around. Everybody got everybody. No no no no. That's not the thing. I told Jessie. Hide a knife in your drawer. Don't walk barefoot. Wear socks, even. Not that long ago, when you think about it. I heard that owl. I heard a train coming. I said think about a letter with a snake wrapped around it. Everything clicked after that. Like it was running on five. Yesterday. No, day before. We thought it was you but it was a dead limb fell on the roof."

He reached down toward Q, who shrunk back in terror. "We take care of what takes care of us," he continued. "Kali'll know. I killed a scorpion yesterday." He grabbed Q by the collar and pulled, the only result of which being that he himself fell over. Collapsed in Q's lap, he seemed to weigh nothing. He smelled, oddly, of ether. He squirmed and struggled but was quickly winded and apparently did not have the strength to rise. As he was now seeming more pitiable than fearsome, Q got up himself and helped the scarecrow to his feet.

Q took him around to the front door of the house and helped him inside, still babbling, though his voice had fallen to a whisper. Inside there were several others, six actually, all as skinny and filthy as the first, three women and three men, each busy at an undetermined task, appearing, at first glance, to be cleaning up the house, but this was belied by the condition of the place, which in truth made the outside look like a pristine campground. The room was covered with trash and odd equipment, plastic buckets with tubes running between them, metal stands and beakers and propane tanks, and the smell of acetone and solvents was overwhelming. A woman who could have been the twin of Q's babbler, except that her head was covered in wild frizzy hair, appeared to be cooking on the stove as she labored near some large pots brimming over with red and blue ooze, but instead of oils and spices the counter was covered of containers of ether and drain cleaner. She and the Others looked at Q with those same horribly bulging eyes. They looked like gaunt, starving cattle, just about ready to give themselves up to the desert, or, as tall and thin as they were, all in a row, like spindly stalks of wheat.

"Told you." the first one said, finding his voice again. "What the cat got drug in by. An eater. A ghost. Got the itch, like us. I told you. I told the yard. I told the barn. I told the helicopter. Turn on the TV. Let's chew the fat. Sit sit sit sit.'

He motioned Q toward a rise in the rubble that might have concealed a couch, and two of the others raced over and began strewing garbage hither and thither to uncover a place for him. Another swept away the plastic bottles, old baseball trophies, alarm clocks and figurines from in front of the television and began looking around it for a switch. But Q begged them not to trouble themselves on his account, as he had just noticed the lateness of the day and should be going. He was backing toward the door as he spoke. But at this refusal of hospitality their attitude changed quite suddenly, and all seven came for him.

He bolted out the door and ran back toward the road he had come in on. He tripped, though, and became entangled in a ball of barbed wire that he had not noticed in the weeds. As he struggled to free himself, he looked back, afraid his Hosts would be on him at any moment. Instead he found that just outside the door they had become so winded they could barely walk, much less run, and were struggling along at a snail's pace, giving him plenty of time to extricate himself. Besides that, however revolting the thought of coming in contact with them might be, he realized watching their wheezing, stumbling approach that the seven of them together couldn't summon the strength to harm him.

And so he walked out at his own speed, looking back only when he had regained the road to see them stopped, panting, far behind, looking after him like impetuous, impotent emissaries from the Land of the Dead.

After a couple of miles the country lane gave out onto a two-lane highway. With nothing in view in either direction, Q decided to turn right, since that was his dominant hand, and set out in that direction. A car passed, and he put out his thumb, but the driver veered to the far side of the road. Then a truck passed, and he put out his thumb again, but the truck, too, gave him a wide berth. A third car passed, and he put out his thumb again, though this time he held out little hope, and this one pulled over beside him rather than turning away.

His hopes were to be dashed yet again, however, for when the driver got close enough that Q and he could see each other through the passenger window, he suddenly sped up again and pulled away. Q realized, now, that wherever he was going he was going on foot, and he slowed his pace sadly and quit bothering to signal to other drivers. There was no need, after all, to tell anyone he was in trouble; he was walking.

He walked until dusk, and many cars passed him, but he made

no signal. When it grew too dark to go on, he walked off the road a little, took off his boots and massaged his blistered feet. Then he lay down in the grass to rest.

He awoke a short time later out of a troubling dream. The dream faded away from him before he could formalize its imagery, but he had a vague sense of its setting, a great, labyrinthine building whose layout seemed to change every time he turned his head. He lay awake under the stars, haunted by this and by the encounter with the Country Folk that day. After a while the stars above him began to turn on an axis, as if the night had speeded up. Then they accelerated their motion until they reeled like a pinwheel and he was no longer certain if it was them that were moving or himself. He felt a great vertigo, as if he were looking down on the heavens rather than up, and this told him he was, again, dreaming. He felt he needed to wake from this dream and tried to move his body and wake himself. He knew where he was; he felt the grass and the earth beneath him, but his somnambulistic torpor was so complete that he could not move a muscle.

Finally it occurred to him that there was nothing to fear from this dream, that no harm would come to him from falling into the sky, and he ceased resisting, and what happened then no one, neither Q nor you nor I, will ever know.

ᴧ

He awoke startled and famished and with no more idea than he had before of where or who he was. He set back out on the highway and followed it without thinking about a destination, for his addled wits could not accommodate such aforethought.

He came at length to a sign of habitation, a large house set back from the road behind a spacious, manicured lawn. Though the place was hidden from the road by hedges, there was no mistaking the plot for yet more wilderness, as the hedges were neatly trimmed and made a noticeable break in the forest. A driveway crossed a culvert and entered the yard through the only break in the hedge, and Q's cravings commanded that he enter.

A heavy iron gate stood at the opening, but it was ajar enough for him to walk through, and so he did, and followed the brick-paved path in toward the house, which was also brick, though fronted by a gleaming white colonnade and windows trimmed with green shutters. The yard was studded with fruit trees and rose bushes and covered, between them, with lush, carefully mown grass, so much of it that Q was struck by the fact that mowing it must be a continuous task.

When he got to the house the first thing he saw was the neatly coiled hose of his fantasy the day before, and he fell on it and slaked his thirst. He sat back, panting, against the brick wall, too spent to even contemplate his next move, but came back to himself when he heard the rumble of lawn mower starting nearby. The sound grew louder, and then the small rider rounded the corner, driven by a portly man in crisp, new denim overalls. The man stopped the mower and eyed Q with curiosity.

"Well, well," he said. "I told Kelly in bed last night we'd soon be visited by one in need of attention. Sometimes I have these visions, but I have to say they don't often come true so literally. Usually there's a need of interpretation, their 'truth' being in some way forced, so that we usually resort to symbols and metaphors to figure, in retrospect, that they were indeed correct. I've always thought of it as a bit of trick, like Tarot. In this case, however, though 'attention' was a bit of an understatement, the premonition seems all but literal. So I guess we best get you tended to."

He got off the little tractor and reached down to help Q up. His grip was firm, and he easily lifted our lanky Hero to his feet and took him inside the house, which Q found to be warm and inviting, with artwork of pleasant rural scenes symmetrically hung about the walls in the huge living room, which was tastefully decorated in Early American style. This room opened into a bright kitchen almost as large as the living room, with windows onto the back pasture reflecting in the gleaming black granite counters. The island in the center was covered with baskets of fresh produce, tomatoes and garlic and bok choy and lettuces and other greens. Seated on stools around this island were three other men and three women, all as fat and jovial as the first, and who, after a first questioning glance at the road-weary Q, welcomed him graciously.

"You all might have thought it was just another dream," said the Host, "but here he is in the flesh."

They sat him down and began busily attending to his needs, and the women began preparing a meal. One of them stopped abruptly, though, wrinkled up her nose and commented that perhaps Q would like to clean up a bit before sitting down to dinner. Q was starving, and the smells coming from the stove were making his mouth water, but the Host told him:

"We eat well around here, Q,"—he patted his ample belly— "but we do have certain, well, rules."

He was escorted, then, to the Master Bath. Here he was admonished, despite the mixed company, to give up his greatcoat, which one of the women carried away, holding it at arm's length. Left alone, he got into the glass-walled shower and washed himself with the sweet-smelling soap, scrubbing with a loofah. Then he turned on the steam unit.

After luxuriating for a few minutes, he got out of the shower and dried himself with a towel from the warmer. Then he anointed himself with the Moroccan oils he found on the vanity and spent some time on his unruly hair. While attacking the tangles with blow-dryer and brush in the mirror he noticed the gnarled scar on his left breast, just over his heart, and touched it questioningly. Images flashed in his head, and he thought the dream he had the night before was coming back to him, but the strange scenes refused to form into a coherent narrative, and he pushed them to the back of his mind as he returned to the creature-comforts of the moment.

He found his greatcoat, freshly cleaned and pressed, hanging on the door. As he was putting it on, he felt something in the lining. Not knowing what it was, he retrieved a pair of scissors from the vanity and carefully removed the stitching that held it in place. He removed the Card from its secure place, glanced at it, and put it in his pocket.

His boots, too, had been cleaned and polished, and he emerged from the dressing area as rather a GQ vision of a railroad bum. He went back to the kitchen, where his seven new friends were just sitting down to a sumptuous meal. The Head of the Table had been reserved for their special guest, and Q took the honor suavely. After a lengthy toast with an excellent Chardonnay to welcome the Guest, all eight of them attacked the roast chicken and fresh greens.

Between bites, Q happily regaled the table with stories of his adventures, filling in the substantial gaps in his memory with likely fictions. They were most interested in his encounter of the previous day, as they were familiar with their emaciated neighbors. Incredible as it seemed, these neighbors of theirs were actually quite well-off and were at present attempting to force a sale of the lovely home they were presently enjoying and the abundant farm it anchored. This place, despite its elegant appearance, was apparently mortgaged to the limit of its value, and the neighbors were negotiating directly with the bank.

Q was astonished and troubled to hear this news, but was quickly reassured by his Hosts that there was a plan afoot. They were building up their stores and changing their crops to meet the demands of a new age. They had consulted with a company called MySanto™ which had provided them with seed for a crop that was to be, they were quite certain, the wave of the future.

In answer to Q's question of what this crop might be, they took him outside to the barn, a large, climate-controlled facility which was crammed full of shrink-wrapped bales of a pungent-smelling herb, each bale labelled with a five-fingered leaf. This new crop, they explained to Q, would have substantial value in the near future, once it was legalized.

Q left his new friends with a full stomach and the warm feeling that their good planning had provided a safety net for their future. They stood at the door of their lovely home and waved good-bye to him as he walked down the driveway and back to the road.

As he was now looking quite presentable, the first car that passed by pulled over and offered him a ride, which he gladly accepted. The driver was a young man of about Q's age who made his living selling seed and equipment to the farms in the area and was happy to have some company on his way to his next stop. They drove for two hours chatting about this job, which the young man felt was the key to his future, and Q told him about his experience at the two farms and their strange inhabitants.

"Yes," the Seed Salesman said after Q had finished his story, "I'm familiar with both of these farms. What they told you means, I'm afraid, that we're in for a downturn."

After this the Seed Salesman seemed to withdraw into this thoughts, and they drove on in silence for some way before turning in to a gas station to refuel and stretch their legs. Q returned from his visit to the rest room, though, to find the Salesman standing by the pump and looking downcast. When Q asked what the problem was, he told Q that his card had been declined. He was quite sure this was due to his Bank's ineptitude, but for the moment did Q have a few dollars he might like to contribute? Q sympathized with the young professional and was sorry to report that he himself was destitute. Then he remembered the mysterious card in his pocket and thought to try it out. To his surprise, the machine clicked on immediately when he inserted it, and soon they were on their way again with a full tank.

Now the young man, impressed at Q's proficiency at the gas pump, began to inquire about Q's profession, and Q had to be a bit clever in his choice of words to avoid saying what was the unfortunate truth, that he did not know if he had a profession or not. He managed to change the topic quickly enough, but he was left feeling a bit empty and not a little jealous of a Normal Person who could readily answer the ubiquitous ice-breaker, "What do you do?" Then, as quickly as they had made friends and had two hours of happy conversation, the car settled into a morose silence, and they sank into the relentless drudgery of the road.

They drove on as the sun set and night fell, finally stopping at a small motel when Q noticed the Salesman beginning to nod, with Q offering to pay for a room with his card. The Salesman insisted that this was not necessary since Q had already bought a tank of gas, but in the end accepted Q's generosity again, when he discovered that the Bank had not yet corrected the problem with his own card.

Q registered for them and they went to their room, a tiny cubicle with two beds and a television, but when Q saw the Seed Salesman open his suitcase, revealing the neatly folded collection of identical shirts and slacks, and take out his crisp leather dopp kit to begin his ablutions, he excused himself for a moment, saying he was going for ice, and went to the desk and rented a second room. He went back, meaning to tell his benefactor what he had done, but when he got to the door he passed it by and went to his own room, where he lay down and did not arise until the next afternoon.

ααα

That morning Espe was awakened by a tapping on her window. She roused herself from the perhaps a little too comfy reclining driver's seat of the Lexus™ to the vision of a State Trooper gently tapping the glass of the window with the barrel of his revolver. When he saw her open her eyes, he tilted his head in shy greeting.

It took her a moment to get her bearings and take stock of her rather compromised position. She rolled her eyes quickly around the car, saw the heap of clothing and papers in the back seat and the litter of beer and whiskey bottles on the floor of the passenger side, and a little of last night's frantic drive across the state came back to her. She'd run out with an armload of random belongings, stopped at an EZ Store for booze, and hit the freeway. Had she a destination? Which direction had she gone? She only remembered M.I.A. blasting on the MP3 player while she guzzled boilermakers and headlights reeled in front of her. Tire squeal and a near miss. Somehow she'd survived long enough to pull onto the shoulder and pass out.

Looking back into the Officer's gun and face, she reached down to her left and activated the electric seat, but she had to let go of the raise switch when she noticed her blouse was unbuttoned and began fumbling to do it up. She leaned up and glanced in the mirror just long enough to see she was a wreck, mascara running off her eyes and her hair frizzed out like the Bride of Frankenstein. She got the blouse buttoned and wiggled her skirt down to mid thigh, trying to smooth out the wrinkles with her hands. Then she looked up at the Cop and tried to smile.

"Good morning," he said cheerfully, voice muffled through the glass. He made a little motion with the pistol telling her to roll it down. She pushed the auto-down and looked out furtively as the glass descended between them and the reek of stale beer, no doubt, wafted out to him.

"I'm the Governor's wife," was all she could think of to say.

"You *were* the Governor's wife," he corrected, "in more ways than one." He winked. "License and Registration please."

It was truly unfortunate—though, then again, what difference did it make at this point—that her purse was on the floor beneath the pile of empty and half-empty bottles, so that she had to dig through them noisily to retrieve it. It was sticky with spill, but she managed to get it open and retrieve the trusty DL. When she handed it to him, he took it daintily by the corner with only two fingers as if it were too filthy to touch or as if it were evidence and he needed to take care not to smudge the fingerprints. He put it in his shirt pocket.

"And the Registration?"

She dug in the console until she found the black plastic case that contained the Lexus™ Owner's Manual and a wad of other papers. Uncertain exactly what the Registration was, she handed him the entire pouch. He looked at the offering without reaching for it, asked her to open it, and when she did he leafed through the contents, again using only his fingertips, until he found the Official Document and removed it. He put it in his pocket with the license. Then he asked her to step out of the car.

The blue strobe of the patrol car, parked behind her, was flashing in the windows of the Lexus™, and now it became a veritable light show as two more of the confidence-inspiring vehicles pulled alongside them and two more cops got out and approached her. "Well, well. Look what the cat drug in," one of them said, and they all three laughed heartily.

The morning traffic had been whooshing by, but now that the police cars had blocked one lane traffic slowed to a crawl and commuter necks craned to see what was going on. Espe tried to turn her back, for she had been a popular first lady, well-covered in the press, and she feared she would be recognized, but the grinning officers understood the gesture and invented reason after reason to demand that she face front. They had her, in parody of a field sobriety test, close her eyes and touch her nose. They made her walk a straight line (in the gravel! in pumps!), and graciously stepped out of the frame when drivers slowed to shoot pictures or video the scene. She winced at the thought that these images would have navigated the globe by the time she was allowed back to the safety of her car.

Indeed, she longed only to be back in her Lexus™ and on her way anywhere but here, and expressed as much to the Officers, trying every mask she had, from weeping damsel to angry authoritarian, to convince them to let her go. But they told the weeping damsel that everything would be fine, they were just going for a little ride, and they told the demanding boss-lady that their hands were tied; they were only following orders from an even more powerful boss.

"You see," the first one told her, "once I pull my car over, and my

GPS logs a stop, and the Dashcam reads your license plate, and my Bodycam shoots you sleeping in your front seat with empties all over the place, if I let you go, I will have to answer to my superiors. So I'm going to ask you to help me out and explain the situation to them, yourself, so that I don't get in hot water. OK?"

At this point the Wrecker arrived, and desperation welled inside her. Afraid to offer them a bribe but also afraid not to, she dropped her purse to the ground then bent over to pick it up. "Oh, silly me," she said awkwardly, bending over as if to pick it up but then clumsily emptying the contents, including three rubber-banded rolls of cash, onto the ground. She left the cash laying there when she picked up everything else. As she had hoped, they pretended not to notice and were careful not to aim their Bodycams in that direction, but the desired result of being sent off with a warning did not happen, and as they were putting her in the back seat of one of the cars and the Lexus™ was slowly being hoisted onto the flat-bed wrecker, a memory of the Old Days came back to Espe. It was in the Old Country, her first country, in her first language. She was quite young, perhaps seven, when the police had come into her house and taken her Father. Her Mother had followed them out, begging for mercy, for the children would starve without their Father to provide, etc. And one of the cops had looked at her and rubbed his fingers together in that universally recognized plea for—when one has them at knife-point—the Other's generosity. And her Mother had had nothing to give, and they had taken her Father away. And with that memory Espe panicked at the thought of being cashless and, leaning toward the Trooper, making sure her face was square in the Bodycam, said:

"Oh, I just realized… I must have dropped some cash on the ground, over there where I spilled my purse."

The Cop's face went cold, for just a moment, before the smile returned and he said, "No problem, ma'am, I'll get it for you." Which he did, kneeling so the Bodycam could catch the entire process of him picking it up, unrolling, counting and placing it in an envelope.

The Wrecker was pulling away now, and the other two cops got back in their cars and left also. Her Arresting Officer came back to the car, got in and sat for several minutes typing on his laptop. Then he put the car in drive, switched off the Bodycam, put the car back in park, got out, opened the back door and beat her until she begged for mercy.

ᗱᗱᗱ

Q, also, was awakened by a tapping sound that morning, though this tapping was on the door to his room, and when he opened it a crack and peered out he saw no Police but only a Maid, a small round woman, who said to him: "Limpia?" which she translated by pointing behind her at her cart full of cleaning supplies, linens and miniature bars of soap and bottles of shampoo. Q raised one finger to indicate his need for a small amount of time to make himself presentable. Then he closed the door, splashed water on his face, put on his greatcoat and boots and left the motel.

The Seed Salesman's car was gone, he noted without regret, and so he walked the streets of the nameless little town where he had landed. Unaccustomed to this sort of "normal" life, he took in the sights, the EZ Stores and junk shops and burger joints and coffee houses, with a bit of wonder. He turned off of the highway onto a small street and was soon in the Old Town, which consisted of three blocks of vintage brick buildings. Half of them were empty, their shop windows displaying dark scenes of empty shelves and rubble inside. The other half had all been repurposed from some previous utilitarian life—hardware, groceries, etc.—into rather pitiful curio shops and bargain centers displaying incongruous arrays of paper towels, potato chips, batteries and bottled water. On each block, however, there was one building that stood out from the rest, being modern, shiny, well-kept and well-trafficked. These were the banks.

He walked through the town, looking down at his feet and the sidewalk moving under them. The store fronts passed by, and occasionally the face of a pedestrian appeared, loomed large, looked him in the eye, and then was gone. These faces, as they stared back at him, he found unsettling, and he wanted to avoid looking at them, but his gaze was drawn to them as if against his own will, and he sought out, again and again, that baffling and excruciating moment when their eyes met, and he thought he saw in those eyes the same bewilderment and fear that he felt in his own.

He noticed something out of the corner of his eye which caused him to stop walking and stare at the sidewalk as if deep in thought. Then he turned and looked in the shop window next to him. The shop was dimly lit, its dingy shelves all but empty. His eyes, however, came into focus on the glass itself, and he saw there a strange figure, a man with long, unruly hair and beard, dressed only in a greatcoat and boots, superimposed over the image of another man, clean-shaven, hair neatly trimmed, dressed in shirt and slacks. The clean-cut one beckoned to the Other, and he went inside.

The shopkeeper sprang into action, fawning over Q as if he were his only customer in months, which indeed he was. Though the shop didn't actually sell clothing, he managed to dig up a pair of pants and a shirt that would fit (for he and Q were much the same size and build), quickly improvised a dressing area behind a curtain, and Q put them on. He paid for them with a wave of his Card over the reader and left the store amid the shopkeeper's fervent admonitions to return.

He felt lighter on his feet now, and he began to nod his head in greeting to the people he passed. He came to a shop whose sign read, simply, "Beauty" and went inside. He emerged shaved and shorn, beautiful, in fact. He began to greet the people he met with friendly smiles and comments about the lovely weather. He stopped in other shops. He bought a wallet to keep his card in. He bought a belt, though his pants fit him perfectly. He bought a keychain, though he had no keys. He bought a music player and earbuds. He bought a hat. He bought a smart phone and a protective cover for it. He bought pens and pencils, a calendar, a notebook. He bought a bag to carry it all in.

And then, fully equipped, hip-hop blasting in his ears and sunglasses over his eyes, a new man, really, he turned back toward the highway to continue his journey. Along the way, however, he passed a used car lot and slowed. There, in the front row, was a 370Z, the very same car (even the same Gun Metallic color his had been) he used to drive to high school as a teenager growing up in Provincial Oaks. And now, as he stared at the Previously Owned Vehicle, gleaming as if it were new, it seemed that the idyllic World of his childhood was reassembling itself, and all that had transpired between then and now, all those years on the street, his brief rap career, his stint in the military, all those breakups and reunions with Lucy, all that was slipping into a realm of misty image, as if it were a story he had read somewhere and that had stuck with him, though he didn't find it particularly interesting.

Just for nostalgia's sake, he took it for a test drive, the obsequious small-town salesman riding shotgun and urging caution as he laid rubber out of the lot. And just on a lark Q had him write it up, argued him down for the sheer fun of it, and then, as punchline to the joke, handed him the Card. The Salesman took it, muttering that credit cards were not the normal mode of transaction for sales of this size and that he would have to take it to the Floor Manager. "Well, take it to the Floor Manager, then," Q responded haughtily. "I don't have all day."

He chuckled to himself as the Salesman bustled off to the office. He settled into his chair and stared out the window at the ranks and files of nearly identical cars on the lot. They were arranged in a neat, nearly perfect grid, so close together one could hardly imagine how any one that was not at the edge could be extracted from it without moving every other one in front of it, except for the front row, next to the highway, where the Specials were parked at compelling angles and festooned with streamers and hilarious effigies that stood over them and fluttered in the wind. Q quickly grew bored of the cheap spectacle, though, so he took out his Phone and began to investigate what it had to offer in the way of distraction.

He had no one to call, of course, nor to text or email, and yet
this first time he logged on there were a host of voice-mails,
text messages and emails waiting for him. There were several
opportunities to upgrade this service or that, and many of them
were so compelling it seemed imprudent to refuse. Many of them,
also, required Social Media accounts, which in turn required status
updates, selfies, and biographical information. This last step in his
becoming truly wired gave him some pause, as he was required to
pick his profession, and then his sub-profession or specialty, from
a pop-up list of possibilities, none of which seemed to describe his
multifarious, unspecific existence. Since he couldn't move to the
next screen without picking something, he chose "Actuary" from the
top of the list, smiling slyly at the trick he was playing by keeping
his real identity a secret, though he was quietly pleased with the
irony that in a certain sense it was true, for wasn't he, indeed, a
Man of the Actual?

All in all, Q was quite proud of all he had accomplished in the
few minutes the Salesman was gone, and he looked up smiling when
the paperwork was laid in front of him. The Salesman, formerly
garrulous and nervously ebullient, was oddly reticent now, seeming
almost afraid of Q as he laid the folder, with the card resting on
top, on the table and then stepped back. There were little yellow
stickers in the pile where Q was required to sign, on the last page
being the final tally of the price, which Q noticed in passing was
several thousand higher than the original, never mind the lower figure
they had negotiated, but he simply sighed and signed, for his Phone
was buzzing in his pocket, and he was anxious to be back in his Z.

$$\partial$$

It had been many years since Q had driven, so he was cautious at
first, by which I mean the first five minutes. The Z's rather stunning
torque to body-weight ratio brings it from a standing start to 60 mph
in under 5 seconds and from 60 to 120 even quicker, so if velocity

is what one desires, then one's desire can be fulfilled forthwith. And speed was exactly what Q desired. He turned onto the freeway and watched, at first with wonder and then with bored expectation, as the miles it would have taken him hours to walk flew by in a blur and as the normal cars he might have hitched a ride in receded in his rear view monitor. And the car's semi-autonomous features allowed him to cruise at 130, one finger on the wheel, while surfing the satellite radio stations and reading his email at once. He felt a fierce pride, even arrogance, at his multi-tasking competence.

His happy ego, however, was momentarily disturbed when the Z informed him in its pleasant voice that he was being passed on the right. He looked over just in time to see a Porsche 911 flying past him. He stepped on the accelerator automatically, but even as the Z announced it was approaching its 7500 rpm red line and that its ailerons were approaching maximum angle, the Porsche continued to pull away, weaving from lane to lane as it passed the normal cars, until it was a mere speck going over the horizon. Q slapped the wheel and cursed his bargain-basement coupe, which suddenly felt as clunky and sluggish as a SmartCar. In his rage, he was quite rude to the Z, even as it seemed to be getting a bit frantic informing him of all the systems that were on the verge of failure.

Q drove several more hours that day, and the miles flowed under him like water. He stopped, now and then, to pick up some new electronic gadget he came across while reading his email, texts, and Instant Messages. Though he had only been on Social Media a few minutes he already had more than a thousand Friends who were a constant source of information about the latest digital products and ever more efficient accoutrements, like battery chargers, universal connectors and colorful carrying cases, and soon the Z's tiny back seat area was overflowing into the passenger side.

And yet, despite the ready availability of Outlet Malls and

the bounty they could offer, all of which was made immediately accessible by the apparently bottomless Card, the euphoria he had felt that first ten minutes in the Z did not return to him, and he found himself tiring of the road, sinking, even, into bitterness and despair. When he posted a Status Update to that effect, though, he found he was not alone and that many of his Friends and Friends of Friends were feeling or had felt the same way and they chimed in by the hundred with consolations and advice on how to regain his Optimism. New advances, for example, in Neurology had revealed the precise regions of the Brain that lit up when one was feeling right with the World, enabling great advances in Pharmacology, and there were many suggestions about new discoveries Q might want to ask his Physician about. When he replied, somewhat ashamed, that he didn't have a Physician, his Friends chimed in with lists of doctors, complete with phone numbers and addresses, near his current location, which all of them uncannily knew with pinpoint precision, despite the speed at which he was traveling.

When he confessed that, in light of a recent experience, he had decided drugs were not the Way, his Friends fell in again with total agreement, again offering testimonials along with recommendations for addiction centers and yoga studios nearby. But Q soon tired of all this self-centered chatter and attempted to move the burgeoning conversation into a more universal realm, offering ideas for the Betterment of Humanity such as protecting the environment and the rights of those less fortunate than ourselves. Again, his Updates were met with sympathy and enthusiastic courtesy. Being new to the ideology game and not really knowing Right from Left, Q made suggestions from every side of the Big Divide, sometimes suggesting in the same post such outrageously contradictory concepts as the redistribution of wealth and limitations on immigration. Sometimes, also, he changed his mind from post to post, saying now that the death penalty was barbaric and should be abolished and then that it should be made universal, but no matter what he said his Friends added their voices to his own. He felt he was starting a movement, several movements, in fact.

But then, quite suddenly, the babble began to bore him. This didn't stop him from posting; in fact, his own posts bored him most of all. It seemed that everyone, himself included, was merely repeating something previously heard, the way one might hear a snippet of a tune on the street and whistle it for the rest of the day, not knowing the song it came from. So he asked the Phone to stop reading posts to him and to book him a suite at the next five star hotel on his route.

ᴅᴅᴅ

Again, the tapping sound. Though this time a little harsher, metallic, more of a clanging, really, as the Correctional Officer walked down the hall, dragging his night stick along the bars as he went, each clang reverberating in Espe's already clanging head. He stopped at her cell to wish her a cheery good morning and to hand her the Morning Paper. "You made the front page, Miss Esperanza," he announced, causing a bit of stir among her sleepy cell-mates, who roused themselves with uncharacteristic enthusiasm and gathered around her bunk to read over her shoulder.

**X Governor's X
Arrested after Drunken Joy Ride
in Stolen State Vehicle**

read the headline over the photo of her standing beside the Lexus™, looking up at her finger on her nose, grimacing in concentration while failing the balance test. To say the photo was unflattering was an understatement. It was hard to believe, really, that this hag—with the frizzy hair, streaked make-up, hollows below her sunken eyes like something out of a horror movie, blouse wrinkled and blotched with booze, buttoned in the wrong holes, falling off one shoulder exposing the bra strap—was the same woman who'd made the power-brokers whimper and drool just by walking past. Voices had dropped to a whisper when interrupted by the click of her heals in the hallways of the Capitol. But look at her now.

"Ooooh looking good, girl," her new friends sang. "Put that in your Hollywood resumé. You goin' places, girl." She cringed and blushed at their ribbing, which went on for some time, but she was glad for their honesty, glad for their utter lack of the sniveling fakery and guile that had become such an integral part of her everyday conversation she no longer noticed it. They had scared her at first, of course, when she was so rudely cast in among them. They had greeted her tears with contempt and promises that if they weren't stifled she would soon have something real to cry about. Even when she'd shown them the contusions around her ribs and midriff (cops usually avoid the face) they had been unimpressed, though there had been a change in tone as they all began to share their scars and stories of their own encounters, few of them as benevolent as Espe's. Several had had ribs broken. Some had seen far worse: pistol whippings, choke holds, feet broken against the curb.

But they had really bonded when the stories had shifted to what had gotten each of them where they were on that particular night. Shoplifting cameras, undercover narcs and suddenly repentant johns got several votes, but then it was Espe's turn. She had tried to get away with telling them that her own case was nondescript, a simple DUI. She had actually thought the car belonged to her. Etc. But these girls knew a soft-pedal when it was in their midst and refused to settle for the easy answer. Even if she thought the car was hers, what was she doing, way out here in the boonies, alone and drunk in the middle of the night? Was she running from something? Where was her famous Man? Was he screwing around on her? Did she catch him with one of those ubiquitous secretaries? Oh, he was faithful, was he? Well then what was she drinking to forget? What was she running from?

And then, before she even knew what she was doing, Espe had told them everything, the whole sick story in one long sentence, from that first morning when she had pulled in to the Bondage shop to the last one when Santo had received the photo and gone wild.

The room had gotten oddly quiet then, and Espe had heard, for the first time, voices from other cells, other rooms. A door closed in the distance. A buzzer sounded.

"Damn, girl," one of them finally said. "Makes that video of me blowin' that john seem like Sunday school." There was another moment of silence during which Espe wondered what she had done. How could she have made such a strategic mistake and revealed her big secret to a bunch of strangers? But then someone started to chuckle, and suddenly the cell erupted in laughter. They high-fived her. They hugged her and kissed her. One produced a pint of gin, another some hash oil. They fought with each other about who got to sit beside Espe during the party. They sang songs a capella and danced to them until the guard came and told them to keep it down or he would get in trouble.

And Espe went to sleep on a bare mattress in the jail, pleasantly high, amid the night smells and night noises of other women's bodies, bereft, destitute, and happier than she'd been in a very long time.

♈

They started letting her out that afternoon. She went to the bail hearing and then was taken to the Bursar to make her bail. She told them that she didn't need a phone call because she would be posting the bail herself, but she would be needing her purse to do so. The Bursar told her it would be impossible, since the purse was locked up in the evidence room and could not be released until Espe herself was released. Espe insisted that she be allowed access to her purse, and the Bursar responded by calling the guard, who took Espe back to her cell, where she waited two hours, after which the guard came and brought her back to the Bursar.

The guard stood by when they handed her the purse in its clear plastic evidence bag. She tried to pay the bail with her debit card, in case she might be needing the cash later, but the Bursar told her the debit card had been declined. So she started counting out the cash. She found, though, that her substantial stack of 20s and 100s had been replaced by an equally substantial stack of ones and after a long spell of counting and recounting discovered she did not have enough cash to make bail and would need a Bondsman.

They took her back to the cell to wait for the Bondsman to arrive, and came to get her after an hour. She signed a stack of papers without reading them, gave the Bondsman all her cash, and they let her go. When she finally left the station it was dark, she was penniless, the battery in her phone was dead; she didn't know anyone in this town and didn't want to.

ᴕᴕᴕ

The next morning, much refreshed after a mud bath and massage, Q regained the road. He spent some time turning off voice commands and text-to-speech, for as helpful as the Phone had been for him the day before, he found he really didn't want to hear it speak ever again.

He drove all that day and into the night, stopping only for gas, until his body was numb from immobility and his mind from the monotonous blur of the landscape passing by. He drove well beyond the point where he should have stopped, because, having finally made up his mind where he was going, he no longer had any interest in the trip itself, only in his destination, and also because the estimated time of arrival on the GPS screen seemed somehow as much a command as a prediction, and he felt obligated to meet or even better it.

Around midnight the freeway widened from two lanes to three, and then to four, five, and even more as he entered the urban sprawl at the outskirts of his City. Despite the late hour, traffic was dense, though still very fast, and the red taillights in his own lanes and the bright whites in the others swirled around him in a blur. Groggy and befuddled, he was at the same time intensely concentrating, as his eyes darted back and forth from windshield to mirror to GPS and back.

He missed his exit, and then he missed the exit that would have corrected for this error. The third possibility the GPS itself missed while recalculating. The fourth he was determined to make, and did, though only by cutting recklessly across three lanes, entering the ramp at high speed, activating the Antilock Braking System before he finally shuddered to a stop at the light at the bottom. Shaken by this, he refused the GPS's instruction to get back on the freeway in the other direction and drove on into the city, turning randomly until it found him a route on surface roads, the upshot being that from the time the GPS showed him five minutes from destination, he was two hours actually arriving.

The checkered flag was all but under him, and still he had not encountered any familiar landmark that would have enabled him to navigate on his own from there. The concrete Sound Barrier on his left looked somewhat like the wall that had been erected, years before, between Provincial Oaks and the railroad, but this one was footed with pristine landscaping and covered with signage. On his right was what appeared to be the wall of a medieval castle, complete with crenelations, turrets, even a moat and what appeared to be archers in spiked helmets keeping guard at the top. And the GPS only added confusion to the confusing scene by directing him to turn directly into it.

He stopped, exhausted and befuddled, thinking the robot had failed him and he was now hopelessly lost, but when he did he noticed a red pinpoint zipping across the hood and realized he was being scanned by a laser. Then he heard a whirring sound and the whine of a hydraulic pump, and a segment of the wall began to open from the top, coming to rest in front of him with a satisfying thunk. A video sign hung above the drawbridge and the newly apparent gate, proudly announcing, in animated letters: Home at last! Welcome to Provincial Oaks.

∂

He drove slowly down the curving, cobblestone streets, between immaculately landscaped lawns anchored by shiny mansions fronted with tall Corinthian columns and leaded glass French doors, seeing nothing he recognized, until the GPS began flashing that he had arrived. He stopped in front of the quaintest, smallest house on the block. Dwarfed by its neighbors and the only one that appeared to have seen better days, with a wooden sign in the front yard that said "Sales Office," the place was yet recognizable as Q's childhood home, subsequently the seat of the Commune he and his parents had founded. He pulled cautiously into the driveway, parked and sat for a moment, still not sure, despite everything, the GPS hadn't steered him wrong.

Then the garage door slowly raised itself in front of him, and the driveway flooded with light. There were two cars inside, the smaller one (was it a Myata?), idling with the brake lights on. This one began to back out and stopped beside the Z. The driver's window lowered, revealing Q's Sister behind the wheel. He pushed the button and rolled down his passenger window.

"Hey Q," she said nonchalantly. "What's up?"

"Not much," he answered.

"You found another Z, huh? Still like the ride?"

"It's OK."

"Well, it must have some zip. You made good time today. At least till you got in the city."

"Yeah."

"Cool. Well, you must be tired. I think Mom ordered pizza. I'll see you later. Let's catch up."

Without waiting for an answer, she backed out into the street and drove away as the garage door lowered in front of him.

a

Once inside, Q found the interior of the house had undergone some changes too. The front room had been converted into a sales office, the walls adorned with photos and artist's renditions of houses like the ones he had seen driving in. Below each one was a sign advertising the model's price with tag lines denoting the way each one was unique: Tudor Luxury, Relax in Your Indoor Hot Tub, This Month's Special, Built-In Kennel, etc. Q noticed that, despite the sometimes significant differences in price and details like column style, glass pattern and paint color, they were actually identical. In the center of the room was an elegant mahogany desk at which his Mother was seated, engrossed in the monitor screen inlaid in the top surface.

"Well, I see you made it," she said, without looking up. "There's pizza in the kitchen. I'm sorry; I know I'm being rude, but once I start a transaction, you see, I have to finish it."

Q walked into the kitchen, which also had been redone, with long rows of shiny new cabinets with granite and marble counters. It had a strange look, though, as each cabinet was a different color or style and each was labelled with a small placard: Early American, Provincial Oak Traditional, Euro-Modern, Antique Shaker, etc. There was a pizza box on the island, and Q was unable to resist grabbing a slice as he walked by on his way to see what sort of changes had been wrought in the rest of the house.

He found his Father in the Den watching a game show on the huge TV which hung over the two fireplaces (one in Traditional stone; one in sleekly modern metal). He glanced at Q and waved an enthusiastic greeting before returning his attention to the screen. It had been a long time since Q had seen his Father in normal clothes, but then, he supposed, it had been a long time since his Father had seen him in normal clothes, and he realized that both of them had changed, just as the house had changed.

He went across to the window wall where he used to look out to check on the weather and the crops. A light came on when he opened the door and stepped out into what was now a diminutive back yard. Beyond the fence, where the communal fields had been, he saw the back wall of another house similar to his own, and beyond that more houses.

He joined his Father on the couch and soon sank into the TV trance with him. When his Mother came in neither of them looked up. She sat down beside them, apologizing for her neglect and cursing the inane inefficiencies of the Bank's new interface, which caused transactions that used to take her only 15 minutes to now take more than 30, and they all shook their heads at the sad fact that all the Systems they depended on every day seemed to be going downhill.

Between the Million Dollar Questions on the game show Q inquired casually about the Commune. "Ah," his Mother said, "a Deprogrammer got in somehow. It wasn't two days after you left that we lost more than half the recruits, and with them all our liquidity, so we had to find another way to keep our heads above water. Then your Father had a dream in which he saw a castle, surrounded by a wall and a moat, where the fields were. We thought it was just another of his crazy ideas, of course, but he got out his easel and painted it, and your Sister said, 'You know, this has possibilities.' So she took a picture of it, put it up on Venture Capital A-Go-Go, and a week later we had the money to build the wall."

"What about the recruits and the adepts who remained?" Q asked, suddenly nostalgic for the friends he'd broken bread with so many times.

"We didn't want to just turn them out, of course," his Mother said, "so we gave them the option to stay on as Security. We gave them knight costumes and toy bows and arrows and had them walk the wall, day and night. That turned out to be a good move, because when people drove by and saw the drawbridge and the guards, they all wanted in. We only have about three lots left. Oh, that reminds me."

She leaned forward, opened the drawer of the coffee table and took out a Card which she handed to Q. It was simple and elegant, gray and translucent, showing the chip and circuitry embedded within. On its face a simple letter:

Q

Q ran his thumb over the letter, feeling intensely proud and happy. Just then a contestant guessed correctly, and the TV went wild with sirens and streamers and flashing lights.

ʔʔʔ

The next day Q woke up early. No one else was stirring except the Maids vacuuming the carpets and mopping the kitchen and bathrooms. Q recognized one of them as his Field Foreman from the Commune and nodded to her. She nodded back and continued her work.

He went outside, feeling meditative and wanting to stroll. But the strolling paths were all gone now, so he walked, instead, once around the pool and then opted for a soak in the Spa. His Sister came out, by and by, in her robe, sipping her coffee, and sat down on the chaise lounge by the tub.

"Long night, Sis?" Q inquired. "You're looking a little rough."

"You ought to see me from this side," she said. "I think I'm getting too old for this life."

"Aw, you've got a ways to go, yet," he consoled.

"Yeah, well, we'll see. Hey, you're coming tonight, right?"

"Yes. I'm coming tonight," he said.

𝕒

He went back up to his room and lay about the rest of the morning. This room hadn't changed much except for the new furniture and paint job. They had also hung some new art, more in keeping with the new decor, and they had boxed up his belongings for the renovation. He found the box in the closet, opened it, and then closed it again.

He took a shower, shaved, futzed with his hair in the mirror for a while, then went back downstairs. His Mother was back at her desk and his Father at his TV, Sis nowhere to be found. He went out and got back in the Z. It was still early, but there was a bit of a drive ahead of him, and he didn't feel like rushing.

He exited at one of the little towns just outside the City, when the little red low fuel symbol on the screen started to flash. He paid for the gas with his own Card, then he went inside, borrowed a pair of scissors from the attendant, and cut the Other One into little pieces.

A homeless woman was sitting on the curb outside the door to the place, staring dully at the ground. She looked up when he came out. "Hey frat boy," she said, "buy me a 40 and I'll show you a good time."

He had seen her before, somewhere. He thought she might have been one of the recruits or one of the workers at the Commune, but he wasn't sure. Not in the least tempted by her offer, for she was haggard and filthy, Q nevertheless went back inside and did as she requested. When he handed her the big can of fortified beer, though, she scorned it.

"You expect me to drink this swill?" she said. "Like you can't afford better? You ought to be whipped for that."

Taken aback but also impressed by the bravado of her response, Q went back in and picked out the most expensive (as he had no other criteria) 40 in the cooler. Then, on a sudden impulse, he stopped at the meager clothing section of the EZ Store and picked out a tee shirt and a pair of tights he thought might fit her.

"I'm going to a show," he said as he handed her the bag. "Want to come?"

She looked up at him, eyes bloodshot and filmy. "I know you from somewhere," she said. And then, "Sure. Why not."

When she came out of the rest room Q was stunned at the change. Merely wiped down with paper towels, hair pulled back, in a cheap t-shirt with a cartoon character on the front, he saw she was younger than he had judged, and also, beneath the road film, rather attractive. Barefoot now, having discarded her ruined pumps along with the filthy skirt and blouse, she picked a pair of beach sandals off the shelf and commanded him to buy them for her, which he did.

᠔

They got to the Dome at dusk. The traffic was so dense that people were simply abandoning their cars in the gridlock and walking, and Q and Espe did the same. The line to get in was equally daunting. The wide entrance ramp thronged with humanity, and they took their place at the end and began the slow shuffle to the door.

Among the myriad faces surrounding them, which were as plentiful as the leaves on a great oak, Q recognized several, old friends from the Commune and even before, from the Road. Up ahead he was surprised to see even his Parents, and marvelled that they had gotten here ahead of him. He waved to them across the crowd, but they didn't see him.

Someone tapped him on the shoulder. When he looked around he found the railroad gang who had fed him and Lucy when they had jumped from the train, and he embraced them, one by one, all of them jittery with excitement to be there, finally. The Old Bawd was with them, grinning through her rotten teeth, and she took Q's hand and leaned in to whisper in his ear: "Before we begin our riotous journey against the years, let me twine crimson pomegranate blossoms for your hair... Better yet, let us have a game of croquet!"

The Troll was among them, too, still in his PT scrubs, but when

Q caught his eye he turned the other way. Beyond him Q saw the emaciated figures of the Meth-heads, and beyond them the Fat Farmers and the Seed Salesman. Horror gripped him for a moment when he spotted the *Custos Scripti*, pointed hat and quiver standing above the crowd, but he was far enough away that Q calmed himself, thinking that no one would dare attempt any aggression at such a gathering as this.

He looked around, worried that he had lost Espe, but she was still beside him. He took her by the hand, and she gave him a suspicious look. "Just so I don't lose you," he said, and she left her hand in his.

They heard a loud whoop and looked back to see Santo pushing his diminutive frame through the crowd toward them. He was wearing a serape, bandana around his head with feathers sticking out of it, leading a group of three or four others similarly attired and similarly whooping. He forced his way up to them and stopped, grinning wildly, to yell "*Muerte a Furhoncle! Vivimos la revolución!*" He pulled a bottle of tequila from under his serape, threw his head back and drank. "And so, my old friend Q," he said, and then handed him the bottle. Q turned it up, drank and handed it to Espe, who did likewise and handed the bottle back to her X. Their eyes met for a moment, and he hesitated, but then he let out a yell, passed the bottle to his comrades and pushed on through the crowd with them in tow.

Now Q was suddenly blinded. A pair of hands had covered his eyes and someone was behind him saying "guess who... guess who it is, Q." He turned around and saw Gwen, with the Pastor standing respectfully a few paces behind. She put her hands on Q's shoulders and looked him in the eye, then threw her arms around him and hugged him close. "I told you. I told you. Didn't I tell you?" she whispered in his ear. Q returned her hug somewhat less vigorously, then pushed her back. "Yes, you told me," he said. She held his eye for another moment, then glanced at Espe by his side. "Nice shirt," she said. "Maybe we'll see you inside," and she pushed on ahead.

The Pastor stopped to shake Q's hand as he struggled to catch up to her. "So glad to see you, Q," he said, then leaned close and told Q in a softer voice that he could join them in an easier entry through the stage door, if he so desired. But Q declined and wished the Pastor good day.

Now there arose a bit of commotion ahead of them. A phalanx of police was attempting to cross the flow of the crowd and all around them people were cheering and clamoring to get a view of whoever it was they were protecting. Q grabbed Espe's hand a bit tighter and pushed forward until he caught a glimpse of the Turntablist walking in their midst. He was beaming, waving, reaching over his harried escorts to touch the myriad hands that were reaching for him as they passed. And beside him, waving and touching hands herself, was Q's sister.

Espe tugged at his shoulder, as she wasn't quite tall enough to see, and Q put his arms around her waist and lifted her as best he could, and she waved and yelled with the rest. He couldn't hold her for long, and when he put her back down she turned in his arms and kissed him.

ᔕ

Inside the Dome the chanting of the Crowd became a silent pantomime of waving arms and open mouths. The dancers came first, leaping and flying like fairies across the stage. Then the Turntablist took his place behind his massive deck and the beat began, perhaps at a pitch just below the level of the audible, so that the Crowd felt it in their bones, a seismic vibration, a pulse.

Smoke rose from the stage, obscuring everything, shot through with lasers and projections, abstract forms settling into images, pyramids and obelisks, Ankh and Ra, wooden masks and clay figures, Kali and Hekatonkheires, Aries with a fistful of spears, Buddha under the cobra's hood, Aphrodite on her shell, lightning strike etching letters into stone, cuneiform scrawl, gods sculpted into marble, Parthenon and Coliseum, a vast desert undulating like the sea, waters parting and closing again, roiling with shields and horses and helmets going under, a whirlwind of fire lifting into the geometry of the Cross and the Figure upon it, standing above the conflagration, high above armies advancing across the mountains and the plains, above palaces and castles and windmills and seacraft, minarets and cathedrals, above victory and death march, winged death and crawling death, the last seal undone and the Book beginning to open.

And then, beneath the great cross, beneath the muddle of history evaporating into the aether, Little A came onto the stage.

The
Private I

I magine a mirror. Imagine a mirror that gives a true and perfect reflection except that gender is reversed. The way most mirrors flip right and left, this mirror flips male and female. Then, imagine this mirror slicing down the middle of a 1952 vintage solid oak desk and reflecting back to the Detective sitting in its wooden swivel-chair the perfect gender-swapped image of him or her self, and you'll have an idea of how Q and Lucy feel sitting across from each other, by utter chance, inside this office that looks like it's been decorated from the set of *The Big Sleep*, with the ridiculous slogan, "Q Private I," painted on the hammered glass vision panel of the equally vintage, equally oaken door.

"It's clever. It made you stand out from the list that came up in the search. Somehow I knew, I guess, knew without knowing, that that I was you. Still, rather a shock."

The word-play elicits a chuckle or two, a good-natured "I see you haven't lost your propensity for silly puns" sort of exchange, with sign-writer and -reader feeling each other out as to just how seriously to take it and, coincidentally, finding something to talk about besides the suspicious nature of the ostensively accidental encounter. "Ah, don't people take coincidences, and puns, far too seriously?" their laughter seems to imply, but with its slight nervous hesitation adding "or maybe not." But is it really so remarkable that a pair of X's should find themselves, after some years apart, one in need of a detective and the other having become one in the interim, sitting across an antique desk from each other, preparing to transact a bit of old-fashioned detective business, preparing to begin the time-honored sequence of mystery, investigation, revelation and payment for services rendered?

Between pleasantries, they check each other out, each attempting to steal glances at the ravages time, stress, frustrated desire and plastic surgery have wrought upon the other's face while the other is not looking, and yet with each quick movement of the eye finding that the other's eye has moved just as quickly up and then down, with all their other little nervous tics—hands darting to faces, noses

wrinkling with sarcasm, lips curling with self-deprecating decorum—
likewise synchronized. It is not that they are identical—far from it,
objectively speaking—but rather that, from all those minutes, hours
and days of their youth spent in close company, gazing into each
other's eyes, naked bodies entwined in reciprocal pleasure, they have
come to recognize in the other an idealized version of themselves,
each kiss a return to the child's narcissistic rehearsal, each entry a
being-entered, each stroke both given and taken, so that the face
and body now sitting opposite appears more familiar than would
their actual face and body in an actual mirror. Such habits are hard
to break, no matter if one or three or thirty years have intervened.

They cross legs, one to the left and one to the right, in a mutual
attempt to appear comfortable and happy about the encounter. Then,
embarrassed at the failure of this gesture, they fumble, one in a purse
and one in a pocket, for cigarettes and light up with identical butane
lighters, quite despite the No Smoking sign, (itself a skeuomorph,
merely a part of the vintage decor, as the rule goes quite without
saying), having each decided that the occasion called for giving in
to impulse and ignoring, for this one moment, the rule.

They exhale in unison, and the smoke rises through the planes
of sunlight that have made it through the clouds and the office
window. It is late for a detective to be still at the office, well past the
hour when your average sleuth has retreated to the neighborhood
bar to forget the sad truth of the human condition the morning's
investigation has uncovered, and the sun is low on the horizon.
The window, which happens to face west, affords a stunning view
of the sunset over the crenellated silhouette of the city, and they
retreat into quiet contemplation of the red-orange and purple light
that cuts under the smog, giving the nicotine time to get into their
bloodstreams and soothe nerves made jittery by the strain of polite
conversation.

The trance is broken, finally, by Q leaning forward and rattling
open a recalcitrant bottom drawer, the one that had been designed,
when the ancient-looking desk was built, to hold paper files but now

serves as stowage for those tools of the detective trade changing times have not rendered obsolete, that is, the gun and the bottle. He takes out the whisky and sets it on the desk, then produces two glasses and pours them each an unwatered shot. He pushes one toward Lucy.

"I was thinking you probably had one of those down there," she says, picking up the glass and sipping demurely. "The desk seems made for it."

"Yes," he says, "predictable, I suppose, but clichés can be a comfort, especially when they come with a buzz."

"Well, everything's better when it comes with a buzz, right?"

"Never before the sun gets below the smog is my rule," Q replies, "but a necessary evil when I'm working late." He takes a drink and holds it in his mouth until he feels it seeping in, slightly numbing his tongue, then swallows and waits for that same feeling to seep into the rest of him.

"I'm surprised to see you so ambitious, a career, a title…. It doesn't seem your style. Not the way I remember you, that's for sure."

"'Career' is perhaps too strong a word, though it is sometimes convenient to have the title, to have an answer to the question that used to flummox me: What do you do? I lived a long time with no simple answer to that question and cherished the freedom, the indolence of the hobo life and the agrarian simplicity of the commune, but I found, in the end, I was craving an Identity, and besides I found that I like the order of the work day and the work week. I like not having to decide what to do each morning. It frees my mind to think of other things, pleasant thoughts and dire ones, problems to negotiate, motivations to uncover. There is, of course, an element of drudgery, for there is no end of mysteries to solve. It isn't like in books. Most cases never really get solved. They just sort of fade away when the client and I both realize that further investigation will only uncover more contradictions, more unanswerable questions. Sometimes I long for a case that will actually conclude, like a novel ending, and let me say, finally, 'the job is done,' but yet it seems, also, that if I ever did solve the case that solved all cases, I would be emptied out. I'd have no reason to get up in the morning and move forward with my comforting schedule."

"Hmmm," she says, sipping. "I don't imagine you'll have that problem with my case, if you decide to take it. It's pretty run-of-the-mill, really. A missing person thing."

A silence falls between them, each looking down at the desktop, sipping their whisky. Finally Q speaks. "I don't usually work for… um… friends. Besides, finding people really isn't my specialty. I can give you a referral…."

"I see," she says, turning her gaze back to the window. The sun is almost down, and it is getting darker, outside and in. "Thank you. That would be most appreciated."

"Of course," he says, pulling out his phone. He says the name of one of his associates. "Your phone?" he asks.

"Oh yes." She takes her own device from her purse and holds it up between them. He leans forward and taps it with his own, as if making a toast.

"Cheers," he says, as her phone assimilates the data.

Outside the office door, which Q turns around to lock with an old-fashioned metal key, they seem to have stepped into a different building. The polished concrete floors, glossy PVC walls and softly luminescent ceiling belong to a different time than Q's cozy wood-toned office. How did he ever find such a place? she wonders. "I didn't find it, actually, but created it," he says, "out of whole cloth. I negotiated architectural control in the lease. It wasn't a hard sell. They're not exactly turning away tenants these days."

This fact is confirmed by the emptiness of the hallway and the other offices that open onto it. The sleek, solid-glass doors they pass on their way to the elevator afford views of bare, vacant rooms, occupied only by random bits of chromium furniture left there by former tenants who had no place to move them. If you look at the glass from the right angle you can still make out the faint outline of signage which had been scraped off, the anonymous, arbitrary names of companies, now either defunct or having retreated to a purely digital existence, which had had enough faith in themselves to believe, for just one moment, they had made it to the point where they could afford the great luxury of a physical location.

"I think of this hallway," he continues, "if you'll excuse a bit of professional bias, as the Corridor of Mistaken Identities."

"How so?" she says. "I would have called it 'the Corridor of Broken Dreams.'"

"But these dreams were all dreams of identity. The people who occupied, however briefly, these offices, were mistaken about who they were. My work has taught me to consider identity as a kind of dream, since both seem to stem from the same primal longing, the same absence or lack. An identity is a dream."

"Your work has taught you this? What a luxury to have room for such philosophical ruminations in the course of the daily grind."

"Not really. All part of the job. I discovered early on that detective work is concerned almost exclusively with matters of identity, with proving and disproving roles, enactments, dreams. Every missing person case, for example, is actually a case of mistaken identity. A client comes to me to locate a spouse or a sibling or a lover who is a lawyer or a drunk or a writer or a crook. But the case always reveals that it is not the person who is missing, only their identity. My client's wife is still sitting there, in the living room, as it were; she is simply not who her husband imagined her to be. He has called her a politician, but she is actually a dominatrix. Or he has told me she is a secretary while she is actually a terrorist."

"A terrorist? You have encountered terrorists?"

"Oh no, of course not. I'm just making random examples. I cannot, naturally, divulge the details of any real case."

"And then, I thought you didn't take missing person cases."

"Well…" Q stammers, thinking quickly how to avoid admitting

he has told her a lie and realizing just as quickly that in his fatuous desire to show off his expertise he has done exactly that, and then he allows, of necessity, the thought to trail off unfinished. "Ah, here's the elevator…" is how he chooses to complete the evasion.

❀❀❀

The street is aglow with sea-green light from the fingernail of sun still visible at its western end. Without thinking, as if from some latent heliotropic impulse, they turn toward it and walk in search of more liquor. But for the occasional car tediously threading between potholes on the ravaged pavement, the street is as empty as the building they have just vacated, prompting Lucy to mutter something under her breath.

"I'm sorry?" says Q.

"Oh nothing," she says. "I was just saying, it's empty like the building, so it must be a street of mistaken identities."

"Ah yes, but the whole city is falling apart like this. A city, a world of mistaken identities."

"Remember," she goes on, "the cities when we were kids, where every apartment had water and electricity and trucks came every day to haul away the garbage? And the streets were full of people going this way and that. And cars, thousands, millions of cars."

"Of course," he says, "and every day someone got killed because people failed to control them properly, being sleepy or distracted by their phones or drunk or dissociated or otherwise impaired. When I feel myself lapsing nostalgic I like to remind myself that there were problems back then, also." As if to drive this point home, a car slams on its brakes to allow them to cross a side street. The driver, jolted awake by the sudden change in velocity, stares up at them in wonder, as if he'd never seen a pedestrian before. "See what I mean. In the good old days we would be lying in the street, waiting for an ambulance now."

"I guess you're right," she concedes, "and I'm not longing for a

388

return, exactly, but still it seems that the city was just, well, nicer, more interesting, fun, even. I used to wear those little shoes with pointy heels that required a perfectly smooth surface to walk on, and I could wear them everywhere. Now I can't leave the house without my hiking shoes."

"Well," Q responds with a sly glance downward, "you still rock a pair of Merrells…."

"Shut up," she says, though, at the same time, does the ghost of a smile lift the corner of her mouth? The answer to this rhetorical question is unequivocally no, he decides, and yet he does, at some level even less apparent than conscious thought, equivocate, and does his heart rate increase, ever so slightly, at the hint of possibility his certainty itself engenders?

"Sorry," is all he can answer, as indeed he is. Sorry that he had the idea to invite her out for a drink, telling himself that moving the encounter to a neutral location, where either of them could, finally, rise from the table and invent another appointment or some other excuse, was an expedient way to bring their meeting to a close. Sorry that she had felt obliged to say OK. Sorry, most of all, that he is incapable of controlling his own tongue, which seems determined to lead him down the very path he fervently wishes to avoid.

The club—one of the three or four Q frequents in the neighborhood—is typical of the new style, tiny front room with bar-top, desultory bartender falling asleep behind it, and three or four stools. At the back of the room is a single, sound-proof door labelled only with a cross, leading to the gloss hall. It is an unwritten law, now, that the halls be sequestered in sound-proof and padded enclosures. There had been too many instances, back when the trend was getting started, of patrons falling into dissociation right at the bar, which was very disruptive to business. Even the bartenders were not immune, and more than one owner had come in the morning to find their liquor shelves emptied, the floor covered with booze and broken glass, bartender and a few last glossies lying in it twitching and still babbling.

When the door to the hall opens, as it does every few minutes with someone going in or coming out to refresh a drink, the thudding bass of the house sampler accompanied by some glossy's entranced speech fills the room, making conversation a difficult and intermittent exercise, a fact which Lucy laments, right off, when they have their whiskies in front of them.

"You're right," Q says, "and my apologies. I seldom have conversations here so I didn't think about it."

The door opens, then, the racket floods in, and they drink, resuming conversation when it closes.

"Sounds like a sad existence, Q," she says, "if your favorite hangout is a place where conversation is impossible. And even sadder that you never even noticed this fact."

"It's kind of like living abroad," he says. "Like if you were living in a country where you didn't speak the language, you might find a bar that you liked even though your conversations there would be limited to the most basic level, ordering drinks, paying, etc. And yet you develop a rapport, even a friendship, with the bartender and the patrons, based solely on banal niceties and subtle gestures of respect. That's kind of what it's like here for me."

The door opens again. A glossy comes out and stands at the bar, looking around dazed for a moment before he can pull himself together to order a vodka fortified with caffeine. Q and Lucy drink.

"I can see that," she says, with a nod toward the door as it closes. "It's a bar where the language is foreign to everyone."

"Ha. I hadn't thought of it that way. But that's pretty good. Pretty good."

"And say, if you're hanging out at glossolalic karaoke bars these days, does that mean you're… you know… practicing again?"

"Oh no, not at all," he says. "Nothing could be further from my mind. Absolutely no desire to go back there, at all."

"So you have no interest in glossing any more, but you hang out in a bar which has absolute zero going for it except the gloss hall in back? Are you being straight with me, Q?"

The door opens as the glossy heads back in, Cafka in hand. They drink.

"Yes, I am being completely straight. I have absolutely no interest in glossing ever again. I've never been through that door and never will. It's just that, you know, a detective needs a bar, and this is what there is, these days. In truth, I suppose, I find it soothing to hear, now and then, in small doses, short spurts, like here, as a kind of background music when I'm thinking about a case or some other problem that needs sorting out. I don't really even listen. And when I remember being here, you know, like the next morning, I never remember the glossing. It goes in one ear and out the other."

"And you're never, after a few drinks, tempted to dip back in, just for old time's sake? I mean, it almost seems a shame. After all, you're the best. The original."

"The original, perhaps, but not the best," he says, faking self-deprecation and then, as if convinced by his own sincerity, feeling it turn real. "Little A was the master, the undisputed God of the genre."

"But Little A came in on your coattails. *Rappin' in Tongues* was the beginning of it all, the album that started the trend. You invented the genre. That was you, your genius."

The door opens as one of the glossies heads to the restroom. They drink. And this time, they drink again. Q leans on the bar and swirls the bit of amber liquid left in his glass.

"Here's the thing," he says. "When you make a great album or do a great performance, people praise you, they talk about you, they remember you. But invent an entire genre and no one will ever know. A billion people will imitate you but not one will know the source. It seeps into their speech, their manners, into the way they live and die, and they never notice a thing and never give a second thought to the ultimate progenitor."

"I know," she says. "It's not fair."

He looks at her, something like a prayer in his eyes. "So who is it you're looking for?" he says.

❖❖❖

"Is it your father?" he wonders aloud.

"Oh for god's sake, no," she says. "I spent my whole life trying to lose that bastard. Why would I want to find him if he went missing?"

"Yes," he says, "I do remember your relationship with your dad was somewhat problematic. Ambivalent might be the word."

"Anyway, he's dead now, thank god."

"Ah. I'm sorry."

"I am too. At least when he was alive I could get away from him for brief intervals. Now, he's inescapable. My mother is gone too, of course. I mean, they'd be like a hundred."

"Of course they would," he says. "I guess I had forgotten the decades that have passed since last I saw them, or you. My parents are gone too, of course."

"Yes. I had assumed. I'm sorry."

The door opens as the glossy returns to the fray, and again the thudding bass and nonsense syllables fill the room. They drink, emptying their glasses. Q motions to the bartender for another round.

"So who is it, then?" he continues, "your 'missing person'?"

"It's a young woman. A friend. I haven't heard from or been able to contact her in over three months."

"I see. So I take it that she and you normally commune more frequently. How often do you normally see each other? How frequently do you typically speak?"

"Practically every day. We're quite close, or at least we used to be."

"Was there, perhaps, a precipitating incident? Did you quarrel? Did one of you touch a nerve somehow?"

She looks down. "Yes, I guess I would have to say that I touched that nerve. We were having a bit of a tiff. I told her I never wanted to see her again, and then I hung up."

"I see. So she apparently has some respect for your wishes."

The door opens, the noise floods in again, this time accompanied by something a bit more distracting, a couple, bedraggled and drenched with sweat, the woman still deeply dissociated, babbling, eyes rolling back, the man looking terrified and trying to steer her to the bar and onto a stool. The bartender, reticent to the point of invisibility until now, comes quickly to life.

"No no no!" he yells. "You can't bring her in here like that."

"But look at her," the guy whimpers, and indeed she is a sight, top torn open and one breast free, hair frizzed out. She thrashes free of her boyfriend's hold and falls to the floor, going into seizure. Q and Lucy have to get up and step back from the bar as she kicks over their stools and wallows on the floor, vibrating and foaming at the mouth.

"Jesus Christ…" The bartender comes out from behind the bar. "Grab her arms," he says to the guy, "and let's get her back in the hall."

"Back in there? You're fucking kidding me. Look what it did to her. And half the people in there are like that."

"Have you never been in a gloss bar before? It's either that door, or that door," the bartender explains, indicating, respectively, the door with the cross and the door to the street. "But she can't stay here." He emphasizes this fact by pointing to the sign, posted prominently above the liquor shelves: "No Tongues at the Bar."

The guy looks furtively from one door to the other, each of them seeming to represent an intolerable fate. "I've been in bars before. Just never one this intense. It's she who's never been in one before. She wanted to see what it was like. I'd heard about this one so I brought her here. Her parents are gonna kill me."

"She'll be fine," the bartender consoles as he leans over and begins pulling the ecstatic soul to her feet. "Just walk her around the block. She'll come out of it." And indeed the seizure has already abated. Though still dissociated, she is lying limp on the floor, staring at the ceiling, and by the time Q and Lucy follow the ragged pair back out to the street she is walking again, with assistance from her worried boyfriend.

❀❀❀

The sun has fully set and the street fallen into darkness, now, broken only by the headlights of the few cars that are out and the cross shaped LED's outside the gloss bars, of which there are several in sight. A fog has descended, also, so that the few pedestrians in sight appear blurred and indistinct, small orbs passing inside a cloud.

"It's funny," Lucy says, "how these bars prohibit the very thing people come to them for."

"Yeah I know," says Q, stumbling over a break in the sidewalk, "like in the old days they would throw you out if you got drunk. Or if you got drunk enough. All things in moderation, I guess."

"Hah," is Lucy's phatic response, as she herself stumbles over the crumbling concrete. She grabs Q's shoulder, and Q puts his arm around her to steady her. She leans into him. "Whoa. I'm as bad as that glossy girl. I think you got me drunk. That bartender would have been throwing me out next."

"Hardly," says Q politely. "At least you can stand up if I hold on to you. And they don't evict drunks any more, anyway. Really, no one gets drunk any more. They have one drink and fall into the gloss, which, whatever else it might do, sobers them up."

"Well, I seem to be getting drunk any more," she says drunkenly. "I could test your rule. I bet if they would throw people out for drinking again, more people would get drunk. Because that's what's fun, right? Disobeying the signs. Making the bartender yell at you and throw you out. The sign they ought to put over the bar would be 'No Drinking.' Anyway, the standing thing. I'm not sure how long I'm going to be doing that. I'm out of practice, I guess, and I've got a feeling I'll be on my back soon." She trips again and slumps into him even more fiercely, as if to emphasize the prophecy.

"There's another bar I know right up here," he says.

394

"Oh, good," she says. "Hey Q, are you still with that—oh, what was her name?…"

Q breathes deeply. "Esperanza. We are still… close. Yes."

"Of course, Esperanza. How could I forget, since I see the name all over the place. Close, eh? Close as in living together or close as in SM pals?"

He rewards her forwardness with a smile. "I do confess Espe and I see each other more on Social Media than in person, these days, though we do share a house on the North side. Her work and mine tend to take us far afield on a regular basis, so we tend not to see each that often, these days. Though we are still a couple, strictly speaking. And what about yourself? Are you and the Pastor still…?"

"Oh Lord no. We were both too committed to our own, um, endeavors, for that to last. I actually don't know what became of him. I assume he's still up there in the clouds, doing God's work and continuing to lead the Church toward world domination."

"Well, I have to admit I'm glad you changed your name back to Lucy. I was never comfortable calling you Gwen. It just seemed wrong. And really, if I am honest, you weren't yourself when you were going by Gwen. You weren't the same person."

"Wait a minute," she says, stopping their progress and turning to face him. "Now that we're starting to talk business, we should take it back to your office, don't you think? So you can take notes. And stuff."

"Ah," says Q with resignation, "I suppose you're right."

Just as Q puts his thumb to the reader on the door to his building lobby, a figure materializes from the fog and pushes himself through the door with them. Lucy, suddenly much less inebriated than she had been only a moment before, pushes him against the wall and cranks his arm up behind him, causing him to scream in pain until she eases the pressure just enough to let him breathe.

"Can we help you?" she whispers in his ear.

"I was just looking, you know, don't mean any harm. I thought this was a bar, you know. I thought there was a bar here."

"This isn't a bar," says Q. "And you're going to have to leave. Lucy, let him go. He's just leaving."

She gives the arm a little push, causing the hapless vagrant, a kid perhaps 20 years old, to scream again, before letting him loose. He backs away from them holding his arm and looking around in terror. "What is this place?" he says in amazement as he takes in the mirrored walls, the motley trio reflected *mise en abyme*, receding figures that shrink, in the furthest reaches, to mere dots.

"It's an office building," Q reiterates.

"What's that?" the kid asks. At this moment, too, the elevator decides to open its door, causing him to ask it yet again.

"An elevator," Lucy answers.

"Elevator." He tries out the word. "What's that?" The question that seems to haunt his being.

Q gives him a nudge toward the door. "They take people up and down in buildings like this. But this one's taking you out." He opens the door and pushes the kid back out onto the street, where he takes off without another word, fading into the murk, clutching his arm.

"I see you've kept your martial arts skills sharp," Q says as they board the mysterious elevator. "Well done."

"I've found the older I get the more necessary they are," she says, her voice dropping a little as she relaxes back into her buzz. She leans into a corner.

"The neighborhood's OK in the daylight," he feels obliged to say. "At night it can get a little wild. We should have been more alert. Though they're harmless, really. Just curious."

"Yeah. If we were their age now, we'd be with them, don't you think?"

Q smiles at this reference to their shared past and, perhaps, shared propensities. "I would like to think I was never quite that clueless," he says in an attempt to steer the conversation back toward banalities, "but you're probably right."

‌‌‌‌‌*❈❈❈*

Back in the anachronism of Q's office, glasses refilled (Lucy having retrieved the bottle from its drawer), now seated comfortably on the couch, they resume the interview. Q sets his phone to record and puts it on the coffee table in front of them. "I hope you don't mind," he says. "Easier and more accurate than taking notes."

"It just seems so out-of-keeping with the room," she says, unlacing her boots and settling in.

"True," he says, "but I've found that oral transcripts carry a great deal more information than a written record, no matter how detailed. Patterns of hesitation, slips of the tongue, changes in pitch and volume can add a great deal of information to an interview."

"Just don't forget to turn it off when we're done."

"Of course. It's only for me to refer to in the course of the investigation."

"Of course."

"Why don't we start with basic facts: name, address or addresses, and any other basic information concerning the missing person."

Lucy sits up straight and, with a hint of pride, recites the data of her missing friend's identity: Name and nicknames, date of birth, phone numbers and media handles, addresses, professions, even such small but telling details as the kind of make-up she wears and the location of certain tattoos.

"And can I take," Q presses, "your apparent familiarity with this young woman to indicate a degree of intimacy? What exactly is your relationship?"

"We are… close. Need I say more? You know I've never been one for the beaten path."

"Yes. And please don't think I am trying to pry, or that I would, in any way, pass judgement on your choice of companions or life-styles. I simply need to understand the nature of your relationship to determine if it might have any bearing…"

"You can assume," she interrupts, "the highest degree of intimacy in our relationship, if you can take that statement without embellishment. We are," she adds with a nod, "about as close as two human beings can be, without being physically conjoined."

"But you don't live together?"

"Not often, no."

"I see." Q sips his whisky. Lucy takes advantage of the pause to do the same. "May I ask, then, when you last saw her?"

"I already told you. About three months ago."

"I understood you to say you merely spoke on the phone three months ago."

"Well, phone or something. I remember talking to her, her face, what she was wearing. Maybe the video was on. It might have even been in person. I can't remember."

"You can't remember if the last time you spoke was on the phone or in person?"

"Sometimes at home I project on the big screen, you know. It's hard to tell the difference if you're not paying close attention."

"So you weren't paying close attention?"

"No. I remember now. It was on the phone. She was on the screen at home. That's it, because we couldn't kiss."

"So you normally kiss?"

"Of course we normally kiss. We kiss like everyone else."

"But a conversation in which you tell her you never want to see her again hardly sounds like an occasion for kissing."

"With us, every occasion is an occasion for kissing. Do you always make your clients feel like they're the ones under investigation?"

Q pauses, sighs, drinks, suddenly remorseful for making this woman, whom he once considered the love of his life and for whom he still feels, obviously, some affection, uncomfortable. "I'm sorry. I don't mean to pry. But I do need to understand the relationship. I need to understand if your friend is missing in the larger sense, ie missing from the culture, missing from life, or if she is missing only to you, if you catch my meaning."

"I catch your meaning, but why should I have to chase it? Her name and data, that should be enough for you to find her or to find that she cannot be found. It would be enough for the police, say. But your questioning seems to cross a line into prurience." She sips her whisky, more to ease the tension her questioning of her interrogator's motives has caused than out of a need for more alcohol, as the room is already spinning.

"I'm sorry," he says yet again. "You're absolutely right. I have enough information now to begin my inquiries. We can end the interview here."

"Oh good," she says, drawing one leg up under her. "Let's just relax and reminisce a bit."

"That sounds perfect," he says. But does he forget or "forget" to turn off his phone as the reminiscence begins?

While daylight had departed from the office with considerable fanfare, streaks of color, bright flashes, the sun seeming to set the smog aflame as it settled into a boiling ocean, it reappears with utter stealth, a foggy gray light coming to consciousness lux by tedious lux, a process so slow and gradual that each moment feels permanent, stable, iconic almost. And yet what is the dawn but process, pure movement, no moment existing except as transition to the next, mutability itself?

If such thoughts could keep the headache at bay, Q would think the more, and he engineers the train of thoughts passing through his mind to continue in this philosophical direction. His getaway, however, is quickly derailed by other encroachments into his sensorium, the rough grain and grit of the wood floor against his cheek, for one, and then Lucy's hand, which he can see beneath the coffee table, draped alongside the couch like the hand of an ingenue trailing beside a gondola as her handsome suitor tests her resistance with honeyed words and melody.

Above the table, he sees as he raises himself painfully to one elbow, she presents a rather different picture, as she sleeps, mouth agape and hair entangled, stripped to her undies which consist, rather too coincidentally, of a vintage 1950s slip, whisky stained and wrinkled, bunched up indelicately almost to her waist by the akimbo position of her still-shapely legs, one of which rests on the back of the couch, the other slouched to the floor, giving a hint that his memory cannot confirm of how their happy reunion had ended. Despite the three decades that have intervened since last he saw her thus compromised, he considers, she still presents a fetching figure, a bit of a paunch (dwarfed by his own), her skin still perfect but for the faintest age-spotting and equally faint scars, noticeable only to one who knows their source.

He rolls over, lifts himself to hands and knees and manages with the aid of the furniture to get to his feet. He is still wearing, for some reason, his shirt and tie, and one sock, though not a stitch else. He finds further clues to his activities of the night before in the ashtray overflowing onto the coffee table, the whisky bottle on its side on the floor, bits of clothing strewn about the room and the general stench of debauch. His phone is on the coffee table, also, and he picks it up to find that the screen will not awaken, the battery spent.

Feeling a sudden and urgent demand, he finds his pants on the floor, still of a piece with his boxers, slips them on, and exits the office for the bathroom down the hall, noting as he does the pointlessness of his modesty, since the floor is vacant but for his office. He returns to find his client still in her ignominious posture, but now with limpid, bloodshot eyes partially open. He turns quickly from her gaze, pretending not to notice that she is awake, and busies himself tidying the office, first dumping the disgusting ashtray in the trash, then sweeping the overflow butts and ash from the table with his hand.

"Getting fastidious in your old age?" she asks, dropping the hiked-up leg and rising to a sitting position.

"Oh, you're awake," he says, still avoiding her gaze as she straightens herself on the couch, pulling the slip down and smoothing it over her belly. "Good morning. Can I get you anything?" His headache and nausea resound through the attempted pleasantry.

"Please do," she says, "give me something."

"What would you like?" he asks, as his sparse inventory of possible gifts and refreshment sorts through his mind.

"Whatever you have," she says, "I want, though nothing you have can possibly be enough."

"I know the feeling. How about a glass of water?"

"Yes, water, of course," she says, and he picks up the sticky whisky glasses from the table and exits the office hurriedly. He goes back to the bathroom, turns on the sink and lets it run until the water turns clear, or nearly so, then rinses the glasses and fills them. Returning to the office, he meets her in the hallway. "Where is it?" she says.

"Oh, it's just here," he says, pointing the way past him to the john. She shuffles unsteadily by and disappears through the door. He returns to the office, places the glasses of milky liquid on his desk, retrieves a vial of bactericide from the top drawer and puts a droplet in each one. Then he plugs his phone into the charger on top of the old metal file cabinet and returns to the task of picking up the room. He quickly discovers, however, that he has no heart for the task in her absence and sits down in his chair to stare at the floor until her return.

She reenters the office in a somewhat more presentable condition, hair combed out if still unruly. She picks up her dress from the floor behind the couch, pulls it on over her slip and reseats herself. Q hands her the water, which she sips and tastes before swallowing. "Quite a night," she says. "I haven't had one of those in a while."

"Nor have I," Q agrees. Then they sit in awkward silence.

"There's one thing you need to know," she finally says. "I didn't just come here to get laid. The case is real. I need you to find this woman for me."

"I see," he says.

"And I can, of course, pay your standard fee."

"I see," he says.

When Lucy's phone buzzes indicating that her car has arrived, Q escorts her back down to the lobby and out the front door. "Stay in touch," she says, and then, before she gets in to the little two-passenger Mercedes, she takes a tube of lipstick out of her purse, pushes her face directly up into his, and applies the makeup while looking intently into his eyes, as he looks back awkwardly. Then she gets in and the car pulls unceremoniously away, lasers scanning the road ahead for the best way through the potholes and rubble.

Q turns as if to go back in the building, activating the door with his thumbprint, but as Lucy's car turns a corner he lets the door close without entering and walks away in the other direction. He walks past the shuttered or ransacked storefronts, small shops—everything from tobacconists to real estate—that had thrived upon the dense, hungry urban population of another age, six blocks to the only establishment left open in the area, a one-room store with walls lined with dusty shelves dotted with a sparse selection of bottles and cans from which Q selects a fifth of whisky to replenish his office stock and a bottle of fluorescent blue rehydator to undo the damage the last has done.

He sets them on the counter but immediately opens the blue stuff and takes a long draught, leaning back, anxious for the dopamine simulators and benzedrine derivatives in the chemical swirl to clear his head. The kid sitting on a stool behind the counter looks up from the comic he is reading, takes out one of his wireless earbuds, and says:

"Hey, you can't do that until it's paid for."

Q reaches into his pocket and puts his card on the counter. The kid looks at the card from his perch on the stool but does not move.

"That's not gonna fix this," he says. "I can't scan an open bottle. It'd be my ass if I scanned an open bottle."

"OK," Q says, feeling, though the hangover, the beginnings of anxiety over what the kid seemed to be implying. "Surely there's a way to work this out to both of our advantage. Let's see. Why don't you scan one of the other bottles on the shelf, then we'll put that back, and I'll take the open one."

"Look man," the kid says aggressively, though he still sits, elbows on his knees, on the stool. "You think you can fool them that easy? They know everything, man, everything that happens. They know this conversation we're having right now. You think you're gonna 'put one over on them'? Think again, man. There's only one way out of this; you're going to have to take that rehydrator as a gift; we'll call it a promotion."

Q stammers, feeling his confidence waiver, even the beginnings of a blush coming to his face, and remains silent as the kid aims his scanner at the bottle of whisky and then passes it over the card. He then bags the whisky and hands him back the card, leaving the half-full bottle of rehydrator sitting on the counter. Q puts the card back in his pocket, picks up the whisky, then stands guiltily eyeing the gratuity. The kid reinserts his earbud and turns his attention back to his rebus, fingertips tapping his knee to a secret rhythm. Finally, wishing wistfully that he could take back his presumptive action, feeling only revulsion for the liquid he had thirsted for so voraciously but seeing no way out other than to accept the shame he had brought on himself, Q picks up the partial bottle, too, and walks out.

He moves forward with determination, in the wrong direction, wanting only to be out of sight from the haughty little bastard of a cashier and out of the store's psychic range, muttering to himself as he walks: "The prick. A normal person would have just scanned it. What's the big deal anyway? They don't care what happens in this backwater store. Little fucker did it just to fuck with me, and I'll never go back there. Is that how they want him to treat their customers?"

He takes another sip of the stuff, looking around to make sure no one can see him. While his first drink had felt cool and refreshing, now it tastes like warm vinegar, almost making him gag. He forces it down, anyway, and then takes another swig, for he knows he needs to clear his head, that part of the problem is that he isn't thinking straight behind his hangover. At the first corner there is a plastic depository, albeit one that hasn't been emptied in years, and he stops, takes a breath, then turns the bottle up and drains it, just to be rid of it. He's fighting nausea as he adds the empty to the pile, and he stumbles on, thinking, for a moment, that he will swoon, but the feeling quickly passes as the stuff seeps through his stomach lining into his bloodstream and begins to take effect, calming his conscience and quickening his pace. By the time he regains his office he has refocused on the matter at hand, the embarrassing incident all but forgotten.

But for the stale ashtray smell, his place seems in great shape, giving no clue to the previous night's debauchery, its nostalgic decor—the simulated leather couch, the patina'd wood of the desk and chair—almost shining in the misty morning light. He replaces the whisky in its drawer beside the pistol and sits down invigorated, ready to begin research on his very first case.

Q and Lucy had met in the railyard, when they were both young, beautiful and strong. He had already been on the street for a year and had learned the ropes, so to speak, but in other ways he was still quite the child. The tall bikers had gotten him drunk and were having a bit of fun at his expense, but she had danced with him, he had fallen into her thrall, and she into his. After a couple of days holed up with her in the boxcar, he would have followed her anywhere. The memory of her sudden departure still makes him wince, and yet in retrospect he must admit she had done him a great favor by forcing him to stand on his own emotional two feet, wobbly as they were, and barring the uxorious relationship he thought he longed for but which would have soured for them both in a week.

Still—he cannot help the bitterness—couldn't she have found a gentler way of breaking it off than simply being gone that fateful morning? Had it been necessary for his development that he ride the rails, those weeks after, wracked with the sickness unto death, not caring if he lived or not, his universe turned gray and bleak and barren by her absence from it? And that, indeed, was only the first of her many abandonings. The last one, when she had jilted him for that smug, self-righteous snake of a pastor, he had thought would be the last nail in the coffin of their relationship, and indeed it had been for three decades now, but then she reappears, and (judging by appearances, at any rate, for he still has no memory of the night before) he falls for her yet again, yet again suffering any humiliation to curry her favor, yet again her obedient dog.

Who would fault him if he were to abandon her now, in her hour of need? Who would say he was being unprofessional if he put her case on the back burner and let it languish in his files, forcing her to inquire, some months hence, as to what he had found concerning her "friend," and having the great pleasure of being able to respond that, sorry, his schedule has been simply frantic and he hasn't had a minute to work on her case?

Lord, he thinks, reading between the lines of his own phantasies, she can still get to me after all these years.

And, he knows in his heart of hearts, he is not going to be able to resist this case since, besides the gloss bars and the occasional game of chess on his phone, he has not one whit else to occupy his time.

The last time he had seen her, outside the Little A show that had been the swan-song of that particular craze, she had been with the Pastor, though even then the relationship was showing signs of wear. It had been a different time, when cities still worked, governments and corporations still had some cultural currency and the Church had not yet taken (or retaken, for those old enough to recall the now-vanished discipline of History and, within it, that era called the Dark Ages) its place as arbiter of all human affairs. It was at this show that Q had hooked up with Esperanza, his Espe. It hadn't exactly been what one would call love at first sight, but they had eased into a relationship of mutual support, only occasionally passionate but always comfortable and mutually beneficial.

As Espe came into his mind he felt a twinge of regret at his indiscretion of the night before, even though he couldn't actually remember it, and yet it was only a twinge, for Espe was not really a stickler for fidelity. Past dalliances had cost him only light whippings under her cat-o'-nine-tails, which hardly counted as deterrence, since this was a punishment that men and, increasingly, women paid handsomely to receive, these days. Though Espe had left the halls of the State Legislature, where she had honed her Art, in disgrace, with Q's support and encouragement she had learned to embrace her God-given talents and started a professional practice which was so popular she soon had to hire a double, and then another and another. She opened a second and then a third storefront. At that point the enterprise caught the attention of the Church and suffered a setback with an Official Denouncement. But Q had had a favor or two (ahem) to call in with the Pastor, and that phone call had changed everything, for not only was the Denouncement denounced but Espe's method was embraced by the Church as Proper Casuistry and was soon being sought by penitents across the globe. Three stores had grown to a worldwide franchise almost overnight. Soon, she scarcely had time to train the trainers, much less the actual practitioners, and the Esperanza™ logo on a bustier, restraint kit or mouth plug had become a universal symbol of quality.

Q, for his own part, had brought to the relationship a none-too-shabby inheritance, thanks to his mother's business acumen and his father's uncanny vision of Provincial Oaks, the former subdivision where Q had maintained his utopian but unprofitable commune for many years, as a medieval fortress, complete with castle walls and moat, anticipating a new, or rather resurgent, architectural trend. Q's 25% stake in the Provincial Oaks redevelopment, which included not only sales of the home tracts but construction profits and substantial monthly fees for maintenance of the common moat, walls and drawbridges, would have enabled him and Espe to live comfortably for the rest of their lives, and upon his parents' death he inherited another quarter, now sharing control only with his sister.

But neither he nor Espe had been suited to a life of indolence. Lounging by the pool lost its appeal within a week. Tennis, polo, yachting and gliding all came to feel fatuous and empty. And so Espe had gone back to work not because she needed to but because she wanted to, because her services were in demand, and that very demand fueled her contempt and gave her role-playing the hint of reality that made her legendary in her profession.

Q, on the other hand, even less comfortable than Espe among the idle rich, had nothing to fall back on. No talent, proclivity or even desire inspired him to act. Having been all over the world and seen things that he never wanted to see again, he had no taste for travel. Never a social butterfly, his friends always having been drawn from society's dregs and established in the comradeship that comes from shared necessity, he found himself now isolated, dependent solely on Espe for human contact, a situation which finally wore out her patience, and when she announced that she would be going abroad for some months to open new franchises, Q wondered if the travel were not discretionary, and realized that he, too, wanted to get away from himself. And so he sat down in front of the big wall monitor with the express purpose of cobbling together an Identity.

He arrived at "detective" by a process of elimination. He surfed contemporary media and examined each role he found there, from political pundit to enthusiastic weatherman, from neurotic comedian to superhero to self-help guru, from evil criminal to philanthropist, from philosopher to pop star, physician to executioner, dancer to commentator, astronaut to diver. His search led, naturally, backward in history, and he quickly ticked off the possibilities of being a chef or a terrorist or an adventurer or mountain climber or cop or cowboy or teacher or comedy writer or killer or lawyer or spy or an average Joe who works at "the office" and has a wife and a passel of kids with whom he is inept but well-intentioned and kind.

He found his role, finally, at the end of the color era, in that golden age of the black and white movie, when suddenly the figure of the detective became ubiquitous. The detective: that character who, for decades, dominated historical fiction but in factual history was all but nonexistent. Q was drawn to the generic qualities of the role, to the emotionally scarred but still timorously hopeful psyche, to the hardened chin that disguised a soul still hoping for love, to the cynical intelligence that saw the self-interest behind the most samaritan of gestures. He saw in the detective a new kind of knight, forever seeking truth and honor in a primally defective world, tilting at windmills, always ending, because of his own tragic flaw, by working for and within the very evil he seeks to overcome. Q was, it came to him, already a detective, for he was seeking an identity in the foul-smelling morass of humanity, searching out the secret truth within a vast text of defensive prevarications. The truth always comes at the end, he saw, bloody sputter on a dying breath, at the moment when it no longer matters, like the secret to a way of living that can only be known, by most, at the brink of death. The detective alone gets to hear the dying whisper; only he gets to see beyond the veil, and what he sees and hears there he can never tell, out of respect for his client's confidentiality.

And so Q identified with this particular Identity and decided to take it on. He did it up right, from the beginning, ordering a felt hat and baggy suits. He even had the tailor match the colors from the old footage, which made him actually look like a black and white image. He ordered a replica of a 1951 Ford coupe. He even lobbied the State to allow it to be human-controlled but was unable to prevail, so he had to settle for riding front left with his elbow on the window and right hand on the purely decorative wheel in front of him.

The office was the last step. He had no problem finding space in one of the more squalid neighborhoods of the city (though he hadn't known, then, that with the rising popularity of the gloss bars this down-and-out block was about to take a downward turn). He had hired a designer and schooled her with a portfolio of his favorite movie sets, and she had recreated them in pastiche, even, once again, matching colors from the black and white images. It had not been an easy matter to find craftspeople who could actually execute the designs, but after dogged searching he did find an old-timer who still knew how to work with wood, and they were able to unearth enough bits and pieces of antique furniture from the basements of about-to-be-demolished buildings to restore a desk. It was with great satisfaction, the satisfaction that comes with having a role to play, that he first sat down at it and saw himself not in a mirror but in the words written on his door in reverse. "Q Private I" it read. (In his haste he had transcribed from film dialogue and not checked spelling. He noticed the error a few days later, while reading a book at the same desk, but he thought the original spelling might confuse potential clients, so he left it.) He took out his pencil and notebook, both custom made from vintage materials, plugged his smart phone into the black desk phone replica, folded his hands on the desk, and then, 22 years later, his first client—that is, Lucy— walked through the door.

Slight exaggeration. Certainly he hadn't sat with his hands folded for two decades as the sun rose and set in time lapse. and the smog turned from brown to red, and real estate values plummeted, and the streets went to hell, and the water turned to poison, and public education was revolutionized (ie, abandoned), and drugs and alcohol lost their appeal to the underclass because the only buzz anyone cared about any more was the dissociation that came from glossing. Certainly he hadn't sat still in his chair, waiting for something to happen, while civilization collapsed around him.

It wasn't as if no silhouette had darkened the hammered glass of his vintage door in all those years. No, they had come, one by one, the husbands with their suspicions of their wives or mistresses; the wives with their suspicions of their husbands' suspicion; the corporate magnates with their suspicions of their underlings and the underlings with their suspicions of their bosses. And, one by one, Q had solved their cases for them, shown them the pictures of the loves of their lives in the sordid thrall of secret desire, shown them the bank statements that proved the venality of the trusted assistant or obsequious apprentice, shown them, in every case, the proof of what they had suspected all along, that their paranoia wasn't paranoid, that their phantasies were real and their realities phantasmatic.

One by one, they left his office wiser but sadder, stricken, heartsick, weeping or masking their grief with rage and grinding their teeth with lust for revenge. They weren't grateful but blamed Q for the truth he conveyed. Far from appreciating the valuable service he had performed, they treated him as if, by enlightening them, he had stolen a prized possession. They sneered at him, lashed out at him with invective or sometimes even attacked with fists or nails. And when it came time to pay the bill, for those who didn't simply stiff him, they did so with distaste and reluctance, feeling that by asking them to honor the agreed-upon terms and not ameliorating their suffering with a humanitarian pro bono, he had added insult to the injury he had already dealt. They threw their phones, like metaphorical wads of cash, onto his desk and looked the other direction while he made the transfer.

So yes, there had been clients but never, until now, a Client with a capital C, never a case that he had felt himself truly involved in, never a conundrum to solve or a missing person to locate which he felt his investigation might actually bring to felicitous conclusion.

For even if the truth he uncovers proves to be the worst imaginable, even if Lucy's "friend" is found, as most are, to be irrevocably lost to infidelity or dishonesty or even death, still Q knows his Lucy, and he will be there to comfort her, and their reunion in shared grief will be at least partial recompense for the loss. As innocuous, as normal as the case seems, somehow he feels this one will be the pinnacle of his career, the one he got into the business for in the first place. Anxious to begin, he puts his phone on the desk, sets it to project onto the wall in front of him and takes the keyboard out of the drawer.

And yet something, some vague premonition, a gray and blurring image far back in his mind, causes him to hesitate, and he stops with fingers poised above the keys. He isn't feeling his best. He knows he isn't his normal astute, ultra-aware self. Despite the therapeutic effect of the rehydrator his headache is returning, and the rest of him is beginning to ache, also, as if from a mild fever. Perhaps a walk, some air and a bite of breakfast are in order before he begins the work day. And so he leaves the office again.

He goes back to the corner store and gets another bottle of rehydrator, red this time, and an energy bar. Neither of them speak as the surly kid behind the counter processes the transaction. Q eats the fruit and grain compote and sips the sweet liquid as he walks back by the boarded-up storefronts, broken glass crunching beneath his feet. He barely notices his surroundings, seemingly lost in thought or daydream, yet he is not thinking about anything. Neither Lucy nor the case nor Espe nor anything else is occupying his mind though, judging by his level of distraction and inattention to his environs, something is.

Halfway back to the office he turns down a narrow alley strewn with rubble and wet from a leaking pipe, a section of which is exposed on the sidewalk like a snake breaking the surface of a stagnant pool. At the end of this alley, directly in front of him, there is a battered brown door with a crude cross painted on, set in a wall of crumbling brick, which he enters. The bartender doesn't look up from his phone as Q walks by and opens the second door, the soundproof one, and, in that moment the door is open and Q is stepping in, the concussive bass rattles the bottles and glasses.

Yes, he lied to her. For reasons which are mysterious even to himself, he hadn't wanted to reveal to Lucy that he still had the yen, as well as the knack, for glossing. For one thing, relevant to this particular instance at least, it will sweat a hangover right out of you. You come to, sopping wet, a bit weak, pale and tousled, but feeling cleansed of all impurities, ready to begin the day or the task at hand with renewed vigor and perfect concentration. He tells himself this, anyway, as he enters the hall and feels the drum beat thudding in his sternum and his own heart syncing to it.

The halls are dingy, dismal places when you first walk in, every surface covered with dirty yellow foam, dimly lit by strings of utility lights, incongruous bits of ramshackle humanity scattered about on the ramshackle furniture, a few broken chairs and some mismatched pews. Some are on their knees in an attitude of prayer, some sprawled in the pews babbling at the sky, and there will be two or three at the altar acting as leaders, though leaders of what is always the question, for the cacophony of language-parts coming from their individual throats lacks both the stereotypy of chant and the synchrony of unison. At first it is simply chaos, but gradually, as your ear attunes, it begins to sound familiar, like a language learned in childhood, spoken at home but not outside it, and later abandoned and forgotten as you make your way into the world. Though not comprehensible in the way that street talk is comprehensible, images flash in the mind and feelings in the soul. The body is exhilarated.

There is a moment, just before the dissociation takes hold, a nether region between two worlds, when one can hear, "understand," in a manner of speaking, and even remember, though the memory is vague and fleeting, next day, like the memory of a dream. Q cherishes this moment, and an important part of his practice is to make it last as long as possible, which he accomplishes with a delicate and quite indescribable spiritual maneuver, unavailable to any but the most gifted adepts. He knows he is in it when the rhythmic voices start to ring like bells and turn transparent, and he knows it is over when he realizes one of the voices he is hearing is his own. This is the beginning of the trance.

Back at his desk, focused and invigorated, fingers now flying across the keys, he is finding his job to be easy, almost suspiciously so. Her name is Antii, (…is it Russian? Lucy didn't know, or said she didn't know…) a name that, as far as Q can tell, is attached to only one living person. Once he finds and saves a selfie or two, he begins to search for the face, and social media and surveillance footage from around the world pops up instantly. In five minutes he has assembled a dossier with hundreds of photos, blog and news mentions, birth and banking records, medical history, even diary entries. The problem is not finding the information but sorting through it, arranging it into a chronology and then deciding which of the myriad details he has assembled are significant. He tries letting the phone's AI assemble a narrative, but it errs, naturally, on the side of inclusion, producing a novel of Tolstoyan proportion but Warholian banality. He knows what she likes for breakfast, that she wasn't breast-fed, that she had her appendix out, that she can swim the backstroke, favors fashionable over sensible shoes, is a good dancer, enjoys comedy shows and walks in the country, but he is not discovering what or, more to the point, where she actually is.

He is interrupted, then, by a call, Lucy's face suddenly taking over the projection. She is obviously suffering from their excesses of the night before, looking uncharacteristically tired and haggard, still in the same rumpled clothes, eyes red and sagging.

"Good morning, Sunshine," Q greets her with irony. "I hope

you're feeling better than I do this morning."

"Oh, sorry," she says, "I must look a fright, though you're looking pretty chipper, I must say. But I had to call, to apologize, I guess, for last night, for taking advantage of you."

"Well, as I remember, it was my pleasure. I'm very happy you chose to come see me. I was actually able to clear my calendar for the morning so I'm working on your case now."

"Oh no," she says urgently, fear, almost panic, coming into her eyes. "Don't do that. That's why I'm calling. To say I was wrong. I should never have come to you. You were right. It's a bad idea to work for friends. And it's not your field. I'm asking you to do something you don't and shouldn't want to do. Anyway I can't afford to pay."

"Ah, don't worry about that," he says, not wanting to say that he cares not one whit about the money. "We can work out a payment plan, or perhaps a trade in kind…"

"No no, really, Q, don't take this case. Don't investigate. If I'm hiring you for something it is to not investigate. I'll come back to see you, socially. We'll catch up. We can be friends, and more, again. I wouldn't want a professional relationship to get in the way of that. Would you?"

"Well…" he stammers, taken off-guard by the sudden change of heart and obvious dishonesty. "It's your case, of course, and if you don't want me to pursue it, I won't."

"Oh good. Thank you for understanding. I'm sorry. I shouldn't have come. I guess I just wanted an excuse to see you again so I made up this thing. It was stupid of me. Thanks for understanding."

"Of course, and please don't think you need an excuse to see me. I'm happy to see you any time. In fact, are you free for lunch tomorrow?"

"Oh, tomorrow? Oh, no, sorry, I have an, um, engagement. No. Can't do tomorrow."

"OK. Of course. At your convenience then." Does a shadow move at the edge of the view? Do her eyes move that direction, just for an instant?

"OK, good. Yes," she says. "We'll do lunch and catch up. I'll give you a call next week."

"I look forward to it," Q says, and she hangs up without another word. "But don't you know, my love," he adds under his breath, to the empty room, as the pastiche of images and texts that comprise the mysterious Antii reappear on his wall, "you can't fire a detective."

She is beautiful, as one would expect, and also familiar, somehow. She reminds him of his sister, as he feels he knows her and yet does not, just as he always felt about Sis. She even bears a passing resemblance to his sister at that age, which is, he detects, 29. She has that look of carrying a secret that his sister always had, a bit haughty, eyebrows always slightly lifted, as if daring you to return the gaze. She has a taste for nice clothes, he discerns from both pictures and shopping history, but seems to have no record of employment, which would indicate an inheritance or other consistent source of income. Bank records show an average balance that never rises above the modest but never falls below a base line, with mysterious deposits appearing, sometimes, just before large purchases are posted. The deposits are cloaked and not trackable by any of Q's tricks of the trade, but he files the data for future investigation.

Lucy shows up in the photos, also, as he finds glimpses of the two of them in evening wear at a concert, or sunning at the beach, or clowning for a tandem selfie in front of some monument or tourist destination. When he adjusts the filters to include Lucy's features, also, he is left with a more manageable field of study, and he can begin to construct a history of their relationship. Data is profuse and frequent over the past few years, mostly captured by surveillance or press at public events—theaters, art openings and the like—or in airports and transportation hubs. The only thing that strikes Q as unusual is that all the photos are in public places; there are no shots of backyard barbecues or toasting with friends or showing off pets in the living room.

Growing bored with the poses, no matter how revelatory they are, he scrolls more and more rapidly backward in time, finally flicking the pad to send the whole lot of them flying by like a cut-up cinema, coming finally to the oldest of the lot, the ur-image, and this one he stops to examine. It is an old (22 years, to be exact) surveillance still from an airport. There are no faces as the pair are captured from behind, the software apparently having interpolated from passport numbers logged in the metadata. It is, as well, an image of very poor quality, grayscale, low resolution, and taken facing the light of an atrium, so that they are little more than silhouettes, the adult woman and child holding hands as they walk down the concourse.

His lips move involuntarily at the revelation. "She's her daughter." He reverses cinematic direction, going a little more slowly since now he knows what he is looking for. There is only the one photo of them at this age, the next being some ten years later, at an art gallery, posed like the rest, but with the added impetus of his growing suspicion he can see the tiny inflections of stance and attitude that reveal the contradictory impulses of deference and rebellion in the younger and proprietary affection in the older. Now that he has the relationship in his mind, in fact, it fairly screams from every photo, and he is surprised he did not notice it sooner. Every image he sees either reinforces his belief or appears neutral; none cause him to question it, right up to the most recent of the batch, another surveillance still, this one from a street camera. Lucy is getting out of a car, leaning back in to say good-bye, apparently, with Antii visible through the car window. The place seems familiar, but all urban streets look like this now, so he drills for the coordinates, discovering to his surprise it's barely a block from where he sits, and less than 18 hours old. It is, in fact, Antii dropping Lucy at his office.

He gets up now and paces. He pauses to light a cigarette and then continues, heart racing as he attempts to read what this writing on his wall is trying to tell him. The only conclusion he can come to is that he and Lucy have a daughter, and she has kept the fact from him all these years. He whimpers and rejoices, by turns, and then, ill-equipped as he is to reason in this moment, he attempts to keep the chain of deductions moving. What are the possible motivations for Lucy coming to him, now, and laying out a fabric of lies seemingly designed to lead him to this exact confusion? Could it be that she wanted to renew their relationship after this long hiatus but felt that would not be possible with this great lie of omission coming between them? No, that doesn't parse, because if she'd wanted a new relationship based on truth she would have simply told him and not complicated things further with more lies.

But then, taking a breath, maybe he is reading this incorrectly. Maybe he isn't the father. Maybe what she is trying to show him is that she has and has had a child by another man for all these years. She might have even had the child prior to their last rendezvous. He struggles with the math and with his recollection, pulls up Antii's birth certificate, checking time and place. Forty weeks is how many months? Well, say 36-40; she might not have gone full term. He pulls up a calendar and counts backward, does a little math with pencil and paper, tries to count the weeks, forgets where he is when a month changes, starts over, finally arrives at a date, at least a no-sooner-than and a no-later-than, then tries to think back, finding only that the era falls in one of the many lacunae in his memory. Then he realizes the meaning of the lacuna, that it was that year they both spent in the hospital recovering from the Sadean nightmare of their mortal injuries, as they lay in induced comas, kept alive by computers and nurses and the charity of the Church... But that's it, of course, the Pastor! That smarmy, power-hungry serpent of a man. Q's lip curls as he remembers his hideous fake smile. The bastard impregnated her while she was comatose!

But no. Alas, no. His anger is deflected, again, by reason and memory, and he calms himself, saddened by the memory of Lucy's (yes, Lucy's, even if she was calling herself Gwen at the time) unseemly displays of affection for the jerk, which had thrown Q into depression and addiction just as he was healing from his physical wounds. She had, of course, been willing. That explains why she hasn't been to see him in decades, and also why she was too ashamed to broach the subject directly when she did. She has a guilty conscience and a need to atone, but lacks the courage to do it directly.

He shakes his head at this sorry state of affairs and sits back down to sulk at his desk. The whisky bottle and glass come out, despite his better judgement, for he knows the intensifying effect distilled spirits can have on rage or grief, the alternating currents coursing through him now. He fiddles with his keyboard, not really wanting to see any more but just to calm his nerves. He turns off the Lucy filter. In fact, he nots Lucy's image, so he doesn't have to see her, and scrolls through images of Antii alone. Is Lucy trying to appoint him some kind of uncle or something? Or even stepfather? From all appearances, he has to admit, there could be a worse fate. He freezes the slide-show on a lovely shot of her looking back over her shoulder, zooming in. She is smiling, posing, even, but it is a wan and knowing smile, not the obligatory happy face, and in her eyes he imagines he sees her history, the tumultuous and emotionally scarring history of a child raised outside the haven of a nuclear family, torn between estranged parents. Does she even know who her father is? He could easily imagine Lucy, embarrassed at the circumstance of the child's conception, keeping his identity secret and inventing some swashbuckling character with an equally swashbuckling and noble reason for his absence, a paternal fiction or effigy for the young girl to bond to. Or, then again, he could also see Lucy simply leaving her daughter in the dark, telling her she had no father, that her mother had been artificially or even miraculously inseminated. But there is knowledge in the eyes of the image in front of him, knowledge and self-sufficiency the broods of suburban normality will never know. She also happens to be the most beautiful creature who ever walked on Earth.

He calls the Ford from the elevator and tells it to come round. "May I ask our destination?" it says.

"We're going to see my Pastor. I'm feeling a need to confess."

"OK," the car answers, "and may I enquire if you mean the current or former Pastor of the Church of the Ostensible Jesus? The current Pastor is in China, with travel time of 38 hours, 56 minutes. The former Pastor and your former associate is at his home in the city, travel time 14 minutes."

"The former Pastor. I prefer to exercise my casuistry with a known quantity. Also, the matter is pressing. I don't have much time."

"Then the known quantity it shall be," the car obliges. "Since time is at issue, I wonder if you would mind walking five-eighths of a block to the corner, so that I don't have to navigate around certain obstacles. This will save us about three minutes."

"OK," Q says as he hangs up. He's at the best moment, the very beginning of the whisky buzz, feeling competent, agitated and aggressive. As he was putting the bottle back in its drawer, too, he had taken out the pistol and put it in his coat pocket, and his right hand is gripping it now.

Leaving the building and turning toward the corner, he encounters the "obstacles" the Ford had mentioned, a half dozen neighborhood slackers milling in the middle of the street. They look dazed and wasted, probably from long hours of glossing and drinking, and appear at first glance to be doing nothing but standing around like zombies. When Q draws even with them, though, he sees what has drawn their attention: a D-class drone has crashed in the street and lies there half mangled, half attempting to sputter back to life. Two of the four rotors are bent beyond function while the other two spin frantically in a futile attempt to drag its body away from the glossies. "Kill it," one of them says, and another pulls a short length of pipe from under his coat and attempts to jam it into one of the functioning rotors. The drone jerks and feints, knocks the pipe out of the guy's hand once, but he finally succeeds in stabbing it through the grill, and now the thing is flopping back and forth, clanging and spitting oil and bits of plastic everywhere, drawing chuckles from the crowd.

Idiots, Q thinks as he passes them. They better pray none of its cameras are still working.

The car is idling at the corner. He gets in the back seat in case he needs to do any work en route, closes the door. It takes off immediately, veering on and off of sidewalks, around the craters and poles. In eight blocks they are on a street of relative contiguity and speed up considerably, the big Ford replica dwarfing the other cars on the road as it whips around them. At the expressway ramp the acceleration is such that Q is thrown against the back of the seat. They pull into the traffic stream, five lanes, bumper to bumper at 140 mph. Now Q's phone is buzzing in his pocket.

It's Espe, in leather, whip in her hand. In the background, over her shoulder, is a man kneeling, dressed only in a light robe which has been pulled off of his back revealing the weave of welts where her whip has been. "Hey Q," she says.

"Yes," he answers. "I'm on a case. What's up?"

"Just checking in. What kind of case? What are you looking into, Q?"

"Oh, you know, missing person thing. Mistaken identity. The usual."

"Oh yeah. Work a day…." She hangs the phone on her bustier, now, to free her hands, Q looking out from this vantage, watching the whip come down on the happy customer's back. "But look, I wanted to tell you…" breathing hard from the exertion; not as easy as it used to be… "…if your girl should stop in on you, you know, one day," lash hitting the back, "that it's ok. You don't have to worry about it, should it happen."

"What are you saying," he says, suddenly suspicious. "How could you know…?"

"Know what?" The whip comes down again; the customer yelps. "Wow. Caught you so easy," she giggles.

"What…?" He is flummoxed, blushing behind his phone.

"Good lord," she says, bringing the whip down again, "it's ok. You know it's ok. In fact, bring her over." The whip comes down. "I'd like to meet her. I think we'd get along."

"Espe, I don't think…."

"And that's best," she says, "but please listen to this one thing." The view fumbles for a moment, and then she appears on the screen again, panting slightly, sweat beading on her forehead. "This case you're on, this case she brought you, let it go. She's messing with your head. Go see your Pastor. Have your philosophical conversation. Then go back to your office and wait for the next case. Or wait for her to come flop on the couch again. Either way is fine. It's good to be that kind of normal. Sit there and pine and lust for her and then come home to me, and I'll help you be good. OK? Tell me you'll do that for me." The view turns back to the kneeling man as the whip strokes his back again.

"But how…?" He pauses, thinking quickly, starting to panic but also deflated. "OK, that's what I'll do. I'll have my conversation. I'll go there and wait. Then we'll see."

"I'm glad," she says as her face comes back to the screen. "See him," she nods over her shoulder. "Know who he is? He's the CEO of Japan."

"Ah," he says, "I was wondering what sort of customer rated your personal attention. Can't he hear you?"

"Yes, he's kind of special. And he doesn't speak English." She brings the whip down again to bring home the point, then comes back to the screen. "Back to work. I just wanted you to know I'm thinking of you. And bring Lucy by. I'm not kidding."

And the screen goes dark.

The gates part magically in front of them, and they drive in, Q and his car, across verdant grounds covered with orchards and roses and labyrinths of boxwood. Even the sky is clear, here, a perfect blue dome decorated with soft dots of cumulus and wisps of cirrus, like a window through the brown smog of the city. The Pastor Emeritus, who probably knew of Q's impending visit about the same time the Ford did, is waiting at the end of the cobblestone driveway, the door to the manse open behind him.

"Q," the Pastor greets him warmly. "What a surprise. It's good to see you again, after all these years. And looking so dapper!"

Q can't help but smile. "It's good to see you too," he lies. "Pardon the intrusion and lack of notice. I need to ask you something."

"Yes, I know you are thirsting for knowledge. You have always thirsted like an acolyte, though you are an adept, and always were. A natural. Well, come in and drink, you who thirst. What I have that is liquid, you shall drink. But remember: drink deep or touch not the stream."

They enter through a vestibule into the large great room, stopping in the doorway to admire the painting on the far wall. It is an imposing decoration, tall and narrow, pointed at the top, fitting precisely between stone buttresses that support an arched ceiling some 60 feet over their heads. At the apex stands Christ, bathed in light and glory, while arrayed below Him is the tangled mass of humanity in its constant state of fall, the very bottom a dark cess pool of broken bodies. Q cranes his neck upward to take it all in. "An impressive replica of the The Last Judgement," he notes.

"Yes, it is, isn't it," the Pastor says humbly. "And yet the replication is by Tintoretto's own hand. When the church of the Madonna dell'Orto, with the Fondamenta de Mori and the rest of Venice, finally succumbed to the rising tide, I was fortunate enough to be chosen as curator of this great work. Since it is not a painting one hangs, shall we say, from a nail in the wall, I built this room to mimic the presbytery of the dell'Orto. One thing that's little known: Tintoretto was awarded this commission, in 1546, only by dint of offering his services gratis, merely to enhance his own glory. Ironic, don't you think, given the subject matter?"

Though quite cognizant of the vanity of human endeavor, Q elects not to reward the Pastor's vainglorious rhetoric with a response. At any rate their revery is interrupted by the butler entering the room from the far side, pushing a cart laden with non-metaphorical refreshments across the marble floor toward the base of the painting, where two leather armchairs have been set up. Q, now ignoring the Pastor's further pontifications, follows him across the room, their footsteps echoing in the vast chamber, and they seat themselves, as it were, in the scene, among the centuries old and life-sized suffering bodies. The Pastor pours from the teapot and motions for Q to help himself to the array of cakes and toast. He also sets a bottle of fine whisky on the table, and this Q does help himself to, unceremoniously spiking his tea, an action the Pastor watches with practiced nonchalance. Q sips with his pinky up from china so thin he is afraid he will break it with his lips, tasting the hobo delicacy, one of his favorite mixes from the old days.

"Ah Q," the Pastor says, "your style is always refreshing. A philosopher's style, quite independent of fashion and propriety."

"I'm sorry if I seem out of character with the room," Q replies cattily, "but it's been a long night, and a long day already, and perhaps some way to go yet."

"Of course I understand your investigatory duties are paramount and, I can only imagine, relentless, so I won't detain you with idle reminiscence and polite pleasantries. How may I help you?"

"You know," Q replies, now stalling himself, sensing that he has turned the conversation slightly to his own favor, "I was thinking the other day how so many things people say actually mean the opposite of their literal meaning. Like when someone says 'pardon me' they really mean 'get out of my way you fool'. Or when they say 'great to see you' they are telling you actually how sorry they are to be stuck in conversation with you again. Or when they say 'may I help you' they are thinking as fast as they can how to utterly thwart you in your search."

"Ah, touché," the Pastor chuckles. "Look how you've already found me out and beaten me at my own game. I should know better than to spar with you in words, you who are famous for your linguistic acumen. And yet in this particular case I would like to venture that your judgement is hasty, that my own interests coincide with yours, for the moment, and that though my 'may I help you' probably isn't motivated purely by altruism, the offer is still genuine. And so I repeat it: What do you need from me?"

"Legitimate, perhaps, but not genuine, since if you are so sure our interests coincide in the question I am about to ask, then you already know what the question is, and why do you not simply answer and save me the trouble of asking?"

"A good question, Q. In reply let me propose another: Do I seem like the kind of person who would assume I could fool a professional detective, nay, the original detective? Should I take at face value the trail of clues you have left on your way to my door, as if leading me toward an over-obvious conclusion? (You really should invest in a proxy server to veil your searches, you know.)"

Q pauses and sips again, resisting the desire to down his cocktail in a gulp and refill with pure whisky. Out of the corner of his eye he can see the writhing figures at the bottom of the painting, their agony perfectly captured by the Master. "Enough of this game," he blurts impatiently. "You know what I want, I know you know it, so give it to me."

"I can't give it to you because you already have it. You already know the answer. Your asking now is only a hopeless plea for me to lie and prove you wrong. You have come to confirm your suspicion, yes, but your suspicion is not what you suspect it to be."

"All right, let's skip over the obvious, then, and cut to the details. What was the exact arrangement? Why cloak the payments if there was nothing to hide?"

The Pastor brings his prayer-folded fingers to his chin as if thinking carefully how to choose his next words. "Let me just say that the Church behaves toward its congregation as a parent to her children, teaching them certain skills, guiding them in the acquisition of knowledge, which doesn't necessarily mean alerting them to every fact in the universe. Some lessons are learned best by the autodidact. Some are best learned by the body and not the mind. Describe it as we may, one knows nothing of a textile until one has spun thread and operated the loom."

"This is starting to sound like a song and dance, empty words. Answer my question."

"Not as empty as you may think. Be careful what you say, (by which perhaps I mean, speak as you will,) for the reality will only dawn when speech has been truly emptied. Surely you, master of tongues as you are, know this. You know it, certainly, when you have entered the trance, though the knowledge remains cloaked and untraceable."

"Your capital is no trance. It leaves a trace, a not unsubtle trace. What matters here is what you actually say when I ask you, directly, 'why cloak the payments? What was there to hide?'"

"If that is the 'matter,' then, I'll simply say 'to thwart the detective.' Nothing cloaks so well as a clue. No knot tightens as inexorably as truth. When the Church, in one of our few flawed gambits, set out to annex Islam, we failed because we opened our arms and made gestures of inclusion. We succeeded only when we embraced, even enhanced, the failure and lashed out, making both sides so angry they fought with sword and word, never realizing the combat itself was the cloak, and no one, not even Ourselves, noticed as we began acquiring their banal means, not their mosques and souls but their PA systems and social media. We forged the swords they fought us with. No one noticed, in the heat of battle, that the logos on the weapons of both sides were the same, and that the real winner of every battle was the One who stayed off the battlefield. It would behoove you to remember that as you enter this conflict."

"So you imagined, from the beginning, that I or some other detective would one day get wind of the fact that the Pastor of the Church of the Ostensible Jesus had an illegitimate daughter? You had to support her merely to be aware of her whereabouts, and to keep her from looking elsewhere for succor. To avoid, in a word, being blackmailed."

The Pastor smiles wanly and takes a sip of his tea. "Ah Q," he says, replacing the delicate cup on its delicate saucer, "you are so close to the truth, and yet that last inch of separation may prove an unbridgeable gulf for you, and you should trust your Pastor when he tells you that would be the sweetest fate."

"Trust you?" Q says incredulously. "You who abandoned me in my hour of need? You who seduced the love of my life and then abandoned her, too, along with your own daughter?"

He smiles again, sighing. "I consider, of course, every woman in the Church to be my daughter, my spiritual daughter, and Antii is no exception, but I am human too, and your arrogance is beginning to stir my own, which is, shamefully, why I'm going to add another clue to your narrative. You see, Gwen and I—I'm sorry, Lucy and I—while we certainly knew each other, every inch of each other, in the biblical sense, our knowledge was of a sort that, while producing ample pleasures, did not leave a material trace. If you think back to those days in the hospital, you will recall the extensive nature of Gwen's—Lucy's—injuries. Suffice it to say that in the ER, the day her mangled and dismembered body arrived, it was all we could do to save her life and restore motility. Reproductive function was not a priority."

Q steels himself, determined not to let his face reveal the psychological tailspin he is falling into. The familial triangle, those three connected points that had been the structural support of his understanding, now appears in his mind as disparate nodes, like stars one had imagined as anchors of a constellation suddenly losing their relationship and hanging in the sky as singular and unrelated objects. "You're saying she was adopted?"

"In a way, yes. Adopted by the Church, at any rate, with your Lucy as Our representative."

"Your representative," Q repeats involuntarily, as he reaches for the whisky bottle and pours himself a teacup full. "I see. And when did this relationship of representation end? Or has it?"

"Without going too deeply into Our philosophy, let me simply say that representation is not a relation that begins and ends. Once begun, shall we say, it has always been. And if ever it ends, it never was. Its diachrony and synchrony coincide. You should think of Antii and Ourselves as in-laws, related in a way that came about by virtue of someone else's marriage, not Our own."

Growing impatient with the Pastor's elliptical discourse, his sphinx-like riddles and oracular fakery, Q lets his vision wander above his adversary's head, again to the Tintoretto. About a third of the way up he notices a detail he had not noticed before: a group of condemned souls washing over the edge of a waterfall or levee. "Didn't God promise Noah that He would not destroy the world by water again? Yet this painting resides here and now by virtue of the inexorably rising sea."

"Well, just remember that change is the only constant, and that all things will pass. The rich man with perfect vision becomes a blind beggar. God, too, by virtue of the fact that He seldom speaks, speaks elliptically. Perhaps He is saying that when the flood comes again, He will have had no hand in it."

Back on the freeway and back under the smog, Q stares out the window at the passing landscape and traffic. If he could roll down his window—something the car would never allow at this speed— he could touch the window of the car next to him. And if that car could roll down its window, he could tap the sleeping driver on the shoulder, though he cannot imagine why he would ever want to do such a thing. He remembers, with sad nostalgia, the days when to drive meant to control the car, days when you had to be attentive to traffic and to the road, when you had to look at signs to determine which exit to take, days when a sleeping driver was an omen of death.

Riding in the back seat of his big coupe, now, reminds him of his youth riding the rails in boxcars. Here, too, all the cars move in unison, controlled as if by a single engine, speeding up, slowing as one, veering in perfect sequence. Unlike the old days when one depended on the consciousness of fellow drivers for one's safety, now it is the road itself that does the thinking, communicating with each car by some kind of telepathy. Like one of those synchronized schools of fish or herds of antelope he has seen in video, they dart forward and brake in perfect unison. A line he read somewhere, in quite another context, comes to mind: There are no accidents.

He is, in a word, depressed. He recalls how every conversation he ever had with the Pastor left him feeling this way, listless and unsure, his carefully reasoned theories turned to insane conjecture, his way no longer clear but clouded and uncertain. He questions, now, even his sacred identity, for what does it matter if the car and office look the part if his mental capacity for detection has been compromised? He imagines every light and every law has been torn from him. He lies down in the back seat and feels he is riding in a hearse, and the daylight seems to darken in response to his mood, though in fact they are just reentering the city.

The trance calls to him. He longs for its atavistic purity, the moil of his mind wiped away, a clean slate as the words change source and begin to form out of the depths of the body rather than the vapor of the mind. But he resists the temptation to return to the bar; once per day, max, is his rule. Another temptation arises in the weight of the iron in his pocket, and he wraps his hand around the gun for reassurance. Suicide is not his way, he knows, but the knowledge that the detective's special tool does present an alternative, should he change his mind, is sad comfort.

The third temptation that arises in his hurtling tomb is the bottle, and he sits up and looks around the back seat in the vain hope he has stowed one here and forgotten. But his search among the crevices and under the seats yields him nothing, and he settles back to finish the ride in morose dejection. As they exit the freeway, however, and slow to the tedious pace required by the ruined streets near his office, he sits up and changes his order. "Keep going," he tells the car, "take me to the shore."

"The usual place?" the car wonders.

"Yes, the usual place."

A couple of families have set up picnics on the beach, children playing in the shallows, searching for shells and oddments, yellow froth of the surf lapping at their ankles. Some older kids have paddled out to one of the half-submerged buildings and are taking turns diving from the roof, hooting and yelling in self-induced terror. One can see all the way to clear water, here, which is why Q likes the place. He's watched many a sunset from the little cafe where he seats himself, conspicuous in his gray flannel suit and felt fedora among the swimsuits and beachwear, sequestered in his eccentricity.

The waiter brings him his customary whisky, and Q takes his life in his hands by ordering a sandwich also, for he is famished. He stares out to sea while he waits for the food. Far out, on a balcony just above the surface, a lone figure is seated, mirroring Q's own isolation. He has often admired the beach bums from afar like this, fascinated by the simplicity of their lives. It takes courage, he thinks, to live in the out-buildings as the waves gradually undermine their foundations and the salt-water dissolves their steel superstructures. There is no warning of impending collapse, no time to swim away. These captains go down with their buildings.

When the waiter plops the plastic triangle on the table, Q first checks it to make sure the seal is not broken, then he opens it and inspects it carefully with eyes and nose, opening it up to check for mold. Appeased, he wolfs it down, chasing it with the whisky, then sets himself to contemplating the timeless motion of the waves, froth running up the asphalt almost to his feet, then sliding back down the slope. His breath slows, unconsciously synchronizing with the rhythmic motion, and the anxiety gradually begins to lift and his mind to clear.

He takes out his phone and begins scrolling through the images again, not looking for anything, really. A pop-up alerts him, though, to an impending shortage of storage capacity, and he notices the large audio file from the night before. He starts to delete it, embarrassing himself by thoughts of what it must contain, but in the interest of leaving no stone unturned decides to make sure. He listens to the beginning, to his apology for turning the thing on, the conversation turning less and less relevant as the whisky flows and their tongues thicken, finally descending into barely intelligible jokes and giggling, then into simian grunts and gasps of pleasure. The sequence ends, though, with a sigh of disappointment from Lucy and Q muttering apologies for his age and inebriation and, after some morose shuffling, a moment of silence quickly giving way to tandem snores. He scrolls through hours of this dead air, the flat line of the sonograph filling screen after screen with emptiness. Around 3 a.m., though, he notices a slight bulge in the line and taps in.

Lucy is talking quietly, just above a whisper, her voice punctuated and occasionally overwhelmed by a background noise which he finally recognizes, with embarrassment, as his own gargantuan snoring. At first he thinks she is talking in her sleep, out of a dream, but then realizes her intermittent interjections are one side of a telephone conversation. "He fell asleep; can't you hear?" she says, and then, "…he's thick headed, especially when he doesn't want to know…" and "…what do you want to do? …waltz in and sit on his lap?" He listens to this muddy five minutes of his unconscious life several times, enough to convince himself that he has no idea what is going on there, scrolls hastily through the rest of the early morning hours, deleting some of the dead air to free the space in case he needs it, then puts the phone back in his pocket and orders another whisky.

He decides to walk the dozen blocks back to his office, leaving the car to fend for itself. He is dully drunk and feeling morose, walking hands in pockets, head down, dragging his feet through the rubble. His thoughts are occupied with nothing so much as their own inadequacy, as step by step he becomes more convinced that his brilliant deductions of that morning were pure delusion and that he completely mishandled the consultation with the Pastor, allowing the duplicitous bastard to dominate the conversation and leave him with nothing but riddles and the humiliating feeling he is not mentally equipped to solve them.

He hears the footsteps behind him but barely looks up as a couple passes him on the sidewalk. They look back at him and chuckle as they pass, and he becomes aware of how ridiculous he must look, stumbling down the gray street in his baggy gray suit, anachronistic poseur, like an aging actress taking the stage with her belly bulging beneath her corset and her wrinkles and sagging skin painted over with makeup. He raises his chin and quickens his pace, glancing at his phone as if he were late for an appointment, though the street is empty now, so his specular sense of purpose is lost on everyone but himself.

He's relieved when he arrives at his office and lets himself back into his private space, but the mirrored lobby leaves him no place to look but at his rumpled self, unshaven and grubby, his suit dusty and wrinkled and his jacket pulled out of shape by the weight of the gun in the pocket. He takes out the gun to let the jacket settle and tucks it, painfully, into his waistband, then tries on a couple of different stances, hands at his sides or in pockets, or one hand in pocket leaning on one leg, or erect and attentive, but none of these images recapture the visage of the competent detective, and he is grateful when the elevator door finally opens.

He hurries down the hall to his office, having by now come to believe in the imaginary appointment he is late for. He takes the dopp kit to the restroom and shaves and washes his face and hands, then returns to the office and puts on a clean shirt and suit, tossing the dirty one on the floor of the closet. He tidies up the office a bit, puts the gun back in its drawer, resists the temptation to pour himself another drink, then puts his phone on the desk, arranges the pencil and notepad conveniently, and sits down to work.

There is, however, no work waiting to be done, besides which the sun's bottom rim is just peeking out below the smog and sending a ray into the window, so he does, finally, allow himself to pour another drink and even light a cigarette as he prepares to watch yet another amazing sunset.

Imagine a mirror. The way most mirrors flip right and left, this mirror flips male and female. Imagine a mirror, and in that imagining you have your mirror, for the mirror is only its being imagined.

Imagine it is late, well past the hour when your average sleuth has retreated to the neighborhood bar to forget the sad truth of the human condition the morning's investigation has uncovered. The sun is low on the horizon. The window, which happens to face west, affords a stunning view of the sunset over the crenellated silhouette of the city. Red-orange and purple light cuts under the smog. Give the nicotine time to get into the bloodstreams and soothe nerves made jittery by the strain of conversation, even if that conversation is only with one's self.

He knows what is coming, knows it without knowing, knows the inexorable approach that every being knows, whisper of the elevator door opening and then closing again, soft footsteps in the hall, and then the silhouette in the doorway, behind the hammered glass, behind the inverted letters of his invented identity, the sign turned outward in a last ditch attempt to bar entry to the featureless figure that is about to reveal itself.

He turns away as she enters, turns toward his stunning view of the sunset, exhaling smoke into the red-orange and purple light. She sits down across from him again, crosses her legs, lights a cigarette. "It really is a great office you've made for yourself here," she says. "The view is stunning, your view of the end."

He is silent for a moment, not wanting to speak, yet what else can he do? "Yes, we are coming to the end, aren't we?" he says to the window. "I am thinking I'll stay here. I'll watch the water rise from here."

"I can see the attraction."

He turns to face her. Despite her being, in the flesh, now in front of him, the glass behind her still bears the silhouette, as if burnt there permanently by photographic process. "You have doubled," he says.

"Yes, in a way. A kind of mitosis."

"She's your daughter."

She sighs, blowing smoke, looking beyond him, out the window. "No, she's adopted."

"But the birth certificate…"

"Forged. A fake."

"Ah." He turns back to the window. A cloud of dust rises in the distance, followed by a rumbling. The floor of the office even shakes a bit. One of the larger buildings in the surf is collapsing.

"She's three years older."

"I see."

"Your mother didn't want to… couldn't keep her."

"My mother…?"

"Yes."

"…couldn't keep her? So she's my sister?"

"Yes, she is your sister."

He mulls this a moment, watching as the dust cloud reaches apogee and then begins to spread and settle. He turns to face her again. "In that case," he continues, "so what? So I have a half-sister. Lots of people have half-sisters. Why the thirty years of secrecy and then this sudden 24 hours of…?"

"At your mother's request. She was, how can I say, embarrassed."

"Ah yes. My mother. Of course it was my mother."

"You know, don't you?"

"Yes, I suppose I do."

"You knew, even then, didn't you?"

"Yes," he says, resigning himself, "though I did not know that I knew. I knew it by the depth of my desire. The eternal abyss of my desire. And then, even in the utter dark of the encounter, I recognized… certain features."

"And you didn't stop."

"No, I didn't stop."

"Why not?"

"I didn't want to."

"And so?"

"And so the case is closed. The investigation ends, as they always do, in the mirror."

"Should I let her in, then?"

"Yes, let her in." He turns back toward the window. The dust cloud has thinned, now, and the sun is cutting through almost too brightly, blinding, yet he continues to stare into it. He hears the door open behind him. Footsteps.

"Q," she says, "meet Antii, your daughter. Your sister and your daughter."

He is trembling as he turns to meet his fate, and yet he never does, for by the time he completes the turn he is blind.

❀❀❀

The astute reader will be familiar with that phenomenon known as cross-modal neuroplasticity, the capacity of an animal to compensate for the loss of one sense by enhancement of the others. Brain imaging studies show the visual cortex in the blind is taken over by other senses, such as hearing and touch, and even contributes to language processing. Thus it is that a person, even an aging man, may come, through blindness, to a new way of seeing. No longer troubled by philosophical debates on the nature of color nor aesthetic decisions of what goes with what, one finds that nature has shifted into a realm of soft grays, glossy obsidians and sudden flashes of white brought on by unexpected tactile contact with low doorways or tilting street signs. Acoustic stimuli—in the form, say, of one's daughter/sister describing tall buildings in the distance or the nearby entry gate to what might once have been an urban park—are routed through circuitry formerly devoted solely to the ocular to a place in the mind formerly devoted solely to imaging, so that with the aid of a simple prosthesis like a stick the blinded man may come to see the pothole in his path in great detail, the cane describing, as it were, a perfect replica of the impending trip hazard, complete with its irregular rim, crumbling walls and bits of gravel and debris in the bottom.

Still, quite despite the all-but-overwhelming amount of compensatory data made available by one's shuffling feet, outstretched arms and the magic lantern of the stick, one will not enter this world of image sans visibility without at least the ghost of a feeling that one has traded down. The world is smaller and more dangerous now. The compensation one receives for safely navigating a pothole is a fall into another just beyond it or a bump on the head from a dangling steel beam. And then there is, especially for someone like Q who has always prided himself on his self-sufficiency, the humbling realization that he is incapable of performing even the most basic tonsorial tasks without assistance. How do you shave or fine tune a collar and tie when you can't see the mirror? How do you brush your teeth when someone else has left the toothpaste out of its normal pocket in the knapsack?

Of all the senses, he now realizes, sight is the one with the greatest reach and prophetic potential, and also, oddly, the one by which we normally measure time. If one's destination is, say, the ransacked store at the end of the block, the sighted person can gauge distance and time to destination in a glance and need not be troubling one's daughter/sister and selfless guide with the child's incessant questions, "how much longer?" or "are we there yet?", straining even further the inverted relationship of helper and helpless they find themselves stuck in. She who wandered aimlessly now must guide, despite her lack of knowledge of the daily shifting environs. He who guided, or at least imagined himself guiding, now follows without question.

For those who can see, they are a pitiful sight, the old man in his rags, bent and broken, eyes turned toward heaven but feet still dragging across the ravaged Earth, and the young girl who, one could say with wry understatement, has rather let herself go, leading him by means of a leash.

"Dear daughter," he says, "literal light of my life, without whom I would have perished long ago, tell me where we've come to now. What is this place? I can smell the sea. I can sense it just below us. Do you see a place to rest here? Some public grounds or shady grove?"

"Yes, Dad. Yes my brother," she replies. "We're in a garden of laurel and olive. There are hanging grapes and nightingales flitting around. I think I just saw a nymph over there. Why don't you sit down here on this comfortable bench." She seats him on a pile of brick in the ruined square (which hasn't seen a living plant in a decade) just out of reach of the waves.

"Thank you," he says. "Thank you for taking care of your blind and helpless father."

"Please, Dad. You flinch when I wave my arm at you. When I point at something you turn toward it. Your pupils shrink when I shine my pen light in them and dilate when I take it away."

"And thank you, too, for keeping me honest and not letting me wallow in self-pity. You know that my infirmity, my lack, is no less real for being psychosomatic. For though I see, and though I know I see because you tell me so, I cannot see what I see. It is as if the neural pathway has been hacked and now sends my visual data to some other person—you, perhaps—leaving me to hear, taste, touch, and nothing more."

"Well, hear, taste and touch our immediate vicinity and tell me where we'll spend the night tonight."

"Why not stay here in this lovely bower?" he says. "I'm tired of wandering. I want to stay here forever."

It's hard to say what happened to the money. It isn't that Q's wealth disappeared, exactly, but the card quit working, and then phone service ceased so there was no way to access the funds or even check the balance. As far as Q knew, the bank had no physical location, so to be out of touch with it was to render his money, effectively, nonexistent. Q pondered, in his newfound darkness, if this meant his wealth was gone or if it was still there but simply inaccessible, the way the debris-ridden streets, the downed poles and semi-collapsed buildings in the surf were still there but simply invisible, his eyes now as worthless as the card and the phone. He does have a bit of old-fashioned cash, which he carried as part of his anachronistic identity, still in his wallet, but this no longer functions, either, for there is no one to exchange it with and nothing to exchange it for.

After Lucy had left them at Q's office for a bit of quality time to get to know one another, the environmental situation had degenerated suddenly and inexplicably. Even the car failed them in their hour of need. When the water had risen into the lobby and the power to Q's office shut down, they had naturally called upon the car to get them away from the city, but it had gone crazy, gotten lost and driven them around the slums for hours, babbling in thirty languages and refusing to follow or even acknowledge the commands they were frantically screaming. It slammed against buildings, crashed through piles of debris, jumped curbs and craters until it flattened all four tires and ripped open the undercarriage. It tried, in the end, to drive itself into the sea and would have taken Q and Antii to a watery grave had not one of the front wheels dropped into a manhole and sheered off. They waded out of the surf and left it there, engine racing, rear wheels churning the water, sending up a cloud of steam, blasting emergency alerts in Swedish and Swahili.

Other vehicles also caught the virus. For the first few days of the father-daughter sojourn mad cars were a constant hazard. They came down the streets at full speed, careening wall to wall until colliding with post or building or another car or casting themselves into the sea like the Ford. Antii, being the eyes for them both, was on constant alert, finally having to subject Q to the ignominy of a leash (which she found still attached to a poor dog that had been run over) in order to be able to pull him to safety when one of the insane things was bearing down. Drones, too, were infected. Great clouds of them settled into the sea like flocks of geese, and rogue singles slammed into buildings, raining debris on the streets below. Once Q and Antii were even attacked by a commercial vacuum cleaner.

After a week of this dystopic terror, during which they imagined themselves humanity's last defense against a race of evil robots, they awoke to an eerie silence. Q, with his newly foreshortened and disordered senses, felt it telepathically: the darkness had flattened and lost its charge. "The grid's down," he said.

"Thank God," his daughter replied.

"Are there lilacs growing here?" Q asks, lifting his face and sniffing the air. "I seem to be catching a whiff of that delicate scent among the headier odors of grapes and olives. Also lavender. There must be a field of that herb nearby."

"How well your nose has compensated for the loss of your eyes, my father," Antii says, "for there are lilacs interspersed among the olives in the grove, and a field of aromatic lavender lies just beyond."

"I thought so," says Q with satisfaction, taking the letter of his daughter's words and ignoring her tone of sarcasm, "and it only confirms my decision to stay here, here in this verdant garden so ironically placed in the ruins of civilization."

"Yes," she answers, "in your blindness your wish is fulfilled. You who were the detective, master of fact, expert in the exposure of truths veiled behind the illusions projected by men's hopeless desire, you have intuited your final resting place and have made your peace by imagining it a place of beauty."

"Yes, a place of beauty indeed it is," he replies, lifting his face again toward heaven, closing his eyes as if to make doubly sure no hint of reality can encroach on his fantasy, "and I can see no reason, beyond death itself, to leave it. But tell me, do I correctly detect an implication in your narrative, that my stay here will be solitary, that I will enter the dark grove of the Furies alone, with neither daughter nor sister but only this pitiful stick to guide me?"

"Yes," she says, "my destiny and my own resting place lie elsewhere. I am fated, like you, but my fate is other than yours. Rest assured, though, that if it is in my power, I'll cover you with dust and pray as is the custom, and I'll hold no grudge that there'll be no one left to do the same for me."

In the weeks and months that followed the death of the grid, they found that rabid machines were not the only threat to their survival in this brave new world. Their fellow humans, which they encountered now and then, in small groups, pairs, or singly, proved to be unpredictable, sometimes offering food and water or otherwise sharing assets, and sometimes quite the opposite, robbing them of whatever they had collected that day, or threatening them with clubs and knives. Q even judged from certain audible and olfactory hints that some were resorting to cannibalism. So they kept to themselves, for the most part, though not without the occasional encounter.

When they, or rather when Antii, would espy a traveler or travelers in the distance, they would stop and try to move to a higher vantage to observe them on their way, scanning body language for signs of aggression, strength and paranoia. If the strangers appeared friendly or, better, weak and helpless, they would approach and exchange news and sometimes barter for food and water. If, on the other hand, the encounter portended the possibility of violence, they would either stay hidden or, in cases where progress was essential, plot the most advantageous or safest means of approach.

After some good and some very bad experiences they became a bit superstitious about these encounters and developed a ritual to help them decide the best course of action. After discussing the scene with her father, Antii would roll a pair of dice she had found and kept for the purpose. Q would call out a number, and Antii would tell him what had rolled (or, in truth, whatever she felt like telling him), and they would proceed according to rules they developed for response to various scores. One die was taken to represent themselves and the other their adversary, so that a six-one indicated far greater strength and combat-readiness on one side than the other, whereas a double five portended a hard-fought battle. Generally, pairs indicated duplicity and thus danger, though the double six was an exception taken to mean victory was assured. Snake eyes meant certain death if the encounter so much as laid eyes on them. If Q's guess at the roll was correct, this indicated the dice had spoken absolute truth, while a bad guess on his part told them there was room for interpretation.

Once, for example, Antii had spotted a diminutive figure coming toward them. She and Q ducked down behind a wrecked car to consider their course of action. Antii rolled the dice on the pavement and asked Q to call the number. He called five; the roll was two, but, after surveying the size and gait of the encounter, Antii tempered the raw omen with reason and told Q the roll was three. "I see," said Q. "The roll is an exact replica of the scene, with the two representing ourselves and the one our encounter. I had, however, called five, which would have been a three and a two, representing only a slight advantage of one die over the other. The roll would suggest, then, that I was being over-cautious by a factor of approximately one tenth (the difference between the two ratios). Further, the fact that the dice have fallen exactly as we and our encounter have fallen suggests a synchrony even more portentous than my correct guess. All in all, I'm concluding the encounter will be safe." And without further consideration Q stood up and stepped out from their hiding place, waving his arm to catch the attention of the Other, who waved back just as enthusiastically.

It was a young girl, the same young girl, Q realized as soon as heard her voice, that he and Lucy had encountered, in a pitiful state of dissociation, at the gloss bar a few months ago. And indeed she seemed still to be speaking in tongues, as her speech was opaque to them. "Can you speak English?" Antii asked, but the girl could only reply with more gibberish. Though her language was definitely glossolalic, she did not appear to be entranced, as she spoke in a normal if somewhat urgent tone, peppering them with incomprehensible questions, augmenting the useless speech by pointing vaguely in the distance or indicating their ruined surroundings with the sweep of an arm. Q and Antii, in turn, answered her with other questions: "Where are you going? Do you mean over there? What is your name?" So that to an observer who was not familiar with either of their languages it would have appeared they were having a normal conversation, quite despite the fact no information was being conveyed in either direction.

In the end the girl threw up her hands and walked away in frustration.

"There's someone here," says Antii. "They've just entered the square. Perhaps a dozen of them." Q turns his head in the direction she is pointing and seems to be sniffing the air. "One of them is coming up to us. The rest are hanging back."

"Hello stranger," Q yells, "as I learn from her whose eyes serve both her and me. I hope you can enlighten us as to the nature of this lovely place, which has so impressed me I can't bear the thought of ever leaving."

"It won't be up to you or me," the stranger, a thirtyish man dressed, like his compatriots waiting at the corner, in a hodge-podge of filthy rags, "but to the Others. This place is reserved, if you get my meaning, for them. They do things here at night."

"I wonder, then, if you would mind telling them that a withered and blind old man is asking their permission to rest here, and that rest is all he craves. Not one whit more will he ask of them but to hide here in the open."

"My messenger is already on his way. We'll know the answer before we have time to wonder. But tell me, blind man, are you the detective we've heard so much about? The one caught out here when the grid went down? We've heard things about you, and about this companion you travel with."

"Being too old and tired to lie, I'll admit my inglorious identity, and my daughter who is now my selfless guide."

"Back off, glossie," Antii interjects. "He's not as helpless as he looks."

This bravado having given the stranger pause, he backs away, but now his minions are moving up behind him, and they begin their own interrogation. "Your not really blind," one of them yells. "Your eyes are following us." And another: "Leave him alone; they say he carries a gun." And another: "What can a blind man shoot? I'll take him now."

Antii gives Q's leash a tug and whispers that they need to be going, and Q stands up obediently and takes a step in her direction. But then the leader comes forward again. "Stay where you are he says. My messenger is back, and they've sent word you can stay. Someone is coming down. It's the Mayor, actually. The Mayor is coming down. Now you've asked for it, you best be here when he comes."

❀❀❀

"I've seen this before," Q had said after the girl's departure. "Sometimes, once in a great while, they don't come out of it. They'll go into the trance and never come out, or rather they seem to come out, but they never get their words back. I think they walk around as in a dream after that, like they are transported to the Tower of Babel. It must be hard, to be inhabited by a language spoken by no one else on Earth."

"It isn't that easy being inhabited by this one," Antii replied.

They wandered on a little further that day, half-expecting to encounter the girl's hapless guardian from the bar, though they never did. They walked aimlessly, day after day, for neither of them had any notion of where they were, the mad car having taken them out of the narrow range of their familiarity with the city, and maps having ceased to exist when the grid went down. Unaccustomed to navigating the world without maps, they had been walking for weeks before it occurred to them they might be retracing their own steps. After conferring on this depressing thought, they decided it best to begin marking their trail, and Antii began writing numbers on the buildings. Starting at one, she used a chalky scrap of concrete to scratch a number and an arrow at each corner they passed. This made for slow going, as her writing tool was primitive and the numbers needed to be large enough to be seen from some distance. Also, they had gotten only to four when, distracted by another encounter, she forgot where she was in the sequence, and they had to retrace their steps to the previous mark to remind themselves.

"Can you do this one thing?" Antii said, exasperated. "I have to be constantly on the alert, looking forward and back and up and down, while you just follow where I lead you. So can you contribute by remembering the numbers? Can you contribute that much to the effort?"

Of course Q enthusiastically agreed, protesting that he was ready

443

and able to take on any task she might assign him, and he set to it with aggressive concentration, holding each number in his mind like a neon image as they walked. Five, six and seven came and went, then eight and nine, and Q was pursuing the blazoned ten when Antii announced they were at the next corner, but that this corner was already marked with a one.

❀ ❀ ❀

They wait an hour for the apparently famous Mayor, and then they wait two, Q and Antii huddled in one corner of the square and the choir in another. "They're staring at us," Antii tells her brother, "like we're some kind of aliens or something. It's giving me the creeps."

"Ah the haunting power of the eye," says Q wistfully. "I think that's what I miss most, not my own vision but the Other's, the invigorating discomfort that comes from being the object of someone else's attention and perceiving it. For while I can sense another's presence by touch or smell or hearing, the ear and nose are blind to the eyes of the interlocutor and so miss the tiny but telling inflections of attitude, the downward or surreptitious or forthright glance."

"Well maybe it's because I'm seeing for two, then, that I'm doubly paranoid, but this crowd hasn't taken their eyes off of us. They huddle and whisper as they look our way. They're plotting something, I'm sure of it. And now they're coming over."

"Don't concern yourself, light of my life," Q replies. "I'm sure they just want to talk."

The crowd approaches them warily, coming within earshot but maintaining a safe distance. "We know who you are," they say. "You're that detective with an unholy secret, and" (to Antii) "you're the unholy spawn of that secret. Get out. We don't want your kind here."

Antii responds: "My father may not be innocent but know we harbor no ill intent and hear my concern, which is only for a bit of comfort in his last hours. My eyes can see that you are sociable folk

444

who can be gracious. Can I ask you be so with us? No, we aren't perfect, but who is?"

"God knows you're a pitiful pair," the group retorts, "and certainly you have our pity and the contempt that goes with it, but forgive us if we prefer to pity you from a distance, in memory and not in sight and certainly not here among us, close enough to touch and, indeed, to smell."

And now Q: "Gentle people, we're at your mercy; hopefully you'll have some. Remember that reputations wax and wane, that my daughter and I were well-regarded once, that the rags we're clothed in are bespoke and bear designer labels, albeit obscured by accumulated filth. Look around us at these ruins. Mere minutes ago this was a great city, and before that a flowering forest. Is it our names alone you fear? I and my anti-I have done nothing to you, and I think you know we intend you no harm now. In a moment of weakness, enslaved to my base and baseless desire, I committed an unspeakable act, something no normal human can bear the thought of, but I had no way of knowing what was up, no reason to suspect that who I would find in the thrall of a nameless encounter would be she who named me. So if intention determines guilt, then I am innocent, and if accident is enough to condemn me, then I am innocent again, since I acted in ignorance of my own intent."

The choir huddles and talks among itself: "What's he talking about? Is he glossing?" "We can't throw them out; they're too gross to touch." "Let the Mayor decide." "I'm getting away from them." "Me too." And they return to their corner.

❂❂❂

Upon discovery that the path they had been taking was circular, or at least repetitive, Antii and Q had mixed emotions. The thought that they had been traversing the same ground over and over for months was, naturally, discouraging, however it also offered hope that the desolation they were trekking through might not be as vast as it appeared, that there might be, in fact, a way out. And so they set about marking their way more rigorously, not only numbering each corner but labelling each side of each corner with a letter (a or b) along with an arrow indicating the direction they had taken, and later, upon multiple visits, with hashmarks to indicate the number of times a particular corner had been visited and a direction taken from it, to avoid as much as possible reiteration of their exploratory routes. After some practice and experimentation with mnemonic devices, Q became fairly adept at holding the numbers in his mind, at least during the course of a day. At night he found himself dreaming about them, and some mornings he was unsure if the number he was seeing was from memory or from oneiric stimulus, so that he sometimes opted for a "safe" number as a starting point in the morning. Thus, if he was unsure if they had left off at 129 or 239 the night before, he might begin the next morning with 150 or 240.

Antii devoted herself to the tracking with increasing urgency, often growing impatient with Q's slow progress and urging him on with the leash, as she was becoming more and more concerned about their shrinking food supply. It had been some time, now, since they had encountered a street-level shop or apartment that had not already been ransacked, and they were forced to climb higher and higher into the taller apartment buildings in search of canned goods to salvage. Sometimes an entire day would be spent laboring up stairwells in search of a still-intact pantry, and this was time taken away from the search for an escape.

These forays into the heights also afforded Antii views of the surroundings which were contributing to a growing suspicion, which she did not share with Q, that they were now on an island. And then the day arrived when, after marking corner #3288a, they came to the shoreline and, looking in all directions, could not find another corner that was not already marked. Even the corners they could see out in the water bore the numbers and arrows of previous visits, with some of the arrows pointing even further out to sea. After that they encountered no more unmarked corners, no more uncharted territory.

"Someone's coming," Antii says.

"Where?" says Q, looking around as if he could see.

"From the sea. They're coming in across the water."

"Who is it?"

"I can't tell. They're still too far away. It almost looks like someone on horseback, riding across a desert."

"A dangerous and unpredictable desert," says Q, "a desert that can swallow."

"Our visitor seems to be handling it with aplomb, riding over the waves without a dip or nod of the head."

"Perhaps it is your sister," Q conjectures inanely. "She always enjoyed horses. She could even ride bareback."

"My sister?"

"Your half sister. I guess you've never known her."

"No, I have not known her. My family remains mysterious to me."

"Well then, perhaps you shall meet her now. I'm glad it's not me."

"Glad what's not you?"

"The one coming in across the sea to meet you. I was on the water once, on a freighter crossing the ocean. I was treated rudely there and have avoided the sea ever since."

"You're afraid of the water?"

"Afraid of what rides upon it."

"Well, what's riding on this particular water is not my sister. I can see now it's gender is likely male. It's wearing a fedora, and it isn't riding a horse but a gondola with a horse's head carved in the prow. Anyway it's getting close, so soon the mystery will be solved."

"Ah, good," says Q with relief. "We're getting to the bottom of it then. And this is always our goal, to get to the bottom of things."

"Like the bottom of the sea?" Antii says. "With its mermaids and sunken cities? With its pools of black oil, which is the blood of the dinosaurs, the sap of extinct species?"

"No, not like that," Q insists. "I meant 'bottom' conceptually, figuratively, to discover the cause, the root, the origin of things, the solution to the mystery."

"Even if that solution is dissolving into the sea?" Antii replies wittily.

"Even if."

"I'll go down and meet our solution, then."

"I'll go with you if you'll be my eyes once again," Q volunteers, "for I feel a portent in this arrival and want to understand what I'm feeling."

"But you're withered and old and weak, as well as blind and addled. I can handle this. Let me be your reason as well as your eyes."

"No, let me come. I feel my strength and my brilliance returning, however briefly, and I feel they will not return again. So for this last, brief scene, let me have reason to reason again."

"Every corner is marked, every road already taken," Q had said. "Our progress is circular no matter which way we turn."

"We are on a circle whose center is everywhere and circumference nowhere," Antii remembered, prompting Q to nod in sad agreement.

"Our philosophy of marking everything has failed us," he added. "We might just as well have marked nothing."

They sat down beside a wrecked car, not out of fatigue but rather from having, simply, no place to go, but had not been there very long before they had another encounter. It was a young girl, the same young girl, Q realized as soon as heard her voice, that he and Lucy had encountered, in a pitiful state of dissociation, at the gloss bar some months ago. And indeed she seemed still to be speaking in tongues, as her speech was opaque to them. "Can you speak English?" Antii asked, but the girl could only reply with more gibberish. Though her language was definitely glossolalic, she did not appear to be entranced, as she spoke in a normal if somewhat urgent tone, peppering them with incomprehensible questions, augmenting the useless speech by pointing vaguely in the distance or indicating their ruined surroundings with the sweep of an arm. Q and Antii, in turn, answered her with other questions: "Where are you going? Do you mean over there? What is your name?" So that to an observer who was not familiar with either of their languages it would have appeared they were having a normal conversation, quite despite the fact no information was being conveyed in either direction.

In the end the girl threw up her hands and walked away in frustration.

Enter the Mayor, an assistant poling his gondola through the shallows among the treacherous ruins. He is strangely attired, in a fedora, as Antii has already observed, but a fedora that has been cut crudely into the shape of a crown, with ragged crenelations scissored into the sides. The rest of his costume is a study in collage, seemingly patched together at random from some costume studio. His jacket resembles a tuxedo on the right side, but on the left it has the epaulet and armored sleeve of a cuiraisser. One foot is shorn with a sandal, the other with a boot. One pantleg is sheathed in heavy leather, the other in flowing silk. One hand is gloved, the other bare, and withal he is covered with a patchwork of pockets and attachments, pouches and anklets, jangling beads and snap-on weaponry. One side of his face is bearded, the other clean-shaven, so that he appears as a feminine youth in one profile and an old man in the other.

When the gondola runs aground he steps out nimbly and wades ashore through the brown foam at water's edge. Besides Q and Antii, the choir has come down to meet him, tittering in awe of the esteemed presence: "He is come. The Mayor has actually come down to meet this pair. Who are they to rate this?"

"I've heard of you, blind man." says the motley Mayor, walking up to Q. "You are as haggard and pitiful as the rumors foretold, and this equally pitiful girl holding your reins, could she be that one to whom you are twice related? A double ignominy for her, it seems, as she must bear both the shame of her birth and the onus of caring for you in your helpless old age. And, tell me, why are you here? What can we do for you? Once, before I acquired by shrewd force this esteemed position, I more resembled you than my present self. I too held out my cup to passers-by more capable and fortunate than me, and I still have a soft spot for the wretched of the Earth."

"There are worse fates," Antii bristles, "than caring for this old man who has become as guileless as child, like believing your own lies, muttering your empty rhetoric in a mirror, pretending to power even as the lights go out all around you."

"May your pride and wit save you from your own desires," the Mayor answers, "as your brother's did not."

"Esteemed Magistrate," Q interjects, "please pardon my daughter's intelligence, which she exercises too freely in defense of her father, who does not deserve it. The favor we would ask of you is slight, and we offer you a great boon in return."

"And what is this favor?"

"Only a short ride in the vessel you came in on, to take me to my final office, one of those big ones out there, at the very top of one of the great structures the sea is now rising into, so that my daughter may be released from me and act according to her own wishes."

"You're right. The favor you ask is small. In fact, it is nothing. We take people out there and leave them often enough, usually as punishment for rebellion. In fact, if I wanted to simply dispose of you, that's how I would do it. But tell me, then, what's in this for us? What is this 'boon' you promise?"

"Why then this whole desolate empire will be yours. You'll be troubled no more with my ambition or my daughter's reason. Further, you'll have the fame of being the only one who knows my final resting place. No other Mayor will be able to say as much. All my followers will flock to you, and you'll hold power for as long as you a place to hold it in."

"Sounds like a good deal to me," says the Mayor. "I'm not sure who these followers are, but it costs me so little I'm willing to take a chance."

"Good. My fate is sealed," he says, and then to Antii: "Daughter, give this man my leash so he can lead me to his craft."

"But I'll come with you," she replies, "to see you settled."

"No. No one can know where I am going now. Else it would not be our Mayor's little secret. Without me holding you back, you'll find your way out. Perhaps there will be something left to find."

"Yes, I suppose I have to," she says. "I'll miss you, as the released prisoner misses the predictable routine of confinement, for a week, and then my fate will be mine alone."

She hands the leash to the Mayor, who turns and begins leading Q out to the boat. Just then, though, one of the group calls out: "Your Honor, we have composed a song in honor of this event. Shall we sing it for you?" The Mayor waves his hand noncommittally without looking back, and the choir lines up and begins to sing:

> A stranger came up, all worn out,
> to the best little square in the City.
> He heard a nightingale in her bower,
> and imagined wine-dark ivy
> and hanging clusters of grapes,
> party place for a goat-foot god
> to dance with nymphs and foster
> an illegitimate child.
>
> He dreamed each morning of pearly dew,
> of red narcissi and crocus wreaths.
> For sister and daughter
> a sleepless fountain
> fed a darling little stream
> to swell earth's bosom

with quick increase,
and our choir found them here.

Here he thinks he'll be fed
by olive trees gently blowing,
an ancient plant
even older than California,
but the horse that came in
from the sea is even older,
bridled by a power
more substantial than the oar.

The crazy choir and Antii stand nostalgically on the shore as the Mayor leads Q through the shallows. The oarsman comes forward and helps the decrepit beggar into the bow. And now it is Q's turn to stand behind the horse, holding, as it were, to the mane as the gondola turns and heads back out through the buildings. The Mayor sits down humbly and lets Q ride as figurehead now, waving his stick and yelling goodbye to Antii and the Choir, who can no longer hear him. He directs the oarsman with his stick as if he can divine where they are going, and they pull up beside one of the buildings which has not yet collapsed, Q following the wall with his hands until he finds a window. It has long since lost its glass, so they pull the boat to in front of it and help Q step through.

Antii and the Choir watch from the shore, 200 meters away, as her Father disappears into the building and the gondola pulls away. She is turning to leave when she suddenly hears him, impossibly loud, and turns to see that he has emerged from a high terrace, twenty stories above the water. He reaches up his arms, still holding his stick, and booms so that all can hear:

"Now the Moon can hear the jackals bleating in the deserts of time—

"Now the eclogues in wooden shoes grumble in the orchard.

"Now, in the budding purple forest, Eucharis tells me it is spring.

"Rise, waters, foam, roll up on the bridge and over the woods, black palls and organs, lightning and thunder, rise and roll… Water and sorrow, rise and unleash the Floods again.

"For since they subsided, real jewels have been turned under and the fields are full of boring flowers, and the Queen, that Witch who lights her coals in the clay pot, has no intention of telling us what she knows, and we will never know."

❀❀❀

Antii was surprised at how easy it was, once unburdened of her lugubrious father, to find her way out of the dead zone. She only had to walk an hour at the brisk pace her new freedom allowed before she began to see unmarked corners, and by the end of the second day she could no longer smell the sea. On the third day she came to the interstate and found it to be a hive of activity, with people and even a few manually controlled vehicles moving along it among a chaos of wrecked cars. Now with the old signs to guide her, she headed out of the city and towards the only place she knew to go.

She asked the people she met what had happened. None of them knew, but already she sensed that the myths were starting to reform. Some said there had been a war. Some said it was a single, anonymous hacker who had brought the whole thing down. But no one had anything in the way of actual information, or at least that type of information they had had in the past, the same no matter who was telling the story, and she quickly learned to take the reports for what they were, reflections of the reporters' fears and desires, and nothing more.

After three days on the elevated road she came to her exit and walked down the long ramp into Lucy's surburban neighborhood. It looked different now, broken and foreboding, with garage doors blasted open and the occasional wreck embedded in a brick fascade, but she recognized enough to get her bearings and was able to find her house without difficulty.

To Antii's disappointment, the house was empty, though a proliferation of candles and other accommodations to the new powerless age indicated to her it had been recently occupied. Hoping against hope, she tried a water tap and found to her amazement that it was operational. She stripped off her rags and took a shower in her own bathroom, a luxury she had begun to despair that she would ever see again. The tub was somewhat foul with mold and mildew and yet she came out of it feeling about as clean as she had ever felt.

In her bedroom she found her clothes still neatly folded in the dresser, and she put on fatigues and the hiking boots she had been longing for these past weeks. She went downstairs and took stock, finding a pantry full of canned goods and bottled water. She ate and sat at the table by herself as darkness fell. Then she went into the living room and lay down on the couch. It was there that Lucy found her in the morning.

Epilogue

Q, long white hair billowing around him, supple garment clinging in the wind, looks down from his particular Elysium onto the no-longer-really-interesting affairs on Earth. He points with his staff at a dust cloud rising at the edge of a sea, and he chuckles.

His brood is gathered around him, and his ancestors also, all the significant links in his chain, above and below, stretching almost to infinity. Almost. They have brought with them their accoutrements, their houses and their lives, their horses and seacraft and wagons and airships, broken statues and battered books, great cities and nations in the constant molt of rise and decline, palaces and churches and lonely mountain caves, teeming valleys, wide deserts and squalid slums.

In this strangely curved space-time, from one point of vantage, specifically Q's, he resides at the pinnacle of history, the apex of a cone of signs, objects, persons and events. From another, specifically ours, he is but a mote in a sandstorm, rendered integral only by an effort of concentration and focus. He will disappear if our attention flags, if we blink, and so, after the manner of all things that insist on remaining things, he buzzes and flits to catch our eye; he throws lightning bolts and clears his throat like thunder; he dances and parades and makes sweeping gestures with his staff. All to no—or at least very little—avail.

The fact of Q's fiction need not concern us, for he differs from those initials which once, however briefly, indicated a living human, only in certain qualities of the prose in which he is remembered. It is quite arguable that Don Quixote is more nearly a "real" character than is Miguel de Cervantes or that Candide possessed just as much flesh and blood as Voltaire, that the conventions of biography accommodate the fictive just as expeditiously as do the rules that govern the production and dissemination of novels. Thus we should consider Q our cousin and view his adventures with all the interested concern we show toward other members of our tribe.

And having done so bid him fond adieu.

Notes

This work was conceived as a neo-picaresque, borrowing stylistically from older works that I admired or, in some cases, despised but was obsessed with. It evolved rapidly into a kind of cut-up, in which my own writings were interspersed with snippets stolen from others. In the Notes below I sometimes say "adapted from" a specific text. This means that I pasted in the text in question and then revised it with impunity to fit my own purpose and context, often quite in conflict with the intent of the original. These Notes represent only the most egregious of the plagiarisms. There are many others an astute Reader may easily discover.

Q

While the basic structure of the opening chapters is borrowed from Voltaire's *Candide*, several of the chapters up to and including the "Editor's Note" are adaptations of the initial chapters of Don Quixote, Book 1. The "Author's Introduction" is an adaptation of Cervantes' intro.

In the chapter that begins "Thus reduced…," the paragraph beginning "A singular disadvantage…" is adapted from Stephen Crane's "The Open Boat."

The first chapter of Book 2, the dialog of Q and the Entropy™ Executive, is adapted from the second book of Plato's Republic.

"The Lonely Camper's Ballad" is adapted from one of the songs in Quixote.

The Brownwater™ Colonel's Story is adapted from "The Writing Lesson" by Claude Lévi-Strauss.

In the chapter that begins "Two days later..." the description of the feast in the second paragraph is adapted from Keats' "The Eve of St. Agnes."

The Bellman's discourse on "The Unhappiest Customer" is adapted from "The Unhappiest Man" in Kierkegaard's Either Or.

In the chapter that begins "Q bade his good-by…" Q's meditation as he walks along the mountain is adapted from the Duino Elegies, #1, of Rainer Maria Rilke.

Little A

The title is a rendering of Lacan's notion of "objet petit a."

The chapter beginning " Q walked out the patio doors" is adapted from Pound's "Kung" canto.

The section that begins "Outside the house Mr. Simpson announced" takes its scenario from The Who's Tommy.

The section in which the dogs are loosed upon Lucy mimics a similar scene in de Sade's Justine.

The Linguist's meditation that begins "On a dark night, full of longing…" opens and closes with quotation from "the Dark Night of the Soul" of St. John of the Cross.

Gwen's discourse that begins "No. As I told you, I am Gwen, Gwen through and through, from my skin to my marrow, Gwen" is lifted directly from Deleuze's *Difference and Repetition*.

The Private I

The second half of The Private I, in which Q wanders blind with Antii, parodies Oedipus at Colonus, with many of the speeches and crowd responses adapted liberally from the play.

BILL LAVENDER is a poet, novelist, and publisher living in New Orleans. *My ID*, his eleventh book of poetry, was published by BlazeVOX in 2019. His verse memoir, *Memory Wing*, called by Rodger Kamentetz "a contemporary autobiographical masterpiece," appeared in 2011. He is the founding director of the publishing house Lavender Ink / Diálogos, and he is the co-founder of the New Orleans Poetry Festival.